T0123279

TURNING POINT

"You don't want to fuck with me right now, Hope," he said, his voice deadly soft with warning.

She shivered at the low tone as awareness cut through her. That was new. She wasn't sure how to deal with this male, so she faced him squarely. Her nipples peaked as flames licked through her, even though it was freezing and there were guns trained on them. "You don't scare me," she said, not meaning a word of it. At the moment, he was surprisingly terrifying. It was as if she didn't know him at all. "If you don't knock it off, I'll kick your ass in front of everybody watching." It didn't hurt to remind him that he would get shot if he made the wrong move.

Also by Rebecca Zanetti

The Dark Protector series
Fated
Claimed
Tempted
Hunted
Consumed
Provoked
Twisted
Shadowed
Tamed
Marked
Talen
Vampire's Faith
Demon's Mercy
Alpha's Promise
Hero's Haven
Guardian's Grace
Rebel's Karma
Immortal's Honor
Garrett's Destiny

The Realm Enforcers series
Wicked Ride
Wicked Edge
Wicked Burn
Wicked Kiss
Wicked Bite

The Scorpius Syndrome series

Scorpius Rising
Mercury Striking
Shadow Falling
Justice Ascending

The Deep Ops series
Hidden
Taken (e-novella)
Fallen
Shaken (e-novella)
Broken
Driven
Unforgiven
Frostbitten

Laurel Snow Thrillers
You Can Run
You Can Hide
You Can Die

WARRIOR'S HOPE

Rebecca Zanetti

LYRICAL PRESS
Kensington Publishing Corp.
www.kensingtonbooks.com

LYRICAL PRESS BOOKS are published by
Kensington Publishing Corp.
119 West 40th Street
New York, NY 10018

All Kensington titles, imprints, and distributed lines are available at special quantity discounts for bulk purchases for sales promotion, premiums, fund-raising, educational, or institutional use.

Special book excerpts or customized printings can also be created to fit specific needs. For details, write or phone the office of the Kensington Sales Manager: Kensington Publishing Corp., 119 West 40th Street, New York, NY 10018. Attn. Sales Department. Phone: 1-800-221-2647.

Lyrical Press and Lyrical Press logo Reg. U.S. Pat. & TM Off.

First Electronic Edition: October 2023
ISBN-13: 978-1-5161-1138-1 (ebook)

First Print Edition: October 2023
ISBN-13: 978-1-5161-1141-1

Printed in the United States of America

This one is for my sister, Debbie English Smith, who reminds me of every tough and sweet heroine in this entire series.

Acknowledgments

As we close up this Seven Arc, I am so thankful that the interest in this series has grown through twenty-one books and three novellas with Kensington. I'm counting the Realm/Witch Enforcers in that total...and there will be more books coming!

Thank you to the readers who've been with the Kayrs family since the beginning, and those who have jumped in with this new era, starting with *Vampire's Faith*. I have many wonderful people to thank for getting this book to readers, and I sincerely apologize to anyone I've forgotten.

Thank you to my truly wonderful family, Big Tone, Gabe, and Karlina for being so supportive as I've written in carpool lines, at practices, and on family vacations. I love you so much and sometimes miss those earlier days when you kids needed us to drive you everywhere. But I'm so proud of who you've become!

Thank you to my always insightful editor, Alicia Condon, who I really miss seeing at conferences since most of them have ended. However, there are new conferences and reader events being planned, and I can't wait to have a drink together again! Thanks also to everyone at Kensington Publishing: Alexandra Nicolajsen, Steven Zacharius, Adam Zacharius, Lynn Cully, Vida Engstrand, Jane Nutter, Lauren Jernigan, Barbara Bennett, Elizabeth Trout, Arthur Maisel, Renee Rocco, Kristin McLaughlin, James Walsh, Jennifer Chang, and Lisa Gilliam.

Thank you to my wonderful agent, Caitlin Blasdell, who has worked so hard on this series from the very beginning, and actually signed me with *Fated,* the first book.

Thank you to my very creative assistant, Anissa Beatty, for her excellent social media work as well as the fun with the Rebels, my FB street team. Thank you to Lisa Ashley for naming Hope's pet, and to Lisa Murray for naming Drew. A huge thank you to the Graves Book Club: Anissa Beatty, Madison Fairbanks, Asmaa Qayyum, Leanna Feazel, Suzi Zuber, Brenda Kay Vann, Amanda Larsen, Joan Lai, Karen Clementi, Marie Brown, and Heather Ates Harris, for their support in the charity auction and for naming Lyrica, who you will continue to see in future books.

Thank you to Writer Space and Fresh Fiction PR for all the hard work.

Thank you to Kimberly Frost, Heather Frost, Asmaa Qqyyum, Suzie Zuber, Madison Fairbanks and Leanna Feazel for Beat Reading this one.

Thanks also to my constant support system: Gail and Jim English, Kathy and Herb Zanetti, Debbie and Travis Smith, Stephanie and Don West, Jessica and Jonah Namson, Chelli and Jason Younker, Liz and Steve Berry, and Jillian and Benji Stein.

Chapter One

The Christmas tree lit the entire main room of the lodge with sparkling green and red lights, adding to the sense of whimsy created by the magical songs humming through the entertainment system.

Hope Kayrs-Kyllwood entered from the kitchen area, holding two heavy mugs and offering one to the woman looking at the tree. "Here you go. This will warm you up," she said, handing over the hot buttered rum.

"Thank you." Lisa Maloney accepted the mug. She still wore the ripped jeans and dirty green sweater she'd had on when she was rescued, but the soldiers who'd saved her had been called to another possible kidnapping, so Hope had instantly volunteered to help ease the woman into her new reality. She'd been through an ordeal, and spending some time in the cheerful lodge with a warm beverage should help.

"I don't even know how to thank your people." Lisa took a sip of the drink. Instantly, color washed across her face. "Oh, this is good."

Hope sampled the concoction. "It's my uncle Garrett's recipe. There's a lot of rum in it, but you're not driving anywhere tonight, so that's okay."

Lisa turned to face Hope. "I'm sorry to be quiet. It's just finding out about immortals has been a shock to my system. Here I thought

I was so experienced and knowledgeable about the world." The twenty-four-year-old teacher from Des Moines shivered. "Those creepy monsters had me. They were kidnapping me, and your people came out of nowhere to stop them."

Hope couldn't imagine the terror. "Yeah, the Kurjans have been kidnapping enhanced females all across the globe, and we're trying to stop them whenever we can." She watched the human closely. Her eyes were clear but her legs fidgety. She wouldn't be able to sit and relax quite yet. Standing was fine.

Lisa's hair was a bright red and her eyes a startling green. There was no doubt she had some Irish heritage, but according to Hope's dossier, her family had lived in the States for a couple of centuries.

"I can't believe that vampires actually exist." Lisa's eyes were still wide.

Hope kept her tone soothing and factual. "I have demon and vampire lineage as well as some witch and shifter, I think."

"Wow," Lisa said. "To think you live among us and I had no idea. How many vampires are there?"

"I'm not at liberty to divulge that, but I can say that I'm the only female with vampire blood in her ever born."

Lisa blinked. "One of the soldiers mentioned that when he asked me to stay here while they went back out to the helicopter. Talk about pressure on you, huh?"

Hope had never known another reality. "I don't feel pressure."

"I'm sure you must," Lisa said. "You're the only one of your kind. Is it a genetic thing?"

Hope savored the delicious cocktail. "Yes. Vampires usually only give birth to males."

"What's an enhanced female?" Lisa looked back at the tree.

Ah. Hope had wondered when the questions would come. Lisa had accepted the reality faster than most. "Somebody with extra abilities. We don't know if you're cousins to the witches or are your own species like vampires or demons." Hope's gaze caught on the many handmade ornaments hung on the massively tall tree.

"This is adorable." Lisa pulled at a pine cone that had been dipped in silver.

"My brother made that last week." Hope admired the ornament. "He turned two not too long ago, and the kid's really gifted."

Lisa gingerly set it back in place. "Two? You have a two-year-old brother? How old are you?"

"I'm twenty-four. Same age as you," Hope said. "It's common for immortal siblings to be born many years apart."

Lisa leaned closer to study a crystal globe ornament. "I don't know if I can go back to teaching high school history and just pretend I don't know all of this."

"You have some time to figure it out. We need to keep you off the Kurjan radar for now." At this very moment, experts in the computer center were working on an exit plan for the woman's current life that would appease anybody who knew her—just in case she needed to hide for a while.

Lisa shuddered. "Kurjans. That's how I pictured vampires. Pale skin, black hair, creepy purple eyes. I mean those dudes were terrifying."

Hope agreed completely. "A lot of them are, I admit. It used to be that they couldn't go out in the sun, but they've figured out a way to protect themselves, and now they can survive daylight for several hours at a time."

"How did they find me?" Lisa asked.

It was a fair question. "Enhanced females set off vibrations, and Kurjan technology has advanced to the point that they can detect them. I can't tell you what they wanted with you because I don't know. We're trying to figure that out." Her people had battled the Kurjans before, and she was trying to avoid another war.

Lisa grasped a hand-whittled guitar ornament. "This is cute. Who did this?"

Fond memories swept through Hope. "My friend Paxton." Her best friend actually. "He wanted to be a rock star when we were young."

Lisa peeked under her lashes. "Sounds like he means a lot to you."

"He does," Hope said, her chest aching. "I miss him."

"Is he one of the soldiers out there fighting for kidnapped women?"

"Oh no." Hope couldn't imagine Pax with a gun. "Paxton is a scientist. His uncle studies the migration patterns of insects and is very fond of butterflies. He took Pax under his wing when we were teenagers, and now Paxton gets to travel all over the world, which is good for him."

Lisa nudged her with a shoulder. "But not so good for you?"

Hope looked at the tiny guitar. "I miss him," she admitted. "My life feels more settled when he's here, but my team just became mission ready yesterday, so we're out on our own soon. There are a lot of enhanced females who need to be rescued, and that's my primary objective."

She felt his absence daily. It had been nearly a year since they were in the same place at the same time, but they spoke often via teleconferencing or by texting nearly every week. His anecdotes about following his uncle around chasing butterflies were often hilarious. Sometimes Hope wished she could be with him, but she had a job to do, and she was good at it.

Lisa reached for another ornament. This one was a framed picture of Hope, Paxton, and their best friend, Libby, when they'd been in elementary school.

"Is this him?" Lisa tapped on his smiling face.

"Yeah," Hope said.

Lisa winked. "I bet he turned out cute."

"He really did." Heat filtered up from Hope's neck to her cheeks.

"So he's the one, huh?" Lisa cocked her head.

The question was like a dash of cold water. "My path lies another way." She absently rubbed the marking on her neck that declared her one of the three prophets of her people.

Lisa followed her motion. "That's a heck of a tattoo you've got there."

"Thank you." The marking wound from her shoulders up both sides of her neck to beneath her ears. The intricate blue design seemed to dance on her skin. She'd worn the brand since before she was born, and she felt the weight of it often.

"Tell me about this Paxton," Lisa said.

"That's about all there is," Hope murmured. "He's a scientist, he's a free spirit, and he's just a great guy. He's sweet."

Lisa rehung the ornament. "He sounds wonderful, and if he turned out as cute as he looks here, I'd say you're missing out if you don't go for it."

Time to change the subject. "What about you?"

Lisa rescued a Santa ornament from tipping over. "My boyfriend and I broke up a year ago. I was thinking about maybe trying a dating app, but I don't know. Now that I know I'm being hunted by super scary, creepy, vampire-esque monsters, I may just lie low for a while."

Hope smoothed out the tree skirt with one foot. "That's not a bad idea. We'll keep you safe, whatever you decide. We can give you a new ID, or you can stay here in Realm territory until we figure things out. I promise we're not going to abandon you now that we've rescued you."

"I appreciate that," Lisa said.

An owl hooted loudly from outside the heavy doors leading to the deck and down to the lake, and Hope moved to open the door. "Hey, Wingman," she called out.

Lisa popped up at her side. "You have an owl for a wingman?"

"It's his name." Hope chuckled. "He somehow adopted me a while back. He's just a friend, or a pet, or maybe neither."

Lisa's eyes widened. "Are you like a witch? You know from those old fairy tales where they have a familiar?"

Hope mulled the question over. "I don't think so. He just appeared one day and hangs around a lot. He does show up at odd times, though." While she did have some witch heritage, she wasn't able to form plasma out of thin air, so her main identity as an immortal probably wasn't as a witch. Unfortunately, she hadn't discovered any talents, so she couldn't figure out what kind of immortal she should identify with. It was quite frustrating.

The bird was beautiful, with thick white feathers and a dark marking around his beak. He was also a good size but flew gracefully when he wanted. "He disappears fairly often," Hope said. "Because he is a predator." Like most people in her world, actually. Her phone buzzed, and she looked down and instantly pressed a button, nerves flaring to life in her abdomen. "Paxton, hi."

His face came into view on screen. Silvery-blue eyes, thick black hair, rugged features with a nice shadow covering his jaw. He looked like a tough-guy wildlife biologist on safari.

Next to her, Lisa sucked in air. "Whoa," she whispered. "Seriously hot."

Hope smiled. "I was just talking to Wingman."

"That bird's weird," Paxton said. Behind him was a beautiful sunlit beach with aqua-colored water that looked too inviting to resist.

She wished she could vacation with him and get out of the snow. "Where are you?"

"I'm in Saint Thomas," he said, leaning back a little bit. "We're in the Caribbean studying the migration patterns of the Gulf fritillary. We're trying to figure out how the little beauty initially arrived here."

Hope assumed he was talking about a butterfly. "Fun."

"Yeah, they're part of the 'brush-footed' or Nymphalidae butterfly family, referring to the short hairs on the front of its legs." His eyes shone as he warmed to the subject. "They like passionflowers, so they're also known as the passion butterfly."

Hope gave Lisa a look. "That's fascinating, Pax." He combined adorable geekiness and rugged sexiness in a way that warmed her heart as well as other parts of her anatomy.

He grinned. "Sorry. I got carried away. But I'm calling you for a reason. Guess what?"

"What?" Hope held her breath.

"We're coming home for Christmas."

Elation whipped through her. "Oh, I'm so glad." She had found him the perfect cutting-edge microscope set and had wanted to give it to him in person. She had also bought brand-new editions of Realm Sudoku, which for some reason he seemed to love, although he never sat still long enough to play. "When will you be home?"

"I think the day before Christmas, but I'll let you know for sure." He looked over his shoulder. "Oh, my uncle is calling me. I have to go. I miss you."

"I miss you too. I'll see you soon." She clicked off.

"You look way too happy for him to be just a friend." Lisa returned her attention to her mug of rum.

Hope let herself bask in the moment for two seconds and then shoved the dream away. "The male has grown up nicely."

"I would say so," Lisa burst out. "Did you see that chest? He wasn't wearing a shirt. Did you notice? Because I sure as heck noticed. That was one heck of a chest."

Hope chuckled. "Yes, Paxton ended up very muscled and good-looking somehow, even though he chases butterflies around the globe." She was grateful that he wasn't part of her world of strategy and war. After his upbringing, he deserved peace. "But we're friends, and we'll always be *just* friends." She knew fate had other plans for her. But the words rang hollow just the same.

Lisa fanned herself. "If you say so, although I think you're crazy, girlfriend."

Hope thought about explaining just as her cousin Collin strode into the room.

"We're on go," he said, securing his duffel bag over his shoulder. "Two women, definitely enhanced. Our first solo mission. The team is heading to the helicopter to take us to the coast. We'll catch a plane there."

Hope put her cup on the table near the tree, her heart beating faster. "Where are we going?"

"Paris." Collin glanced at his watch. "We're wheels up in twenty minutes."

Hope thought through mission parameters. "I have a go bag and will meet you at the hangar."

"You've got it," Collin said. "Liam is acquiring weapons, and I'll assist him. See you there." He strode out of the room.

Lisa blew out air. "Wow. What is it with these immortal males? I mean, dangerously sexy."

Hope blinked. "I guess." He was her cousin, so she'd never really looked at him that way. "Lisa, you're safe here, and you can stay as long as you want."

"Thank you." Lisa leaned in for an impulsive hug. "You're going out there to save two more women like me?"

"That's the plan." Hope slid her phone into the back pocket of her cargo pants as anticipation trilled through her veins. Finally, she and her team would have a chance to work on their own and make a difference. She would not fail those women. No matter what.

Chapter Two

Hope reshuffled her dossier on the table in the Gulfstream jet and looked at her team. They were about seven hours into the nine-hour flight, and several had napped on the way.

"Okay," she said. "I've reviewed locations, and I have a plan to take both women." She looked at her team of four. "This is our first solo mission, and we're going to do it completely by the book. First, I want to talk about any new enhancements you may or may not have. Libby, how's the shifting going?"

"Perfect," Libby said. Liberty was a feline shifter, a cougar to be exact. And she'd been able to shift since she was sixteen, so she'd mastered the skill. It was difficult to understand how humans failed to see the animal lurking inside her. Her blondish-brown hair showed a myriad of colors, and her eyes were a catlike bourbon brown.

"All right. Just remember that if you're ordered to shift, make sure the team's out of the way. The sonic boom you emit can be uncomfortable." Hope barely shifted her gaze to her cousin Derrick, who was Libby's partner.

He rolled his eyes. "Yeah, let's not forget that again, Libs. As for my skills, I'm fully prepared with fireballs, and I have been working on forming ice out of air, but I'm not quite there yet." As a vampire-witch hybrid, his skills came from his mother, Brenna, who was a witch. Witches created and threw plasma balls by transforming air to fire using quantum physics Hope just wasn't interested in. Even though he was mainly a witch, he looked just like his vampire father, Jase, and he had his dad's copper-colored eyes and muscled physique. Regardless of lineage or looks, immortals normally only inherited the powers of one parent.

Hope nodded. "That's good, though. Fireballs come in handy— we just have to be careful if we're in the tunnels again." She studied the twins, who sat at the far end. They were the spitting image of their father, Conn, and both had full vampire attributes, to the consternation of their mother, Moira, who was a powerful witch. The seventh sister of a seventh sister, Moira was a unicorn in the witch world. She kept trying to talk Conn into having more children so she could get a witch or two in there, and Conn was fully on board, but it could take eons for immortals to procreate. "What about you two?"

Liam shook his head. "I'm at full vampire strength, but I haven't gained any additional skills as of yet. I feel like I should be able to halt people in their tracks the way Uncle Talen does, but it hasn't happened yet."

"That's okay," Hope said, calculating how best to use his abilities in Paris. "You're young. You probably won't get that powerful until you're in your fifties. What about you, Collin?"

He shrugged. "Just vampire strength and speed. I've been trying to control the weather a little bit like Uncle Jase, but nothing so far."

It'd be fascinating to see what skills they picked up through the years. She didn't have any extra strength or speed yet, but she was still hoping, although it wasn't looking good. So far, she was the only vampire in the world who caught colds and became ill, but she wasn't going to worry about that now.

"You'll get your abilities," Liam said quietly, reassuringly.

She kept her face placid. Liam was usually more about business and fighting than soothing anybody's fears. It was nice of him.

The twins looked exactly like their father, with thick dark hair and electric-green eyes. Hard-cut muscle showed on their bodies.

Part of Hope's job as a strategic leader was to help them fit in to a human neighborhood if necessary. It was difficult with their looks sometimes, but she had chosen clothing that should help.

"All right, Collin," she said. "You studied the dossiers on the enhanced females we've been assigned. What do you have?"

Collin leaned his head back against the luxurious leather chair. "Two sisters—Natalie and Annette Toussaint, twenty-two and twenty-five years old respectively. Natalie works as an art curator at a small private country club, while Annette is a pilot for the government. We discovered their enhancements the other day after hacking into yet another of the Kurjan devices placed all around the world. However, I think the Kurjans are starting to use satellites in their hunts by tracking the vibrations of enhanced females. If that happens, we're in real trouble."

Hope appreciated the detailed information. "Derrick, is there any chatter from the Kurjans today?"

"No," Derrick said. "Nothing yet. We don't know if they've caught wind of the enhanced females, but considering we hacked into their technology, I'd be shocked if the Kurjans weren't headed the same way we are."

"We just have to be faster," Hope said, her adrenaline flowing freely. This was their first solo mission, and they couldn't fail. "Okay. I'm going to set up in the building on Boulevard Saint-Germain."

They'd trained all over the world during the last five years—sometimes with other teams on real missions, sometimes on practice missions—and Hope knew exactly where she wanted to be.

"I'm going to send two teams out. Derrick and Libby, you're on Natalie. Liam and Collin, you're on Annette. When we arrive, they should both be at work, so I'll finish studying the schematics of their workplaces, and we'll come up with a plan." She didn't like kidnapping anybody, but sometimes there wasn't time to cajole potential victims into taking shelter at a safe house.

Her phone dinged, and she lifted it absently to her ear. "Kayrs-Kyllwood."

"Hi, it's Božena Jílek."

Hope went still, and her head jerked up. "Hi, I wasn't expecting your call yet."

"He's coming today," the woman said quietly, dropping into her native language of German. "I just received a message from him with a purchase order. An impressive order."

Hope sat back and dropped her pen. "Today? Are you sure?"

"Yes. He'll be here at 2:00 P.M. I don't think I can do this, Ms. Kayrs-Kyllwood."

Hope rapidly recalculated the trip. "You don't have a choice. You owe me, and you know it." She'd saved the woman's life a couple of years ago, and she was fully prepared to call in the debt.

Božena sighed. "I understand. He placed a large order, like I said."

"You can give him the products, but you have to throw the tracking dust on him as he leaves."

"He'll know it was me."

Hope would have the bastard in custody at that point. "That's irrelevant. I'll take him in, and you'll be safe. You won't have anything to worry about." Her heart hammered against her rib cage. She couldn't believe this.

"All right, but I'm leaving town the second he exits my doorway."

"That's a good idea. Thank you," Hope said. "After this, we're even." She clicked off, her eyes widening on her team.

Collin straightened. "What?"

"I found him—our hacker. He's going to be in Nuremberg in just a few hours." Hope couldn't believe it. Finally. She'd been chasing this guy for two years.

"Are you sure it's the hacker?" Libby leaned forward. "I was starting to think he didn't really exist—except he's taken a bunch of our money."

"Oh, he exists," Hope said. "Finally. We're going to nail him."

Liam didn't twitch, and his lids were still at half-mast. "What about the sisters in Paris?"

Hope knocked her fist against her head. "You're right." She wanted to save those women, but this male had been causing havoc, and she knew, she just *knew*, he was a Kurjan soldier or spy. If they could get him into Realm territory and question him, what might they discover? The guy might be the key to taking down the entire Kurjan nation, or at least forcing them to the negotiation table.

"All right." She quickly shot off several texts issuing orders. "There's a Realm team in London. I'm sending it to get the sisters. We're going after this guy."

Libby shared a look with Derrick. "Are you sure this isn't personal?"

Of course it was personal. Hope clicked through a map of Nuremberg. "He's stolen our money, taken out some of our resources, and even hacked into personal Realm business. I knew when we took out his computer control room in Scottsdale, he'd need to restock and resupply." In fact, she'd been counting on it.

"When did you contact Božena?" Collin asked.

"The second we confiscated all of his equipment," Hope admitted. Božena was one of the foremost dark computer retailers in the world. A woman who owed Hope a favor. She'd known when she had destroyed his Scottsdale headquarters that he'd have no choice but to turn to the woman, but Hope hadn't realized it'd be this quickly. He must have more funds available than she had thought.

Collin secured a knife in his vest. "Enhanced females have always been our priority."

Hope glanced at her cousin. "I agree, but the London team can get them. We finally have a chance to get this guy, Collin." It was personal, and it had been since he'd hacked into Uncle Dage's schedule a few months ago. "He's ours now." Since he was most likely a Kurjan, she'd then be in a position to negotiate with the

Kurjan leader for his release. It was time to find peace for everyone. "We can't fail. Everything is on the line."

The plane started to descend, and she secured her seat belt. She'd barely gathered her belongings when they landed in Nuremberg and rolled to a stop. As always, Liam was the first out of the plane door, scouting with his weapon, making sure they were safe before leading everyone to the waiting vehicles.

Dark SUVs drove them past the imposing brick castle that dominated the Nuremberg skyline and to the Realm control room, which looked like one of the many two-story townhouses in the area. Hope sent her team off and locked herself in to prepare.

Finally, she was going to catch the hacker. They'd been playing a game for years, and she was ready to win it.

Holding her breath, she engaged the computer system and zeroed in on the tracking dust. There he was. For a second, she just stared. He was one little blue dot on her screen. "He's headed into the tunnels outside the computer store in the old city." Which was actually camouflaged as a soap-and-sundries shop. "You know your entry points," she advised the red blips on the screen. Her teammates were already in the tunnels that had been built beneath the old city centuries ago.

Her team was the best.

Adrenaline raced through Hope's veins. She typed rapidly on her keyboard and scanned the three monitors in front of her before tapping on her ear communicator. "He's moving west, fast." She couldn't believe they might actually catch this guy.

"On it," Liam said.

She brought up a map of the entire area. "Affirmative. Derrick, I need you and Libs to come in from the south. He's going through those tunnels underground, the ones we mapped out last year that are about thirty clicks from that tea store we visited during training."

"Copy that," Derrick said. "And *you* went into the tea store. I don't do tea."

She could hear the barely veiled excitement in his tone. "Libs? Status?"

"Moving fast. Feel Kurjans in the air. Hate abandoning the original objective and hope the second team can get there soon," Libby said tersely. "Going dark now."

Hope frowned. She'd had to switch objectives because this bastard was within reach. For two years, she'd hunted him using every ounce of strategy and technology she could find and had come close several times, but never like this.

The microphone crackled. "You need to report this to headquarters," Collin said, ever the hall monitor. He and his twin, Liam, might look alike, but their approaches couldn't be more different.

"I know," Hope muttered. She quickly fired off a couple of texts to Realm headquarters in Idaho. Not that anybody could get to Nuremberg to help or stop them right now. "Everyone go dark as you move." The Kurjans had excellent equipment, and if any were in the area, they might be able to hack the comms.

Glancing out the window, she could see the castle in the distance, could hear the sounds of revelry from the Christmas market below, where shoppers were enjoying glasses of glühwein as they browsed the stalls. Was this fate? That she had been on her way to Europe when she'd received the call? Although she had chosen not to believe in fate. Well, much.

An argument in German caught her attention, and she leaned toward the open window. It was early in the afternoon for the alcohol to be affecting tourists already. She listened as two brothers argued about a Christmas present for their mother.

That was cute, even though the men sounded as if they were in their fifties.

Christmas music poured through speakers, and in the distance, the odd droning of a German official vehicle hinted that the police were near.

Movement showed on her screen. "Okay, he's down one more level in the tunnels. Go east," she ordered the two teams.

Finally. They'd have this criminal. She could feel it. Then the sound of an explosion ripped through her headset, and she dropped to her seat. "Call in, now. Everyone!"

Chapter Three

"He threw something back. Some sort of flash grenade," Libby said, coughing. "We made it to cover, but visibility is hampered by debris."

"Our team is fine," Collin said. "Where is this asshole?"

Hope swallowed and leaned closer to the screen. "He's to the north, just ahead of you."

"We'll get him," Liam snapped.

"We're close," Libby said. The young feline shifter was one of Hope's best friends and as stealthy as a missile.

Her team had trained long hours, and they worked hard; she knew each of their strengths better than she knew her own. She typed rapidly and twisted the map on the screen, widening it even farther. "The subject has to turn left by that stack of bricks on the second level down, right under the castle," she said. "We marked it last year while scouting." Though many folks were aware of the tunnels, most of them had been blocked off. Not to her people.

Derrick cleared his throat. "I hear tourists buying chess sets ahead. There aren't supposed to be people in these tunnels."

Hope took a deep breath. "Go dark and evade," she said. "Call in when you're clear."

"Let us know if you need backup," Liam said, his voice a low growl like his father's.

The team went dark again. Hope hated that part, even though she could watch their blips on screen and could engage the cameras in their vests. She did so, flinging those images to the far-right screen. The blips gave her more information right now.

Nervous, she spun the silver band on her right ring finger. Paxton had given the ring to her for her birthday years ago, and she always wore the piece. Gulping, she glanced at the gold band circling her left ring finger. Drake was the leader of the Kurjan nation, and he'd gifted her with it a while back, telling her she'd be his queen and together they'd make peace between the Realm and the Kurjans.

The queen of the Kurjan nation? What did that even mean? He might intrigue her, but was he really her fate? If the male she hunted was a Kurjan, as she suspected, she'd have some leverage in dealing with Drake. She needed answers.

Hope typed rapidly, watching the blue blip. Two years was a long time for anybody to elude her. She'd first caught wind of him through an internet search that had led to several skirmishes in the vampire and demon worlds. Then he'd siphoned off funds from both kingdoms, and he'd somehow managed to hack into the King of the Realm's personal schedule three times in the last month alone.

The breach had been discovered in time, and the schedule had been changed. If this jerk wanted to kill her uncle, she'd hunt him to the end of the globe. "Libs and Derrick? You're getting closer to him. Be ready for him to launch more explosives at you."

She'd spent weeks following the money trail of her prey to first Prague and then Nuremberg after she'd found his secret headquarters in Scottsdale and confiscated his entire computer system. Which had, unfortunately, wiped itself before she could find anything except two obscure files referencing a group called the Seven, who she was determined to protect. She was glad

Božena had followed orders and coated him with tracking dust. The woman was no doubt already out of the country now. "Go faster, teams."

Collin sighed. "You need to report this mission, and you need to do it now."

"I already did," Hope said. "I'm not stupid."

She'd take a gamble or two, but she wasn't going to risk the wrath of the King of the Realm, also known as her uncle Dage. She thought fleetingly about contacting another one of her uncles, Garrett, since he was a member of the Seven, but quickly discarded the notion. After she caught the enemy, she'd call G.

The Seven was an elite group of warriors tasked with ridding the world of a true monster, a Kurjan leader named Ulric. It wasn't Ulric she was chasing today, but no doubt it was one of his soldiers. The only description she'd gotten from an arms dealer in Iran was that her enemy was male, tall, and pale—just like the Kurjans and the members of their religious order, the Cyst.

"Tell us the rest of it," Liam ordered, obviously forgetting he was three months younger than Hope. Twice as big, though.

She swallowed. He had every right to ask. "Last week, one of my sources hinted that he might be here taking a meeting with Christopher Larkin about the Seven, but I thought it was unlikely. I just texted Larkin, and he reluctantly admitted he'd been contacted," she explained. Larkin was thought to be a psychic vampire, and since he was four thousand years old, it was possible. But he only gave readings in exchange for trucks of gold or baskets of diamonds.

Silence came over the line.

She sighed. "I can hear you judging me."

It was Collin who spoke first, and his voice was rough with anger. As the mellow cousin, he rarely lost his temper. "You have clear orders to stay away from the Seven. Period."

"I haven't disobeyed orders. We received concrete intel that an enemy of the Realm was going to be here buying illegal computer components." She'd also had a hunch they'd find the Interloper.

Yeah, her hunches were psychic, so were they really hunches? "If you ask me, fate has intervened again."

"Damn fate," Libby muttered.

Hope could agree. She thought through the weapons she had at her disposal, mainly her cousins. Though young, they were deadly and they were strong. She had to take back control of the mission. "Derrick," she reminded him. "If you throw fire underground, there's going to be a smoke problem. You need to keep that in mind."

"Affirmative," Derrick said.

"Liam and Collin, you come in strong from the other side," Hope ordered, typing rapidly, trying to find the best place for them to take this guy.

"Not a problem," Liam said.

"Got it," Collin said.

She tracked her swiftly moving team by their dots on the map. Liam and Collin worked perfectly together, sweeping each area before they went forward, moving in a synchronized dance. Derrick did the same with Libby, but he stayed slightly ahead of the shifter no matter what, willing to get shot to prevent her from being harmed. Hope admired that in him, but she didn't want to see any of her cousins hurt.

"Hope." Liam's low tone came over the line. "I'm thinking maybe it was more than a hunch, considering you got your source to toss tracking dust on this guy."

She winced. "You know I'm always prepared."

Triple sighs came through the line, along with a small chuckle from Libby.

Hope winced. "Honestly, I didn't think we'd actually find him here." She'd been chasing this guy all over the world for the last two years. She leaned forward. "Wait a minute, he's gone south." There was no tunnel to the south. It looked as if his body was moving through solid rock. "Twenty feet ahead of you, Derrick and Libs. He somehow turned left." Liam and Collin approached from the other direction. "Ten feet ahead of you, guys, there's a doorway. There's a passage or something."

"We don't see it," Derrick said. The sound of tapping and pounding came over the line.

"It's solid brick," Collin muttered.

Panic rose in Hope. "It's not. I can see him moving." She'd made it her mission to catch the man she'd dubbed the Interloper, and she was the best strategic planner in her generation. She didn't know how and she didn't know why, but she felt like her first big test was to catch this guy. "There's got to be a way in. Derrick, if you have to use fire, do it."

"Copy that. Forming now," Derrick said calmly.

Good. "Throw it at the brick. I'm telling you, there's some sort of tunnel in there." As Hope watched, her quarry climbed up and emerged out onto the street. She flipped on an external camera feed. Maybe she could actually see him instead of just following him as a freaking blue dot. "Damn it, he's exited the tunnel in the Christmas market." She yanked a bulletproof vest over her head and reached for her weapon.

"Don't do it," Collin snarled. "Hope, you're not covered. You need to stay there."

"We're losing him," she said, cocking her gun and then yanking a jacket over her vest and weapon. She hurried toward the door.

Something blasted over the line. "We'll find the tunnel," Derrick said.

"We're headed back and will rendezvous with you," Collin said, his tone grim.

Hope snatched a combat knife off the weapons table and shoved it into her boot, pulling her phone free to watch the blue dot. "He's right below me."

"Hope Kayrs-Kyllwood," Derrick snapped. "Do not even think of leaving that control room."

She unlocked the doors with their multiple bolts and dashed into the hallway, running full bore down the steps out into the

Christmas market. Tourists milled around, looking at the colorful booths with cups of glühwein in their hands, chatting happily. She kept her phone in her hand and followed the trail of the enemy through the crowd, dodging out of the way of an elderly man moving fragile Christmas ornaments on a rickety cart.

"Hope, where are you?" Liam called. "We're headed back out. We'll be there in about three minutes, tops. Do not engage this guy on your own."

Ignoring his command, she ran down an alleyway, turning, headed toward one of the many nearby buildings with their curved copper roofs.

The Interloper was quick, but she saw a way to cut him off.

"He's moving toward the east corner of the Albrecht-Durer-Haus in about thirty seconds," she said. "If anybody is near, green light granted on taking him down." Or she would do it. She ran, watching the tracking device. He was so close. Finally.

Her quarry turned suddenly around a booth and cut through another alley. She dropped into a full run, going as fast as she could, avoiding tourists and wine on her way. Her heart rate sped up. He turned down a blind corner where the town had just erected several new Christmas market tents that weren't normally there. They completely blocked the way.

She had him now.

The crowd pressed around her, and she searched frantically for a glimpse of him before glancing down at her phone. Somehow he'd managed to get around one of the booths. She followed, smiled at a man who tried to sell her a pretzel, and ducked behind the booth and down another alley.

The snowy cobblestones fought her boots and kept her slightly off-balance, and soon the sound of the crowd disappeared. She hissed an updated location for her team. Her prey swiftly took another corner, fast. A quick look at the map on her phone confirmed she could intercept him. She veered the other direction and then saw him slip behind a brick building where there was no escape.

They were alone in the alley. She slid to a halt on the rough, snow-covered cobblestones.

"Stop," she yelled, pulling out her weapon and instantly firing green lasers—the ones that harmed immortals—into the brick building next to him. He paused, his back to her. She moved cautiously toward him, speaking to her team. "I've got him. Get here fast."

He was bigger than she expected for somebody who moved so quickly and gracefully. He still faced away from her, at least six and a half feet tall, with solid muscle and a broad back—short for a Kurjan but unusually broad for one as well. He'd dressed in black cargo pants and a dark sweatshirt and wasn't even breathing heavily after his run.

A hat covered his head. Yet there was something about him. "Turn around," she ordered, her voice trembling just a little. She couldn't believe she'd caught him.

Slowly, he put his hands down at his sides.

"I will shoot you," she said, meaning every word.

Slowly he turned around, and she took a step back. Her vision filled with silvery-blue eyes, black hair, and a roughly chiseled face.

Her breath stopped. The entire world tilted. "Paxton?"

"Hi, Hope." He looked behind her, his gaze scouting the area.

She set her stance as memories assailed her. Pax playing with a stuffed dragon when they were toddlers. Him defending her to a bully. His lips lowering to hers for her first soft kiss. Years later, that same mouth taking hers after a motorcycle ride—not so softly. She still wore the silver ring he'd given her as a child and the pink quartz necklace he'd bought for her as a teenager. For luck.

He edged toward the side. Paxton was supposed to be a scientist working with his uncle. But what exactly had he been doing? Her best friend was a traitor.

The betrayal wasn't sharp; it didn't cut like a knife. It was the full swing of a baseball bat, right to the center of her heart, smashing the silly organ into useless bits. "It's you."

His body bunched to attack. "Yeah."

Without hesitating, she fired three times, hitting center mass.

Chapter Four

He couldn't believe she'd fucking shot him. Paxton Phoenix sat on his ass on the frozen cobblestones, his back to a brick building as fury slid through his veins. Oh, she hadn't damaged his heart, and she could have. He'd practiced shooting with her enough to know that she could have easily put him in the hospital for a month.

Instead, blood poured out of his left shoulder, the right side of his rib cage, and his gut. Then she'd nailed him in the left thigh, forcing him to go down. He met her furious glare squarely. He'd always known that someday it would come down to this. Oh, he hadn't expected to get shot, but he'd been certain that sooner or later he'd see this stark betrayal in her indigo-blue eyes.

To her credit, she kept her stance wide and the weapon pointed at him, right between his eyes this time, but she was pale and she was shaking. Her nose was turning red.

He couldn't help himself. "Hope, you need a heavier jacket."

Both of her eyebrows rose, and her chin dropped. "Are you kidding me?" she snapped, her full five-foot-two frame vibrating. She was small and compact—definitely feminine. "You're a traitor, and you're worried about my jacket?"

Amusement bubbled up even as pain throbbed throughout his body. He sent healing cells to the injuries and calculated how quickly he could get past her without hurting her. "Yeah, you still fall ill sometimes. You need a jacket," he retorted, gratified when color flushed into her face. At least she wasn't so pale now. For a moment, he'd been concerned she'd pass out.

"You're supposed to be a scientist," she spat.

Not really. Not even close, actually. He didn't like her pointing the gun at him, but he didn't want to scare her. Being on the ground, bleeding like this, threw him back into his violent childhood for a second. The world tunneled in, and he exhaled slowly.

"Pax?" she asked.

"I'm good."

She tapped her ear communicator with her free hand, pushing back her thick auburn hair and revealing the blue, winding, prophecy mark that rose up her neck on both sides. "Liam and Collin, I need your assistance. Libby and Derrick, tear down the temporary computer headquarters—I don't want the computers left exposed—and lock up. We may need the location again in the future. Meet at the rendezvous point at the corner of Lacenster in fifteen minutes." Fury now lit her eyes.

Great. He wasn't in any state to take on both Collin and Liam Kayrs, and he knew it. He'd trained with them as teens, before they thought he'd turned to science, when he'd actually been training all around the globe. He sensed them before they turned the corner and advanced, both halting near Hope, shock on their faces.

"Paxton." Liam was the one who spoke first.

"Hi, guys," Paxton said sardonically.

Both males took several steps forward, putting their bodies between him and Hope.

"You can't think I'd hurt her," he muttered.

They both stared at him, their expressions stone cold, looking more like their father, Conn, than ever. They were about Pax's size in muscle and mass. He was quicker for some reason, and he would have to use that to his advantage. He didn't want to hurt any of them. He was learning to infiltrate minds and cause pain like some of the older demons could, but he'd never harm any of his friends like that. It just wasn't fair.

Collin studied him, his green eyes flat, hard, and cold. *"You're* the traitor?"

"Looks like it," Paxton said. He was shocked and impressed that Hope had been able to catch him. It had taken her two years, and he'd worked hard to avoid her, even though he knew this showdown had to occur at some point. Fate was fate...and she was a bitch.

Liam barely twitched. "Why?" he asked shortly.

"You wouldn't understand," Paxton said. His leg was healed. He slowly pushed himself up, pressing a hand over the still-bleeding wound in his side. She'd nicked a rib, and it had splintered into his lung, where the healing cells were still hard at work. Hope hadn't said a word, but he could feel her pain from his betrayal. It dug deep inside him, lodging deeper than any blade ever could. "I'm sorry," he said.

"Don't be sorry," she snapped, trying to move up between her cousins. They instantly took a step toward each other, putting them shoulder to shoulder, with Hope completely hidden behind them. Her attempt to shove them out of the way almost amused Paxton, but the pain surrounding him was too great.

Finally, she just edged to the side and looked around Collin's broad back. "Why, Paxton? It's a good question, and one you need to answer."

"I can't explain it to you. If I could, I would." Pax calculated the best way to get beyond the twins.

"Fair enough." Liam was the first to move toward him, yanking out a pair of zip ties.

Heat filled Paxton's chest. "You think you can tie me?" He really didn't want to physically hurt anybody.

Liam rolled his eyes. "You haven't trained, Pax. We have. Don't make this harder than it needs to be."

So they still thought he was a nerdy scientist. Interesting. He'd assumed they could see the killer lurking inside him, but maybe people just saw what they wanted. "I'm stronger than I look," he warned the young warrior.

In answer, Hope lifted her weapon and aimed it at his forehead. "I am happy to fry your brain for the next six months, Paxton Phoenix. Just say the word."

He read the hard determination in her gaze. The female wasn't bluffing. She would actually shoot him and leave him to repair his brain over several months. Giving her a look, he turned and let Liam zip-tie his hands at his back. The pat-down was brief and revealed two knives and a gun as well as a flash drive. Liam spun him around and tossed the USB to Hope.

"You'll never hack it," Paxton said, challenging Hope, wanting to see more color in her face. She was starting to shiver in the cold, and he didn't like that. Her anger would cause her to warm up a little. He was happy to provide her with a focus.

"That's what you think," Liam said, yanking him by the arm toward the side of the alley. "We're going around back, and we're going to avoid the market. I want to hurt you, Paxton," he said, his voice low. "So please give me the chance to put a bullet between your ears. And you know what? This little knife you just gave me? We both know I could use it to take off your head."

Paxton heard the truth in his ex-friend's tone. "Even so," he snorted, "you can't take off my head. You all know the king will want to talk to me about this."

Liam brightened. "You're right. Dage hasn't had a good kill in a while. I'm sure he'll take you apart limb by limb, and then he'll kill you."

A small sound of distress came from Hope and shot through Paxton like another bullet. She most certainly didn't mean to make the sound, and it was killing him that he was hurting her.

She made a quick call on her phone to arrange transport as they maneuvered through the alleys behind the quaint townhouses of Nuremberg. A light snow started to fall, and he glanced again at Hope. "Somebody find her a heavier jacket."

Collin slowly turned his head and looked at Paxton, no real expression on his face, but a *what the fuck are you thinking?* glint in his eye.

Paxton couldn't explain even if he'd wanted to. The breeze picked up, and his instincts went on full alert. "You get that?" he asked.

"Shit," Collin said.

"We have incoming," Liam said to Hope. "Get behind me. Get behind me now."

She obeyed instantly. While Hope was the only female vampire alive, for some reason she hadn't gained immortal strength yet. When she was injured, she stayed injured longer than she should. Her fighting skills were pretty good for a human. Against an immortal right now, she wouldn't win. However, as Paxton could attest, she was a hell of a shot.

Instinct had Paxton looking up. "Sniper to the east," he bellowed, partially turning to shield Hope.

The first bullet hit Collin square in the chest and threw him several feet back before two Kurjans ran around the stucco building, guns in their hands. They were almost seven feet tall, their black hair tipped with red, skin ghost pale, and lips bloodred. Once, they'd been unable to venture into sunlight, but they had evolved, and the day was overcast. These two wore black uniforms with silver designations on their breasts.

Liam took a bullet to the shoulder, dropped, and stumbled to his feet, already firing toward the two. Hope fired at the one on the left, and Paxton ducked and rolled, trying to come up in front of her. She nearly shot him in the ass.

"Get out of the way," she yelled. "You're not trained."

He never should've let Liam bind him. "Release my hands now," he snapped.

"Why, because your friends are here?" she hissed.

The twins fired again at the Kurjans, and the two in front of them went down. Another bullet pinged from high above. "Sniper still active," Pax yelled. "Hug the building."

"They're your people, aren't they?" Hope pressed her back to the bricks.

"No, they're not my people," he said. "Undo my hands now."

She rested her head back and took a deep breath. "No. Just let us handle things."

"There are more coming," Liam said, plastering his wounded brother against the building. "How bad are you hurt?"

"I'm fine," Collin said, his face pale. Even though a bulletproof vest covered his wide chest, he'd been close enough to the laser that it would've hit hard and formed a strong enough metal disc that he probably had a couple of ribs broken. "Move," he hissed.

Hope exhaled. "I'll take lead."

"The fuck you will," Paxton said. "That's it." He dove on the ground, hitting his right shoulder and rolling in a perfect somersault to grab a knife out of the downed Kurjan's boot. Quick motions had the zip ties sliced open and him standing, reaching for one of the unconscious soldier's weapons. The farthest Kurjan started to stir, and Paxton kicked him square in the temple, making him flop down. "I'm on lead," he growled.

"Oh, screw you." Hope lifted her weapon.

He looked at her over his shoulder. "You shoot me again, baby, and you're really going to regret it."

Fire lit her eyes, turning them a violet blue that didn't exist in the ordinary world.

"Are you kidding me? His hands are free." Liam glared at Paxton and lifted his gun to aim. "He might figure out how to shoot that thing."

"We need him for now. Let's go," his brother said through clenched teeth. Sweat dotted his brow, and healing vibrations cascaded from him.

"I know this city like the back of my hand," Paxton said. "Hug the wall, and then we're turning south." They didn't have any choice but to follow him—and he was just fine with that. Once he got them to safety, he'd have to figure out a way to gain his freedom. For now, he wasn't going to let them die.

Until about ten minutes ago, they'd been his friends, his family. He led them easily through the labyrinth of narrow alleys, almost to where he'd heard Hope order transport to be waiting. His skin crawled, and he held up a hand. The breeze stopped.

Two Kurjan soldiers jumped down from the nearest roof ahead of him and two from the rear. He instantly went into battle mode, firing his gun and slashing with his knife, rushing them. A bullet hit his wrist, and the gun flew out of his hand. He dropped into hand-to-hand with the nearest soldier while Liam did the same. A quick pivot, and he slammed the knife into the soldier's throat, slicing furiously until he freed the head from the body. Kurjan blood spurted across Paxton's neck, instantly burning him.

Liam dispatched the other soldier, and the Kurjan's head bumped across the rough cobblestones.

Pax could hear shots behind him where Hope no doubt fired, and hopefully Collin did as well.

The sound of breaking bones came from behind him. Okay, so Collin had dropped into hand-to-hand.

A series of darts struck Paxton's neck. "What the hell?" He yanked several out and looked up in the direction from which they'd come. This was a kidnapping attempt? Shit. They wanted Hope.

"Darts," Hope bellowed. "Everybody get against the building."

The darts were coming from a sniper position high above, so Paxton instantly moved where she ordered. She must have seen the shooter.

Her eyes were wide on him, and she was cradling her arm, snow covering her side. Had she fallen? "When did you learn to fight?"

She hadn't seen anything yet. "Your arm?" he growled.

"Broken." She winced. "Trying to heal it now."

"More darts incoming," Liam yelled. Then he groaned and fell to his knees with several bullet holes in his temple, face, and neck. He dropped forward onto the stones, blood seeping from beneath his face.

Paxton turned and fired perfectly through the air. A groan sounded, and then a crash echoed.

Everything wavered and went dark around Paxton. "What was in those darts?" He looked around. There were four fallen Kurjans as well as the one off the roof. There would no doubt be more coming. "Were you hit?" he asked Hope.

She was holding her neck with her good hand, and she'd gone stark white pale.

Panic clawed through him with a force he'd never experienced.

"Damn it." Collin reached down and hauled his brother over his shoulder.

Hope sank to her knees, pitching forward.

Paxton forced the darkness away and caught her before she hit the cobblestones, ducking his head to toss her over his aching shoulder. She sputtered and then fell unconscious as the drug in the darts must've taken effect.

Collin leveled a grim look at him. "You hurt her, and there won't be one inch on this world where you can hide."

Paxton ignored the threat and turned, loping into an unsteady jog as he led the way out of the labyrinth. Each step was excruciating, and the darkness kept coming for him as the drugs moved through his system. He stumbled, and the scent of vanilla beans and orange spice wafted around him.

Hope's scent.

He growled low, dug deep, and kept moving. They finally emerged onto a quiet street where an innocuous off-white van waited silently, the delivery driver long gone.

Collin tossed Liam in the back with a low groan.

Paxton gently flipped Hope over, cradling her easily against his chest. Possessiveness pummeled him, stronger and more primal than any drug from a dart. He'd never made himself look down deep inside where his monster lived, but today the door to that hellhole cracked open, and the beast roared, rattling his very bones.

"Give her to me." Collin reached for his cousin.

Paxton bared his teeth as that possessive predator inside him protested. She was *his*.

Collin caught sight of his expression and reached for his weapon.

"No." Paxton gently handed her over, sensing more Kurjans coming. "Go. I'll fight them off." He turned to run back toward danger, and the darkness finally took him.

He went down, landed hard on his elbow and then his face. Collin didn't try to break his fall. Pain exploded, and the gleeful blackness opened up its jaws and swallowed him whole.

Chapter Five

"I can't believe I was out for the entire flight home." Hope sat on a plush leather examination table in her aunt's lab, having blood drawn. Her head hurt, and her tongue was swollen. When she'd regained consciousness after arriving at Realm headquarters in Idaho, her arm was already in a cast.

"I set your fractured ulna while you were out. Now I'm going to look at the components in those darts," Emma said, inserting an IV needle into Hope's arm. "Here's a nice concoction that'll help you feel better."

It was nothing new for Emma to take Hope's blood, but today she just ached. Her head hurt, and she couldn't grasp the thought that Paxton had betrayed her, had betrayed all of them, actually. It didn't make sense. She desperately needed to speak with him.

Emma smoothed Hope's hair away from her face. "We'll figure this out, honey, I promise."

"I know." Hope tried to force a smile for her aunt, who was also the Queen of the Realm. She was their chief scientist, and she spent more time inside the lab trying to cure diseases than she did outside it. Her hair was raven black and her eyes sparkling blue, and as usual, she wore a goofy T-shirt, frayed jeans, and tennis shoes beneath a white lab coat.

The door opened, and a large figure came inside. "Are you all right?" asked Hope's uncle Kane, moving to her and looking into her eyes.

She blinked. He was actually her great-uncle, but when one lived forever, it was necessary to condense titles. "Emma? You called Uncle Kane?" she whispered.

Emma swallowed. "There's nothing wrong with a second opinion."

Except there was. Warning ticked down Hope's spine. Emma hated anybody messing with her equipment, so she must have been more worried than she appeared to be, to call for a second opinion.

Kane stared at the sling. "Heard you broke your arm."

Hope swallowed. "Yeah."

"You try to send healing cells to it?" he asked.

Duh. "What a great idea," she said, trying to cover her sarcasm but failing miserably. "Maybe the drugs are slowing down my healing cells." Her voice wasn't as level as she'd hoped. All immortals had healing cells to repair injuries, but hers weren't working. Never had, really.

"When was the last time you fractured a bone?" His eyes glinted with intelligence.

"Many years ago in a bike wreck," she admitted. So there was no way to determine if she had healing cells. They didn't work against colds or the flu, basically because most immortals weren't susceptible to such illnesses.

"You want blood?" Kane's fangs dropped.

Emma didn't look up from her microscope. "No. No blood until the drugs have completely exited her system. I'm not taking any chances."

"Huh." Kane stalked over to the microscope and nudged Emma aside.

Emma glared at her brother-in-law. "Kane, give me a break. It's my lab."

"I'm still the smartest person on the planet, last time I checked," Kane said absently, having to lean down to look into the scope. "Plus, you called me."

Emma rolled her eyes. "I'm real glad to hear those self-esteem classes are working for you."

Hope shifted uneasily. "Kane, have you been down to see Paxton?"

Her uncle straightened and looked over his shoulder at her. "No. You're not going, either."

"I don't think I can go near him until I calm down a little bit." Hope sighed, her chest hurting. "I don't even know what to think."

Kane looked around the spacious lab. He wore a black silk shirt tucked into black pants, and even relaxed, his muscles played as he moved. His hair was Kayrs dark, his eyes violet, and his intellect unsurpassed. "You know, I'm surprised your parents aren't here, or your grandparents for that matter."

"I kicked them out," Emma said simply. "They were driving me nuts, and you're the next to go."

Kane straightened to his full height just as one of the many pieces of lab equipment on the wide granite counter beeped.

Emma hurried over to it and then turned as a printer spit out several pieces of paper. She read through each page rapidly. "Riveting."

"What?" Kane leaned over her shoulder.

She handed him the papers.

Hope held a hand to her stomach. "What did they give me?"

"Quite a few interesting components in those darts," Emma murmured. "The one that knocked you out was xylazine, which is used by veterinarians to sedate large animals, usually horses."

"*Damno is totus ut abyssus,*" Kane said. "It's also a street drug, which is probably where the Kurjans got it. They no doubt wanted to kidnap you."

For goodness' sake. Hope knew Latin, so it was silly that Kane still swore in the language when around her. "We've suspected they've had a bounty out on me for years. Am I going to be okay?"

"Sure," Emma said.

Hope narrowed her gaze. "What else was in the dart?"

"I don't know," Emma said.

Hope was quiet for a moment, her lungs stuttering. Emma knew everything about drugs. "What do you mean you don't know?"

"There's a very, very small ingredient my equipment couldn't identify." Emma frowned, gazing off in the distance as her amazing mind no doubt went to work.

"Hmm," Kane said as he read over the sheet. "We'll need to do further testing. Let's use the robust flame ionization detector."

"Out," Emma said. "I know what I'm doing." Even though he was a good head taller than she was, Emma put both her hands on his chest and pushed him toward the door. "I appreciate the consult, and I'll be in touch once I have more information."

"Jeez, fine," Kane said, stomping off. "Call me when you need me."

The tension in the room dissipated with his departure. "I swear, your uncles." Emma sighed.

"My mom was just as bad." Hope chuckled.

"Yeah, Janie's a sweetheart," Emma said, her expression softening. "I probably shouldn't have kicked her out when I kicked your dad out, but Zane's pacing was upping my anxiety."

Her parents were still overprotective even though she was twenty-four years old. "How much of this unknown compound remains in my blood?"

"Not much," Emma said. "The second tests show that it's dissipating quickly, whatever it is, but I still want to identify the compound. It's something I haven't seen before."

Hope flopped back on the comfortable table, her hair spreading out over the pillow. Her arm ached, but she didn't care. "That can't be good."

"No, it can't. I need to take another sample from Paxton."

Hope swallowed. "How is he?" She felt like an idiot for asking, but if his head was pounding as bad as hers was, well, he probably deserved it.

"He's not talking," Emma admitted. "He's just sitting there looking like Pax."

Her heart hurt. "They have him in a cell?" Hope had to talk to him. None of what had happened made sense. Paxton, her best friend for life, wouldn't have betrayed her like this. Something was off. It had to be.

"Oh yeah," Emma said. "He's definitely in a cell."

Hope didn't know how to ask the question, but she'd never shied away from the truth. "Are they going to torture him?"

"I hope not." Emma's brow furrowed. "I just can't believe he's the one who hacked into Dage's schedule. It doesn't make a lick of sense. He probably has it on his Realm app."

"No, he doesn't," Hope said. "We put protocols in place three years ago so only a few of us have Dage's schedule at any one time. Even my parents don't have it unless they ask for it."

Emma's eyebrows rose. "I didn't know that." Not surprising, considering the queen lived in her lab. "I'm glad. Sometimes I worry about Dage."

"He always worries about you." Hope forced a smile. "And, Emma?"

"Yes?" Emma reached for Hope's wrist to take her pulse.

"How much faster did Paxton come out of the drug than I did?"

Emma finished and made a notation on a tablet she kept on the counter. "According to your cousins, Paxton was conscious and swearing at them within two hours." She scanned Hope's forehead with a thermometer. "No fever. Apparently, Pax didn't like the way they trussed him up for the long flight home."

Hope exhaled slowly and waited until her aunt met her gaze. "I should be stronger than all of them, since I'm the only female vampire in the entire world. I have the blood of almost every species in my veins." She paused and looked down at the cast and sling holding her arm to her chest. "I can't believe you set my arm." She should have been able to heal a simple fracture herself. "Why am I not strong and fast like they are?"

Emma pressed her lips together and studied her. "You still have a lot of time to come into your strength. You're young yet."

Hope sat up again. She had to face facts. "I figured I'd gain strength by the time I turn twenty-five next year, but there's nothing new. I hadn't realized it fully until I started training with my team. I'm not like them. Plus, you had to actually set this bone." She said the last on a whisper.

"It's doubtful you'll go from where you are now to full immortal vampire strength in just a year," Emma mused.

Exactly, and it was time to stop waiting to figure out what was wrong with her—especially since this broken bone proved irrevocably that Hope lacked immortal abilities. "That's unacceptable. If my fate goes anything like my mom's did, then I'll need to meet my destiny when I'm twenty-five." She wasn't ready.

Emma took a piece of candy out of her pocket and slowly unwrapped it before popping it into her mouth. "We've studied your blood your entire life. There's nothing wrong with you on a genetic or cellular level."

"Then why do I get sick?"

"It's a question I've been asking since you were born," Emma said. "Your chromosomal pairs are those of a vampire. Your tissues, blood, muscles, and everything else I've ever studied are those of an immortal."

Yet Hope caught colds, now broke bones that she couldn't heal, and often suffered from headaches. "I've been thinking about this since I formed the squad, and there's only one theory that really works."

"After setting your arm, I have a theory too, but I don't love it," Emma muttered.

Hope already had an inkling of what that theory would be, but she needed to hear the only doctor she'd ever known say the words. "You know, don't you?"

"I don't know anything," Emma admitted. "However, I have spent decades studying the issue and trying to figure out a way to make you stronger."

"Why haven't you ever told me?" Hope asked.

Emma shrugged and chewed on the candy. "Why would I? I didn't have any hard and fast answers. Hoping that you'd get stronger and be invincible by the time you hit twenty-five seemed to work for both of us. But apparently, we've both been ruminating on the problem a lot lately."

"Ah, crap," Hope said. "We're on the same track, aren't we?"

Emma chuckled. "You haven't said anything, so I can't confirm or deny that."

Hope chewed on her lip, feeling much better now that the IV had dripped whatever magical concoction Emma had created into her veins. Her headache was slowly subsiding. "Liam and Collin have a vampire-demon father and a witch mother."

"Yep," Emma said, reaching into her pocket for a piece of candy to toss to Hope.

Hope caught it one-handed. As usual, it was butterscotch. "However," she continued, "the twins are vampires. They have all the characteristics of vampires, not demons or witches, even though they could've easily gone the other way."

Emma nodded. "Yep. Immortals can only take on one aspect of their heritage. That's why Derrick is more witch than vampire, even though his father is one of the most powerful vampires alive. His mother's pretty tough too."

Hope's thoughts turned traitorously to Paxton. He was much more a demon than a vampire, which pleased him, since his mom had been a kind demon and his dad an asshole vampire. "So I can only inherit the traits of one part of my entire heritage."

Emma took out another piece of candy. She was obviously feeling uneasy, or she wouldn't be pounding candy like a two-year-old. "That's what I surmise."

"You know what that means, right?"

"Maybe," Emma allowed.

Hope just had to say the words out loud. "My traits are those of a human." Her mother was human while her father had all sorts of interesting ancestors. When humans mated immortals, they always, and that meant *always,* had immortal children.

"Never in the history of the immortal world have progeny from an immortal ended up human," Emma said, her tone reassuring but her eyes giving her concern away.

Hope ripped open the paper protecting the candy. "True. But there has never been a female vampire, either." Vampires only made males. Period. Except for her.

"That's true," Emma said.

"So I'm human. Or mostly human." Hope shoved the treat in her mouth. "What does that mean for me?"

Emma rolled her neck. "Being human isn't so bad. There are a lot of great ones out there."

That wasn't the issue. Hope glanced down again at her offending arm and then back up at her aunt. "Am I even immortal?"

Emma slowly unwrapped another piece of butterscotch candy. "I have absolutely no idea."

Chapter Six

Paxton sat in the well-guarded cell, his head still pounding from whatever drug had been in those darts. It felt like the backs of his eyeballs were trying to force their way through the front. Even so, he kept a bored expression on his face as he sat on the rough dirt floor. He had to make sure Hope had been able to heal her fractured arm, and so far, nobody would give him the answers he needed.

They'd left him in there all day, no doubt as an interrogation tactic. What they didn't know was that he could remain still for days and not give a fuck. His training had been more extensive than anybody would ever realize. A door opened in the distance, and heavy footsteps sounded down the long hallway, stopping in front of his cell, which was covered and protected by steel bars that even he couldn't open. He looked up as three figures loomed on the other side. "I wondered if the trifecta of power and glory would appear at the same time."

He was being a complete jerk, but when faced with three of the most powerful badasses on the planet, a guy had to have some pride. Plus, they knew him and might be able to get into his head. He had to prevent that at any cost.

The King of the Realm, Dage Kayrs, stood on the far left, tension and boiling fury in every line of his body. Even though he was hundreds of years old, his hair was mostly black, his eyes silver, and he could probably take down an ancient redwood with his pinky finger.

Next to him stood his brother, Talen Kayrs, who was the strategic leader of the Realm and had probably racked up a body count Pax couldn't imagine. He was also Hope's grandfather but still looked thirty with his dark hair, golden eyes, and dense muscles. One barely there silver strip showed in his hair from his surviving a plague years ago.

On the right stood Zane Kyllwood, the king of the demon nation, Hope's father, and the one currently emoting so much rage that Paxton could feel his skin heat.

"You almost got her killed, Paxton," Zane said evenly, his voice soft but filled with danger.

Paxton stood, determined to face these three on even ground. "Bullshit."

One of Zane's dark eyebrows rose. His hair was just as dark as Dage's, but he had sizzling green eyes that, right now, weren't anything close to human. If he walked out into the human world, they would know they had immortals living among them. "Excuse me?"

"That Kurjan squad wasn't there for me, Zane. They were there for Hope. I don't know how they knew she was there. How is her arm?"

"Don't ask about her damn arm," Zane snapped.

Paxton studied him, knowing better but still trying to slide into his mind. It was a new talent, one he was developing at a fairly young age. Many demons had the skill. Unfortunately, the ability to teleport had been taken from them years ago, before he'd even had a chance to see if he could accomplish the feat. The ability would be handy right about now. He mentally pinpointed Zane's love for his daughter and tried to get inside his mind.

Zane's chin jerked up. "Nice try, kid. Stop, or I'll fry your brain so it'll never be the same."

"Then tell me about her damn arm," Paxton said softly, more than ready to try again.

Talen cocked his head to the side. "You know, I might just have to kill him before we get the information we need."

"If anybody's going to kill him, it's going to be me," the king said.

"Oh, fuck no," Zane said, moving closer to the bars. "He's mine."

Paxton knew he should be feeling fear right now. But truth be told, he just didn't give a shit any longer. He'd broken Hope's heart, and she would never forgive him. That was pretty much the end of him caring about anything. "How about you all have a go at me?" he offered, hoping he'd feel better if somebody knocked him out.

"You want that?" Zane muttered.

"Sure. You can go in alphabetical order. And, Zane, if you really are itching, then we can go in reverse alphabetical order. First names only, since you all have Ks for last names." It was something that had always impressed Paxton. There were times, especially when he'd been younger, that he'd wished he could've been one of them. His father had hated his guts. So wearing Paelotin's last name had never felt right to him.

It was Zane who spoke first. "You really don't think I'll take you apart?"

Paxton turned his focus entirely on Hope's father. "I'm surprised you didn't do it eons ago," he admitted. "Do you know how many times I snuck into her room over the years?" Sure. It was mostly to hang out or for comfort when his father had beaten the crap out of him. But even when he'd gotten older, he'd snuck past the guards and the cameras to visit her.

"Of course I knew," Zane exploded. "Do you honestly think I don't know exactly who comes into my house?" The air grew hot and heavy with tension. "I knew you were there every time, Paxton. But you know what? Even when you were way too old to be sneaking into my girl's room, I trusted you."

It was like a blow to the solar plexus, and Paxton took it without wincing. Without even giving an indication of how squarely the punch had landed.

Dage studied him for a long time, silent, as Talen did the same, while Zane was so still it was difficult to determine if he was even breathing. But of course, he was. The guy probably didn't even know that Paxton had learned all about the work he'd done as the Ghost, who most people thought was only a legend now. He wasn't. Zane had been an assassin long ago.

The trio might be intimidating, but Paxton would never let any fear show. "How is Hope doing?"

"She's doing better," Zane said. "Emma has her hooked up to a bag of something, and she says the headache's going away, although she has not been able to heal the fractured arm."

Paxton barely hid his surprise that Zane had answered him finally.

"The twins told me how you stood in front of her and tried to save her," Zane said. "Are you or are you not working with the Kurjans?"

"Not," Pax said.

Zane's gaze probed deep, and Paxton slapped shields into place over his mind. "Now would be a real good time for you to tell me what you've been up to," Zane suggested, not so quietly. "Rumor has it you were able to fight way better than the twins expected."

"I got lucky." The urge to tell him everything nearly overwhelmed Paxton. But he'd been trained by the best. He knew how to kill, and hell, he pretty much knew how to die. Right now, he couldn't tell them anything. "So long as Hope is safe, I don't really care what you do with me," he said honestly.

"Why'd you hack into my schedule?" Dage asked. "If you'd just called me, I would've given it to you."

Paxton kept his lips tightly together. It had been so easy to hack into the system until Hope and Chalton had upgraded it. "I wasn't going to kill you, King," he admitted. "I just wanted to know where you were."

Zane cocked his head to the side. "It's almost like you want me to beat the crap out of you."

If there was one thing in life Paxton knew, it was that he could take a punch. He'd spent the first half of his life taking them from his worthless father. Ironically, it was Zane who had rescued him. Zane and Talen, actually. "If that's what you need to do, feel free," Pax offered. He deserved it.

"It may come to that," Zane said grimly. "First, we're going to have a nice little chat with your uncle. The absent-minded professor has been your guardian this entire time—surely he can give me some answers."

Paxton's ears heated. "Why talk to him? He doesn't know a thing."

"Bullshit," Zane countered. "We're ripping apart your life right now, Phoenix. I'm going to know absolutely everything about you by tomorrow, and your uncle is right in the middle of your life. I took you to him, remember?"

Yeah. After Zane had saved Pax's life. "Leave my uncle alone. He doesn't know anything. He's a guy who studies butterflies."

"My ass," Talen grumbled, finally speaking. "I say we see how he stands up to torture."

For the first time, Paxton let anger sizzle in his eyes. "You touch my uncle, and we're going to have a problem."

Talen's smile wasn't nice. It wasn't even fierce. It was cruel. "I'll bring him to you in a box." With that, he turned and strode away. The king gave Zane one long look and then followed his brother.

Zane remained on the other side of the bars. "Tell me your motivation for this fucked up mission was to keep Hope safe."

Now Paxton couldn't help but let the emotion show on his face. For just a second, he felt no need to hide from Zane. "Everything I've done in my entire life was to keep that female safe. You of all people should know that."

Zane lifted one eyebrow. "I told you once, many years ago, after I beat the hell out of your dad and kicked him out of headquarters, that we make our own fate."

"I remember," Pax said softly.

Zane shook his head. "So exactly what kind of fate did you just make for yourself?"

"You wouldn't understand if I told you, and I'm not going to say another word. So if you want to come in here and go at me, let's do this, Zane."

If Paxton had thought Talen's smile was cruel, he'd been mistaken. The one that instantly lifted Zane's lips shot a chill through the entire room. Zane leaned to the side and tapped on a keyboard. The bars slowly rolled out of the way. Paxton braced himself. When the demon king came at him, he probably wouldn't see it until he felt the first strike.

"Let's go," Zane said.

Paxton jerked. "Is this a trick?"

"No. Get out of the cell."

"All right. You want to fight in the hallway? We'll fight in the hallway." Except he wasn't really going to engage. Zane had saved him when he needed it, and no matter how screwed up things had become, Paxton would never lift a hand against the warrior. "You hit first. You are kind of old." Yet Zane looked thirty and could destroy anybody in his line of sight.

Something ached in Paxton, speaking to Zane like that, but he also couldn't back down. He walked into the hallway.

"Move," Zane said. "Get out of here."

"And where am I... Okay." Paxton strode down the hallway, expecting an attack from behind. His gut churning, he strode up the stairs into the main lobby of headquarters. The Christmas tree in the corner glowed light blue, with handmade ornaments hanging from every branch. Too many presents to count were stacked all around the green boughs.

The double doors leading outside were within reach. He paused. "What is happening?"

"Get out, Paxton. I think if you stay here any longer, Talen or Dage is going to come back. Believe me, they definitely want a piece of you."

Confusion filled Paxton's head, but he moved toward the exterior door, shocked to freely walk out into the snowy Idaho evening.

What had just happened?

Chapter Seven

Paxton caught wind of Hope's scent as he walked along the lake from vampire to demon territory. There was a wide sidewalk where guards patrolled between the two compounds, but right now, none were visible. That was odd.

This entire situation was messing with his mind. Had that been their intention? If so, it was working; he hadn't felt this off-balance in at least a year. Then he caught sight of the woman, and the world narrowed in focus. His heart started to thrum, and his blood heated.

She sat on the hood of his dark blue truck—she must have wiped the snow off it. She wore a heavy jacket and thick pants, but even so, her nose was pink, and her hands were shoved in her pockets.

He didn't increase his pace, needing to get his raging hormones under control before he reached her. Even from a distance, he could see the shocking blue of her eyes glimmer through the night. She shivered slightly, though she was wrapped up while he wore only jeans and a black long-sleeved T-shirt, keeping his hands in his pockets. He was such a cold bastard that even Mother Nature could no longer touch him.

She tensed as he finally approached, looking at the darkened house and then at her. "Is my uncle here?" he asked.

"No." She shook her head. "I knocked and I rang the bell, but nobody answered."

Good. Hopefully Santino had found safety in the underground bunker and was not being tortured by Talen right now. "You have to know that I didn't mean for you to get hurt," Paxton said quietly, his gaze catching on the sling barely visible around her neck. She sat tipped to the side, as if her arm was folded beneath the jacket. "Wait a minute, you still haven't healed your arm?" Irritation slashed through him.

"No," she said, "not yet."

He was unable to stop himself from taking another step toward her. "Why?"

"Because I just didn't," she said, her small chin lifting. Several streetlights shone down and fully illuminated her, showing her pale face and fragile bone structure. Not to mention the unfathomable blue of her eyes that matched the prophecy markings on each side of her neck.

"Are you telling me you still can't heal your arm?" he asked, not feeling the cold, even though it had to be about zero degrees Fahrenheit. It was probably too chilly for her to be out, but he knew she wouldn't come inside the house. The woman was there for answers, and he didn't have any to give to her.

When she didn't answer him, he stepped even closer so his legs were touching hers as they dangled off the side of the hood.

"Hope?" He put command into his voice this time, even though his brain was still mushy from those drugs.

"I can't heal it, all right?" she snapped, her tone tense as frustration lowered her brows.

Shock kept him immobile. He knew that she caught illnesses sometimes, but he figured that even somebody with slower healing cells would be able to heal a fractured bone in a day. His fangs slowly slid down. "You need blood?" He pushed his shirt sleeve out of the way so he could get to his vein.

"No," she said, holding up one hand.

"Don't make me force you." He'd do it, too. In order to heal her, to make her feel better, he'd do pretty much anything except tell her the truth.

Her delicate jaw firmed. "I can't take blood, Pax, or I would've already taken it from my dad. I mean, give me a break." She might sound snippy, but he could feel the pain vibrating from her. "Emma doesn't want me to take anything until the drug from the darts is completely out of my system. It might react negatively with vampire or demon blood."

So the darts were filled with more than just a tranq. Great. He frowned, the nape of his neck itching as the night air finally began to clear his head. Being casual about it, he glanced around the neighborhood. Ah-ha. That made more sense. "How many snipers are trained on me right now?" he asked. "Merely curious."

"My team of four plus me," she admitted. "I had to fight to get Dad and Dage to treat me like an adult. I'm a little irritated with you right now as well."

So this was a setup. Good to know. He figured she wouldn't have been able to just sneak out of the Realm hospital and into demon territory, but his mind wasn't working quite as fast as it should. "Did Emma determine what was in the darts?"

"Mainly a horse tranquilizer, but also something she couldn't identify."

Shock kept him quiet for a moment. "There's something Emma can't identify?" That was pretty much unheard of. The queen knew every compound there was.

"Yes." Hope looked small and defenseless on his truck.

"Well, fantastic," he muttered. "Whatever was in those darts is in my system too. Is that why you couldn't heal your arm?" Yet he'd had no problem healing his wounds from the laser bullets.

She shook her head. "I don't think so, but I don't know for sure. There's really no way to tell, is there?" She tapped a finger on her lips. "Unless after I heal this..."

"No," he said softly, his voice determined. "You will not break another bone and use yourself as a test subject."

Her eyes flared. "Considering you're a traitorous bastard, I don't think you are in any position to give me advice, much less tell me what to do."

The woman wasn't wrong. He did notice that she was still wearing the silver ring he'd given her so long ago, and he'd bet everything he had that the pink quartz necklace was still hanging between her breasts. It gave him an odd satisfaction that he had no right to feel. He was balancing on a razor-thin line, and there was absolutely no doubt he was going to fall over into the abyss, but for now, he'd make sure she was safe.

"Do you want to come inside? It's too cold out here for you."

"Yeah, right," she snorted. "The snipers wouldn't like that."

He shoved his hands farther down in his jeans pockets so he didn't reach for her. "All right, so obviously you're supposed to be getting information from me. How did you get them to agree to this?"

It was unthinkable that Zane would let his only daughter so close to Paxton after everything that had gone down.

"I didn't give them much of a choice," Hope admitted. "I needed to talk to you, and frankly, we all need answers. I'm an adult, and I'm good at what I do." She was, and he was proud of her. She probably had the best strategic mind of anybody he'd ever met. "Why don't you trust me, Paxton?" she asked softly.

He blinked and then shoved his mask back into place. "I do trust you."

"No, you don't, or you would've told me what you were up to." She leaned toward him, reaching with her good arm for his. He could sense someone's finger tighten on a trigger nearby, but he didn't care. He didn't make her remove her hand. "Come on, Paxton. It's me. I don't believe you would want to hurt my uncle or that you would be working with the Kurjans against us."

"I'm not working with the Kurjans, and I'd never harm Dage," he said. "You have to know that."

She nodded, her eyes luminous now. Were there tears in them?

His heart took the pain as if somebody had stabbed him. "I wouldn't do anything to hurt you, Hope. I hope you believe me." He didn't elaborate, but things were about to get a lot worse, probably for all of them, because he was certainly failing at what he needed to do.

She tightened her grip, her nails digging through his thin shirt. "Paxton," she whispered. "Please tell me what's going on. Does this have to do with your uncle and the Defenders?"

He barely kept from reacting. Instead, he forced an indulgent smile to his lips, one that would irritate the hell out of her. "The Defenders? Who in the world are the Defenders?"

"Don't play stupid with me, and don't treat me like I'm dumb. Do you think our computer experts are not tearing apart your entire history right now? They know you're part of the Defenders. They know your uncle is a member of the Defenders. Come clean now, Paxton, or I swear they'll decide you're a traitor and slice off your head."

Spirit and heat filled her face, and for a moment all he could do was stare at her. She'd been adorable as a kid. As a woman, she was downright fucking gorgeous, even while she was pissed off and wounded and sitting on his favorite truck.

"Is this about the Seven?" she asked.

Heck, she was smart. She was so freaking smart, he didn't know what to do with her sometimes.

"I know only what you do about the Seven," he said. Which frankly wasn't nearly enough. He did know that the Seven Warriors had broken the laws of physics to create three prison worlds to house a dangerous Cyst, one of the spiritual leaders of the Kurjan nation. When those prison realms had been destroyed, all the worlds had gone out of whack, including Earth, which was why demons were no longer able to teleport. The Seven had a final ritual in mind to kill Ulric, but unfortunately, it involved using Hope.

He'd vowed with his own blood to prevent that from happening. He'd been more foolish than courageous, and that was how he'd ended up in this clusterfuck.

"I think you do know more," she said. "I think this is all about the Seven, but it doesn't make any sense. Why did you hack into Dage's schedule?"

Because he hadn't had a choice, but he couldn't tell her that. She wouldn't understand, and he didn't blame her. "You did a good job with the questioning, sweetheart," he said, "but it's time for you to go home." He looked toward the tree line. "Where's your escort?"

"Escort? I'm not going anywhere," she said, smacking him on the arm.

The impact was ineffectual. Yet irritation still ticked within him, not so much at her but at the people who had sent her to talk to him. They knew he was dangerous, and they knew he'd been working against them, and yet they'd sent her in like a sacrificial lamb? Sure, the snipers were good, but he was quicker than anybody knew. He looked slowly around to identify each position and then tuned in his senses to the soldiers in the forest. There were even three behind the house and two inside the home. If he made a wrong move, there'd be a lot of shots fired, but he still had a chance to take her. They never should have allowed her anywhere near him.

"Don't put yourself in danger like this again, even if the people around you are stupid enough to think you can handle it," he said curtly. "Do you understand me?"

Her temper was rare, but when it flared, it was glorious. She kicked him hard, right where she'd shot him in the leg earlier.

Residual pain echoed through his muscles, and he growled. "All right, fine." He yanked his hands free of his pockets and grabbed her good shoulder, pulling her in. She started to protest.

"You think you know me. You don't. Stop treating me like the scared kid who used to hide in your room."

That sweet little chin firmed. "Or what?"

* * * *

Oh, she knew it was a colossal mistake to challenge Paxton, especially with so many snipers focused on him, but she just couldn't help it. She needed to let go of the image of the boy he'd been and face the warrior he'd become while she'd thought he had been studying insects with his uncle.

"You don't want to fuck with me right now, Hope," he said, his voice deadly soft with warning.

She shivered at the low tone as awareness cut through her. That was new. She wasn't sure how to deal with this new Paxton, so she faced him squarely. Her nipples peaked as flames licked through her, even though it was freezing and there were guns trained on them. "You don't scare me," she said, not meaning a word of it. At the moment, he was surprisingly terrifying. It was as if she didn't know him at all. "If you don't knock it off, I'll kick your ass in front of everybody watching." It didn't hurt to remind him that he would get shot if he made the wrong move.

She hadn't even realized he was dangerous until she'd seen him fight in Nuremberg. Pax was faster than any other soldier his age, and he had seemed perfectly in control and more than prepared to take down the Kurjan squads. "I don't want us to be enemies," she said honestly, her heart turning over. "But if you do, have the balls to say so right now."

"Or what?" He threw her words back at her quietly. His eyes blazed a glittering green in the harsh glare of the streetlights— which was his tertiary color. Those colors emerged during times of stress or deep emotion.

She gulped.

He looked down at her, creating a huge shadow in the light behind him. When had he gotten so big and so broad? His body looked harder than rock, dense and impenetrable. "It's time for you to go home," he said, turning away from her.

Oh no, he didn't. She kicked him again in the leg—right where she'd shot him earlier.

He didn't turn quickly as she expected. Instead, he pivoted slowly to face her. She knew instantly she'd made a mistake.

He curled one impossibly strong hand around the nape of her neck and one beneath her knee, pulling her butt forward and tipping her back. She gasped, but he ignored the sound and pressed her down, partially leaning over her but not putting any pressure against her wounded arm.

His jaw looked cut from granite. "I think maybe it's time you learned I'm not the scared little kid who won't take what he wants." His heated palm cradled her neck as his thumb caressed the side of her jawline.

She couldn't move and she couldn't think. Flames licked at her skin, and she forgot all about the soldiers surrounding them as his mouth took hers. Her eyelids fluttered closed, and sparks flashed, hot and bright, as desire lit her nipples on fire and landed between her legs in a firestorm. She had never felt like this—so sensitive and so needy. Paxton Phoenix was the only reality in the entire world.

A bullet impacted the back of the truck, but even then, Paxton didn't stop kissing her. His tongue delved deep, tasting of cinnamon somehow, and his lips moved fierce and firm on hers. She made a soft sound, and she could admit later that it was more of a surrender than a protest.

With his hand still at her nape, he pulled her back into a seated position, and then slowly released her and took a step away. He studied her for one long moment. "Tell Liam he's fixing this truck since he just put a bullet hole in it." With that, Paxton turned and strode to the doorway of the house and disappeared inside, not looking back once.

Hope pressed her fingers to her trembling lips. Even at her age, she'd learned that single moments, tiny slices in time, could change everything.

Her world would never be the same.

Chapter Eight

Since it was well after midnight, all of the lights were off in Hope's house as her protective escort of six left her at her door. Her sprawling ranch house sat in the middle of demon territory, several houses down from her parents' home in a nice cul-de-sac in front of the quiet lake. She opened the door and walked inside the comfortable home she was temporarily sharing with Libby.

Their Christmas tree twinkled in the corner, and several presents for Hope's baby brother were already wrapped and wrinkled under the tree after he'd done his best to shake them the other day.

As usual, there were blankets, pillows, books, notes, pens, and more of Libby's belongings strewn around the living room. Hope was too tired to clean up after her tonight.

Zane Kyllwood clicked on the lamp from his seat on the sofa near the fireplace. The jumble around him was uncharacteristic, and Hope knew her father must have had to struggle to refrain from organizing the chaos.

Hope couldn't help a small grin, even though her head was still aching. "Libby's kind of messy."

"I'm well aware," Zane said. "She always has been. How are you?"

She couldn't read his mood, which worried her. "I'm okay. My head still hurts, but the drugs are wearing off, so it should be all right soon. Any word from Emma on the ingredients of whatever they shot into me?"

"Not yet." Zane appeared relaxed, but it was a deceptive pose Hope knew well. Her father could leap into action in a millisecond. "How did it go with Pax?"

She didn't have a read on that situation, either. "I'm sure you already know." Besides the snipers, there had been cameras and microphones aimed her way, no doubt.

"I do, but you know him better than anybody else. What's going on?"

She tilted her head. "I'm still trying to figure out why you let him go." In her heart, she somehow still trusted Paxton even though she knew that was probably insane, but as the king of the demon nation, her father wasn't one to take risks. "Do you trust him?"

"Absolutely not," Zane said. "Neither should you."

"So you're running a con on him. He's got information you need, and you didn't think you could torture it out of him?" She tilted her head. "That's interesting."

Zane looked briefly away and then back at her. "There's always been a steel core in Paxton Phoenix, so torturing him would take a lot of time. Anybody can be broken, Hope. You know that." He shifted his weight. "But yeah, I didn't want to be the one to do it. Pax would do anything for you. Well, except tell you the truth."

She shook her head. "Things have gotten so crazy."

"They usually do," Zane said soberly. "I want you to stay away from Paxton, because things are about to become very difficult for him, and I don't want you caught up in it."

It figured her father had a plan. There was no way he'd just let Paxton loose. "What's going on with him? I can't put the pieces together." She was thought of as a strategic genius, and yet the puzzle of Pax eluded her.

Zane stood and stalked like a lazy panther around the sofa, then pressed a kiss to the top of her head while pulling a knife from his back pocket to place in her hand. A new Kurjan-designed knife that could split in three and slice off a head. "Keep this with you on missions."

She'd wanted one of those. "Thanks." The metal chilled her palm.

"Paxton is no longer your problem, honey. You need to go back to your main mission with your squad...and put some ice on that arm." Without waiting for an answer, he strode out the door. "Lock this behind me," he called out.

She rolled her eyes and locked the door. There were more guards around her home than at an international airport. If her father thought she wasn't going to figure out what Paxton was up to, he had lost his mind. One of two things was certain: either Pax had gone dark and she would be the one to take him down, or something had gone horribly wrong and she had to be the one to save him.

Either way, she was all in.

* * * *

Paxton's head was killing him. Whatever had been in those darts had been meant to take him out for longer than it had. He couldn't believe the Queen of the Realm hadn't yet identified the exact mix of the compounds, but he had no doubt she would figure it out eventually. Hopefully it wasn't something that could actually harm Hope. She appeared more fragile than ever, which just pissed him off.

He'd kicked the soldiers out of his house and then sat in the dark for two hours after Hope had gotten her sweet butt off his beloved truck. He didn't have much time left, and if he got this next move wrong, he'd never forgive himself.

So he forced himself to turn on the lights and start a crossword puzzle, hating every second of it. When his eyes had gone blurry, he casually moved the papers out of sight and began to write. Then he stood and swiped the papers into his pocket.

Finally, when he was sure there was nobody still lurking outside, he walked down the stairs, through the basement, and slid open a panel that revealed a door in the concrete. He made quick work of the keypad before moving inside to find his uncle and his dog, two of the three beings on this planet he actually cared about.

Santino looked up, his curly white eyebrows out of control, his faded blue eyes worried. "Pax, you're okay." He stood up and rushed forward to hug him, his head not quite reaching Paxton's chin. "I was worried about you."

"I'm fine. Nothing to worry about," Paxton said. "There was an attack squad in Nuremberg. I think they were after Hope, not me, but I'm not sure." He leaned down to pet his dog. The collie had been with him since he'd moved in with his uncle, and a healthy diet and a little bit of vampire blood once in a while kept him young. It was a pretty cool way to keep a dog. "Thank you for not eating the soldiers." He scrunched the dog's ears. Gibson yipped and then ran around in a circle and darted out the concrete door. There was a doggy door upstairs, and no doubt he needed to go outside. "Did you hear them coming?" Pax asked.

"I did," Santino said. "So I just brought the dog in here and waited them out. When we built this place, we built it right. Neither king knows this underground lab is here. I'm so sorry about this disaster."

"Time for apologies is over," Paxton said, walking into the next room, which held a computer bank almost as good as the one the Realm had. He had made a deal for additional components since his other lab had been taken out by Hope, and those would be available to him within the next week or so.

Santino pulled a chair up to the banks of monitors. "Three more enhanced women have gone missing in Prague. I was going to send you there while you were in the area, but then the attack happened."

"Do we have anybody on it?" Pax stared at the monitor.

"We're going to feed the info to the Realm and let them take care of it. Our forces are, well, nonexistent." Santino threw back his head and laughed, the sound strained.

Every muscle in Paxton's body felt as if it was stretched too tight. He'd been headed down this path for too long, and he hadn't found an off-ramp. His head was killing him.

The door on the opposite side of the room opened, and Henric Jones walked in, followed by Charles Fralep. Their homes were connected via the tunnel.

Paxton instantly felt the hair rise on the back of his neck. He didn't know when and he didn't know how, but he was taking off Henric's head the first chance he got. The male was a hybrid who looked more like a vampire than a demon. He had brown hair, metallic eyes, and a broad body.

"I heard you had some trouble in Nuremberg," Henric said.

"I took care of it," Paxton said shortly. His time was running out. His fists clenched at the thought, and he quickly relaxed them. Control. It was all he had.

The vampire glared. "Good, because the time's coming near for the ritual, and you know what you have to do."

Paxton kept silent but ground his back teeth together.

Santino looked from one to the other, his jaw slack. "When we started the Defenders, I really thought we were doing something good."

"We are," Henric snapped. "We're saving the fucking world. Don't you think that's something good?"

"I don't think you're going to be able to save yourself," Paxton said quietly.

Henric's head swung, and whatever he saw in Paxton's eyes had him blinking. Just once, but that was enough. "I don't think you understand who holds the power here."

Paxton flicked a glance at Fralep, who was a purebred demon with buzz-cut white hair and dark black eyes. "Power is fleeting and often changes hands, in my experience."

"Not this time," Henric retorted. "More importantly, why did they let you go?"

"I don't entirely know," Paxton said. "My guess is they don't think I'm a threat to anybody they care about. Dage didn't seem too bothered about me hacking into his schedule." Yet the Realm's response didn't feel right at all, and his instincts told him something was coming for him—hard.

"We saw what happened," Henric said. "You saved the female in Nuremberg when you could've taken her. No doubt the king, actually both kings, are aware of that same fact."

Yeah, there was no doubt about that. The two kings most certainly had eyes everywhere. "Exactly," he retorted, drumming up some anger. "You wouldn't have gotten two feet with her. They had a squad of four on the ground and no doubt reinforcements close. And I've already told you repeatedly: I will not kidnap Hope."

"We just need her blood." Fralep patted his flat belly. He smelled like pepperoni, as always, and it was really fucking annoying.

"Sure you do," Paxton said. "You just want her blood and the blood of the three Keys." What a bunch of complete bullshit. The Defenders had kept their secrets through the years, even from him. He didn't even know who was involved in the other cells across the world, and sometimes he doubted Henric did, either. They were autonomous for a reason.

Henric strutted closer to the screen. "Why else would we hack into King Kayrs's computer system? When we recruited you for this mission, we thought you could get into the lab."

"I can," Paxton said easily. "But all samples, especially those of the Seven and the Keys, are secured by a system that even I can't hack."

"We're going to have to make our move soon," Henric said. "Never forget how dispensable you are, Paxton."

He'd never been anything but. "I'm more than willing to die to make the world safe," Paxton said easily, yanking his puzzle book out of his pocket and shoving it onto an open shelf beneath his computer. "I didn't think I'd make it this long. But anything else you have planned, besides stopping the ritual, will take you straight to hell."

"That's doubtful. Also, if you'd stop playing stupid games all the time, you'd get more accomplished," Fralep said, standing shoulder to shoulder with his friend and gesturing toward the game book. "I want a plan to finally obtain those blood samples from the lab. Otherwise, we'll go after Hope and the Keys themselves."

Paxton chuckled, and the sound was dark. "There is no way you'll reach the three Keys."

According to legend, the ritual that could kill Ulric required the blood of three female Keys and the Lock, who was Hope. He had spent enough time around the Queen of the Realm to know that she had combined the blood of all four females multiple times, trying to figure out how that concoction would actually kill Ulric, who was immortal.

Centuries ago, the monster had killed a hundred enhanced females in a secret ritual that had strengthened his outer body so his head could not be cut off, unlike the rest of the immortals. Legend said that only the blood of the three Keys would take him down. Not even the legends spoke of what Hope's role was as the Lock.

Henric snarled. "I don't need to be the one to infiltrate the Seven's headquarters. We know where they are now. Allowing that information to leak out would take care of the issue for me. In fact, I think I'll send that information to the Kurjans very soon."

Santino shook his head. "I thought you were a much better male when we formed this group. We came together to combat the violation of the laws of physics perpetrated by the Seven when they built those other worlds." His sigh was tortured. "You've gone down a dark path."

"And we're going to keep going down that path," Henric said smoothly. "Paxton? I do hope you remember what happened last time you forgot to whom you owe your allegiance."

Sprawled deceptively calmly in a heavy rolling chair, Paxton just looked at him, not giving the bastard the satisfaction of an answer. Even so, that damn clock was ticking down, and he'd have to make a move soon.

A light glinted in Henric's eyes that Paxton hadn't noticed before. It was deep and dark and swirling with madness. "I'd hate to have to teach that lesson to the Lock."

Paxton exploded out of his chair with blurring speed, grabbing Henric's shirt and twisting, shoving the man against the rock wall. He leaned in, his gaze penetrating as he attacked the male's mind.

Henric paled and then snarled, striking upward to break the hold. "Get out of my head, you freak."

Paxton didn't release him. "Freak? I don't think so. I'm the killer you all created, and don't you ever forget it. I've done everything you asked, and for a while, I did so willingly. But the line has always been crystal clear. Hurt Hope, and you die, and I ain't gonna go slow. You don't want to threaten her again, Henric. Trust me."

"Paxton," his uncle said wearily, "let him go. We're in this, right or wrong."

It was definitely wrong, and every one of those males was underestimating him if they thought he was under their control. Slowly, Paxton released the jerk and took a step back, withdrawing the demon mind attack. He was getting better at those.

"Tomorrow night," Henric repeated, straightening his shirt, hatred darkening his face. "Or we go with plan B." He turned and swept out of the room. Fralep gave Paxton a dirty look and then followed him. The door shut quietly.

"I'm real sorry about this, boy," Santino said. "I should have stuck with studying butterflies."

Pax scrubbed both hands down his face. "It's a little late for that." There was no doubt Henric was done waiting.

Paxton had put him off for years as they'd slowly infiltrated the computer system of the Realm and hunted for the Keys, who were hidden away. They had found them all. In other words, they had found the headquarters of the Seven. It was all coming together too quickly for Paxton to handle. He needed to stop and think. He had no problem dying for the cause, but Hope's life had been at stake for more than two years.

She didn't even know.

He looked at his uncle and dropped back onto his chair. "We have no choice. I'll break into the lab tomorrow." Without looking, he reached between the pages of his crossword puzzle book beneath the desk and finished the last fold on a piece of paper he'd been working on for six months.

It was time.

Chapter Nine

The atmosphere of Hope's house calmed and settled after her father left. She'd truthfully told him over a year ago that she could no longer create dreamworlds, and his relief had been palpable. However, she hadn't shared her thoughts about why.

It had to be Paxton. She'd only been able to form the worlds when Paxton was near her. Now she was older and stronger, so hopefully he didn't have to be in the same room with her, just nearby. There was only one way to find out.

She went to her bedroom to ditch her clothes and change into yoga gear. Her mind was spinning and dull at the same time, and she was so tired she could barely think. But she had to figure this out. She had known Paxton her entire life, and he wasn't a traitor. The mere fact that her father had let him go today showed that Zane hadn't condemned him completely either. Oh, they didn't know what he was up to, and it didn't look good, but Hope had to have some faith.

Her arm hurt, and she cradled it against her rib cage, willing healing cells to go to the fracture, yet nothing happened. She didn't feel any different. She couldn't even feel those cells. What if she were human, and what if she actually could die? She honestly hadn't considered that to be a possibility until very recently. She knew she couldn't heal herself as others did, and she sometimes caught human illnesses, but she'd never imagined she could actually die. What if one of those bullets today had hit her in the heart or the head?

Would her chromosomal pairs save her? Was she just like an enhanced human? Skilled somehow but still susceptible to death?

She shuddered and moved closer to the wide bank of windows that faced the lake. Snow drifted down lazily, covering her deck, and she shivered and pulled out her meditation pillow to sit. She eyed her bed, which looked so warm and inviting, but it was not to be. She had something to do, so she dropped into place and tried to clear her mind.

Calmness took much longer to reach than usual.

Finally, she found herself walking along the rocky, uneven ground next to a lazily rolling river. The sun was high in a blue sky, and it warmed her face. She looked down to note that her arm was still broken. She blinked, wondering if she could fix it in the dreamworld. Nothing happened. In fact, it hurt even worse.

She wandered for a while, picking her way along the grassy bank, trying to let the imaginary sun warm her. Across the river was an outcropping of rocks, and on a ledge sat her book, the green book she'd been trying to read her entire life. She thought about crossing the river, but it looked cold.

Besides, anytime she'd gotten near the book, it had somehow disappeared on her. She figured she'd be able to read it when she turned twenty-five, which for some reason seemed to be a magical year for her people. It was the year her mother and father had mated, and it would probably be the year she chose a mate as well. She was months away from that, so she didn't bother getting her feet wet trying to reach the elusive book.

She looked around at the tall trees. They were pine and some spruce with maybe a tamarack thrown in. Across the river were birch. Sometimes, her dreamworlds held fantastical trees and a colorful ocean, but this time she'd decided to go with realism.

A small sandy embankment spread out into the river, and she walked down it, feeling the rocks beneath her bare toes. She probably should have worn shoes, but who cared? There she took a seat and waited, concentrating on Drake. The minute she thought of his name, he appeared across the river, his eyebrows up.

"Oh," she said. Huh. That had never happened before. Usually people were right where she put them.

He lifted his shoulder and strode easily across what appeared to be shallow water. He wore the black uniform of the Kurjan soldiers. In the last year, he'd grown even more. He had to be about six foot seven or maybe even eight. His skin was still pale, and his eyes were still green with a purple rim, but his black hair had grown out to his shoulders.

"At least you didn't drop me in the river," he said, approaching slowly, his gaze piercing.

She stood and dusted pebbles off her butt. She knew enough about the Kurjans' ranks to see that he was now the leader of the nation, according to the many silver medallions on his left breast. "Hi."

"Hi." His lips twitched, and he looked around. "Just us here tonight?"

"Looks like it," she said. She could bring in Paxton or Libby, and maybe Drake's cousin Vero, but she chose not to involve anybody else.

He reached out and clasped her good hand. "It's been a rough year without you."

She nodded. "I know. For some reason I can't create the dreamworld unless Paxton is near."

Drake took a step back. His face was chiseled and sharp, his body tall and lean. He was definitely muscled and strong, as she had always known he would be. "Paxton Phoenix is here?"

"Well, not here," she murmured. It was so odd to be seeing Drake again.

"Why is your arm in a sling?" Puzzlement wrinkled his brow.

She watched him closely. "We were attacked by two squads of Kurjans in Nuremberg earlier today. Were they after me, or were they after Paxton?" She'd been mulling the situation over and hadn't reached a conclusion. "In addition to a bullet, I took darts filled with ingredients we don't recognize. How about you tell me what you're up to?"

"Oh, they were definitely after Paxton," Drake said easily. "I know he's your friend, but he killed my father, and he's going to die." Drake's voice remained low and steady but determined.

She gulped. Paxton and her uncle Garrett had killed Dayne in a battle three years earlier. "I know he killed your father, and I'm sorry about that. But it was during a battle after Ulric had kidnapped Garrett's mate. They were only fighting to rescue her. You know that, right?"

"I don't know much of anything," Drake admitted. He shoved his hands in his pockets. "I'm sorry, but Paxton's fate is not negotiable. Now answer my question about your arm."

She swallowed. For years, she'd kept from Drake the fact that she could become ill. It was silly, but she hadn't wanted to appear weak to him. "The drug in the darts could mix dangerously with vampire blood, so I'm not taking any until it dissipates. What was in those darts, anyway?"

"The unit was tasked with securing Paxton and bringing him to me. They did not use any darts." Drake shook his head. "I didn't order anybody to shoot you with drugs." His frown darkened. "Damn it. This wasn't me."

She searched his face for any sign of deception and didn't see it. "All right."

He stepped closer to her, blocking the sun. "Not all right. Heal your arm yourself."

It was time to be honest with him. "I can't. I don't have the healing cells that most immortals do."

He took a step back to better study her. "Just now? Or have you never had them?"

She felt exposed. Vulnerable. "I don't think so."

He studied her for several long moments. "When you mate, you'll gain the cells, then. Where are you living these days?"

"I'm back in Idaho," she admitted, her heart opening. He didn't care that she was deficient. Good. It was common knowledge that the Realm headquarters were in northern Idaho, so she wasn't giving anything away. She also knew where he was. "How is Canada?"

"Cold," he said. "We're training hard outside. I have to tell you, it's freaking frigid."

She smiled and kicked a rock. It had been a rough year, not seeing him. They'd known each other since birth, and she'd always thought they would have something to do with fixing the world. But sometimes she felt so tired, she wasn't sure. "I guess you're leading the Kurjan nation?" She'd wondered about that.

"I guess I am," he said. "I'm a little young, but I'm doing my best."

"And Ulric?" she asked. Hopefully Drake had taken care of the monster, but something told her he hadn't.

Drake looked up at the sun, closing his eyes. "Ulric is still knocking on my door," he muttered. "He's in charge of the Cyst, and many of my people listen to him. We waited so long for him to return to this plane, and he survived circumstances that would've killed any other being. That has earned him both respect and incredible power."

"That's understandable." She looked up at the sun, able to stare directly at it. Ulric led the Cyst, who were both the spiritual leaders and the most deadly assassins in Drake's world. While Kurjans were pale with dark hair that had red tips, the Cyst were pale with a shocking white strip of hair down their heads. "Do you need us to help you fight him?"

His lips twitched. "No. I don't need the Realm's assistance, but thanks."

"Sure," she said, feeling silly. But she did have quite the fighting force on her side. "Drake, we have reports that enhanced women

are still being kidnapped around the globe. Is that true? Is it you?"
She already knew it was the Kurjans, but she couldn't figure out
his part in the kidnappings, if he had one.

"No, it's not me," he said, taking his hand out of his pocket
and ruffling his hair. His fingers were long, probably longer than
Pax's, but Pax's hands were wider.

It was odd, or maybe it wasn't, that she kept comparing them.
She had done so her whole life. Right now, she was extremely
angry at Paxton, and she wasn't too happy with Drake. "Who is
taking the enhanced females? It has to be Ulric, right?"

"I believe so," Drake said. "I'm working on it."

She felt for him. "Why? What's his grand plan?"

"I don't know." A breeze picked up and wafted shiny blue leaves
across the river. He laughed. "Those are pretty. Everything else
looks so real."

"I thought I'd add some whimsy." She had a feeling that Drake
didn't have much whimsy in his life, and she'd always wished
she could lighten his load. She didn't think it had been easy for
him, being the only son of the Kurjan leader and then having to
step into his father's shoes when he was so young. She had once
thought that the three of them, four including Libby, would save
the world. She'd been naïve. Right now, she didn't think Drake
and Paxton could coexist in the same world. Paxton probably
wanted Drake as dead as Drake wanted Pax.

"Stop worrying so much," Drake said, his grin widening again.
"I think it's time we met in person, don't you?"

Heat wandered through her along with curiosity. "We have
met in person once."

"I remember," Drake said. "That was the first time I ever
thought there might be peace between us, when your soldiers
captured me and then let me go."

"You were just a kid," she said.

He snorted. "We were both kids. Remember how much
trouble we got into?"

Yeah, she'd been grounded forever, if she remembered right.

"I don't have a lot of time to mess around," Drake said. "You and I are fated, and it's about time we met. Don't you think?"

She looked up at him, letting the weight of his words sink in. "How do you know we're fated?"

He brushed her hair back from her shoulder. "Come on, Hope. It's always been you and me. If we're ever going to have peace between our people, and if we're ever going to actually take Ulric down, which is something I now want to do as well, then we have to do it together." His gaze flicked to the rocks where the green book sat open. "Don't you agree?"

She thought about it. She thought about Paxton's betrayal, and she felt the weight of destiny pressing in. Could she trust Drake? Her mind told her to trust Drake rather than Paxton. Yet her heart was telling her something else. "I don't know."

Drake leaned down and kissed her, his lips soft. It was a nice kiss. "You're meant to be a queen. You have to understand your place in the world."

She didn't care about being a queen. She believed her role was to broker peace. "Yes, I do."

Chapter Ten

Early in the morning, Drake studied the map on the wall of the small control room, noticing the different energy signatures and vibrations going throughout Spokane, Washington. It wasn't a place he would've thought to find several enhanced females, but it'd be an easy place to reach.

Most soldiers weren't up yet, so he had the place to himself.

His fingers still tingled from holding Hope's hand the night before, and he marveled at the memory. Not much moved him. She was powerful and would make the perfect queen—and if that brought some peace to their people, so be it.

First there would be retribution and rivers of blood. It was the only way to avenge his father's death.

The outside door opened, and power instantly slammed inside. He knew who it was before turning, so he didn't bother.

"You found three more?" Ulric clomped down the stairs to the lower level, where Drake stood.

"Yeah. Spokane, Washington," Drake said. "I'll send a squad in about an hour."

"Good."

Drake spared a glance at the Cyst leader. He'd regained all of his strength, despite being held in a horrific prison world for a thousand years. His appetite was unseemly, ranging from food to females. But at the moment, he was revered not only by the many Cyst in the coalition but also by the Kurjans—his people, who should be looking to Drake.

"How is your house coming along?" Ulric sneered.

Drake looked squarely at the Cyst leader. He had grown even broader, wider, and stronger as he recuperated. He stood at least six foot nine and was probably the largest soldier Drake had ever seen. He was pale, unnaturally so, even for a Cyst, and one long line of white hair bisected his otherwise bald scalp and was braided down his back. His eyes were a terrifying hue of so many colors, Drake couldn't choose just one. "My house is lovely, thank you."

Ulric snorted. "To think you believe that you'll make a Realm female happy just by giving her a house. She can't live here. She can't live the way we do. You know that, correct?"

"She'll live any way I want her to," Drake responded. Hope had been his from the moment she'd been born; they were destined for each other. Not only did he feel that in his gut, but fate whispered the truth on the wind. "You know the only way to take down the Realm is from the inside."

Ulric glanced at the screen. "They still don't know the plan, do they?"

Drake shrugged. "I don't believe so. As far as I know, they still think your grand scheme is to kill all enhanced females." Which was just stupid. The Kurjans needed to mate enhanced females just as the vampires and demons did. "It's a good way to cause war between the shifter, demon, and vampire nations. They won't be able to help themselves once we've finished this campaign."

"Have you ever thought that your mate will try to stop you?"

"Of course she'll try to stop me," Drake said. "Don't be ridiculous." Sometimes he didn't have patience for ancient soldiers who were unable even to text on an iPhone. "She'll make a fine queen, and she'll learn her place soon enough. She'll be an excellent mother, and the power our sons will hold shall impress even you,

General." Not that he gave two shits whether he impressed the general or not, since he fully planned on killing him once he figured out how.

Ulric leaned down and typed rapidly on a keyboard to bring up a square on the monitor. "Paxton Phoenix is back in Realm territory. To think you almost had him in Nuremberg."

Blood rushed through Drake's veins with the need to exact revenge. Paxton would die, many times over. Drake would bring him back each time, until at some point he'd finally give up. His fangs dropped low with a need to taste blood.

"I thought you were going after the girl in Nuremberg," Ulric said evenly.

"I was actually following the girl to get to Paxton," Drake admitted. "I'm not ready for Hope yet. We might as well let her have the freedom she enjoys as long as possible." Because there was no doubt, once she was his, that would change.

Ulric seemed amused, and yet anger, as always, flowed from him. Furious seemed to be his default setting. "Are we prepared for the attack on the Seven headquarters tonight?"

"Yes. The Defenders in demon territory came through with the intel." Drake clicked on another monitor and surveyed the location an hour from Denver. "Soldiers are in place, and air support is ready to go. We have missile lock." Even though the scientists had enabled the Kurjans to spend a limited time in the sun, they were stronger after dark. "Go time is midnight."

"Good." Ulric rubbed his wide jaw. "Don't forget. I need the Intended in one piece."

Drake brought up the picture of Destiny Applegate-Kayrs. She was such a little thing to be both a Key and Ulric's Intended. "The squads have her picture." Although he didn't really care. If she died, another Intended would take her place, and fate would stamp another female with Ulric's mark. "Legend says the three Keys will have the ability to destroy you. I'd think you'd want to kill all three of them rather than mating one." The other two were also at Seven headquarters, which made it all so convenient.

"If the other two are dead, her power as a Key is ended." Ulric stared at the stunning brunette. "Mine."

The door opened again, and Vero walked in. He and his unit had just returned to headquarters the day before, having been stationed outside of Homer for the last year, first creating and then using a training facility for soldiers. "Harold just took another complaint from the women we have here in storage. They need to be put into warmer quarters. The cabins we've been using aren't insulated well enough."

Drake looked at his cousin. "Then insulate them." He didn't have time for this, and Harold did nothing but irritate him. Why hadn't Vero left the loser in Homer?

Vero stood tall. "If it were that easy, I would. Humans aren't the only ones affected by the supply chain problem, cousin." Anger and something deeper glowed in Vero's blue eyes. He was an anomaly amongst the Kurjans, who never had even a hint of blue in their eyes. After Vero's father had been killed, he'd spent a lot of time with the females, which might've softened him. He had a kindness that didn't belong in their world.

He'd finally grown to almost six and a half feet, still short for a Kurjan male. Although his chest was broader than Drake's. They had trained long hours with every weapon until Vero was as fierce a warrior as Drake could make him. It was either that or let Ulric kill the guy, and Drake needed family support. He liked that Vero had created an excellent fighting force for the Kurjans. It was needed.

Ulric snorted. "Why are you so worried about human females? We mate a couple to our people, we inject the rest, then let them go. The hypnosis works, right?"

"Yes," Vero said. "The hypnosis works. They don't know that they were taken once we let them go." His face was stone cold, and his eyes had gone flat, but Drake could still feel the emotion coming from him. The young warrior didn't like the current campaign, but that was too bad. He would follow orders.

Drake looked back at the screen. "Find them blankets and then send a squad to Spokane."

* * * *

Hope sat in the conference room and looked at her team of four, trying to focus even though her head ached from the nightmares that had plagued her. She needed to see Paxton. Her focus shot back into the room as Collin's report concluded.

Why hadn't anybody told her this news yesterday? Sure, she'd been unconscious all day and then went on her own mission to deal with Paxton, but her team should've checked in. "We lost them?" she asked.

Collin's face was impassive but fury glowed in his eyes. "We did. The other team got there as soon as they could, but the Kurjans got the two enhanced females in Paris."

"The sisters?" Libby whispered.

A muscle ticked in Liam's jaw. "Yeah. Our team was about fifteen minutes behind the Kurjan squad."

Guilt swamped Hope. "Those women should have been our priority."

"Maybe not," Liam said. "Paxton's been working among us freely, and we didn't know it. I'm not saying that those women aren't important and we won't go find them, because we will." His jaw hardened. "But we needed to know about Paxton."

Libby plucked at a piece of paper on the heavy onyx table. "I didn't have any idea," she mumbled, her gaze down.

"Neither did I," Hope said.

Collin shook his head. "I was pissed when we first saw him but, I mean, it's Paxton."

Derrick leaned back, looking more like his father, Jase, than ever. "Well, exactly, it's Paxton. I mean, what do we really know about him? He was friends with Hope and Libby as a kid. With all of us, really. Then he went off with his uncle to study butterflies and the history of ancient cultures. That's what we thought, anyway."

"We were wrong," Collin said.

"Yeah, we were," Derrick agreed. "So it begs the question, do any of us really know him? We are all surprised, and our first instinct is to defend the guy and say something's going on that we don't understand, but we don't really know him." He emphasized each word.

Hope sat back, her mind reeling. "I know him."

"Do you?" Derrick asked, leaning forward. "Why? Because you were buddies as kids? Because he stepped in front of you when his psycho dad tried to hurt you? That was a long time ago, Hope. He's been with Santino and his group longer than he was without them, and apparently he's been training, and training hard, while he's been away."

Liam's shoulders went back. "Yeah, the male can fight. He wasn't even breaking a sweat after he took down those two Kurjans. I'm not sure we could have contained him without the darts."

"Speaking of which," Libby said softly, "has Emma figured out what's in them?"

Hope's head was still aching. "Not yet." She'd called her aunt first thing in the morning, but Emma didn't have news.

"That's not good," Derrick muttered. "Kurjans with a concoction we can't trace." He dropped his gaze to the sling holding Hope's set arm against her body. "So you can't take any blood until we know for sure how the blood will react to whatever is still in your system, right?"

She nodded. "Yeah."

Libby slid a bottle of pills across the table to Hope.

Hope reached and turned it around. "Advil?"

Libby stared at the bottle. "After you texted us about this new theory, I ran to the pharmacy at the nearest town, and the clerk helped me choose the right painkiller for you. She said that one would help."

Derrick's eyebrows rose. "She didn't think it was odd that a twenty-something female had to ask about human painkillers?"

"I told her I was Amish," Libby murmured, her tawny gaze directed at Hope. "Take the pills. If you're human, we'll figure out how to keep you alive. It's okay to be human."

No, it wasn't. She shouldn't be mortal. "I'm a prophet, with the marking and all, and I also have vampiric chromosomal pairs, so I don't see how I could be completely mortal." Hope opened the bottle. "Do I take them all?"

Libby wrinkled her nose. "The clerk said to start with two, and if that doesn't work, up the dosage but never take more than what the directions say."

Hope tossed two of the round pills into her mouth and swallowed.

Liam leaned forward. "Do you feel better?"

"Not yet," Hope said. While the Realm hospital had some serious painkillers that would probably kill a human, simple ones like these were unnecessary and thus not stocked.

"It'll be okay." Collin straightened in his seat. "We'll figure this out like we always do."

Hope tried to believe him, but doubts still ticked through her brain like marching ants. "I appreciate the support, but we have to find those two women we lost. Do we have any sort of bead on them?"

"No," Collin said. He was their resident computer expert and even now had a laptop open in front of him. "They were gone when the other team got there. Satellite images confirm a Kurjan squad took them. It looks like they headed first to Germany. Then we lost them. We don't know how they got the women out of the country."

"We're losing too many of them," Hope said. Hers was by no means the only squad out trying to rescue enhanced women before the Kurjans kidnapped them. But her little force was deadly precise and would soon rise through the ranks, she was certain. "Has anybody reached out to other squads to figure out if they know more than we do?"

"We just got the intelligence report from Dage," Libby said, nodding toward the computer. "I don't think anybody knows anything except that Ulric is definitely collecting enhanced females. We don't know why the legends seem to be coming true, and nobody even knows the basis for the legend."

Hope sighed. Ulric hadn't been put away just for the damage he'd wrought but because he had some sort of plan to kill all enhanced females, even those mated to immortals. It didn't make sense to her. She cleared her throat. "I spoke with Drake in a dream last night in one of my dreamworlds."

Libby jolted. "You did what? You didn't bring me in?"

"No. It was just the two of us," Hope said. "Now that Paxton is back in the territory, apparently I can get into the dreamworlds." It didn't make a lick of sense, but for some reason, she only was able to do that when he was around.

"Maybe it's something about his energy," Derrick said thoughtfully.

"What do you mean?" Hope asked.

He shrugged. "I don't know. I've been studying energy for a while. That's kind of what we witches do. It has to be something like that. Something in you must respond to him in a way that opens the dreamworlds."

"I wonder if that means he should be there with you," Liam said, his gaze unrelenting.

Hope ignored the menace in her cousin's tone. "Maybe, but we don't exactly trust him right now, do we?"

"Absolutely not," Liam responded. "Yet I don't like you being alone with a Kurjan either."

Hope felt heat rising into her face. She'd kissed both Paxton and Drake the day before, and she shouldn't trust either of them. "It's just a dreamworld. He can't get to me from there. Nobody can. I can bring myself out of it at any point."

"Well, there's that," Derrick mumbled. "Did you ask him why they're taking enhanced females?"

"I think there's a war going on within the Kurjan nation," Hope said.

"What do you mean?" Derrick asked.

She leaned forward. "I think Drake had to step up as leader when Dayne died, and he and Ulric don't like each other. I think Ulric is actually kidnapping the enhanced females, and Drake wants to stop him."

"Yeah, because he's a good guy," Collin bit out.

Irritation rose within Hope. "If he wants to stop Ulric, he can't be all bad." It was time to level completely with her team. "Drake wants to meet me in person, and I think it's time."

A chorus of "oh, hell no" went around the entire table.

Chapter Eleven

Paxton leaned against a tree outside of demon headquarters as the sun sparkled off the snow blanketing his surroundings. Christmas lights had been strung around every eave of every home, twinkling merrily, even though it was almost noon. It seemed as if lately the demons and the vampires were competing to see who could decorate with more lights and outside whimsy, such as deer and presents and even a snowman. He wished he could get into the spirit, but considering he didn't have much chance of surviving the next week, he wasn't feeling it.

An overlarge Santa bobbed and ducked in the determined wind, taking Paxton back to a Christmas when he'd been about five years old, playing with LEGOs given to him by Hope's mom. His father had loomed over him, drunk and high, and had kicked the LEGOs across the room before turning his fists on Pax.

He shivered and wrenched himself out of the past. It was over. Sometimes the nightmares took him, and even now, he couldn't help but search for threats around him, hoping his imagination didn't add any to the count.

His pose was casual, but he could spring into action in a moment. Although it probably wouldn't matter, considering there were snipers on two rooftops and at least one he could sense in the trees. The heightened security was no doubt because of him, but it was rare that Hope went anywhere, even in Realm territory, without being covered by at least two soldiers.

He actually liked that fact; it helped him to sleep better at night when the nightmares weren't plaguing him. There was no doubt in his mind that the Kurjans would make a move to take her, and the security in place made it nearly impossible to reach her.

Although he'd always thought he'd be the one standing in front of her. At the end of the current day, Henric would probably blow off his head. It was a risk he had to take.

She walked out of the building flanked by Liam and Collin. That was good. Libby trailed behind her, chattering with Derrick, who was forming plasma balls and tossing them back and forth between his bare hands. The second he caught sight of Paxton, he winged one his way.

Pax stepped easily out of the line of fire and partially turned to watch as the small golf ball–sized orb crashed harmlessly into a snowbank and heated its way through until sputtering out.

While his bet had been that Liam would lose his temper and rush him, he hadn't expected Derrick to duck out from behind Hope and run full bore at him. Interesting. Derrick was young at about twenty-two, but as a demon-vampire hybrid, he was quick.

Paxton set his stance and absorbed the impact, ducked his shoulders, and threw the heavily muscled male into the recesses of the forest. The kid hit a tree, and the tall spruce came down. Pax grinned. He had purposely aimed for the tree with the sniper, who yelled as he landed on his back. The guy was up instantly with his weapon pointed at Pax, who turned around to face Hope.

"Anybody else?" he asked, sounding bored. He actually wouldn't mind a good fight, but hurting one of her team would just piss her off, and right now he needed her cooperation.

Liam's chin dropped as if he were going to charge.

"No," Hope said softly, her laptop bag over her shoulder. "Everybody just stop. Paxton, what do you want?"

"I want to talk to you," he said.

"Absolutely not," Liam exploded, predictably.

Libby walked around and marched right up to him, ignoring Collin's hand on her arm.

When she reached him, her eyes were blazing. "What are you up to?" She put both hands on her hips.

He wished he could tell her. Instead, he stared down at one of his oldest friends. Libby had grown to be about five foot eight, with tawny brown hair and usually mellow brown eyes. She was fit and compact like a shifter, and she could go from human to feline in a second. The anger in her eyes dug deep into his heart, making it ache.

"Libby, I need to talk to Hope," he said, trying to keep his voice gentle.

She punched him then, full-on in the gut. He took it, not tightening his abs. Oh, he could have stopped her, and they both knew it, but he figured she deserved one good hit.

"Feel better?" he asked.

"No," she spat, looking like she wanted to stomp on his foot. In fact, knowing Libby, she would. Derrick lumbered out of the woods, snow falling from his head. His growl held menace as he stood next to Libby in a defensive position.

Hope sighed and moved toward Pax. "Everybody carry out your assignments. We all have work to do today. We'll meet up again at five."

"I'm not leaving you with him." Collin instantly tried to put himself in front of her.

Every muscle in Paxton's body tightened, preparing to attack. Yet he kept his stance relaxed. "Get out of my way," he said, unable to help himself.

"Oh, I'm not leaving her with you," Collin sputtered.

Pax didn't lift even an eyebrow but cut his gaze to Hope and then back. "You are, or you're going to leave bleeding. I suggest you move now."

Only Hope's sharp calling of Collin's name stopped him. "You guys, I mean it. Everybody to work. I've got this," she said, exasperation evident in her voice.

Liam checked out the snipers on the nearby rooftops, not bothering to hide the direction of his gaze. "All right," he called out. "Feel free to shoot the asshole. We're okay with it. Come on, D." He slung an arm around his cousin's snow-covered shoulders. "Hope can handle herself."

The team unwillingly stomped off toward Realm headquarters in vampire territory.

"Was any of that necessary?" Hope asked.

At least today she was wearing a heavier jacket. It was white and puffy and matched the mittens on her hands. He was gratified to see that she wore heavy boots as well. Oh, he had no doubt it irritated her because she wanted to be as tough as the other warriors, but she wasn't, and she needed to stay warm. Even now, her nose was pink, and her lips were turning blue.

"What do you want, Paxton?" she demanded.

"I want to know why you look exhausted and your arm still is in a cast." He didn't like that there was only one arm showing; the other one must have been against her body. He could smell the plaster, actual plaster, like for a human fracture. "You should take blood and just heal it."

"That concoction is still in my blood," she admitted. "I dropped by Emma's lab first thing this morning."

He took in the dark circles beneath her stunning eyes. Eyes shouldn't be violet, but hers were. "You look tired."

"Gee, thanks." She turned to walk toward Realm headquarters.

"Let's go by the lake." He captured her hand and felt the snipers settle into firing positions.

She looked down at his hand enfolding hers over the mitten. "What are you doing?"

"We used to hold hands all the time."

She sighed and tugged a small photo album from her bag. "This is yours. We found it when searching the stuff in storage that your father left behind." She handed over a thin blue book.

He stilled, then opened it to see a picture of his mother smiling at the camera with him on her lap. She'd been so beautiful. As a pure demon, she had white hair and black eyes, and she held him as if he mattered, tucking him close. There were three photos of the two of them, and she'd titled them: Our New Life, On to an Adventure, and The Two of Us. Pax's heart ached.

Hope tightened her hold on his hand. "She loved you. A lot."

"New Life?" Was it possible she'd been trying to leave the asshole? Maybe. Pax wondered what might've been. A hard rock in his gut started to unfold. He hadn't even realized it was there. Leave it to Hope to help him, even when she was angry with him. "Thank you for this." He secured the little book in his back pocket.

"Sure." She was so sweet, even when she didn't want to be. He loved that about her.

He started walking, heading around the building toward the long sidewalk that ran the length of the lake. "Come on, we used to walk here all the time."

She fell into step with him, surprisingly not yanking her hand away. It felt good to be connected to her. Sorrow hit him, and then fury. He would miss this. His body had been aroused around her since he'd become a teenager, so that wasn't new. Neither was the feeling of inevitability.

"What's your plan now, Phoenix?" she asked, her voice holding a tone he couldn't quite identify.

There was nothing wrong with going with the truth. Well, most of the truth. "I want to get my blood tested, and I figure nobody will shoot me if you walk into headquarters with me," he admitted. "I need to know if the drugs are still in my blood, and Emma didn't come chasing me with a needle today."

"Emma's busy." They walked in silence for a little while with the wind stinging their cheeks. Whitecaps rose on the lake, but with the bright blue sky, the area was stunningly beautiful. Somewhere in the distance, Christmas music lifted sweet notes into the sky. For the briefest of moments, he could pretend he was a normal soldier out for a walk with his girl.

With the only girl he'd ever love. That was for sure. Even if he managed to live past the next week, which was highly doubtful, there would never be anyone but Hope Kayrs-Kyllwood for him. Whether she knew it or not, she lived in his heart and always would.

"Are you going to tell me what's really going on?" she asked.

He thought about it. He couldn't. For a moment his vision wavered, and he caught himself. What was that? "We really do need to figure out what was in those darts," he said. Whatever it was, it was messing with his head even worse than his head was normally messed with. If she only knew what he was dealing with. Well, she'd probably be furious, but she had every right to be.

"I had several nightmares last night," she said. "And then couldn't fall back to sleep." So that explained the dark circles under her eyes.

He stiffened. Her nightmares should not be ignored. "Tell me about the dreams," he said.

"No."

He tightened his hold on her hand. "Tell me about the dreams, Hope. Now."

"Fine," she hissed. "Man."

There was a time she would've told him automatically when she had a bad dream, before he'd been gone for the last year. He missed those times when communication was so free-flowing between them. When she came to him if she had a problem. He rubbed his free hand over his chest, which suddenly hurt.

"I dreamed about missiles and fire and blood and death," she said slowly, her voice barely loud enough to be heard.

He stiffened. "Here?"

"I couldn't see a location," she whispered. "I still reported the dreams to my dad and Uncle Dage, but I don't know. It could have been a battle from years ago, Paxton, or it could be an attack coming for us tomorrow."

It sucked that fate gave her visions but failed to add any context. It didn't seem fair, but then life never really was.

"We've traced your activity for the past several years but can't find what you were really doing," she admitted. "I mean, you've managed to amass quite a fortune, and yet you're not about money. I know that, Paxton. You also have hacked into many of the Realm's computer systems and databases. Finally, your dossiers on the Seven and their mates and the three Keys are impressive."

She looked at him squarely, still walking. "I could tell you'd compiled all of that data. Your fingerprints were all over it. We hacked into the files early this morning. You should know that."

"I do," he admitted. "I had safeguards in place that alerted me."

"Why didn't you wipe the files?"

He shrugged. "Who says I didn't?"

The Realm computer experts were phenomenal, even better than he was. It had taken him a long time to figure out his strengths: he was a fighter, and he was a killer. He wasn't a computer guru. Although he was pretty damn good.

She smiled. "I always thought that you would be a scientist, not some vigilante."

He felt like a traitor. "I know. Me too."

She turned back to watch the snow starting to fall in front of them, glancing at him sideways from time to time as if she wanted to see his face. "I also saw videos of the battles you undertook with the wolf shifters as well as the panthers down in Africa. You're probably one of the fastest and most brutal fighters I've ever seen. You killed without hesitation or remorse." She didn't sound put off by his exploits. In fact, her tone had gone a little breathy.

Was she becoming chilled? He had to get her inside.

"I'd like to say I killed the bad guys," he admitted. "But yeah, Hope, I didn't go the way I thought either."

There had never been a time he really wanted to study science, but he hadn't had enough faith in himself to be an actual warrior or soldier. It had taken desperation and the prodding of his uncle's cronies to make him into one. He didn't like them, and he would probably kill them if he had the chance, but he was who he was because of them.

"Why don't you take those skills and work for the Realm?" she asked softly.

He snorted. "After all this, you think the Realm will take me as a soldier?"

Her shoulders hunched. "No. But can't you explain any of this? I mean, come on, Paxton, what is going on? The little that we know of the Defenders is that they want to prevent Ulric's death. How can you want that?"

"No. They want to prevent the final ritual that is intended to kill Ulric. There's something off about that ritual, and you know it, Hope. You know the Seven screwed up the laws of physics, and they changed this world. I should be able to teleport, and I can't. Shifter kids are having psychic visions of things that happened long ago, and it's screwing them up because they think those things are happening right now. Even the fairies can't teleport to other worlds anymore." He tightened his grip on her hand, needing her to understand. The crossword puzzle book felt heavy in his pocket as if in warning. "If we let the Seven actually perform the ritual in order to kill Ulric, we could destroy the entire world. All of the worlds."

She was silent as they reached the rear of the main Realm headquarters building. "I have to trust that the Seven know what they're doing."

Pax shook his head. "That's just stupid."

Her eyes widened, and damn if she didn't punch him in the throat. Hard.

He moved without thinking, drawing her in, curling his fingers around her nape. If this was one of his last moments, he was going to make a memory to take with him to hell. He kissed her, just wanting one heartbeat in heaven. He was risking getting his head blown off by a sniper, but it was worth it. So fucking worth it.

Because she kissed him back. Passion, need, even anger all poured into him from her. She was innocence and sin wrapped together, and her taste sank into his body, into his blood, into his soul so hard and fast he'd never be free. Nothing mattered but pulling her closer against him as thunder roared in his ears.

She gave a soft little moan against his mouth, and he felt it to his core. Right to his aching cock. He skimmed a hand beneath her shirt at her waist, and smooth, soft, silky skin filled his heated palm.

The female was absolutely perfect.

Her breath caught, and she leaned into him. He gave in to temptation and caressed up, covering one breast. For a tiny thing, she had surprisingly full breasts. He swept his thumb beneath her bra, swiping a rock-hard nipple.

Her gasp jolted him back to the present and their location. His body was on fire, and the beast at his core was raging against its chains with the need to take. To finally make her *his*.

He pulled away first, his hand catching her jaw and forcing her to look him in the eyes. Hers were a violet blue tinged with amethyst. "I don't know what happens next to me, but you have to promise. You will not mate a Kurjan." They both couldn't sacrifice their lives.

She swallowed and stepped back, her eyebrows rising when he allowed her to move away from him. "I'm not promising you anything."

Chapter Twelve

Hope's body had never been so alive. Never. Paxton had kissed her before, but not like that. Nobody in the world kissed like that. She was twenty-four years old, had spent some time dating and kissing, but that was unreal.

It was fire and ice, promise and threat. Her nipples were hard as diamonds, and her entire body felt soft and needy. On the edge for Paxton.

She'd loved the boy and now wanted the adult male. More than she would've thought possible.

"I'm not going to allow you to sacrifice yourself," he said, his jaw set so hard it had to hurt as he removed his hand, leaving her breasts aching and needy.

Even so...*allow?* "I haven't decided what I'm going to do, but I don't see any of my choices being a sacrifice." It was shocking her voice still worked while her mouth tingled so wildly from just one kiss.

His hand descended on her shoulder and curled, showing restrained strength. The same hand that had just been on her breast, making her needy. "You care for Drake." Pax's eyes went flat. Hard. Deadly.

Her mouth opened, but no sound came out. Who was this male? She cleared her throat. "You know I do. We've all been friends since childhood." Yet she didn't know Drake the way she did Paxton. She didn't want to hurt anybody, but fate always had a plan. Of course, Hope could make her own fate.

"You shouldn't trust him," Pax said, his voice a low growl that licked along her nerve endings.

What the heck was going on with her? She had to focus. "Let's get back to you and what you've been doing. Tell me why. Just why?"

"The Seven has to be stopped," he said.

She wished his betrayal was just about money, but in her stomach, in her gut, in her soul, she knew it wasn't. His life hadn't been easy, and who knew what kind of pressures his uncle had put on him.

His activities centered on the Seven and their upcoming ritual. He really believed what he'd said about the Seven messing with the laws of physics, and she wasn't entirely sure he was wrong. The Seven had changed life on this planet when they'd undertaken the first ritual in order to put Ulric away by creating a prison world across dimensions. "I want to understand," she breathed. "But I have to know the truth."

He released her and stepped back, shoving his thumbs in the front pockets of his jeans. "I've never lied to you."

Her mouth gaped open. "You haven't lied to me? You've been part of the Defenders for over a decade."

"True," he allowed. "But I never lied to you. I just didn't tell you everything." He tilted his head. "Though I guess that could be considered lying."

That was one thing about Paxton. He always saw both sides in the search for fairness.

"Why didn't you tell me?" she asked, her heart still aching. "I thought we told each other everything."

His gaze dropped and then returned to hers, meeting it squarely. "I thought they were right. Still do. The ritual should not happen, and I won't risk your life." He sighed. "Also, my uncle took me in, gave me a dog, and was kind to me. I care about him, and I wanted to be loyal. It didn't mean I wasn't loyal to you."

"It feels like it," she said, her gaze searching. Even angry with him, even hurt, she looked to him for comfort. She always had, and it was a difficult habit to break.

His gaze softened. "I know, and for that, I'm sorry. You have to know that everything I've ever done was with the idea of protecting you, even if it doesn't seem like it, and even if I totally screwed up. I'm sorry if I've hurt you."

He was so earnest and so honest that her heart just rolled over. She knew Paxton would never hurt anybody on purpose, or at least nobody he cared about. "In doing our deep dive into the Defenders' records," she said, going slowly, "we discovered that the group plotted to kill my uncle Sam years ago."

Sam was supposedly the Keeper of the Circle, which meant that he had to find the location where the final ritual was to take place. It irritated the ever-living heck out of him because he didn't want any part of the ritual and didn't want to be the keeper of anything. Yet he'd do his duty.

"Paxton," she prodded.

He nodded. "Yes, I argued against it, but the Defenders, once I was out of the room, took a vote on whether or not to assassinate Sam." He looked at the comfortable lodge as if he didn't see it. "To be honest, I almost wish they had voted yes."

Her head jerked back in shock. "You wanted them to kill Sam?"

"No, I wanted them to vote yes to kill Sam." He shook his head. "I would never have let that happen. So at that point, I would've been forced to defy them and either get myself killed or at least be able to warn Sam or your father. Instead, they listened to me and voted not to kill him. I wasn't as good at strategy then as I am now."

Well, of course not. He'd been just a kid.

"I'm glad they voted no," she said. "And I'm glad you're not dead." She chewed the inside of her lip and huddled into her coat. "I don't know, Paxton. I'm still pretty mad at you, and I think you could be wrong about the ritual."

She had learned that nothing came without a price. What price must be paid for destroying Ulric? Why did they have to kill him? Sure, he was evil and he deserved to die, but did he have to? Could they not...? Her mind started to hurt, so she shut it down. She knew they couldn't lock him away in any prison here on earth. It would be impossible to contain him, and she also knew that there was no way they'd be able to create another prison world. "I've thought through all the possibilities, and Ulric has to die, even though we don't understand the ritual yet."

Paxton's expression didn't alter. "I felt you create a dreamworld last night," he said. "I've always been able to sense when you were doing that." She knew that was true. "I would've tried to get to you, but there were more snipers covering your home last night than ever before. Why didn't you bring me in?"

"I didn't need you."

He jolted. "You always need me."

"No, I don't. Haven't needed you for years," she lied.

The door opened, and Dage Kayrs stepped onto the snowy deck. "Paxton," Dage drawled, his gaze dropping to their joined hands. "I suggest you release her before I take off your arm."

Shockingly, Pax didn't so much as twitch. Instead, he cocked his head to the side and stared at the king. "We're in the middle of something, King. Give us a minute."

Hope's breath quickened, and she hurriedly jerked her hand away. The last thing she wanted was for Dage to kill Paxton right outside the lodge with all the Christmas decorations proclaiming it a merry place.

There was no doubt Paxton could fight, and he'd probably even do some damage to Dage, but the king was hundreds of years old, plus...he was the king.

Irritation and something else glowed in Dage's silver eyes. Admiration? Respect? Yeah, it was there. Oh, he was pissed. There was no doubt about it, but he was looking at Paxton as if he'd never seen him before. "Where do you think you're going?" he asked.

"To the lab," Hope said, grabbing Pax's hand again and all but dragging him up the stairs and past Dage to the interior. "We both want to have more blood taken. We have to figure out what this drug is. I don't feel so great."

Instantly, Dage turned all business. "All right, let's go."

As he led the way down to the lab, Hope was unsurprised to see fierce-looking armed soldiers along the way. Paxton loped easily beside her, not seeming bothered by the fact that every one of them wanted to put a bullet between his eyes. Her heart hurt, but she couldn't find a solution to their problems.

Emma was already waiting for them in the lab. No doubt somebody had signaled they were coming. She also looked tired, and her dark hair had escaped its clip to fall around her face. Her lab coat had what appeared to be coffee stains on the left sleeve. "You two want to give more blood?"

"Yes," Hope said just as Paxton said, "No."

"But we will," he added. "We need to know what they shot into us—I'm concerned." He flicked his gaze to Hope and then back.

Emma nodded. "As am I. I haven't identified that ingredient yet. Let's see if the drug is still in your systems." She drew blood from both of them and directed them to the waiting room outside her main lab. "You two go rest on one of those comfy sofas and try not to get shot. I'll need a few minutes."

Pax brushed Emma's arm once. "Thanks, Queen." He slid an arm around Hope's shoulders. "Come on, Hope." He led her into a waiting room where plush leather seats awaited. A TV was already droning on about Christmas sales.

Unsurprisingly, Dage leaned against a far wall near several of his soldiers.

Pax pulled Hope down to sit next to him on a sofa. It felt right to be next to him, even though they were so disconnected right now. "What did Drake want last night?" he asked without preamble.

She jolted. "He wants to meet me in person."

Across the room, one of Dage's dark eyebrows slowly rose.

"I think it's a good idea," she said.

"Hell no," Paxton and Dage said at the same time.

Amusement ticked through her. She couldn't help it. Why was everyone's reaction the same? "I've been training since birth—I can handle a Kurjan."

Dage's gaze firmed. "Honey, he's the leader of the Kurjan nation. You know, the people who sent that squad after you the other day?"

She shook her head. "I don't think so, Uncle Dage. The Kurjan nation is experiencing an internal war. I think some of the Kurjans are following Ulric and the Cyst, but I don't think Drake is. It wouldn't hurt to meet with him."

"Wrong," Paxton said, his voice a low growl.

"You always knew it would come down to this," she said forcefully. "We have to negotiate peace between us and figure out why they're taking enhanced females. Drake didn't know anything about it."

Paxton sat back and closed his eyes. "That's insane. There is no way he doesn't know what's going on within his own nation."

Hope looked toward her uncle. "We could choose the place, and I could be well covered. I think we should do it."

"I'll consider it," Dage said.

Paxton sat straight up and looked at the king. "You have lost your mind."

"Maybe." Dage slightly turned his head, his eyes flashing blue and silver. They unfocused for a quick heartbeat and then mellowed. "I'll go see what's taking Emma so long." He stalked toward the door like a predator out for a stroll.

That was interesting. Hope had seen that look on his face before. Mates could communicate telepathically after a while, and there was no doubt her aunt and uncle did so. Had he just gotten a message from her? If so, why?

"I'm not letting you go see Drake," Paxton said softly, a thread of steel in his tone.

She looked at him, marveling once again at the stark planes of his face. She'd always known he'd be handsome, but she hadn't had any idea of the raw sexuality that would be inherent in each line of his features. It was fascinating. "You couldn't stop me if you wanted to," she said.

"Humph." He looked back toward the closed door.

Dage returned, walking smoothly with a smile on his face.

"You have good news?" Hope asked, perking up. Maybe the drugs were out of her system.

"I do." Faster than a blur, Dage's right hand rose, and something sharp pricked her neck. She heard Paxton growl, and then darkness consumed her.

Chapter Thirteen

Hope didn't know how long she floated before cool air brushed her skin. Her body felt relaxed and very warm. She blinked several times, then opened her eyes to find herself in a hospital bed, not in Emma's lab but in the actual hospital wing of headquarters. The bed was soft and comfortable, and heated blankets covered her. She stretched as her mind came slowly awake.

"What in the world?" She started to sit up.

"Hold on, hold on. I've got you," her mother said as the head of the bed began to lift so she could sit. "How are you?" Janie asked, her blue eyes worried.

Hope blinked. Seeing her mother was like looking in the mirror, even though her mom was a quarter century older than she was. Janie had been human but became immortal when she mated Zane. She didn't gain additional strength or speed, but she'd live forever, and she'd probably always look young—and she had serious psychic abilities. Probably stronger than Hope's, or at least on a different frequency.

"Mom?" Hope pushed her hair out of her way. "Why am I in a hospital bed?"

The room was quiet, with the shades open to reveal the lake and the dark sky. Snow had fallen on the ice, covering the entire water mass. The moon shone down, making it look magical.

"I was sitting with Paxton," she said slowly.

Janie leaned forward to rub her hand, where the silver ring he'd given her still rested. "I know. I need you to take a deep breath and tell me how you're feeling."

Hope did as she was told, inhaling slowly and calming her body. "Actually, I feel fine. I kind of had a weird headache for a while, but I figured it was just stress. It's gone now."

Janie nodded. "I bet."

"Wait, what's happening?" Hope looked around. "Where is Paxton?"

"He's in the other room," Janie said quietly.

The door opened, and Emma walked in, moving slowly, her tennis shoes squeaking on the sparkling clean tiles. "Hey there, sunshine. How are you feeling?" Her blue eyes matched Janie's.

Hope looked from one to the other. "I think I'm fine." Images filtered through her memory so fast she nearly gasped. "Wait a minute, did Uncle Dage shoot me with a tranquilizer?" How did any of this make sense? Was she dreaming now?

Emma snorted. "Yeah, he can be pretty quick when he wants." Even though her voice was light, stress lines fanned from her eyes. "He did shoot you. I have to give it to him—even at his age, he's unbeatable in speed." Her smile didn't reach her stunning blue eyes.

"What is going on?" Hope asked, still cradling her wounded arm to her chest.

Emma brightened. "It looks like the unknown compound from the Kurjan dart is dissolving in your bloodstream. So I'd give it a day, maybe two, just to be sure, and then you can take blood and heal that arm."

Janie leaned forward. "Unless you can heal it yourself."

"I've tried, Mom," Hope said. "Nothing." She hated to see the worry on her mother's face, but she also wasn't going to lie to her.

Janie patted her arm. "I've been mated for twenty-five years, and I still can't really create healing cells."

"Me either," Emma said. "It could take hundreds of years to develop that ability. We'll get there."

"Yes," Hope said, plucking at a loose thread on the blanket. "But you were both human enhanced females when you mated. I actually have vampire and demon as well as shifter blood in me. There's probably some witch thrown in too."

Emma read her tablet. "I suppose so."

"Then why can't I heal myself?" Hope asked. She shook her head. "We know why. It's because I'm human. I'm actually *human*," she said to her mom.

Janie winced. "I know. I spoke with Emma about it. And frankly, honey, it does make some sense. Every immortal being of mixed heritage only takes on the aspects of one species. There can only be one, and I guess your body went with human. It's okay. We'll figure it out."

"You mean I'll mate an immortal and become immortal through him?" Hope grumbled. That was not the way she wanted to go.

"We don't know that," Emma interjected, her ever-present tablet in hand. She started pressing on buttons, looking up at the monitor above Hope's head and then back at the tablet to make more notations. "You could just be slow to develop. Immortals live for thousands of years. Maybe you're still in the infant stage. Maybe you'll gain strength and speed and healing cells when you turn a 100 or 120 or 132. Who knows, honey? Just take a deep breath."

"But what if I die?" Hope asked, voicing the question that was on everybody's minds.

Emma and Janie exchanged looks.

"We don't know," Emma admitted. "I'd like to do a lot more tests on you. But the only way to know for sure is to try to kill you, and that is not happening. Ever."

"Great," Hope muttered. Now she'd never get out of Realm headquarters. There'd be guards on her for the rest of her life, however long that might be. She snorted. This entire situation was ridiculous. "Where is my brother?" She could use a hug from the two-year-old right about now.

"Baking cookies with Sarah and Max," Janie said.

That just figured. Hope stretched her good arm. "Would you please tell me now why Uncle Dage knocked me unconscious?" Her mind would just not catch up. "I have a vague recollection of being under, but I'm really confused. Where is Paxton?"

Janie reached into her jeans pocket and pulled out a folded piece of paper. "When you left the lab earlier, Paxton slipped this to Emma."

Hope reached for it, curiosity riding her hard. The paper was well worn, and she unfolded it gently.

EMMA, I'M PASSING THIS TO YOU WITHOUT LOOKING AT IT BECAUSE THERE'S AN IMPLANT BEHIND MY LEFT EYE. I BELIEVE IT'S THE SAME TECHNOLOGY THAT WAS USED ON KARMA REESE SEVERAL YEARS AGO. THEY CAN SEE WHAT I SEE AND HEAR WHAT I HEAR, AND IF THEY DON'T LIKE SOMETHING, THEY CAN HIT A BUTTON, AND MY HEAD WILL EXPLODE LIKE A MELON.

Hope's throat went dry. Each word had been written in a different ink and a different thickness. How long had it taken Pax to write this? She continued to read.

THREE YEARS AGO, THEY INJECTED A BOMB IN HOPE'S HEAD. A CLUSTER BOMB, MINUSCULE, KURJAN TECHNOLOGY. I DIDN'T KNOW. SAVE HER. DON'T WORRY ABOUT ME. PAXTON. ALSO, WHEN YOU GO AFTER THE DEFENDERS, AND THERE ARE SEVERAL DIFFERENT FACTIONS AROUND THE WORLD, MY UNCLE WAS NOT IN ON THIS TRAVESTY.

Hope looked up. "He's been living with this for years."

"It looks like it," Janie said.

Hope scrubbed her hands down her face, her entire heart shuddering. "I should have known. He hates puzzles, and all of a sudden he has a crossword or Sudoku book with him constantly? He was writing this note and camouflaging the action the entire time."

"How could you have known?" Emma asked. "He's been away. We thought he was on some scientific mission with his uncle. We had no idea he was training or fighting so brutally."

Janie leaned forward. "This explains a lot, but it also tells you that Paxton isn't the boy we knew and loved. You understand that, right?"

"Oh, I definitely understand that," Hope said, swearing she could still feel his lips on hers and his hard body bracketing her. Her skin was electrified, even after brain surgery. Had she ever needed anybody like this? It was a little terrifying. She looked at Emma. "How is he? Did you get the device out of his head?"

"I did," Emma said. "The thing exploded right afterward and destroyed half of the machinery in that lab."

Panic slid through the haze of whatever drug had been used on her this time. "Is Paxton okay?" Hope asked, her voice hoarse.

"Yeah, he's tough," Emma said. "I had him partially shielded. One side of his body was burned, and his healing cells are sluggish. I'm afraid the Kurjan drug is affecting his ability to repair himself."

Hope struggled to rise. "I have to see him."

"Not yet," Emma murmured. "He's still under."

Hope frowned. "You put him back under?"

"I did, so I could treat the burns. Also—" She swung her gaze to Janie and then back at Hope. "While that compound in your blood is dissolving, it's actually gaining strength in his."

Hope blinked. "So he's getting worse?"

Emma finished tapping on her tablet and straightened. "I don't know. It's odd. The compound seems to affect people differently on a cellular and possibly genetic level. I've never seen anything like it. The good news is that you will have dispelled it soon. I'll keep conducting further tests on Paxton." With a quick hug to Janie, Emma turned and strode from the room.

Janie stared at her daughter. "You really care about him, don't you?"

"Don't you?" Hope asked.

"Yes," Janie said. "I always have. Even when he was a scared little kid who jumped every time I tried to give him a cookie. I thought we were doing a good thing when we sent him to live with his uncle Santino. To think we had no idea about the Defenders." She rolled her eyes. "What a stupid name."

"He feels horrible about joining them," Hope said, not quite sure if that was true. "Although he does have concerns about the Seven and the ritual."

Janie reached out to smooth the blanket over Hope. "I do as well and I'm not even involved, but you are, and we don't know what that means." Her gaze turned piercing. "Do you have any idea?"

Hope rolled her neck, trying to ease some tension. "No. If I did, I would tell you. But I believe the ritual has to happen, or Ulric won't be stopped. We have to do something about the enhanced females who are being kidnapped." She rubbed her eyes. "I wish I understood his goals. None of it makes any sense, and of course the legends are all fragmented. Even the Kurjans don't know." She stilled after she spoke the words, knowing what they gave away.

Her mother sighed. "I knew you had returned to the dreamworld," she said softly.

"How?" Hope asked.

Janie looked around the comfortable hospital room. "I feel it. There's a change in the air, and I've always caught wind of it." She grimaced. "It happened the other night, and honestly, I tried to join you. I tried to hop right in."

"Now that would've been something to see." Hope grinned. "I've tried to pull you in before, but I couldn't."

"I know. After I turned twenty-five, I've never been able to get back in. I don't like that you're doing it, but I understand." Janie sighed. "Back when I had the dreamworlds and thought I could broker a world peace, I refused to stop and think of all alternatives. But, you really need to be careful. If you are truly human, then you could die in a dreamworld."

Hope gulped. "I know, but you were human too, Mom."

Janie didn't have an answer because it was true. She held her daughter's hand. "I know you. I know you're full of light and, very appropriately, hope. I used to be that way too, but the Kurjans, they don't want peace. Or if they do, their peace doesn't look like ours. I need you to keep your eyes wide open."

Hope flipped her hand around to entwine her fingers with her mom's. They had the same hands. "You trust me?" she asked. "You're not going to beg me not to go back into the dreamworld?"

An unwilling smile lifted Janie's lips. "I would if I thought it would do any good, but I also know how determined you are. You're going to find your own path, which is what I always wanted for you. I'll worry, but in the end, I do trust you. Just know that sacrificing yourself is not the right path, no matter who you are."

Sometimes Hope forgot how smart her mother was and how insightful she could be. "The green book is still there," she offered.

Janie blinked. "Oh man, I hated that book. The closer I'd get to it, the farther away it seemed to be. I had hoped I'd be the one who could read it. Do you think you'll get to read the pages?"

Janie's dreamworlds had been a lot like Hope's, and that book had always been there.

"I hope so," Hope breathed. "I felt even closer to it last time, and something tells me I will get my hands on it."

Which would be amazing because then all the riddles would be answered. She would know what to do. She knew it contained her story and Janie's and those of all of the chosen females through the years, maybe some of the males, though the book felt very feminine. She needed to get her hands on it to see what happened next. "Thank you for trusting me."

"Of course," Janie said. "You are my daughter. After all, saving the world is kind of what we do."

Chapter Fourteen

Paxton came to with a snarl, leaping up and instinctively going for the biggest threat. His hands closed around a muscled neck, and he shoved a male soldier back, twisting his leg around the guy's knee and taking him down. Paxton landed on top of him, and the guy smoothly rolled until Pax was beneath him. He grabbed Paxton's head, lifted it, and smacked it down onto the ground.

"Would you knock it off? I'm trying not to hurt you here," Zane snarled.

Pax looked up to find shockingly emerald and slightly pissed eyes staring down at him. It took him a second to realize he was only wearing boxer shorts. "What happened?"

"Good, you're back." Zane grabbed him by the shoulders and pulled him up, shoving him none too gently toward the bed. "At least sit down."

Paxton's vision went blurry, and he sat, noting pain down his entire right side. He looked down to see the flesh raised and bumpy. "Did something explode?" He looked numbly around the innocuous hospital room.

"Yes," Zane said shortly. "The device in your head was detonated."

Huh. Paxton rubbed his eye, which for the first time in too long didn't feel as if needles were poking into it. "So they didn't lie.

The thing really did explode, huh?" He stilled. "Is Emma okay?" There was no doubt in his mind that Emma had been the surgeon performing the extraction.

"She's fine," Zane said, watching him closely.

Fire rolled through him. "What about Hope? Did they get the cluster bomb out of Hope's head?"

"Yes," Zane said. "It was no bigger than a dime. Pretty incredible, really."

Paxton scrubbed both hands down his face, still feeling her soft mouth beneath his. "I've been terrified for years, but they wouldn't let me get close enough to warn anybody. Until now, when they want me to make a move."

"How did they get in her head?" Zane asked.

Paxton felt dizzy, but he remained upright, facing the recrimination he deserved. "One of the nights I was home a few years ago, we watched movies at my uncle's. I don't know what happened. We were drinking some wine and watching the movie, and we both kind of fell asleep. We woke up when the movie was over and that was it. I didn't sense anything. I didn't feel anything at all." He frowned, having gone over the night in his mind a million times as he painstakingly wrote that note.

"I've brought your uncle and his cronies in for questioning," Zane said quietly.

In Paxton's world, questioning meant interrogating, probably torturing. "My uncle was out of town," he said evenly. "He was in the Baltics at that time, hunting down a seer who supposedly had information about the Seven ritual. I think Henric operated on us. It wasn't Fralep. He doesn't have the hands for it. It was definitely Henric."

"I've brought them in as well."

Paxton stood, the floor chilly beneath his feet. It was nice to feel anything right now. He figured he'd be dead. "You have to know that the Defenders have many cells in different locations throughout the world, and even after all this time, I don't have a line on any of them. They're traditionalists, autonomous, and each has a different mission. Mine was concerned with the Seven. For now, I want a shot at Henric."

"I'm sure you do," Zane said. "I'll give you a go after I'm done."

"I'm really sorry about this," Pax said. "I got word to you as soon as I could. I had to be careful because I really do believe Henric wants Hope dead."

Zane straightened, coming off the wall. "Why is that?"

"Because she's the Lock. If she's not around, the Seven can't perform the final ritual," Paxton admitted. "I have them convinced that if something happens to her, another Lock will show up. That they can't just end this by taking her out."

"It's a good strategy," Zane admitted.

He'd been plotting for so long. "Yeah," Paxton said. "So now their grand goal is to kill everyone. The Seven, the Keys, the Lock, and even the Keeper of the circle. I think. I'm not privy to what they're really planning, but that's been my fear."

Zane's gaze narrowed. "Paxton, I've seen some of the missions you went on. You know there are cameras or satellites everywhere. You could have killed all of them and not built up a sweat."

"I know," Paxton said, the constant ache in his chest starting to unravel now that Hope's brain was clear. "But they have safeguards, or at least they did. Henric has somebody out there I've never been able to find. If he doesn't check in with that person on a regular schedule I've never figured out, then Hope dies. I couldn't take that chance."

Zane scrutinized him. "I need you to tell me everything you know about the Seven, the ritual, and the leader of the Kurjan nation."

"Gladly," Paxton said. "Unfortunately, even after all the research we've done, the fights we've encountered, and the training I've undergone, all we know is that the Seven, many of them being your relatives, are planning a ritual that will somehow kill Ulric. They need the blood of the three Keys, and Hope has something to do with it—my guess is it'll take her sacrifice. Something like this requires a price. Nobody knows anything more than that, which means it's all probably bullshit."

Zane snorted. "No, there's always truth with the bullshit. We just don't know what it is. Hope wants to meet Drake in the real world. She thinks she can broker some kind of peace. What do you think?"

"I think the Kurjans want war," Paxton said honestly. "If there's to be any peace, as far as they're concerned, it means they're the only ones left standing." He knew that to his soul.

When Zane spoke next, his eyes darkened, going from green to greenish black. That could be mesmerizing to some, but it was a warning to Paxton. "Hope believes there is a fight within the Kurjan nation, and our source inside confirms that."

"Maybe," Paxton allowed. "But that doesn't mean Drake wants peace with us. He may just want to get his people under control. If I were you, I wouldn't let Hope get within a foot of him. You know she saw him the other night in a dreamworld." He hated reporting her activities, but the more people protecting her, the better.

"Did she now?" Zane asked. "She's an adult, and she's a strategic genius."

Paxton sighed. "I'm aware of that. However, she's always had a blind spot for Drake, and she believes she's got to follow her fate and find peace. She'll sacrifice herself to do it, and while that may be okay with you, I'm not going to let it happen."

He pivoted slightly, putting himself toe to toe, chest to chest, against one of the most powerful immortals ever to walk the planet. Zane was born and bred to lead the demons, and he was as deadly as they came.

Instead of lashing out, Zane just regarded him. "As much as I would like to encourage you on that, you have a bigger problem to worry about, Paxton."

"What is that?" Pax asked.

"The concentration of that drug in your blood has increased. It's not disappearing in you as it is in Hope. She should be clear of it by tomorrow. So obviously it was made just for you."

"Great," Pax muttered, even as he relaxed at the news that Hope would be safe from the drug. It wasn't a surprise. There was no doubt in his mind that Drake had been planning to get rid of him for years. "Why am I not dead, then?"

"We don't know," Zane said. "Emma's researching around the clock, trying to figure out what it is and why it's interacting with your system differently. There's something in your genetic makeup that has reacted oddly with the drug, and obviously the Kurjans had a sample to work with to create a weapon specifically designed to injure you. There's one avenue we might have to pursue."

Paxton remained still and stoic, but inside, for just a second, he flashed back to that terrified little kid living alone with his father. When he thought he had himself under control, he forced himself to go cold. "I guess it's time to see good old Dad."

* * * *

Paxton stood outside the jail bars and surveyed Henric and Fralep as well as his uncle. His uncle looked relatively unscathed, but the other two men were bleeding, wounded, and damaged. The interrogators had not gone easy on either of them.

His phone buzzed, and he lifted it to his ear. "Phoenix."

"Hey, it's Oscar. I'm still in San Diego—no luck with your father. He was here a month ago."

"Thanks." Pax ended the call and sent off a series of texts to other sources around the world. It was time to call in a few of the favors he'd earned in the last few years. Then he concentrated again on the occupants of the cell.

As he watched, Henric turned to the side and spat out a couple of teeth.

"Paxton," Santino said, hurrying for the bars, his faded blue eyes wide and worried. "Are you all right?"

"I'm fine, Uncle," he said. "You're getting out of here. Come on." He tapped in the code on a keypad, and the door slid open. He reached for his uncle's arm and pulled him out before securing the locks again.

"Why am I being let out?" Santino asked, his eyes wrinkling in confusion. "I told them everything I know, but still, I am one of the Defenders."

Pax had always thought it was an incredibly stupid name. The Defenders, his ass. "You told both Zane and Dage everything you knew, and you didn't do anything to Hope, Uncle."

It had taken him a while to figure out that his uncle had been duped. His soul was pure, and when he'd found out what had been done to both Paxton and Hope, he'd been horrified. Since then, he'd seemed to shrink in size as if he couldn't bear the weight and responsibility. Soon there'd be nothing left of the guy.

Paxton patted his shoulder. "We're okay. None of this is your fault."

"I'm to blame," Santino exploded, his arms sweeping wide. "I got you into the Defenders. None of this would've happened if I hadn't agreed to go along with them. We should have just gone and studied insects around the globe as I'd been doing before." His eyes filled. "It was a good life, and I miss it. I could have given that to you."

There was no question Paxton would never have that life now, so he didn't tell his uncle the lie. His path had been set long ago, and even if it hadn't, the training in the last few years had ensured he could only be a killer. Hopefully the Realm would put him to work in the unlikely event that he survived the next battle.

"I don't regret a thing," he lied to his uncle. "You gave me a home, and you gave me a dog, and I have skills that will help me to do what I need to do." He cleared his throat. "The Defenders are working with the Kurjans. Did you know?"

"No. I'm not on the inside." Santino sighed and looked down at his bare feet. They must have taken his shoes. "What do you have to do?"

Pax couldn't find the right words to explain because he didn't fully understand it himself. "If I knew, I'd tell you, but it's no longer your concern." It was the one thing he could do for the man who had saved him, who had given him a home when he truly didn't have anybody who was just his. "You're going back to your life of science. They need you to study the migration patterns of butterflies because they think the Kurjans might use them as a distribution system."

Santino perked up. "Distribution system. For what?"

"I don't know," Paxton said. "I just had a meeting with Zane, and according to him, several Kurjans have been conducting trial runs in the Sahel desert, using painted lady butterflies to do their dirty work."

"Ooh, the painted lady migrates the farthest of all the butterflies. She's a beauty, too."

Paxton couldn't help but smile. "There are guards waiting to take you back to our home. I want you to go. Word of your innocence will be out by tomorrow, but for now, we don't want to take any chances."

Santino looked over his shoulder at the other two men in the cell. "What about them?"

"They're not leaving yet," Paxton said shortly. "Go home, feed the dog, and I'll be there to see you soon. Stay out of the tunnels."

"I never want to go back there as long as I live," Santino said sadly. "In fact, we should move."

"Fine by me," Paxton said. "The Realm techs cleaned out the entire tunnel, which is now empty." All the computers and everything else had been confiscated by Zane and his soldiers. Even so, there was no need to bring back bad memories.

Santino threw both arms around him, hugged him, and lifted him. Apparently the old guy had some strength left in him yet. "I am so sorry. Please tell Hope I'm heartbroken about everything."

"Hope's strong, and she's fine. She's already forgiven you," Paxton said easily. He didn't know if that was true or not, but he knew Hope well enough to believe that she'd forgive Santino the minute she saw him. That was just her nature. "Go. I'll be home later."

"All right, sounds good. I do need to investigate the painted lady butterfly," Santino said, scurrying down the hallway.

"Make sure somebody gets him some boots," Paxton called out to the guards. Then he turned back toward the other two in the cell. "Looks like you took a fist to the teeth, Henric," he said cheerfully.

Henric glared at him. "This isn't the end."

"Oh, I believe it is," Paxton said. "Right now, we're rounding up the rest of your group." As far as he knew, there were only twelve of them in this Defenders cell and most were currently on missions out of the country. But the Realm forces were good—they would find them all. Then they'd move on to the other cells.

Fralep looked at Henric out of one eye because the other was swollen shut. "I told you we should have beat him on a regular basis."

"Santino wouldn't let us," Henric said. "We didn't really have any leverage until we got that thing in his head."

Pax let the killer they'd created show in his eyes. "That was Kurjan technology, as was the minuscule bomb you put in my woman's head."

"Your woman," Henric snorted. "She's not going to live long enough to be anybody's woman, and even if she were, I think the Kurjans have dibs, don't you?"

Fury clacked through Paxton on the heels of rage, but he let his expression go to pure boredom. "Which one of you has been working with the Kurjans?"

"It doesn't matter," Henric said. "They want the same thing we do. To stop the ritual."

Paxton's gut turned over. "You're a traitor."

"No, I'm not," Henric said. "I did the right thing for our people, and while I might be temporarily indisposed, we have others, Paxton. So many. Some close to you."

Paxton took the blow to the gut but didn't move, didn't even twitch. "Tell me more."

"Oh, I think you know. There's only one person in the world who would've agreed to blow off Hope Kayrs-Kyllwood's head if I didn't report in. Just one. Even the Kurjans want her alive."

"My father," Paxton said, something tearing inside him.

"He hated you with everything he had," Fralep said, chuckling. "He saw a weakness in you that I never could figure out. You were a dumb kid, but you grew up to be a pretty decent fighter. Yet I've never seen such raw hatred. He'll be coming for you."

For the first time, Paxton let a smile tilt his lips. "I'm going for him first." Then he opened the door to their cell, noting how they both stiffened. They were about to regret making sure his training was so good. "After you tell me everything you know." He shut the door. "Who's first?"

Chapter Fifteen

Hope knocked softly on the door to Paxton's house, acutely aware of the disapproval emanating from the soldiers in the trees around her. It wasn't easy being the only female vampire on earth, not to mention the demon king's daughter and the vampire king's great-niece. She was accustomed to people watching her. She was not used to the waves of disapproval.

Obviously, word had not yet gone out about what Paxton had done or that none of this was his fault. Still, she couldn't help a tiny slice of hurt that he hadn't somehow figured out a way to talk to her. Of course, he had been gone for the last few years, probably by design. The Defenders seemed to have known what they were doing.

The door opened, and he stood there, all six foot six of him, broad, muscled, and mean. If he was surprised to see her, he didn't show it. Instead, his gaze rose to the trees across the icy street. "I feel Liam," he murmured.

"Yeah, but Liam's on your side," she said. She'd at least managed to tell Liam what had been going on.

"There are several out there who aren't." He grasped her arm and drew her inside the warm home, putting his body between her and the trees. For several moments, he stood there, making himself a perfect target.

"Would you knock it off?" She punched him in the kidneys and stepped away.

He didn't so much as twitch. "I thought I'd give them a good chance."

Slowly he shut the door and turned back to face her, leaning against it. It struck her then how different he was from the boy she once knew. He'd had an entire life she knew nothing about, and the knowledge hurt. It was also intriguing. She'd loved him since she was a child. Loved him as her best friend, as her confidant, as her trusted protector.

This was different. This was something new and something she could not indulge. "I wanted to see if you were okay," she said.

"I'm fine." He leaned down to look into her eyes. "How are you feeling?"

"I'm good. I didn't even know that thing was in my head," she admitted. She'd taken more of the Advil, and that had helped as well. "I'm sorry you had to carry that fear for the last year." She knew Paxton and understood he had always felt responsible for everybody around him. It must have killed him, knowing there was a bomb in her head. "I'm okay now, though."

Heat rolled from him, warming the entire room. "I'm sorry, Hope."

"Sorry for what?" She lifted her chin. "Sorry I got a bomb put in my head? Sorry you've been lying to me for years? Sorry you joined the Defenders, which is a group that apparently wants to kill all of my uncles?"

His silvery-blue eyes flashed to a sharp and sizzling green and then morphed back again. Vampires had tertiary colors, and his had always been green. It emerged only during high-intensity moments or extremely emotional ones. "I did what I had to do, and I never would have killed one of your uncles. Besides, only three of the Seven are your uncles."

"They're pretty much all my uncles," she muttered. "Some of them are ancient and a million times removed, but I'm related to almost everybody on the Seven. You wanted to destroy them."

He sighed, but he didn't deny it. His phone buzzed, and he scooped it off the table near the door, reading the screen and then shooting off a couple of texts. "He can't hide forever." Pax tossed the phone away and zeroed his focus on her.

"You really believed everything you said the other day, didn't you?" she asked quietly.

"About the final ritual being stopped? Yeah, I did. I have looked at this from every single angle there is, princess, and the only way it makes sense is that the Lock is there to balance the scales for Ulric's death. You and I both know that any ritual, *anything* involving altering physics, demands a high price."

She blinked.

His gaze narrowed. "You knew, didn't you?"

"I suspected," she said. "It doesn't make any sense unless a sacrifice is made. I figured that was probably my life." She expected him to commiserate with her or to vow that he'd figure something else out.

Instead, he pivoted suddenly, lifting her by the hips and slamming her against the door. "You will not accept such a fate. Do you understand me?" His voice was all the more frightening for the soft tone he used.

Heat traveled through her so quickly her ears rang, her heart thundered, and her thighs softened. What was happening? "Paxton, put me down." Her voice emerged breathy, as if she'd been running for hours.

"I don't think so," he said. "I think people have been going along with what you want and what you think for far too long. If you were mine, there's no way in hell you'd be wandering around demon territory right now."

His? "Listen, Pax." She shot both hands up to nail him beneath the jaw.

He didn't step back. In fact, it didn't even look like he'd felt the blow. Instead, his head lowered until his eyes were right above hers. His scent of leather and the forest wafted around them. "You're a brat, Hope. I might adore you, but I won't accept that."

What did that mean? She opened her mouth to give it to him just as one of his broad hands tangled in her hair, twisted, and pulled her head back. Her breath caught in her throat, and she latched onto his shoulders for balance, feeling the muscles play beneath his shirt. Hard and fluid.

Then his firm lips were on hers.

Fire seared through her, zinging from her mouth to her breasts right to her core. Her abdomen heated, and butterflies winged in every direction. She moved into him, even though her brain told her to stop.

She moaned, and he pressed her jaw with his thumb, forcing her to open. For him. For Paxton Phoenix, who was much more dangerous than she'd ever imagined.

Then he dove in, all wildfire, all danger, his tongue taking control. The growl rumbling up from his chest and into her mouth, down her throat, to her every nerve was all demon Primal and savage.

He easily held her aloft, his free hand flexing on her hip with barely restrained power.

She'd had no idea desire could be painful.

Gasping, she pulled back, her lungs needing air. For the first time in too long, she really looked at him. His handsome face and calm demeanor masked a deadly warrior. A true predator. And right now, she was in his sights. Her body did a full roll.

His smile was quick, gone as quickly as it had arrived. It was the smile of a male in control of his environment. One prepared for violence, and one who held her easily off the floor.

Watching her, those green eyes a chromatic warning, he tugged the button on her jeans free.

Her eyes widened...but she didn't stop him.

Slowly, so slowly that she could hear the seconds ticking by, he flattened his heated palm against her abdomen and caressed down, slipping his fingers into her panties. She panicked and stiffened, but then he found her.

Her mouth opened on a gasp. She was wet and ready...and so far out of her element she couldn't think. Her hips jerked as if she'd been shocked. Desire ripped through her, pinpointed right where he touched her.

She let her head go back on the door. His fingers parted her, and one slipped inside, while the other rubbed against her clit. He tilted his head, watching her, learning her. Then he sped up, and she gasped, riding his fingers. As if he knew her body better than she did, he flicked her clit. Hard.

The world exploded. She shut her eyes as the orgasm tore through her, taking even her breath. She rode the waves and then slowly came down, sagging against him.

Stunned.

Then somebody knocked forcefully on the door, right against her back. She jerked her head up, nailing his jaw.

"What?" Paxton snapped, removing his hand and quickly zipping up her jeans. Her bottle of Advil fell out of her pocket, and he caught it, handing it over with one raised eyebrow.

"It's Zane. The intel you secured from Henric was good. The Seven stronghold is being attacked. We need the teams in the air, Hope. Now."

Paxton slowly lowered her until she stood on her own. "I'm on your team now. Period."

* * * *

Hope settled into her chair as the monitors came up, managing her team from two miles away from the battle zone. It was the first time she'd had either Paxton or her father on the team, and the weight of that responsibility felt like boulders on her shoulders. She forced the thought of Pax's kiss, of that freaking devastating orgasm, out of her head. She had a job to do. The entire area was already alight with missiles and fighters as her team rappelled down from two helicopters.

"Squad one, go to the south, squad two to the east," she ordered, typing rapidly. "We have two more helicopters in the air, ready for wounded."

She tried to keep her voice level, but the idea of her uncles or her aunts being injured or worse made her voice hoarse. She also knew that Paxton wasn't in top form, but she watched him through the screen, holding her breath as he moved swiftly toward the enemy. As swiftly as her father did.

Combined, they were a frighteningly deadly duo.

Two Kurjans emerged from out of nowhere and attacked Paxton. He dropped to the ground, and she barely bit back a scream until she noticed that he'd slid on purpose to slice the Achilles tendons of the nearest Kurjan. In one smooth and impossibly strong motion, he leaped up, stabbed the second Kurjan in the eye, manacled him around the neck, and then kicked in the temple of the other one trying to get up.

Zane turned to engage a Cyst that had come out of the fire as Garrett ran full bore out of an underground bunker with Dessie in his arms.

"Helicopter one," Hope bellowed. "Set down to the north two clicks. We've got incoming."

As she watched, Collin tossed Garrett an ear communicator that he snatched out of the air and stuck in his ear while he kept running.

"Garrett, head north, we'll run interference for you." She typed and gave terse orders to her squad. "Libby and Derrick, I want you to intercept," she said. "There are forces coming from the east, and Garrett needs to get to the helicopter."

He was limping, and she couldn't tell if Dessie was ever breathing. The idea that Garrett's mate wasn't moving chilled

Hope to the bone. She gave orders, trying to clear an evacuation path for all of the Seven. Ivar was next, with his mate on his back, and then Benny and Karma appeared, each holding a small child with twin girls running between them. They were missing a kid.

Hope scrambled, typing rapidly, looking. There was Adare and his mate, Grace. She held the other little boy as they ran, apparently following Garrett's instructions. There wasn't time to throw any of them an ear communicator, so Garrett was directing. She moved her team and caught sight of more dark forms following.

"There's another Kurjan squad just dropped from the south," she announced.

They were definitely outmanned. Two more Realm helicopters dropped additional soldiers, and it was a melee on the ground. Knives flashed, laser guns fired, and blood spurted. She tracked her team, knowing somebody else would be tracking the other teams closer to the site. She was positioned far from the action because she was most likely human. Not immortal. That thought infuriated her, but she sucked it up and focused on protecting her team.

Liam went down, and Collin threw him over his shoulder. "Wounded. Half of his neck is gone," Collin said tersely. "I'm taking him to the helicopter."

Hope typed rapidly. "All right, fill in. Libby, where are you?"

"I'm here," Libby said tersely. "I need to shift."

"Green light given. Do it with maximum exposure."

"Got it."

Libby ran into the midst of several Kurjan soldiers and shifted. A sonic boom sent them spiraling through the air. In one swift motion, she turned, caught one, and ripped off his head with her sharp teeth.

Still missing some of the Seven members, Hope typed and moved the satellite angle to see better. A thump sounded outside her door. She was in a small temporary building they'd put far enough away that she wouldn't be hurt, and there were two guards on the door. Another thump. Oh, crap.

She turned just as the door burst open to reveal a six-foot-eight Kurjan soldier with blood on his face, smiling, his fangs yellow and sharp.

He let them retract. "If it isn't the Lock," he rasped.

She casually turned and pulled her weapon from her right boot without seeming to move. It was a gift she'd had since she was young, although she'd worked for years to perfect it. Unfortunately, the Kurjan blade was in her other boot, and he'd see her go for it. This would have to do. "You're missing the fight," she said.

His smile was cruel. "Perhaps, but there are several of us who are scouting farther out just in case. We had a bet against you being here, but our leader thought you'd be part of this."

"Drake or Ulric?"

"Does it matter?" the Kurjan asked. "Either way, my future is set. I'm bringing the queen home." He moved toward her, so tall she had to tilt her head to see his eyes.

With a battle cry, she rushed forward and stabbed him in the stomach.

He grabbed her hair and threw her across the room as blood arced behind him. Swearing, he pulled the knife out, brandishing it. "Queens don't stab."

"I'm not a queen," she said, ducking and rolling. She came up firing with her gun, hitting him several times in the chest, neck, and square between the eyes. She aimed for the brain. He went down sputtering and yet still moving. She'd shot him in the brain, for Pete's sake.

He let out a furious roar and leaped for her, hitting her center mass, lifting her up and throwing her against the wall. Pain crashed down her spine. Her head fell back, and stars flashed behind her eyes.

Shrieking, he threw her down on the floor and kicked her hard in the ribs. Several shattered. She rolled, gasping in a pain so great it shocked the air from her lungs. The earth stopped moving

Wincing, crying, trying to remain conscious, she managed to roll over and sit up.

He glared down at her, bullets popping out of his skin. "I can't wait till you're in my territory. You'll learn how to behave," he said, blood dribbling out of his mouth.

"I know how to behave now," she hissed despite the pain filling her entire body. In one jerky motion, she reached into her other boot and lifted out the special knife, the one created by the Kurjans, then threw it with unerring accuracy toward his neck. It lodged in his throat, and in a whisper of sound, flicked open, its many blades slicing in every direction. His eyes, purple and swirling with red, widened in shock, and he took a step back. Then his head rolled right off his body.

Holding her damaged ribs with her damaged arm, she crawled back to the computer and pressed the button. "Headquarters needs backup now."

She barely got the words out before darkness ripped through her head, and her chin dropped to the desk with a painful thud before she slid to the floor.

Chapter Sixteen

Buzzing filled Hope's head, made her ears tingle, and shot through her veins. She was cold and a chugging sound echoed all around her. Slowly, she opened her eyes to find herself in one of the Realm's attack helicopters, secured against the side while sitting on a wide bench. She was flanked by Paxton and Zane. Residual pain echoed through her body, but she didn't feel nearly as bad as she should.

"Who gave me blood?" she asked, trying to focus.

"I did," her father said, as the sound of healing cells popped around him. "There wasn't any choice. I hope the other drug is out of your system, but you had ribs crushing your lungs." He kept his eyes closed as he spoke, but tension emanated from him almost as strongly as the waves streaming off Pax.

She looked around to make sure the rest of her team was in one piece. Libby and Derrick sat across from her, while Liam and Collin took up the rear bench of the small copter. Everybody was bruised and bleeding, but alert. Healing cells filled the cabin, and she wished once again that she had the ability to summon them. Everybody in the copter was as young as she was except for Zane, and they all had the skill. She really did fear she was human.

"Status?" she croaked out.

"We got them all out," Paxton said wearily.

She focused more closely on him. Their legs were touching, but it was because his were slightly spread as he repaired what looked like a broken knee. It was twisted the wrong way. Her stomach lurched. His shoulders were so wide they also touched hers, and she wanted to lean into him but refrained. Pain poured off him, sharper than the others and with an odd signature she didn't recognize. The Kurjans had inflicted some serious damage on him—or that drug in his system was still working to harm him.

"How bad are you hurt?" she asked.

"Same as everybody," he said, his knee twisting around to where it should be.

She sucked in air, making more sound than he did. God, that had to have hurt. "What about the other teams?"

"We didn't lose any," Zane said quietly. "We've got the Seven and their mates safely on the way to Realm headquarters. We've decided to put them there instead of demon headquarters for now. It's more central, and we can keep a better eye on them. Plus, the guesthouses are nicer."

"Any injuries?" Hope asked, gingerly stretching her arm out. The healing cells from the borrowed blood had healed the fracture. Her wrist felt shaky but not nearly as bad as when the bone was broken. "Hey, you guys took off my cast."

"You didn't need it," Pax muttered.

She glanced over to see the remnants of the plaster still on his fingertips. He must have torn the thing right off her while she was out.

Libby rubbed at a bruise above her right eye that was more of a goose egg. "Word came in that two of the Seven's mates were injured, but they're taking blood and should be okay."

Hope chewed on her lip. "I like the idea that they'll relocate to headquarters and not remain out by themselves." She was now more convinced than ever that they needed to perform this ritual. "We need battle plans in place to take Ulric."

The tension in the craft rose while the temperature dropped
She shivered. It was suddenly freezing.

When nobody answered her, she said, "Well?"

"No ritual," Paxton said tersely.

"I think I agree," her father said.

Hope looked at the rest of her team.

Libby shrugged, blood matting her golden-brown hair. "I don'
know what to say. They'll keep coming until we end this, but we
don't really know *how* to end it. In addition, we're losing enhanced
females left and right."

Hope let the vibrations of the helicopter settle and organize the
energy flowing through her. "I don't see that we have a choice
We need to kill Ulric." She knew it in her heart. "Whatever's
going on, the enhanced females are being taken because of him
He is behind all of this." She wasn't one to advocate killing i
there was a peaceful solution. "Our other alternative is to reach
out and negotiate peace."

"The Kurjans aren't going to negotiate peace," Paxton said as
even more pain wafted from him. She was in tune to him and
always had been, so she tried to take some of his agony away
It was a skill she had been working on, one she'd never quite
mastered, but they were close enough that she felt she could take
some of his pain away and ease his suffering.

"Stop it," he growled.

Interesting. "No," she retorted.

Instant invisible shields went up between them. "I told
you to stop it."

Zane finally straightened and opened his eyes, looking around
Hope toward Paxton. "What is she doing?"

"She's trying to take my pain," Paxton said wearily.

"Tattletale." Hope looked up at him. He was pale, far too pale
and it looked like there was blood at the ends of his hair. Maybe
down his neck. Kurjan blood burned. "You need to wipe that
off," she said.

"I'm fine," he said.

She looked around at her group. "Anybody else have Kurjan blood on them? We should have a wet wipe around here somewhere."

"It's in my hair," Libby said. "But it doesn't burn there. I'll take a shower when we get back."

"You need any help?" Derrick joked.

Libby snorted. "Like you would know what to do with a woman in the shower."

The group chuckled as some of the tension abated. Hope shook her head at them. They were the best of friends, and while she would love to see friends turn into lovers, the feeling just wasn't there. They teased each other like brother and sister. Although it would be fun to see a witch and a cougar shifter in love. The relationship would be explosive.

Liam finished repairing a cut to his skull, his skin stitching itself together. "Nice job with the Kurjan soldier, by the way."

Hope splayed a hand across her sternum. "Thanks, but he broke all my ribs."

"Yeah, but you killed him." Collin joined his brother in grinning at her. "That was pretty freaking impressive. That guy was twice your size."

Warmth filled her. She might not have super strength or speed, but she had taken out a Kurjan soldier. "He started it," she said, her lips twitching to a smile.

Libby chuckled. "Well, you finished it."

She was nowhere near the fighter that her friends were, but she had protected herself.

"I'm proud of you," her dad said, nudging her with a shoulder.

"So am I," Paxton whispered.

Now she was just going to get a big head. "You all did a good job on the field," she said. "I was proud of all of you. How come we didn't have intel on the attack a week ago?" she asked. Thank goodness Pax had gotten the information from Henric in time.

"I don't know," Zane said. "We're going to have to check with Hunter and figure out why he didn't know."

Her cousin Hunter was undercover in the Kurjan nation, and he stayed close to Vero, who was Drake's cousin. "I think he didn't know because Drake didn't orchestrate the attack," Hope retorted "He and Vero stay right on Drake's heels. They have been at the main headquarters for several days. I feel they would've known if he'd ordered this attack."

"They've only been back a couple of days," Paxton corrected "This campaign took weeks to plan." He shifted his weight and his leg popped again. "Stop giving Drake the benefit of the doubt.'

Libby rolled her eyes. "Boys," she mouthed. Hope couldn't help but grin.

It was incredible, really. Hope's body hurt. Her head was aching and she was worried about everybody she knew, and yet Libby could always make her smile. She was the best of best friends Her other best friend was obviously cranky and still in pain. He wouldn't let her help, and frankly, she hadn't developed the ability yet, although she'd been trying. So maybe she wasn't so human Maybe there was a chance for her after all.

She steeled her shoulders and looked at her father. "Dad, the Seven are now in our territory. We have all the ingredients to take down Ulric." She held up a hand when he started to protest. "I'm not saying that we go kidnap the guy, even if we could. What I am saying is that it is time for the vampire and demon nations, the entire Realm actually, and the Seven to get on the same page. We need to work together and figure out what to do. If a peace treaty is the way to go, then that's what we do. If war has to happen, then we agree first. The time for different factions is over."

He looked at her, his green eyes somber. "I think you're right."

Libby perked up. "Hey, don't forget the shifter nations. We made a promise that if we went after Ulric or did anything, you would let Jordan know." Jordan was the leader of the feline nation, and Libby was loyal to him.

Zane nodded. "I'm aware. We should let the witch nation know as well."

"Don't forget the Fae people," Derrick said, grinning. Fairies were known to be a bit explosive and unpredictable.

"Ah, damn it," Zane muttered.

Streaks of pink and gold highlighted the sky as the helicopter landed. Hope blinked. It was later than she'd realized, or rather, earlier. Anyway, it was no longer dark.

The door opened, and she stepped out, nearly falling back when a bundle of energy rushed at her. She laughed and leaned down to pick up her younger brother, happy that she could do so without her arm killing her.

"Where have you been?" he asked.

She cuddled him close. "What do you mean where have I been? I was out doing tough girl stuff."

He leaned back to look at her, both of his chubby little hands cupping her face. "You are a tough girl," he said.

"Yes, I am." She kissed the top of his head.

At two years old, Andrew Scott Kyllwood, also known as Drew, was pretty much the cutest thing on the planet. He had Zane's black hair and Janie's blue eyes, and already he could speak at a fifth-grade level. He was kind, and he was funny, and he was all his father's son.

"Dad!" he yelled, partially turning in Hope's arms.

Hope tossed the boy to Zane, who easily caught him and swung him in a circle. "How quickly they move on," she said, looking over to see her mom lounging against the outside of the hangar. The crew would unload the craft before putting it to bed.

"Hey, Mom," she said, walking up to give Janie a hug.

Janie wore a thick green sweater and light jeans, looking young and a mite tired. "Hi. Your brother was not willing to sleep in today," she said, rubbing her head. She looked at Hope and then over at Pax. "Paxton, you're too pale."

Pain pinched the skin by his generous mouth, but he still appeared ready to fight, his body tense and prepared to uncoil. "I'm okay, Janie." Pax strode toward them, looking graceful and deadly. He dropped a quick kiss on Janie's head. "I just need to rest." He continued walking away, tossing over his shoulder, "I'll be back in a couple of hours to review the campaign. I just need to go heal a few things."

Janie's brow wrinkled, and her gaze sobered. "I've never seen him so pale. Is that drug still in his system?"

"As far as I know," Hope said, giving her mom another hug. "I'm going to go walk with him." Without waiting for an answer, she issued instructions to the rest of her team. "Let's recoup and meet around noon. We can have lunch in the conference room and figure out our next steps."

She should give them the day off, but she could smell war on the wind, so she followed Paxton, surprised when he didn't slow down. "Pax, wait up."

"How about we talk later, Hope?" Dogged determination settled hard on his face as he slogged through the snow.

"How about you tell me how bad you're feeling?"

He looked down at her. "I feel crappy. I think it's more than just getting a couple of bones broken and being stabbed a few times. It's whatever's in my blood. I'm going to go home, take a shower, heal my injuries, and then drop by Emma's lab on the way to our meeting."

"That's a good plan," Hope said. "Can I do anything to help?"

His grin was quick, but at least it was there. "Not unless you want to hop in the shower with me."

If he had any idea how tempted she was, she'd probably end up in that shower before she knew it. Instead, she slapped his arm lightly. "Knock it off. We're going to war, unless I can find a way to broker peace." They had to forget what had happened earlier against the door.

He stopped in the middle of the snowy street. "I like that you've always wanted to find peace." He slid his thumb along her jawline and tugged on her ear. "I wish I could be positive as well, but I don't feel peace coming for us."

Her skin was electrified, her entire body heating from that one little touch.

His watch dinged, and he glanced down. He straightened, stiffened, and somehow looked more distant than ever.

"What is it?" she asked.

"It was a message from a source," he murmured. "I'm going to miss our lunch meeting."

She tried to read his watch, but the message had already faded away. "Why? What's happening?"

He eyed the forest and the trees, obviously looking for snipers. They were always about, especially these days. "A source has located my father. It's time he and I had a little chat."

Chapter Seventeen

Still burned, battered, and bleeding from a wound in his head, Paxton found his father in a dilapidated bar outside of Cabo San Lucas. Known only to locals, it was a place for drinking and not much else. The flight had taken more than five hours because of rough weather, though the harsh sun had been blinding as it ripped through the clouds from time to time. His head was still aching from the glare.

The ocean rolled in the distance as Paxton opened the flimsy wooden door and walked inside, instantly feeling the warmth of the many bodies scattered inside the rough building. Bottles of cheap liquor were piled high behind the scarred wooden bar.

As he stalked across the dirt floor, the stench of body odor, puke, and stale beer filled his nostrils. But he didn't care. He approached the lone figure sitting on a stool at the far end of the bar, a broad male hunched over a glass of rotgut.

The more Pax moved, the more his heart rate finally picked up. The drug was still poisoning his system, and he thought idly it might be shutting him down pretty soon, so he had to get his affairs in order. Unfortunately, one of those items included dealing with this asshole from his past. As he got close, his father lifted his head.

Slowly, that dark gaze, already filled with hatred, swept Paxton from his feet to the top of his head. "Huh, guess your brain didn't explode earlier, did it?"

The implications of that statement shot through Paxton. Even though he had heard the truth from Henric, there was a part of him—that scared kid from long ago who had wanted to impress his father—that hadn't wanted to believe it. His own father had been more than willing to see him dead.

"How did you find me?" Paelotin asked, swigging back the rotgut.

"I've at least had an idea of your location since I turned sixteen years old," Paxton said. "Didn't matter who I had to bribe or beat up. I kept track of you."

"Not very well," Paelotin said, motioning to the bartender for another round.

The bartender, a short human who had to be about ninety years old, shuffled over, his girth barely clearing the narrow space behind the bar. He poured some unidentifiable liquid into Paelotin's glass and went away.

"So you really wanted me dead," Paxton said.

"Huh. Actually, I didn't give two shits," Paelotin said, looking at his drink. His raw hatred belied his words.

"How long have you been working with the Kurjans?" Paxton asked evenly, pulling out a stool when all he wanted to do was choke the very life out of the monster in front of him.

"Does it matter?"

Paxton wasn't sure whether it did or not. "If you don't remember, then don't worry about it." He motioned for the bartender. The guy came over, his thin gray hair oiled back with a thick paste, and he poured Paxton a glass, not looking up, then shuffled away.

"The Defenders contacted me when the Realm kicked me out," Paelotin pointed for the bartender to just come and leave the bottle. The guy did so with no expression.

Pax eyed the bottle. Most of the label had been worn off. "You were a soldier for the Realm. How could you just switch alliances like that?" The Kurjans had killed Pax's mother. How could his father hate the Realm and Paxton more than the evil scum who had killed his mate?

"The Kurjans made it worth my while. I figured, why not? They at least were offering money while the Realm offered nothing but disappointment." He looked Paxton up and down. "I could've trained you well, but they took you from me, although, let's be honest, I didn't much care. I figured you'd be a scientist or something. Are you?"

"You know exactly what I am," Paxton retorted. "You've been in contact with Henric this whole time."

Paelotin poured more into his glass. "Henric knows what he is doing. He may be a scientist, but the guy's a strategic genius. He got you to work for him, didn't he?"

Paxton couldn't argue with that.

"Plus," Paelotin continued, "he got Santino, that moron, to work for him as well. Well, for a while. You know your uncle tried to get out."

Paxton tipped back his glass, trying not to wince as the liquor burned down his throat. Stuff tasted like pure acid. "Santino tried to leave the Defenders?"

"Oh yeah," Paelotin said, wiping his mouth on his sleeve. "Something about Sam Kyllwood and a vote to kill him. I think he finally realized the stakes. He told Henric he wanted out, and of course, Henric made threats. Said he had people watching you and would kill you."

Paxton's chest hurt, but he didn't rub it. He refused to show any unease to his father. "Santino's a good man." No doubt he would've sacrificed himself to save Pax. "Unlike you. You've never sacrificed for anybody, have you?" The anger still flowed through him, but he wouldn't let it show. He would never give Paelotin that satisfaction. "I waited a long time to talk to you," he said.

Paelotin snorted. "We don't have anything to say, boy. You chose the Realm over me."

"Of course I did," Paxton said. "You're a loser who beats kids and works for the enemy. One of the biggest regrets of my life is that I have your last name. I could change it."

It didn't really matter, because his mother's name was Pankov. So as a demon, when his mating mark appeared on his hand, it would be a *P*. For years, he'd felt it itching on his palm, but the marking hadn't appeared yet. Something seemed to be holding him back, but he sensed it would happen soon. He kind of liked his last name. It was unfortunate he shared it with this miscreant.

Paelotin just looked at him. "I can't believe you're here actually trying to be threatening. You're lucky I didn't kill you when you were young. I should have."

"You tried," Paxton said softly. "And failed."

Paelotin chuckled. "Yeah. Deep down you're still a crying little bastard though, aren't you? You may look all tough, and you may be able to fight, but we both know you're nothing but garbage."

"Do we know that?" Paxton asked calmly, his gut turning. Yeah, he felt worthless sometimes. That was because his father's words still rang in his head. But now, he was bigger than the bastard. Tougher and most certainly deadlier. "You're the one who got kicked out of the Realm. Talk about garbage."

"You just had to protect that little bitch."

Paxton grabbed him square on the throat and squeezed. "I strongly recommend you don't talk about Hope like that. I came here to chat, but I'm also fine with killing you."

"You think you could?" Paelotin lifted one arm and struggled to shove Paxton's hold off.

Paxton could have easily grabbed him again, but he reached for his drink first. He needed answers, and he needed his father to be able to speak. "Who's your contact in the Kurjan nation?"

"They're all my contacts." Paelotin's chest puffed out. "I work with different ones at different times."

"What about Drake?"

Paelotin grimaced. "The leader? Yeah, we're best friends."

"You want to level with me," Paxton said, downing his drink in one gulp. The cheap liquor hit his stomach and flashed out, burning as it went. What was in that stuff? He poured himself another shot. "Start talking, or you're not going to like the results."

"What are you going to do, boy?" Paelotin asked. "I am more than ready to fight you. I spent half my life hitting you. I miss those days."

It was odd he didn't even want payback. This was for Hope. "Don't forget you liked to kick too."

"I surely did. Obviously not enough. I should have killed you when I had the chance."

Paxton had expected the vitriol, but even so, he had to wonder. His memories of his mother were good. She was only around until he was maybe three or so, but even Hope had gotten to know her a little bit. She was soft, and she was sweet, and then she was gone. "What did my mother ever see in you?"

Paelotin looked at him and laughed. "Not much. She didn't have another option."

What the hell did that mean? Paxton never heard the story, though he'd asked many times. She had died at the end of the last war. His mother didn't really know anybody from the main headquarters of the Realm because she worked as a soldier for an international squad, just like his father. "How did she die?"

"I killed her," Paelotin said calmly.

Paxton coughed. "She died in a battle with the Kurjans."

"There was a battle. But..." He shook his head. "She wanted to go back on a promise and, well, I couldn't let her."

Paxton's ears rang, his stomach hurt, and his vision blurred. "A promise?" he asked. "What promise?" Whatever was in his system was slowly killing him, no doubt as the Kurjans had planned. "The Realm's good at what it does; they would've known if you'd killed her." This was just another of his father's mind fucks.

"No. We were in the middle of a battle with some very, very, very angry Kurjans, with a couple of the Cyst thrown in. It was easy to fake her death, Paxton. Don't be a moron."

"You killed her? You really killed her?"

"Oh, with great pleasure."

Everything inside Paxton wanted to attack, but he needed to remain strategic for now. There were facts to discover that could help Hope. "You always were a damn coward," Pax muttered.

With that, Paelotin charged him. They flew off the stools, landing hard on the dirt-packed floor. People around them scrambled out of the way, some fleeing the bar, some just sidling away as if a brutal fight was a common occurrence.

Paelotin's first punch nearly knocked off Paxton's head, but he rolled with it, pulling his father with him. He punched upward twice and then scissored his legs around this monster from his past and flipped them over, punching twice more.

He could've done immeasurable damage, but instead, he secured his father hard against the ground. Not once in training or in battle had he inflicted more damage than was necessary, and though he might want to kill this bastard, he wouldn't stoop to that. But he would get answers.

His father fought his hold for several long moments and then gave up, panting.

"Why?" Pax asked, his voice rough. "Why do you hate me so much?"

Paelotin, his teeth bloody, managed to smile. "Because you're not my son, you little prick."

Cymbals crashed in Pax's head. "You're lying."

"Nope. Total truth." Even wheezing, Paelotin laughed.

That was a good truth. "That explains the pictures I found of my mother." The labels conveyed a different meaning now. She'd been taking him into the Realm, the two of them, for a new life. He was glad to know she'd tried to leave and save them both. "Does Santino know?"

"No." Paelotin snorted. "The absent-minded professor doesn't know about any of it. He's truly one clueless bastard."

Pax relaxed. Good. "Then who's my father?"

The smile widened, and air bubbled out with blood. "Ask King Zane Kyllwood. Didn't you ever wonder why he took such an interest in you?"

Chapter Eighteen

Hope cuddled up on the sofa in Paxton's empty house, watching an old movie. She'd made herself at home, microwaving a huge bowl of popcorn and opening a beer. Through the years, when Paxton was home from his travels, she'd spent many an evening watching movies on that very sofa, so she knew exactly where to find the threadbare blanket she always used to keep warm.

It was sad he didn't have a fireplace. Most houses in the subdivision had fireplaces; in northern Idaho, it got freaking cold. At least the blanket helped.

Several ancient texts and tomes were spread over the coffee table. For years, she'd spent every spare hour reading through legends and prophecies and found several that hinted at what must be done to kill Ulric. Her name was mentioned as well as the importance of the Lock, but there was a frustrating lack of detail. It was accepted that the blood of the three Keys was needed, but Hope was sure the Lock would have to give more than blood. Otherwise, there would be just four Keys.

Unless somehow, the blood of the Lock activated something in the blood of the Keys?

Ugh. Her head started to ache, so she removed the Advil bottle from her pocket and took three pills before sliding it back into place. For so long, all she'd had were questions. She picked up her phone and dialed.

"Yo," Collin answered. "What's up?"

"I'm just giving myself a headache trying to read these new books you found." Well, new to them. One was bound with what looked like human skin from a thousand years ago. "Do you have a line on any additional volumes?"

The sound of a television set being turned down came over the phone. "Yeah. I'm bidding on several right now in online auctions and I have a squad infiltrating a mansion in Iberia in about three hours. The owner collects ancient books, and he wouldn't ever entertain an offer to look at his collection, much less buy it."

Hope took a handful of popcorn. "So you're stealing it?"

His chuckle was low. "Half of the books you have were stolen. The owners didn't give me a choice."

She winced. "Did you at least leave reimbursement?"

"No. Most didn't need money. I did, however, leave them an IOU and a promise that I'd return the books along with a couple new ones. I figured we could raid the Realm libraries for something interesting once we're finished."

"So long as we don't harm anybody while stealing." She coughed. There was too much salt on the popcorn. Oops.

He drank something, most likely grape soda. Both twins had inherited their fondness for the stuff from their uncle Dage. "Don't worry. I've trained all my thieves very well. They can get in and out of pretty much anywhere without having to hurt anybody."

"Good. Thanks." She reached for her beer. "Why don't you have a date or something tonight?"

"Why don't you?" he countered.

That was a fair point. Considering she was currently torn between two males, adding a third to the mix would be insane. "All right. I'll see you tomorrow." They'd had to reschedule their strategy meeting for the following day. She clicked off, turning the movie back on and watching until her eyes became blurry and her head started to nod.

When the outside door opened, she stiffened and pushed pause on the remote. Paxton prowled in, looking as if he'd been tossed through a wood chipper. There were contusions and scrapes all over his face and arms, and his bottom lip had swollen.

"Hope," he said, walking inside, his gaze not meeting hers.

She had figured it would be bad when he'd said he was going to meet his father, but she'd never imagined it would be this bad. Why hadn't he healed those injuries? He was so pale, he looked almost ghostlike. "I should have gone with you," she said, her heart hurting for him. Though she'd known the reunion wouldn't be pleasant, she hadn't expected the raw devastation in Pax's eyes.

He glanced at the movie and then back to her face. His body was hard and cut, and tension rolled off him in waves. If she didn't know him, she'd fear him. "It's three in the morning. Why aren't you in bed? You were in a battle not too long ago."

"It looks like you've been in a couple since then," she said, scooting over on the sofa. Had the male even had a chance to heal his injuries from the first battle? If she remembered right, his father was well muscled and had beefy fists. It wouldn't have been an easy fight, even for someone as skilled as Pax. And no doubt, since Pax had wanted answers, Paelotin wouldn't have given them. Not without a good beating. By the look of Pax's knuckles, he'd punched hard and fast. "Come sit down, Paxton."

There was something off about him, an energy she couldn't read. She had been attuned to him since they were toddlers, and right now, he was as distant as someone across the globe, even though he stood right next to her. "I'm guessing it was bad?"

"Worse than bad," Paxton admitted, dropping onto the sofa. He scrubbed both hands down his face. His knuckles were raw and bloody.

"Why didn't you heal those on the ride home?"

"I couldn't." He stretched out his hands and looked at them.

Shock reverberated through her, and she pressed a fist against her mouth. "Is it my fault?"

He turned, looking at her. His eyes were an electric silvery blue. "Why would this be your fault?"

"I don't know." She threw up her hands. "We kissed, and we kissed big-time. Maybe I somehow infected you with whatever's wrong with me." Her ears rang, and she couldn't focus to figure out what she was trying to say. Her face heated when she thought about the orgasm. It had been spectacular.

He snorted. "You can't infect me with being human, Hope. Come on, we know that's what's going on with you. No, that's not my problem. That drug the Kurjans injected into me has just gotten stronger. It's flowing through my veins, spreading into my muscles. Emma is attempting to identify the unknown compound, but..."

Anger roared through her so fast she had to grasp his thigh for balance. "We'll figure this out. I'll go talk to Drake."

"No," Paxton said, turning and yanking her onto his lap. "You will not go talk to Drake. I will fix this somehow."

"We'll do it together," she said, cupping his jaw. He had raspy whiskers and a definite shadow. There was nothing soft about Paxton Phoenix, and for a moment, just a brief moment, she missed the sweet little boy he'd been. "Did you find out who your father was working with in the Kurjan nation?"

"No. He gave me some low-level names. I don't think anybody higher up met or talked with him." Pax's voice was demon hoarse and he seemed to rock in place.

"Tell me about your father," she said.

His scoff moved his huge chest. "Well, now that's the problem, isn't it?" Gingerly, he lifted her off his lap and placed her gently on the other end of the sofa.

She rubbed her arms, suddenly chilled. "What do you mean?"

Pax's chin dropped to his chest. "I shouldn't have put you on my lap. I'm sorry. Oh God, this is so screwed up."

She stilled, knowing the world was about to crash around her. "Did you kill him?"

"No," Paxton said, "I didn't. He is in a holding cell right now. I beat him up pretty good, but I got him out of there."

The pain in Paxton's eyes was palpable. "Pax, whatever he said, ignore him. He never knew you."

"Oh, he knew me a little bit," Paxton said, the sound desolate.

This was getting out of hand. There was a desperation in his eyes that she had never seen before. "I think I should call my dad." Zane would know what to do.

"He's not here," Paxton said wearily. "He returned to the battlefield with two squads to see if there was anything left of the Seven's documents. He wanted to be one of the people to sift through the rubble for some reason."

"Oh," she said softly. "How do you know that? Were you looking for him?"

"You could say that," Paxton said dryly, putting up invisible shields around himself.

She couldn't see them, but she could feel them. "Pax. Don't let whatever your dad said hurt you and drive people away. Let me in. I can help you." Her heart was breaking, and he was acting as if he didn't care.

The expression in his eyes was bleak. "I think maybe your instincts have been right all these years—we weren't meant to be together. It would be abnormal."

She blinked, her body reacting as if he'd punched her square in the solar plexus. She had never said that they shouldn't be together. It was just that her fate lay on a different path. Her duty was to find peace, and it was one she accepted willingly. "You can't listen to that guy. I don't care what he said to you."

"Oh yeah?" Paxton asked. "He's not my father."

She jolted. "Seriously? Huh." She thought back. She couldn't remember much except that his mother had been a nice demoness. She wasn't around for long. "Wouldn't somebody have known?"

Paxton tilted his head. "I don't think so. They kept to themselves when they weren't with separate squads off fighting. So they weren't close to your parents. They weren't close to anybody. They just did their jobs and then came home. It's entirely possible they weren't mated."

"But that means your mom was probably mated to somebody else," she said. "I don't understand."

"I know," Paxton muttered, "but it doesn't necessarily mean she was mated to somebody else. There have been times, as you know, when unmated immortals have procreated. I guess I could have been one of those babies?"

Elation roared through her. "Well then, that's good. We hated that guy. It's good he wasn't your father."

Paxton looked away. "Maybe not. When I asked him who my father is, he told me to ask your dad."

"Huh?"

"He insinuated that Zane Kyllwood is my father," Paxton said.

Hope's entire world came crashing down.

Chapter Nineteen

Pacing back and forth in her bedroom, Hope could not settle down. Was it possible that Paxton was her half-brother? Sure, they'd been close as kids, and she'd always felt a pull toward him, but she'd kissed him, and she'd felt that kiss to her very toes, if not deeper.

For a second, she let herself indulge in the fantasy that they weren't related, and this love was the real kind that lasted centuries. The passionate and wild kind. Now that the possibility might be gone, she realized how much she had wanted it.

Pain sliced into her. She loved him.

She pressed her fist to her mouth. None of that mattered—and she had a destiny to follow, anyway. They'd have to forget what had happened and move forward. She'd been inexperienced and Paxton very good at touching her, and that's all there was to it.

This was insane. She wished her father would hurry up and get back from the battlefield, but his team had gone dark so she couldn't even reach him.

Time to get on with her fate. It would be smart to meditate before she sought out Drake, but at the moment, she was exhausted. Her body had been beaten up, her heart had taken a hit, and even her brain hurt, so she just slid into bed and let the dreams take her. While she understood that Paxton would sense she'd entered a dreamworld as he always did, at the moment, she didn't care.

This needed to happen.

For a while, she wandered around, going from world to world until finally she arrived in one of her favorites from years gone by. The ocean was pink, the sand a light blue, and the trees were made up of wispy wands. Even the sky was an incredible shade of green, darker than any forest. There were no clouds, and the sun was high.

She found a series of rocks that looked like diamonds. This was new. She liked the addition. So she found a flat one and sat scanning the area for her book. It was located near the forest on a flat sapphire-colored rock, closed and barely vibrating. She couldn't help herself. She jumped off the rock and ran to it, her fingers just touching the leather-bound cover before it whisked away just out of sight. She looked around and then found the bound book up in a tree, open again, the pages facing her but much too far away to read.

"If you don't want me to read you, why are you here?" she yelled

A chuckle came from down the beach. She crossed her arms and turned to watch as Drake strode toward her, wearing his soldier's uniform, as usual. His hair was getting longer, and amusement danced across his hard face.

"Yelling at books is never wise. What if they yell back?" he asked

She snorted. "That would be hilarious."

"I like this place." He looked around. "The diamond rocks are new. Pretty. Do you like diamonds?"

She lifted a shoulder. "Yeah, I do. I like things that sparkle. Obviously." She swept a hand toward the pink ocean, trying to center herself in this moment. This was where she was supposed to be, not with Pax.

"You've always liked sparkles," he said. "You need to go for substance, though."

"Is that you, Drake?" she challenged.

He nodded. "We both know it is."

Possibly. Her life with Paxton was now in the past. If he was her brother, she'd love him as such, forever. Even if he wasn't, her path was set. Peace might save millions. She kicked at a loose pebble on the sand and watched it roll away. "I have to know. Did your people attack the Seven stronghold yesterday?"

His jaw hardened. "No, it wasn't me. I'm not saying my people didn't do it, but it wasn't me."

"It was Ulric?" she asked. Concern filtered through her. Just how much danger was Drake in? She didn't want him to be harmed.

His stance widened. "I'm getting things under control, but they're not there yet. Were any of the Seven hurt? I haven't even heard that much."

"No," she said. "They're all safe. We got them home."

He wiped his eyes as if he had a raging migraine. They were deep and green with that purple rim, which seemed to glow brighter every time she saw him. "I'm pleased they weren't hurt." He glanced down at her, taking her hand in his large one. "You weren't in battle, were you?"

"Actually, I was," she said. "Just with one guy, though. One of your soldiers. I had to kill him. I'm sorry." She winced. Hopefully she hadn't killed one of his friends.

Drake's lips twitched. "You killed a Kurjan soldier?"

"I did," she said. They had to get on the same side in this new war. "I didn't have a choice. I hope he wasn't a friend of yours."

Drake's brows drew down in a fierce frown. "You should not be in battle. You know that, correct? You are to be a queen."

Amusement and irritation clashed within her. "I'm not really cut out for the whole queen thing," she said. "I'm a strategic planner, and sometimes that means being on the battlefield—or at least a couple of miles away." She could help the Kurjans with that.

"That ends now," he said. "No more, Hope."

She didn't like him dictating to her, but she also didn't have time to fight. "We can argue about that later. For now, I'm trying to find out—is there any chance for peace?"

"Between us, you and me? Definitely." Drake leaned in and stole a fast kiss.

Her lips tingled, but guilt grabbed her. "I don't mean peace between us," she said, her mind reeling from the events of the last couple of days. "I mean our people. If we agree not to kill Ulric, can your people agree to stop coming after the Seven and the Keys as well as me?" It was time she applied her strategic ability to every area of her life.

Drake rubbed his chin, studying her intently. "I can definitely take that to my people, but you still have a decision to make. Fate is calling us both. Peace means we mate. I'll make you happy. I promise."

"I know." She'd always known it was her duty to catch peace with both hands and hold it tight, and Drake had been put in her dreamworlds for a reason.

"We're meant to be together, Hope."

She'd always known that to be true. She cared about Drake even though they had never spent much time in the same place. Confusion blanketed her. She wanted to share the fact that Paxton thought he might be her brother, but that would feel like a betrayal and she couldn't do that to Pax. As if Drake were reading her mind, he brushed a piece of hair out of her eyes. When had the breeze picked up?

"How is Paxton? Has he recovered from the darts as well as you have?" he asked.

Should she tell him that Pax had not recovered? "No," she said, taking a chance. "There was something in those darts that is hurting him. It's poisoning his blood and hasn't disappeared as it did in mine. Do you know why?"

She studied Drake's facial expressions and his eyes, trying to find an answer.

His eyes remained clear. "No, I have no idea. I don't even know what was in the darts," he murmured. "You know I want Paxton dead, but not from a silly drug. I plan to be there as he breathes his last breath. He'll pay for killing my father."

A chill swept down her back. It was time to stop waffling. "Find me the cure for Paxton, promise you won't kill him, and I'll mate you immediately."

Drake's gaze darkened until the purple rim swallowed up the green. "I accept half of your terms. While I don't know what was in those darts, I'll tear the Cyst world apart to find a cure." He was quiet for a moment. "Ulric is working on his own. In fact..."

She touched his arm. "What?"

"I'm not opposed to him being killed," Drake said slowly as if savoring the idea. "I hadn't really thought it was possible, but I don't need him, do I?"

"No. You don't." Hope grabbed his arm, her mind calculating different scenarios as fast as a computer could. This was an idea she'd never contemplated. What if she and Drake worked together to bring down Ulric? If the Realm and the Kurjans focused on a common enemy, that would make them allies. If they could learn to trust each other, then going forward, they could live together in peace. "Would you set him up for us?"

Drake clenched his jaw before speaking. "I just might, but first I have to know that you can actually kill him. Do you have a viable plan?"

She winced. "We're still trying to figure it out. I was hoping you would know of a way."

"I don't. I am familiar with the same legends you have learned, the ones that say he's impregnable. That only the blood of the three Keys can kill him, along with the blood of the Lock. You." His gaze flew up to the tree where the book glowed in the sunlight. "To be honest, I always thought the answer would be in that annoying book."

Hope sighed. "So did I." She had to get her hands on those pages so she could find some direction. The smartest people on the planet couldn't figure out her role, and even her instincts weren' helping her. The answer was in that book.

He studied her for another moment. "You and I have alway: known it would be up to you, Paxton, and myself to figure thi out. Maybe what we're supposed to do is combine forces and take out Ulric. A temporary truce, if you will." He spoke slowl] as if puzzling his way through the matter. "What do you think?

"I don't know," she said, "but I'm all for it. If we could only b sure we can kill that monster." The last thing she wanted was fo Ulric to learn that Drake had betrayed him. Ulric was powerfu and more ancient than all of them put together. He would no hesitate to kill one of his own. If Drake went down, who would take his place? She didn't know him well, but he seemed to b a kind person. Or at the very least, one open-minded enough to envision a new future. She had to protect him. "We need to plan.

"Agreed," Drake said. "How about you bring Paxton in, and we'll come up with a plan? I give you my word that I won't exac revenge upon him until Ulric is dead, and then I'll give Paxton fair chance. This destiny, one of many I'm sure, has always com down to the three of us."

That was what she had been trying to say for nearly two decades If they worked together to destroy Ulric, perhaps Paxton and Drak could then reach an alliance. Or at least a wary agreement no to kill each other. "Okay. How about tomorrow night?"

"All right." Drake glared at the book and sighed, turning hi focus to her. "I'll discover what I can about the drugs affectin Paxton. Maybe there's some sort of antidote." He stared at he for a long while. "I can't wait until you're mine, Hope."

She turned to see a crown full of emeralds, diamonds, and sapphires cresting the waves of the pink ocean.

A crown.

Fate couldn't be more obvious than that.

Chapter Twenty

It was after midnight when Zane Kyllwood returned from the battlefield outside of Denver. Paxton lounged against a mature cedar tree across from Zane and Janie's house. It was a two-story with a lot of glass and stone, and he actually didn't mind standing guard outside it. Much of his time as a youth had been spent making sure the house and its occupants were safe.

Zane parked his vehicle in front of the home, stepped out and stiffened before turning and instantly spotting him. It was like a physical punch of power.

Paxton shoved away from the tree and strode across the street to meet him, noting they were the same height and had the same black hair. He wasn't as thick as Zane yet, but he probably was exactly as Zane had been at his age. He'd never noticed the similarities between them. It made sense, since they both had demon and vampire lineage, so what was there to notice?

"Paxton," Zane said, shutting the door. "I have intel that your father is in a cell."

He felt like puking. How was he even going to ask this question? Did he truly want to know the answer? "Paelotin is in a cell," Pax corrected. "I brought him in. He's been working with the Kurjans and was their liaison with Henric, but he didn't have any high-up contacts. Or at least those higher up didn't let him know who they were."

Zane took in the bumps and bruises still showing on Paxton' face. "It looks like it was a tough takedown."

"It wasn't easy," Paxton said. "I dropped by to see Emma before waiting for you out here. The Kurjan concoction in my blood i worsening. The drug has infiltrated my muscle fibers and should be hitting my organs next."

Zane's body tightened. "Shit, Pax, what are we going to do about that?"

Paxton shrugged. "I don't know. She doesn't even know what it is. It may kill me. It may make me stronger, but at this poin it's just giving me a freaking headache, and I can't heal myself."

Zane swore. "We require more information." He rubbed the whiskered shadow covering his chin. "We'll create a plan to infiltrate the Kurjan stronghold in Canada. That's where the scientists are. We'll need to take one," he said thoughtfully.

Paxton stepped back, surprised. "You'd start a war over me?"

Zane's eyes blazed in the darkness. "Of course I'd start a war over you. Don't be a dumbass."

A rock dropped hard into Paxton's stomach. Why was that Crap, could Zane actually be his father? "That's insane. You can' start a war because of me."

Zane rarely showed expressions, but a quick scroll of confusion crossed his face before he focused fully on Paxton. "They fired drugs into one of mine. That is war if they don't give up the information on how to save you. You know that."

One of his. Paxton kicked snow off his boots. He just needed to ask the question. Why was he so afraid? If the guy he had revered for pretty much his entire life turned out to be a dishonest prick then he was better off knowing it. "Are you my father?"

Zane stilled, his shoulders going back. Then he cocked his head...slowly. Paxton fought the urge to tackle him to th snow. This violence inside him would never go away, no matter how hard he tried.

"What the hell are you talking about?" Zane finally asked, looking at him as if he'd lost his mind.

Peace unfurled in Paxton's chest. It took everything he had to keep from running away, grabbing Hope, and escaping this place. If he never knew the answer, he could keep loving her. Man, he was a sick fuck. "Paelotin said that he is not my father, and there was a definite ring of truth to his claim. I asked him who was, and he said to ask you."

Zane's brow cleared. "Pax, I have absolutely zero idea what you're talking about." He leaned against the car. Perfectly casual. "Do you believe he's not your father?"

Paxton swallowed. "I sure didn't take it as bad news until he implicated you as my real father."

"Just to be very clear, I am not your father. That jerk was obviously messing with your head." Zane snorted and slid an arm around his shoulders. "Let's go inside. It's cold out here. I could use a drink. We need to figure this out."

"Did you even know my mom?" Paxton asked.

"Not really," Zane admitted. "When I took over the Demon nation, things were pretty disorganized. Your folks were both with the international fighting squads, and frankly, I didn't get a chance to know either of them very well. I met your mother a couple of times, but never when she was around your father, so I didn't get the sense of anything wrong between them."

"He said he killed her," Pax said, his voice low. Even though he'd been just a kid, he felt responsible.

Zane opened the door to the house, and warmth instantly washed over Pax. "I told you a long time ago to stop taking blame for things you didn't do. Remember when Hope fell off her bike?"

"Yes." But that *had* been Pax's fault. He should have made her get off the bike and avoid the jump. "What if Paelotin is telling the truth?"

"I've seen the battle report. She died during a skirmish with a rogue squad of Kurjans."

Paxton walked inside, inhaling the smell of chocolate chip cookies. Almost of their own volition, his feet took him to the kitchen, where a big platter lay on the counter. He reached for one because that's what Janie would expect of him. The treat was still warm and delicious.

"Hey, those are my cookies," Zane said, shoving him aside.

"Janie always says I can have a couple," Paxton mumbled around the cookie.

Zane opened the fridge and reached in for two beers, popping the top off of each and handing one to Pax. "Yes, I know. If I kept you from the cookies, Janie would just yell at me." He sighed.

The painful knot in Paxton's gut slowly unraveled. Thank God he hadn't kissed his sister. To banish the thought, he drank the entire beer down in three long gulps. He could not go there ever again in his head.

Zane munched on another cookie. "We'll have Emma perform a DNA test tomorrow. It's entirely possible Paelotin is lying about not being your father. The guy's a real ass."

"Agreed," Paxton said. "It felt so good when he told me that I didn't come from him. Although, no offense, I didn't want to come from you either."

Zane snorted. "I think I understand what you mean, but I really don't want to talk about you and my daughter right now, if ever. If I could talk her into going to a nunnery, I would."

Paxton snorted. "It's difficult to be a strategic genius when you're in a nunnery, but if anybody could pull it off, it would be Hope. Oh, crap." He covered his mouth with his hand. "I told her we might be siblings."

Zane frowned and slapped Pax's hand when he reached for another cookie. "I told you these are mine."

Pax shoved him and managed to snag two cookies before Zane could secure the entire tray. "I told you Janie would want you to share."

Zane laughed. "You told Hope you might be siblings." He finished his beer and put the bottle on the table. "Oh, I wish I could have been there for that. I bet the look on her face was hilarious. I can't wait to tell Janie."

Pax eyed the remaining cookie.

"Don't even think it." Zane snatched it in a blur of motion.

"Whatever." Paxton happily ate the last one still in his hand. There were probably more in the fridge or the cupboard, and he knew it. "I have to say, Zane, I'm real glad you aren't my dad."

Zane nodded, his expression sobering. "I would've been proud to be your father, but it would make things a little more complicated. What are your intentions toward my daughter?"

Paxton choked on the delicious treat. He quickly swallowed. In all their time together, Zane had never asked him anything like that. Nor had they talked about the fact that Paxton had been working against the Realm, although it hadn't been his choice. "I want to marry her and mate her," he said honestly, unable to lie to the man who had once saved his life.

"What does she think about that?" Zane asked.

"You should probably ask her," Pax said, ducking into the fridge for two more beers. He handed one to Zane. "But I'm worried that she'll sacrifice herself to the Kurjans, thinking that will bring peace. Drake has her fooled, but he's not a good guy."

One of Zane's dark eyebrows rose. "Are you sure he isn't honorable? Could it be that you are just feeling possessive?"

Pax took a smaller drink of the beer this time. "I'm definitely feeling possessive, but I'm not wrong about Drake. The Kurjans don't want peace, and he doesn't understand Hope. He doesn't understand what she needs."

Zane placed his beer on the counter. "And you do?"

Pax looked up and met Zane's gaze squarely, his chest settling and his body finally relaxing. "A hundred percent, I do." A tension rode the wind and prickled Paxton's nape. A dreamworld had just been breached. He could feel it, and his entire body stiffened. "I need to go, King. I'll catch you later."

Zane watched him, his gaze serious. "All right, Paxton, you do what you need to do. Let's meet tomorrow for the DNA tests. I'll get blood from Paelotin tonight."

Pax didn't much care how Zane would go about that. "All right, I'll catch you in the morning."

Keeping his face stoic, he turned and strode out of the house, noting the pummeling snow. The lazy drifting flakes of earlier had disappeared, and the skies had opened up. Freezing shards of snow joined the wind in a melee that hampered visibility.

He turned and prowled farther down into the cul-de-sac, surrounded by watching trees, their boughs heavy with the white powder. The snow cut into him like barbed sleet, and he ducked his head, shoving his hands in his pockets. As he reached Hope's house, he could feel the tension heightening.

He could sense the vibrations, and fury ripped through him.

When he turned the knob on the front door, his anger escalated further. She'd left the fucking door unlocked.

Nobody shot at him from the trees, so apparently Zane had given orders for the guards to leave him alone.

Good.

Without calling out, he walked inside and kicked off his boots, heading unerringly for her bedroom, where he stopped, just watching her, his heart turning inside out.

She lay on the far side of the bed, small, curled up beneath the covers, having left a lamp on to softly illuminate the room. It was a pink glass lamp that she had found in an antique store a while back. He'd been one of her guards at the time, though she didn't know it. She had thought she was out unobserved for a fun day of shopping.

The woman always slept like that, curled on her side at the edge of one side of the bed, almost as if making room for him. When they were younger, she had. Even though the blankets covered her, she was shivering. He moved into the room and shut the door, looking for another blanket. The room felt warm enough to him, but she'd been through a lot lately.

Her thick auburn hair was spread over the pillow, and it moved like silk when she made a small sound of distress. The air was electrified with both power and heat. She shouldn't be cold.

Irritation cut through him, and he walked around to the other side to sit next to her. "Hope, wake up." He grabbed her shoulder and gently shook her.

She didn't awaken.

"Now." He put command into his voice.

Her lids slowly opened, and those incredible blue eyes focused on him. For a moment, he could only stare at her, taking in those wide intelligent eyes, that thick auburn hair. His entire body clenched, and he fought the fury pounding through him. "Tell me you were not in a dreamworld meeting Drake." He'd always felt it when she opened a dreamworld. Somehow. The very air changed around him from calm to menacing. Each. Fucking. Time.

She faltered, and the lazy smile of welcome spreading across her face stopped midway. Her eyes widened as she no doubt caught his mood, and she scrambled to sit up, pulling the blankets to her. Bruises still marred her pale face from fighting the Kurjan soldier the day before.

"Hope, what were you thinking?" he asked, his voice low and raw.

She blinked once and then twice, coming fully awake. "I was doing my job."

"Meeting with the enemy is not your job." He was tired of watching her flounder and put herself in danger. He was furious that she wouldn't listen to him, and he was just about done with acting like anybody other than exactly who he was. "By the way, we most certainly do not share a father." His fingers closed around her upper arms and pulled her close. He tried to be gentle, but he felt aggressive. His hand curled around the back of her neck. Her eyes widened, and her gaze dropped to his mouth.

So he gave them what they both wanted and kissed her.

Chapter Twenty-One

Fire lit Hope from within. As Paxton kissed her, he was rough and commanding in a way he'd never been before. Throughout their lives, she'd sensed the barely veiled dominance in him but had figured he'd never let himself lose control, especially with her. She figured deep down he knew she would take another path in life because she really had no choice.

He poured flames down her throat, his hands sweeping her arms, branding every inch of her skin. His growl was rough, and the sound rumbled deep inside her, burning right to her sex. He was wild and it was dangerous. She was on fire. Her control fled while his seemed to solidify.

Those flames burned through her good intentions to fulfill her duty. And for a moment, a brief, devastating, wild moment, she let herself just feel the aggressiveness in him and the wild response in her.

Paxton was somebody she couldn't resist. With just his mouth and the slightest touch of his broad hands, he took control of them both, creating a storm of desire that no woman could resist, much less one who cared about him. Who had peered into his soul.

Every nerve ending in her entire body flared awake as if just waiting for the command from Paxton to do so.

His fingers clenched her hips, digging in. Her nipples hardened within her tiny camisole, but the material wasn't rough enough for what she needed.

What did she need? For once, she wasn't sure.

He leaned back and bit her bottom lip. The sharp sting tore through her, shocking her with her response. "Paxton," she breathed, her panties dampening.

His smile was wicked. "I'm done waiting for you to figure things out." Then his lips were on hers again, his tongue taking her mouth like he owned it. Blood pounded in her clit, and she moaned, letting him tilt her head to the side and go deeper with his conquest.

He leaned into her, his body one long line of solid steel. The muscles and raw strength in his arms thrilled her.

"Paxton," she moaned against his mouth, and he kissed her deeper, making her forget whatever it was she'd been about to say.

He took complete control in a way he never had before. She softened against him, unable to do anything else against such a hard body, and then reached up for his thick hair, tangling her fingers in the strands and holding tight. He pulled back to let her breathe and scraped his teeth along her jawline, wandering down to bite the soft skin where her neck met her shoulder. Her entire body shuddered, and she gasped, sliding her hands down to clutch his biceps. Her hands were too small to wrap around them, and even that thrilled her.

She had to think.

Need uncoiled inside her, hot and furious and demanding. This was wrong. He wasn't for her, but she had never needed anything more in her entire life.

Her body contradicted her mind, and she caressed his neck. His tough-guy, strong, impossibly warm neck. She should stop this.

She threw that thought away as those sharp teeth scraped dangerously along her clavicle, and then she felt the sting of a bite right above her breast. That sting zinged through her entire body as sharp as any laser bullet, shooting right to her sex. She whimpered and tried to get closer. He was pure, raw heat and coiling danger, and he was somebody new and different.

Or maybe it was just Paxton fully unleashed.

His fingers were deadly, unrelenting as they stroked over her body, over her breasts. The pads of his thumbs were rough as he drew them across both nipples. She shuddered, wanting so much more.

"God, you're beautiful," he growled, throwing the covers off and grasping her rib cage, laying her down and covering her. Even though he kept his weight off her with his elbows, he blanketed her, completely pinning her to the bed. A delicious little thrill zipped through her entire body, electrifying her from within.

She didn't know what to think.

He was demanding ultimate surrender, and she couldn't give that to him. She couldn't give it to anybody, but she had never been so tempted. Had never felt more feminine.

"Pax." She gripped his face and held tight. His whiskers burned her palms, adding to the erotic sensations already whipping over her skin. "We have to stop." Her body protested, and she tried to ignore it.

He lifted his head, and his eyes were a sharp, silvery, metallic blue with green striations.

For a second, she couldn't speak. Everything inside her wanted to submit to the primal demand in them, and she wasn't a woman who submitted. "We can't do this." Her voice trembled. With fear? With need? Maybe both.

He didn't answer. Instead, he suddenly moved to the side, planted his heavy hand in the center of her chest and swiped his palm down her body in a hot caress that had her biting her lip to keep from begging for more. "You tell me to stop, I'll stop. If not, you're giving me this."

She opened her mouth, and just as his fingers brushed over her clit, she couldn't help but arch into his hand. "Paxton," she whispered, shocked, needy, stunned.

His gaze searched her face, his jaw hard, his nostrils flared. "Yeah. You're giving me this, Hope." In one quick movement he had the little shorts off her, and then his mouth replaced his hand. She cried out, arching into him as ecstasy ripped through her. She would never be the same.

And she needed more.

She craved.

He dropped to his knees beside the bed, grabbed both her legs and tossed them over his shoulders. What was happening? This was too much, and yet it wasn't enough. She cried out, knowing without a doubt that if she told him to stop, he would.

She didn't want this to stop. Ever.

She bucked against his mouth, and he planted one hand on her abdomen, holding her down.

He reached up and tweaked her nipple and then soothed it before moving to her other breast. There was enough bite in his touch that she was moaning, moving against him, needing more.

He raked her clit with his tongue, lashing mercilessly, and then slid two fingers inside her. She couldn't breathe. She couldn't think. She could only need, and Paxton was the only person in the world who could subdue this fire.

"Paxton," she moaned. "Hurry up."

He looked up, his whiskers scraping her needy clit. Sensation sliced through her, tightening every muscle. "You'll take what I give you, Hope, and you'll learn patience."

The words should have pissed her off. Instead, a traitorous trembling rolled from the top of her body to the bottom of her feet, making her clit pound even harder as that shudder passed through.

He moved down again, sucked her entire clit into his mouth, and then went at her like a male possessed.

He was tongue and teeth and lips and fingers.

She didn't know which one was coming when they were all over her, and still it was not enough. He drove her up fast and then played with her on the edge until she was bucking and nearly crying in her need for relief.

When panic was hitting her, and desperation was making her plant her heels on his back and press against him, he finally let her fall over. She crashed hard, live wires uncoiled inside her, tossing her off that ledge to be broken into a million pieces.

She cried out loudly, and she was pretty sure it was his name she shrieked. Her body rippled with something way too close to pain to be called mere pleasure, and yet she couldn't stop shuddering wildly with the climax. She came down slowly, her heart thundering so loudly she was sure Libby could hear it on the other side of the house. Oh man. She covered her eyes. Had Libby heard that?

Hope came back to the cool air brushing her skin, lying there stunned, satiated, and vulnerable. Paxton stood and gazed down at her. The look in his eyes showed need and lust, desire and something deeper. Much deeper.

She blinked and slowly forced herself to sit up, dazed. She could have stopped him, and she had chosen not to. They both knew that.

His chin lifted, giving him the look of a warrior about to charge. "I'll take your taste with me until the day I die." He pulled off his shirt.

She blinked at the raw play of natural strength. She could see the animal deep inside Pax—the warrior who'd taken on a squad of Kurjans by himself and hadn't broken a sweat. His muscled torso was wide and tapered to ridged abs so tight it was shocking bullets didn't bounce right off them. "What are you doing?"

"I'm not leaving you." His jeans were next, and she tried to look away, but there was a lot to look at in those dark boxers.

"Paxton." She should feel foolish. Instead, she felt satiated, stunned, and still aroused. She shook her head, torn between reaching to take what she wanted and being the responsible person she needed to be.

He lifted her as if she weighed nothing, pulled the covers back tossed her in, and curled in behind her. "We're just gonna sleep baby. We both need it."

Had Paxton Phoenix just called her *baby?* She should not like that. Not at all. Yet pleasure unfolded inside her. Man, she was screwed up. She should make him leave. But as she settled into his magma-hot body, every muscle in her body relaxed and settled and submitted as if this was exactly where she should be.

She didn't know what to say. What had just happened? She wanted to roll over, kiss him, and take care of the raging hard-on pressed against her butt. A shiver took her. His arm tightened like a band of iron beneath her breasts, and he pulled her closer to him, so much bigger and stronger than she'd ever be.

His lips wandered over the top of her head, and she felt that touch through her entire body. "Pax? I've never done that before."

He paused. "Good."

She shouldn't care, but she did. "I've kissed people but not much more."

His body was a shield around her. "Why not?" There was curiosity in his tone as well as a definite growl of possessiveness

She swallowed, feeling way too vulnerable. "I guess I figured it would be like cheating on someone." On her future mate. Or fate. "Plus, it's not like I've had a lot of alone time in my life." She was quiet, her mind spinning.

His thighs were solid heated rock behind hers. "Ask the question."

How did he know her so well? It didn't matter. They weren't dating and never would. She'd agreed to Drake's terms. "You were good at that. Have you been with a lot of females?" She told herself, again, that it didn't matter.

"No. Nobody." His lips moved lazily down to her ear. "There's only been you. My entire life."

Her heart pretty much exploded—then ached. She wanted happiness, to be with him, but if she could save the world from another war, she had to do so. "Pax—"

"Go to sleep, Kyllwood. We'll figure it out tomorrow." His voice was already drowsy, and then he dropped into sleep, still holding her as tightly as she could ever want.

Chapter Twenty-Two

Paxton came awake instantly, as he always did, keeping his eyes closed and scanning the surrounding area for any threats. He was in a warm bed, and the scent of Hope was all around him—orange spice and vanilla bean. How she smelled like that, he'd never figured out. There was no bodywash or lotion that came close.

While his body was relaxed, his cock ached and throbbed. To be so close to her, all night, was more than his body could take. He took a deep breath, feeling her snuggled against him. In the night, he had rolled onto his back, and she had curled into his side, one thigh over his leg, her hand splayed on his abdomen. Her face was tucked into his neck, and she was breathing softly. She had all but wrapped herself around him during the night, as if she didn't want him to go.

He had no intention of going anywhere.

He could hear the icy snow falling outside, and he could hear the guards near the lake patrolling the territory. The soldiers in the trees didn't make noise, but he could sense them. Would they report back to Zane that he'd stayed the night? He didn't know and frankly, he didn't care.

Clothing rustled at the other end of the house where Libby must have been getting ready for the day. His hearing was shockingly good; it had saved his life more than once.

Slowly, the hand at his abdomen curled and traced his abs. "You stayed all night," Hope murmured, her lips soft against his skin.

He was planning to stay forever, but he probably shouldn't tell her that, at least not yet. She still thought she was going to go save the world on her own or with their mortal enemy, but she was wrong. That wasn't going to happen.

She lifted her head and blinked, her eyes drowsy and her pert nose wrinkled. "We need to talk."

Those were the last words he wanted to hear, but the first ones he'd been expecting. "Go ahead and talk."

She licked her lips. His entire body shuddered, and he fought a groan. She sighed. "When I was in the dreamworld the other night with Drake, I learned a few things. When I told you that the Kurjan nation was at war, I was right."

He was unable to stop himself from smoothing an arm down her back and curling it at her waist, pulling her even closer to him. She was so soft and small. He hated having to fight her to keep her safe, but he'd do what he needed to do. The idea that she'd met with Drake by herself irritated the hell out of him. She was fragile, possibly human, and she had to be more careful. He'd been as patient as he could be with her, but no more. She'd be tough to lock down. He'd do what needed to be done. "Good. If they're at war, they'll leave us alone."

"They're not leaving us alone." She stretched against him like a little cat, nearly killing him. "Ulric is searching for enhanced females, and he was behind the attack on the Seven. Drake wants to take him out, and he is willing to help us to do it."

Paxton would trust Drake as far as he could throw him, but he forced himself to listen. He needed to get all the facts. "Tell me more."

She bit her lip. "Drake is willing to help us with the final ritual In fact, he's more than willing to betray Ulric, but we need to provide proof to him that we actually know what needs to happen at the ritual."

"We don't," Paxton said shortly. Her fingers traced little patterns on his abs, and he was about to lose his mind. It felt right to be talking over strategy with her in bed, but it was downright painful to remain relaxed and not roll her right over and finish what they'd started the night before. She was everything he could ever want in the world. He wanted to give her space and time to figure that out, but even he had a limit. It was quickly approaching.

"We have to figure it out, Paxton. It's the only chance we have." She avoided his gaze as if she didn't quite want to look him in the eye.

He stiffened. "Hope, what is it?" She began to push away from him, and he held her in place. "You're not moving until you tell me."

Exasperation had her blowing out air. "I don't like this whole bossy, dominant, alpha, I'm-a-vampire-demon-hybrid bullshit."

"Yeah, your body says otherwise." He wasn't letting her off the hook. "Whatever you're not telling me, you need to say right now." He shrugged. "Or later. Either way, we're not moving till you do."

She rolled her eyes, temper darkening her cheeks to damask pink. "Fine. Drake wants us both in the dreamworld tonight so we can plan. Come with me, or I'll go myself."

He didn't like that. Being threatened wasn't his thing. However he also wasn't going to let her go in alone. "Okay, tonight at midnight. We'll go talk to the Kurjan and see what he thinks If he has a plan, I'll listen to it, and then we can take it to both kings." It was the right thing to do, even though the last person he wanted to see in the entire world was Drake.

Hope smiled. "See? Was that so hard?"

Paxton didn't really have an answer for her. He didn't like any of this.

She cleared her throat. "He still wants to kill you, and I know you want to end him, but you both have to agree to a truce until we kill Ulric. Then maybe we can broker another truce."

There would be no truce, and if Drake found a chance to kill Paxton, he'd take it. Yet Paxton didn't want to remove that glimmer of hope from her pretty eyes. "Okay."

Her gaze studied his face. "You're still pale. How are you feeling?"

"Weird," he admitted. He still had cuts and bruises from the brawl with Paelotin, and yet he didn't feel weak. He just couldn't quite get his healing cells to work. It had to be whatever drug was still in his system. His gaze traveled across her face. She was adorable in the morning, and his heart thumped. Hard. He leaned down and kissed her nose. "Do you want to finish this or what?"

Her eyes widened, and panic glowed in them. He could barely keep back a laugh.

"No." She scrambled away from him, and he let her, glancing at the clock. He was probably already late.

Allowing her to escape him for now, he got up from the bed and reached for his jeans. Within minutes, he was dressed and turning to look down at her. "I'm having more blood taken by Emma, and then Paelotin and I are going to have another chat about my real father."

"Thank goodness it wasn't my dad." She blushed and hugged the pillow. She looked a little lost and a lot vulnerable and adorable.

He snagged the pillow and tossed it away before grabbing her arms and hauling her toward him to plant one hard kiss on her lips. "We're not done here, Hope. Don't think for a second that we are."

With that, he released her, exited the bedroom, and strolled through the house, smiling at Libby, whose jaw dropped when she saw him. "Morning, Libs." It was rare to see the shifter speechless, and he enjoyed every second. He was outside and headed down the snow-covered street before he heard her move. He didn't envy Hope the morning discussion. But what did he know? He'd never had a girlfriend, and he'd never really had a morning after, so

maybe women liked to talk about that stuff. He had no idea. Wha‍
he did know was he didn't have anybody to talk to.

As he walked to Realm headquarters, he nodded at severa‍
soldiers, who all returned the nod, so apparently word had gotte‍
out that he wasn't a traitor. At least that was something.

Entering the lodge, he jogged down to the main laboratory‍
wishing once again he had the ability to teleport. It was unfai‍
that all demons had lost the ability because of the Seven. He kne‍
he wasn't the only one feeling angry, and he wondered just ho‍
safe the Seven would be in Realm territory. Both kings had issue‍
decrees that they were to be left alone, but they'd hurt peopl‍
because of what they'd done. Teleporting had been a part of life‍
and now it was gone.

Paxton wished he could teleport into Kurjan territory and hav‍
a little talk with Drake by himself. Unfortunately, that wasn'‍
going to happen. He opened another door, and Emma looked up‍

"Hey, you're here to donate more blood," she said, he‍
eyes cobalt today.

"I am." He walked over to her, pulling up his sleeve‍
"Take all you need."

The woman gave a happy hop. She was one of the kindes‍
females he'd ever met, and yet she was a menace with a syringe i‍
her hand. He wondered if there was anybody who'd ever met he‍
who hadn't had blood taken. At least she was good at it. Withi‍
seconds, she had inserted the needle and was extracting blood.

"How are you feeling?" she asked.

"The same," he admitted. "I can't heal myself, but my strength i‍
still there. My speed is still there. I'm not impacted in any other way.‍

She tapped on the needle and pulled it out. "I should hav‍
results for you in an hour. Dage interviewed Paelotin at demo‍
headquarters and took his blood. Since I already had yours here‍
I conducted a quick paternity test. You probably already kno‍
this, but Paelotin isn't your father." Sympathy darkened her eyes‍
"Neither is Zane."

"I know."

She exhaled. "I haven't found a match in the database yet; it might take some time. What's your plan now?"

He looked at her, a cold slice of fury centering in his chest. "Now I'm going to have a nice little discussion with Paelotin. One or both of us may require your services afterward."

Her head jerked as she took in his meaning. "Pax."

"Thank you, Emma. I appreciate it." He turned and strode out of the lab, squaring his shoulders. He was more than up for another fight, and this time he wasn't leaving until Paelotin told him everything. It was a long walk to demon headquarters. He made plans—bloody ones—on the way.

Chapter Twenty-Three

Hope stretched her neck and put her arms over her head, trying to loosen the tight muscles in her shoulders. She stood on a blue grappling mat in the gym in the east wing of demon headquarters. The new gym was state of the art and had several grappling rooms as well as training areas.

Libby stepped inside, her hair in a ponytail, her feet bare, and her yoga pants printed with dancing animals. "Hey," she said.

"Hey," Hope said, trying to act normal when she felt like a total dork. "Thanks for meeting me. I, uh, missed you this morning."

Libby looked anywhere but at her. "I went for a run. You know. Cougar. We like to run."

Hope sighed. "Thanks for answering my text. I wanted to work out before we meet with the team later today."

"No problem." Libby placed a water bottle over to the side and danced on the mat, automatically graceful without trying.

Hope pulled one arm over her chest in another stretch.

"So," Libby said, still dancing, "you were kind of loud last night."

Heat rose into Hope's face, probably turning her a strawberry color. "I was worried about that."

"I'm all the way across the house." Libby chuckled. "I saw Paxton this morning and thought you might need some alone time." She snorted. "He didn't look embarrassed at all. Unlike you right now."

"Paxton is better at hiding his emotions than I am." Hope dodged in just as Libby leaped agilely to the left. Hope sprawled across the mat, then rolled and came back up.

"That was quick," Libby said. "Nice."

"Thanks," Hope said dryly. She didn't have a chance against the cougar shifter, but she always gave it her best.

Libby chewed on her lip. "You need to go for the legs."

"I know that," Hope said, feinting for the legs, which was what Libby wanted.

Just as Libby started to jump over her head, Hope leaped up, locked her arms around Lib's waist, pivoted, and took her down.

"Nice." Libby moved easily out of the way. "I didn't expect it."

"That was the point."

Lib danced for a while, looking for an opening. "We should probably talk about this. How was he?"

Hope rolled her eyes. "Give me a break. I didn't sleep with him."

"You did *something* with him."

"Well, I did sleep with him. He stayed the night," Hope admitted. "But he's done that before."

Libby shook her head. "So, what? Are you guys together now? I mean, what about your grand fate plan and all that?"

Hope wanted to chuckle and tease with her friend, but her chest felt heavy. "I don't know. I just got carried away and, I mean, it's Paxton, except it wasn't Paxton."

Libby rubbed her eye. "What do you mean it wasn't Paxton?"

"He turned into full-on vampire-demon-hybrid pain-in-the-ass last night," Hope said. "All of a sudden, he was a warrior instead of our friend."

Libby tipped herself into a handstand and started walking across the room on her hands. "Pax *is* a warrior. I saw him fight, Hope. He's definitely been training the last several years, and from what

I can tell, most of it was live training. You need to know that. He's not the same kid who would run scared to us as a child."

Hope's thighs carried his whisker burn this morning. She shivered, her body still sensitive. "I'm fully aware of that fact. He proved it all over again last night."

"What about Drake?" Libby easily flipped her legs over and landed in perfect form.

"I don't know," Hope said. "Every time I talk to him, I feel like we could make a difference and prevent war. But he also has some grand scheme that I'm going to be queen of all the land."

Libby dropped into a deceptively casual pose before she turned and kicked Hope in the thigh. Hope went down and came back up, dodging in to tackle her friend to the ground.

Libby rolled easily away. "Nice tackle."

"Thanks. Good kick," Hope said, her shoulders feeling better. Her arm was finally completely healed.

"It might be nice to be queen."

Hope chewed on the inside of her lip. "I wouldn't mind being queen. But I want to actually work, not just, I don't know, tell people what to do. I don't even know what a Kurjan queen does."

"Has there ever been a Kurjan queen?" Libby asked.

Hope thought about it. "Not in a long time, I think." She'd never heard of one, but Drake had had a mother a long time ago. Had she been the queen?

"So couldn't you just decide what you want to do?"

Hope shrugged. "I think the Kurjans are stuck in the last century, especially in their view of females."

"Then you can bring them into this century," Libby said. "However, I don't think you should sacrifice yourself to do that. If the Kurjans need to be brought into the current century, we can figure out a way to do it. If you want to be with Paxton, then you should follow your heart, not some duty you've put on yourself."

Hope didn't know what to do, but she couldn't get the previous night out of her mind. She still felt the imprint of Pax's mouth on her. Everywhere. "I needed to see if you were okay with all of this." She sat and stretched out her legs. Libby had a heck of a kick even when she was pulling it.

Libby dropped into a split and stretched back until her head rested against her thigh. "Okay with you becoming queen of the Kurjan nation?"

"No," Hope said.

Libby leaned forward, her chest lowering all the way to her other leg. "You sacrificing yourself and saving the world?"

"No."

"Because you don't care if I don't want you to die?" Libby asked, her tone pointed.

Hope sighed and stretched out her left leg, leaning over it and wincing at the still echoing pain. "Of course I care."

"Then don't sacrifice yourself," Libby returned.

"I don't think it'll come to that," Hope said, not really knowing whether that was the truth or not. "I'm asking if you're okay with what happened between Paxton and me last night."

Libby straightened up, her eyes a warm honey. "What exactly did happen?"

Hope cleared her throat. She'd never kept secrets from Libby, and now wasn't the time to start. So she told her, holding just a few of the details back. By the end, Libby's eyes were wide.

"Wow. Go, Paxton," she said. "Maybe his new warrior pain-in-the-ass attitude isn't quite as bothersome as you said."

"I didn't say it wasn't a turn-on," Hope protested. "But what I've learned with all these vampire and demon males around is if you give them an inch..."

Libby snorted. "They take the entire territory."

"Exactly," Hope said. "It has always been the three of us. I just wanted to make sure you were okay with what happened."

Libby reached out and slapped Hope's foot. "Of course I'm okay with it. It's always been you and Pax. I never even considered any other possibility."

"What if I mate Drake?" Hope asked quietly. When she wa
younger, she'd wanted Libby and Pax to be together if that happened
because then they'd be safe, and their little group would still b
together. Now, she didn't like the thought. Hated it actually. Sh
didn't want to think of Pax with anybody else in the world, which
was just as screwed up as screwed up got, because she was th
one considering mating Drake and becoming a freaking queen
"What about you and Pax?"

Libby wrinkled her nose. "I really do see Paxton like a brother
Even if you two don't end up together, he is definitely not my path.

Relief filtered through Hope. "Okay. I was just curious. It woul
be nice to see both of you happy."

Libby sobered. "Paxton won't be happy unless he's with
you. Even though you're all caught up in this grand scheme
there's nobody else for him. Honestly, I'm not quite sure there'
anybody else for you."

Hope would miss these talks with Libby if she actually move
away. "I think there might be better reasons to mate and marr
than just love," she said.

"Not if you look around us," Libby murmured. "Look at you
parents. Look at mine. Look at everybody we know. They're i
love, and it makes them stronger. I understand duty, and I've alway
had your back. Whatever you decide, I'll support you. Besides.
Her grin lit up her face. "Has Paxton even asked you to mate?"

"No," Hope said. Interesting. He never had, had he? "He jus
kind of talks like that's what he wants."

"Hmm," Libby said. "You might want to think about that." Sh
glanced at her watch. "Oh, we're going to be late."

Hope sat back, thinking through the last several days
Paxton hadn't ever asked her, now had he? Maybe it wa
something to consider.

Either way, it was time to debrief the team.

* * * *

Paxton walked slowly down the stairs to the sublevel of demon headquarters and opened the door to the long hallway that held the cells. He had no idea where Henric and Fralep were being held now, but they were probably still at the main headquarters.

The cells here at demon headquarters were a little rougher, cut into the rock and fronted by solid, transparent glass that couldn't be broken. He kept his thumbs looped casually in his jeans pockets as he looked inside. Paelotin sat on the floor, which was hard onyx marble that also didn't shatter. Nothing could break that surface, and Paxton had seen groups try as part of their training. Bones broke when smashed against that floor.

It came in quite handy.

He nodded at the guards down the way, and they returned the gesture, not moving. Good. He tapped in a code on the keypad, and a door snicked open just far enough for him to walk inside. It rolled silently closed behind him.

Paelotin stood to his full height, his fangs dropping low. "Surprised to see you," he said.

It was a gift not many vampires had, the ability to speak clearly and enunciate each word with their fangs extended. But Paelotin had mastered it years ago. Paxton knew that expression well. When he was a child, it hadn't boded well for him. Now, he couldn't give two fucks. "Had a nice talk with Zane Kyllwood," he said, keeping his voice low and controlled, like always.

Paelotin threw back his head and laughed. "Oh, I bet that was a good one. Did he deny it? Did he deny that he's your father?"

"Not only did he deny it, we conducted a DNA check just to be sure," Paxton admitted.

Paelotin stopped laughing, and his eyes hardened to that mean, sharp, hate-filled glint he'd always had. "It doesn't matter. There's no way you're getting within two feet of the princess, even if she' not your sister, and you know it."

He'd gotten a lot closer to Hope than that the night before. Bu Paxton saw no reason to share that fact. "It's time you told m everything you know about my mother."

Paelotin snorted. "Boy, I'm not going to tell you anything."

"I was hoping you'd say that," Pax said calmly, pulling hi hands free and rolling his shoulders.

Paelotin laughed again, the sound grating in the small cel "I've beaten you since you were five years old. You couldn't tak me then, and you can't take me now."

"Maybe," Paxton said, still softly. "But I've spent the last thre years learning how to take my enemy apart, and you don't com close to what I've already dealt with."

"Is that a fact?" Predictably, Paelotin charged.

Paxton neatly sidestepped him, and the man smashed into th clear wall. He bounced back and turned, swinging shockingl fast and catching Paxton in the side of the jaw. Pax's body didn' move, but his head jerked back. Pain exploded through his head But he forced a smile. "Is that all you've got?"

Paelotin charged again, and this time, Paxton took the hi midcenter. Ducking, he wrapped his arms around Paelotin' stomach and twisted, flipping the man off his feet and shovin him hard to the ground headfirst. Something popped, and Paeloti screamed, kicking out and nailing Paxton in the nose.

Pax retaliated by grabbing the offending ankle and twistin until several bones fractured. Then he continued to twist. Bloo spurted. Paelotin bellowed and punched out, hitting Pax in th shin. Paxton dropped him on the ground, and without missin a beat, kicked him in the ribs. He was wearing steel-toed boots Paelotin growled, jumping up in another tackle that threw then both against the back wall.

Paxton almost casually dropped both elbows onto Paelotin' shoulders, knocking him to his knees on the hard surface. The

Pax punched him in the nose and the teeth, hearing cartilage crunch and enamel shatter.

"You know, I don't really give a shit about you," Paxton said, not feeling much of anything. He should hate the useless bastard, but he just didn't. "However," he said, "I'll never forget the time you tried to hurt Hope."

As he said her name, he stuck one finger right into Paelotin's eye, blinding him. The warrior shrieked, scrambling to reach for his face. Paxton tossed him to the ground, kicked him several times in the groin, and then dropped with a knee on his broken ribs. Paelotin shrieked.

Paxton smiled, in complete contrast to the violence he'd meted out. "Okay, so we're going to try again. How about you tell me about my mother?" he suggested softly.

Chapter Twenty-Four

"We can't find them," Collin said, typing rapidly on a keyboard. "They're gone."

They sat in the smaller conference room in demon headquarters, one that was used by different teams at various times.

Hope put her head back and sank onto the heavy leather chair. "We are unable to trace the sisters from Paris," she repeated, her stomach lurching. "Natalie and Annette Toussaint." The Kurjan had them, and who knew what was happening to them.

Libby reached over and patted her hand. "We did what we could. We had to catch..." She winced. "Paxton."

"Agreed," Liam said from across the heavy oak conference table. "We had to catch him, or we wouldn't have known that there was a bomb in your head. I'm sorry about those two females, but we will continue trying to track them down."

Collin waved a hand, and a map came to life on the wall at the end of the table. "I found another enhanced female. She is in Florence, Italy."

"Send the note to another squad," Hope said. "We have too much going on here to go to Italy."

"Agreed." Collin typed something quickly.

Hope's phone buzzed, and she looked down, her body stiffening as she read. "I've been called to the main Realm headquarters."

"All of us?" Derrick asked, fire oscillating up his arms.

"Show-off," Hope retorted. "No, just me."

Libby's eyes widened. "It must have something to do with the Seven."

"It must," Hope said. She pushed back the chair and stood. "Sorry to cut our meeting short. Let's just stay on track. Keep trying to find the two females we lost and make sure the one in Italy is protected."

They had finally figured out how to hack into some of the Kurjans' vibration systems that were being used to locate enhanced females. Even so, the Kurjans kept getting to them before the Realm. "We also have to figure out what their new technology is. We've hacked into one system, but obviously they have others."

"I think it has to do with satellites," Collin said, turning away from the computer bank. "I've analyzed their current system, and I think somehow they're able to use satellites to catch the vibrations emitted by enhanced females."

Hope rubbed her left eye. Even though the bomb was gone, her head still ached a little bit. "Great. All right, let's put a report together, and I'll submit it to both my father and Dage. We may just have to shoot their satellites out of the sky."

It was tantamount to declaring war, but considering the Kurjans had fired upon the Seven and blown up their headquarters, she had a feeling war had already begun. "I believe we're at war," she said honestly, her gut hurting.

Everyone in the room nodded. All right, so at least they were on the same page.

"Everybody stay on your current tasks," she said. She turned and walked out of the room to find two guards waiting at the front door. "Apparently I have an escort," she said dryly to nobody in particular.

They were both huge and silent, a pair that she recognized bu didn't know well. They walked along the path to the lake, an she entered through the rear entrance of Realm headquarters t find her father and Dage and Talen arguing loudly with her uncle Garrett and Logan.

Huh. It was more power than she had ever seen in one plac at one time, and at the moment, it was angry power. She though about leaving, just returning to her house, but instead stood ther and put her hands on her hips. When nobody seemed to notic her, she finally whistled loudly.

In unison, five hard, dangerous, intelligent gazes focused on he She forced a smile. "Hello, male relatives of mine."

It was interesting to see Talen and Garrett arguing, considerin they pretty much looked like the same person, as father and sor Same with Zane and Logan, who were brothers. Dage stood apar from everyone as usual, but as the king of pretty much everybody that wasn't out of the ordinary.

"Apparently, I'm some sort of strategic mastermind," sh drawled. "How about y'all tell me what you boys are arguin about." Considering they were all her relatives and all older tha she was, her comment showed a lot of bravado, but she was in n mood for theatrics.

Her father spoke first. "That's quite the offer, Hope. But th Seven are here, and they're having a meeting and..."

Ah, now she got it. "The Seven don't want the three of you i there." Garrett and Logan were members of the Seven, but th other three males were not.

She indicated Dage, the King of the Realm; Zane, the king o the demon nation; and Talen, Dage's younger brother and the mo: stubborn and yet strategically brilliant soldier ever born.

"Exactly." Talen was the one who answered her.

"Well." She looked at Garrett and Logan. "I guess you tw were sent to deliver the bad news, huh?"

It wasn't funny. She should not feel amusement, and her lips should not be twitching. She tried to keep a straight face when all she wanted to do was chuckle. There was something about incredibly stubborn and dangerous males that was just cute when they got all riled up with each other, especially if they were family.

"We don't need any additional energy in the strategic meeting," Garrett said slowly. "We've got the Seven, we've got the three Keys, and now we have the Lock. We've been busy creating bombs armed with their blood in the hope that we can kill Ulric with them. Now we need to plan the attack, and don't worry, just the soldiers are going. Hope deserves to be part of the planning, and we need her brain, anyway."

"You are not taking my daughter into that group without me there," Zane growled, threat in every syllable of his words.

A shiver danced down Hope's spine, and she lost the smile and all of the amusement.

Dage's chin lowered in a way that would have anybody backing away. Anybody except for his nephews. "I'm the King of the Realm. Anything that happens in this entire world is my business. Especially"—he flicked his gaze toward Hope—"when it involves my niece."

Talen just started walking toward the door. "Done talking."

Garrett threw his hands up, while Logan cracked a smile. "Told you we wouldn't talk him out of it," he said.

"Shut up," Garrett said, following his father.

Zane gestured Hope in front of him. "Let's go. Let's see what they're up to."

Hope was more curious than anything else. Though she remained in contact with the members of the Seven, she didn't think they had any additional knowledge beyond what she had compiled. In other words, nobody knew how to kill Ulric.

She walked down one flight of stairs to the largest conference room. All members of the Seven were now inside, as well as Dage, Zane, Talen, and Hope. At the far end of the table sat the

three Keys: Mercy, a half fairy mated to Hope's uncle Loga
Kyllwood; Grace, an enhanced female mated to the ancient Adar
O'Cearbhaill; and Dessie, an enhanced female and Ulric's possibl
Intended, who was mated to Uncle Garrett.

The three females couldn't be more dissimilar in looks an
temperament, and yet they all had the birthmark with the mystica
key. Logan sat next to Mercy in an unmistakably protective stance

"Howdy, Lock," Mercy said, kicking back in her chair, he
mismatched green and black eyes twinkling.

"Hi, Aunt Mercy," Hope returned, grinning. The stunnin
woman wasn't old enough to be Hope's aunt.

Dessie smiled. "We're finally going to figure all of this out."

"I hope so," Hope said.

Grace, her brown hair atop her head, remained quiet as usua
Her soul was a soft and quiet one, and she used photography t
depict scenarios that nobody else saw. Her gaze landed on he
mate, who gave her a barely perceptible nod. Her answerin
smile was sweet.

Garrett folded an arm around Dessie. "We have all the bloo
bombs we could ever need. Does anybody know how we can us
them to kill Ulric? I don't like the idea of just magically shovin
them down his gullet. What happens then?"

Benjamin Reese, one of the oldest hybrids in the room, an
possibly one of the craziest, shook his head. "It's our only optior
Down the throat."

Ivar Kjeidsen, an ancient hybrid, tapped his long fingers on th
table. "My mate has been working on different equations, hopin
to form another prison world, but it just doesn't seem possible.
His mate was a brilliant physicist who was more at home wit
a whiteboard than nature. He looked at Seven members Quad
and Ronan Kayrs. "You're all related, so shouldn't you be o
the same page?"

Quade shrugged. "We created the prison worlds in defiance c
the laws of physics, and our young nephew, the king, doesn't like it.

Benny snorted. "Well, we did fuck up the universe, so I don't blame him." He gestured with his chin at Garrett Kayrs and Logan Kyllwood. "I know the two kings aren't happy about Garrett and Logan being part of the Seven, but they have good heads on their shoulders, and you can trust them. The blood bombs will take care of Ulric. We will finally kill that bastard."

"Just how exactly are we going to do that?" Hope asked.

"That's the problem now, isn't it?" Dage drawled. "Even if we captured him, do you honestly think just pouring blood down his throat will do it?"

That was too easy. Hope looked at the piles of ancient texts scattered across the table. "No." She didn't know how, she didn't know why, but she knew that wasn't the answer. "I don't think that's how we kill Ulric."

"Then how?" Dage asked her softly.

She thought for several long moments. "I really don't know." Her gaze caught on a scaly black book whose pages had yellowed with age. "I haven't seen this one." She'd pored over every old book she could find for years.

Mercy nodded. "We found that in Glacier National Park about a month ago. I was in the process of copying it for you when we were attacked. Smell it."

Benny rolled his eyes. "Don't smell it. The thing has been underground forever."

Hope leaned forward and took a deep whiff. "Spiced oranges? Weird." The cover was the skin of an animal.

"I think it's dragon skin," Mercy whispered.

The open page showed three Keys, painstakingly drawn, a river of fire, and a Lock. It was the Lock's shape that caught her eye. Different symbols and several archaic languages made up the text. "The Lock is in the shape of a heart," she mused, flipping the pages quickly. "Where's the rest of the book?" It appeared as if it had been torn in half.

Dessie threw her hands up. "I wanted to stay in the park and find it, but Mr. Bossy Pants said it was too dangerous and that we were going home." She smacked Garrett in the chest.

He easily caught her hand and held it against his heart, his metallic-gray eyes amused. "Don't think I won't spank you, witnesses or not."

"Get a room," Logan drawled.

The picture, a thousand years old, almost glowed on the worn parchment.

Excitement rushed through Hope's blood, and she reached for her phone to shoot off a quick text to Collin. "So far, Collin has located all of our resources. If anybody can find the second half of this, it's him." The team would be ready to go. "We're close." She sat studying the one clear page.

"What?" her father asked.

She looked up. "I don't think the heart shape of the Lock is an accident." Did this mean they had to shove her entire heart down Ulric's throat? What could be more of a sacrifice than giving up her heart? Most immortals could regrow a heart, but if she were truly human as they suspected, then she'd die. "We have to find the rest of this book." There had to be another way.

"You're the heart of all of us, sweetheart," Zane murmured.

That was sweet; he obviously hadn't come to the same conclusion as she. He was her father, and no way would he agree to take out her heart, even to kill a monster. She'd have to figure that one out on her own. For now, she looked up at the assembled group. "Paxton and I are meeting Drake in a dreamworld tonight. He has agreed to a temporary truce because he wants to help us take down Ulric."

She sat back to let the fireworks commence.

Chapter Twenty-Five

If Paxton had ever been more uncomfortable in his life, he couldn't remember it. This was seriously unreal. He sat at the far end of Hope's bedroom on the floor, his legs extended and his back against the wall. She perched on the bed, the very bed where he'd brought her to orgasm last night. He tried not to look at it just so he could keep his body under control. Those sweet sounds she had made still echoed in his brain.

Her parents sat in a seating area over to the right near several bookcases. Two soldiers stood on either side of the door, both armed and deadly.

"You tired yet?" Paxton asked Hope.

She was dressed in yoga pants and a shirt as she sat up in her bed. "Not even close. How about you?"

"I seriously want to stab myself in the neck," he muttered.

Zane cut him a look. "If you think we're sending you two solo into some dreamworld with the Kurjans, you're insane. You need backup, and we're here."

"That's not how it works," Janie said, looking at her daughter. "You know that, Zane. We used to meet in dreamworlds. Once you're there, you're there. Their bodies will be here. But we have no control over what goes on inside the dreamworld." Her gaze was concerned as she looked at her daughter.

"If we're all in the same room, maybe she can take us all in," Zane said.

Both Hope and Janie shook their heads at the same time.

"Dad," Hope said, looking both adorable and frustrated. "I've tried to bring Mom in before, and I can't. For some reason, it' just the people I used to bring in when we were kids. I'm sorry, but if we do this, you're not coming." She held herself stiffly. "I'm twenty-four years old. Get out of my bedroom and go back to your own house."

"I'll keep her safe," Paxton said. "I can't imagine Drake trying to hurt her in a dreamworld. But if he does, I'll take him out." He spoke with absolute conviction because he meant each word. "This might even be a trap for me, but don't worry. I'm ready." He'd always been prepared to destroy Drake if necessary.

Zane looked at Paxton, his green eyes blazing. "What do you think? You've been in these dreamworlds with this guy. Do you think there's any chance he'll really turn on Ulric?"

Paxton wanted to say no. He wanted to say that there was no way the Kurjans would ever pursue peace and that the Realm should go to full-out war. But he'd always been honest with Zane except for hiding his involvement with the Defenders. "I honestly don't know," he said. "My gut feeling is that no, he doesn't want peace, and he won't work against Ulric. But it is possible." He rolled his ankle, which was still a little sore from his fight with Paelotin earlier. What he wouldn't give to have his healing cell back. He should deal with what was happening to him, but first he needed to ensure Hope's safety.

Hope glanced at the soldiers. "I can't sleep like this."

Zane jerked his chin at the soldiers. "All right, you two, outside."

They left, shutting the door without saying a word. Hope gave Paxton a look, and he tried not to smile. This was so freaking awkward.

"How are you feeling?" Zane asked him.

"Okay. I still can't heal my wounds, and my blood feels sluggish."

"Has Emma said anything?" Hope asked, her blue eyes so dark, they were violet again.

Pax shook his head. "I called her before I headed over here, and she doesn't have anything. My blood is still changing, and she thinks the fibers of my muscles are somehow being altered. So there's something in the drug that's affecting me in a way we don't want." He kept his tone flat and emotionless because he wasn't going to allow the Kurjans or the Cyst to mess with his head.

He had every intention of asking Drake about that compound once they were in the dreamworld, even if he had to beat him to get an answer. It'd be a good fight, and he was pissed off enough to make it work. They'd shot the same shit into Hope, but she seemed fine. So had the drug been made specifically for him, or would it work on any vampire-demon hybrid? If so, what was in Hope's blood that had beaten the effects of the drug? Emma was working on the problem constantly and would hopefully know soon. While Pax hadn't lost strength before today, he was feeling weaker now. His power was diminishing.

Hope glanced at her parents. "I can't go to sleep with you here. You can't come into the dreamworld, and you know it. So could we just all act like adults? Why don't you two go home?"

"I'm not going anywhere," Zane snapped.

Janie sighed. "You're being overbearing."

"That's my job," Zane returned.

Paxton nodded. It was Zane's job to keep Hope safe until it was his. Sure, he'd always considered it his duty. But she hadn't given him the right to make her safety his full job yet. But she would.

Zane crossed his arms, looking way too large for the love seat where he sat with his mate. "I'm not going anywhere. So you might as well get nice and sleepy."

Hope rolled her eyes.

Paxton couldn't blame him. He didn't want to let Hope out of his sight either. It was time to take control of the situation. "Relax your body and go to sleep. Let's get this over with," he ordered.

Hope gave him a look but snuggled down in the bed and curled onto her side. "What did you find out about your mother?" she asked.

"Not enough," Paxton admitted. "Paelotin told me everything he knew, and it wasn't much."

"Tell me," Hope mumbled, her voice sounding sleepy.

Paxton shut his eyes, putting his head back on the wall. "She approached him when she was about six months pregnant and said that her mate had died in the war. She didn't believe in the virus that negated mating bonds, so she figured she'd never mate again. Instead, she paid him a lot of money to pretend to be mated to her. Apparently, the deal was that if he ever found somebody he wanted to mate, she would move on and allow it."

"Why did she want to be with the demon nation?" Hope asked.

"After the war, it was the safest place to be for a lost demoness according to Paelotin," Paxton said. "He doesn't have any idea who my real father was." No doubt Paelotin didn't care.

"I've been trying to track that," Zane said. "All I know about your mom is that she lived within the demon nation for almost a hundred years and then just disappeared. There's no record of her for the next hundred years until she showed up at headquarters right after the war. At that time, we wanted all the soldiers we could get, and she was skilled. Then she was killed before I really had a chance to get to know or investigate her."

Paxton didn't open his eyes. "It's not your fault, Zane."

"I know. The war had just ended, and I was taking over the demon nation when all of that happened," Zane said. "Still, I wish I had known. I wasn't around them enough to realize they weren't really mated."

"Nobody was," Paxton said. "They didn't even fight in the same squads. Frankly, I don't remember spending much time with Paelotin until my mother died. He certainly didn't like me."

"I'm really sorry we didn't realize what was happening, Paxton," Janie said. "We were around you a lot, but Paelotin stayed away. Now we know why."

"It's fine," Paxton said. "Everything worked out the way it was supposed to. But I would like to know who she was, and I'd love to find out who my deceased father was." It'd be nice to find family out there.

"All I know," Zane said, "is that she was born in Paris in one of the demon strongholds there. She learned to fight young, even though female demons are so rare, and then during the first war, she disappeared. Somehow she resurfaced when the demon nation became part of the Realm and I took over. It isn't unusual for demons to go missing or to take off, especially when there are wars involved." Zane sighed heavily. "The demon nation was pretty fractured before I brought us into the Realm."

Paxton opened his eyes. "That's pretty much all I know about her too. Did you discover if she had any family?"

Zane grimaced. "No. She didn't have any siblings from the records I found, and her parents both died in the first war. So she was pretty much alone. That could be why she paid Paelotin and thought she should join the Realm. I don't know." He shook his head. "She could have done so without pretending to be mated."

"Yes," Janie said. "But you have to remember she grew up in a demon faction where she had no autonomy. Before you ruled the Demon nation, Zane, it wasn't the same for females. Your uncle was a real jerk, and he wouldn't have given her choices in her life. She probably didn't realize how much things had changed when she first approached Paelotin."

Paxton sighed. "He killed her. I got the truth from him earlier today. She did discover that things had changed, and she was going to leave with me. That's what he said, and so he killed her and made it look as if it had happened during a battle."

Zane stiffened. "Why didn't you tell me?"

"I just found out today," Paxton said.

"You let him live?" Hope asked softly.

Pax looked at her. "I told you to go to sleep."

"I'm trying. But you're talking," she said.

He sighed. "All right. That's fair. Yes. I let him live for now. He's not standing, and he'll be coughing blood for the next week despite his healing abilities. But I decided to let him live until we figure out our next move with the Kurjans. He gave me all the information he had, but on the off chance there's something in that tiny brain of his that he didn't think was relevant, I want him alive until we kill Ulric. He was a go-between between the Kurjans and Henric for quite a while, and we may need to ask questions that I don't even know yet."

"What then?" Hope asked.

"Then he dies," Paxton said, his tone hard. He wasn't going to start lying to her now. He took a deep breath and rested his head again. "All right, everybody be quiet," he told the room at large. "It's time to go meet the Kurjan."

Chapter Twenty-Six

Hope finally dropped into sleep and wandered through different worlds until she reached the one she wanted. Instead of choosing an ocean or a river, she chose a nice quiet lake this time. She wondered why she always needed water in the dreamworlds, but she didn't want to force a change. There was something about water that calmed her.

The lake was a deep aqua, the sky a burnished gold, and the sun beautiful and bright. She decided to make the trees all cedar, and their delicious scent wafted around her. It was as calm a place as she could create. Pressure built from outside the world, fierce and strong, and she allowed Paxton inside. "Give me a minute. I was setting up the place." She threw up her hands.

"If you're in here, I'm in here." He scouted the area, his body on alert. "Pretty lake."

"Thanks." He was lucky she had brought him in wearing jeans and a black T-shirt. "Knock it off, or I'll put you back into jean shorts and a cutoff shirt."

He rolled his eyes. "I'm glad you have a better sense of wardrobe these days." He looked around, no doubt for a weapon.

"There's nothing that can be used here, Paxton. That's no[
how this works," she said, although she probably could create a
knife out of nothing if she wanted.

She blinked twice, and Drake and his cousin Vero instantly
appeared. Vero was a couple of years younger than Drake,
but he stood tall. He'd filled out in the last few years, and al
pudginess was long gone.

He looked around. "Ah, come on. Why am I in the
dreamworld again?"

"Sorry." Hope studied him.

He was an anomaly in the Kurjan nation, with his blue eyes
and completely black hair, absent any red tips. She had felt sorry
for him before because he'd always seemed a little lost. Now, he
flanked his cousin, his gaze fixed on Paxton.

Drake's gaze traveled Hope's form, and then he looked a[
Paxton, not hiding the hatred glowing in his eyes. "I meant the
truce until we kill Ulric, and then I'm coming for you."

Paxton lifted his chin. "Any time and any place."

"I want you at full strength when I kill you." Drake growled
"You're looking very pale. Is it from the drug that Ulric
shot into you?"

"I'm fine," Paxton said shortly.

Hope jolted and looked over at her friend. He did look pale
She had gotten used to the change already, and yet he was almos[
as pale as Drake. "Are you feeling all right?" she asked.

"I'm fine," he repeated calmly.

She had to take him at his word, although she figured he wouldn'[
show any weakness in front of the Kurjans.

"Did you find out anything about those drugs?" she asked
Drake, ignoring the tension momentarily.

"No, sorry." He kept his gaze on Paxton. "You really
don't look well."

Vero hadn't moved his gaze from Paxton and looked prepared to
take any measure necessary to protect Drake. It was interesting tha[

he was now the guard dog. He had seemed so sweet and sensitive before. Besides, Hope didn't figure Drake needed protection.

"So you want to fix the world?" Pax drawled. "I guess you're ready to kill Ulric."

Drake cut a look at Vero. "I was going to bring you in on this."

Vero was silent. Interesting. Hope watched the interplay. Paxton had no doubt made the claim just to see if Vero knew anything. Apparently, Drake had not shared his concerns about Ulric.

"Have you figured out how to kill Ulric?" Drake asked when his cousin didn't reply.

"Not yet," Hope admitted. "We know it'll take the blood of the Keys and probably the Lock, but we haven't figured out if that will do it. We think maybe if we get a bullet of the stuff down his throat, it will mingle with his blood and destroy him." She perked up. "Do you have any ancient texts or legends that would give us more info? We've found some recently, but I was thinking there might be a lot more."

"We have a few," Drake said shortly, focusing once again completely on her. "We've always been more of an action-oriented society, not one of books. I could start sending scouts out, but we're stretched a little thin right now with my faction fighting Ulric's. There are more Kurjans joining the Cyst than I would hope."

"So you want to take him out," Paxton drawled. "That seems rather disloyal of you."

Hope searched Vero's expression for any hint as to what he was thinking, but he had learned to mask his thoughts well. "What's your plan?" she asked, hoping Drake had one.

He smiled. "A temporary treaty with the Realm, of course."

Excitement started to drum through her. If she could negotiate a treaty between the two nations, she would have fulfilled at least part of her fate. Anything temporary could turn into something permanent. This was good. She smiled. "All right, what are your terms?"

"They're simple," Drake said. "One, you kill Ulric and then give me a year to consolidate the power of the Kurjan and Cyst nations. Two, immediate acceptance into the Realm and everything that entails. If we're attacked, we have your full defense behind us. Three, full access to all Realm satellites and data regarding the Kurjan nation and the Cyst. Four, all information regarding all enhanced human females in the world shall be shared. And five—" His gaze warmed. "We commingle our peoples in the same way treaties have been cemented in the past. You mate me, Hope."

Paxton instantly stepped in front of her. "The last one's a no go. Probably the third one as well."

"That's nonnegotiable," Drake said.

Hope cocked her head to the side. "You and I have a deal, remember?" She ignored the way Paxton's body stiffened. "Find out what drugs are in Pax's system and get me a cure. Then I'll mate you."

Drake lifted one powerful shoulder. "You and I have been destined from the moment you were born. I think you know that. Treaties have been consolidated by matings for much longer than any of us have lived. That part is nonnegotiable."

"No," Pax growled. He glanced at her over his shoulder. "No way will I allow you to mate this guy."

She couldn't help it. "It's not like you've asked me."

"That's it." He clapped his hands hard, and the dreamworld disappeared.

Hope sat upright in her bed.

He stood, all angry demon male. "What the hell was that?" he snapped.

Both Zane and Janie moved off the loveseat.

"What happened?" Zane asked.

Pax spared him a glance and looked back at Hope. "Are you kidding me? I've wanted to mate you since I was two years old. It has always been my plan. I've been waiting for you to show up."

"Why didn't you ever ask me?" she asked, knowing full well she could have asked him.

"Because I didn't want to hear you say no," he growled even lower, making his tone demon hoarse. "You're still thinking about sacrificing yourself for this damn nation. It's ridiculous, and those thoughts need to stop now."

Anger trilled through her, and she shoved herself out of the bed, stomping across the room to poke him in the chest. Just who did he think he was? "Now listen here."

Before she could get another word out, the air tightened and exploded outward. The comforter flew off the bed, and the books plummeted down from the bookshelf. Even the papers on her dresser whirled away.

Paxton turned. "What the—"

Drake suddenly appeared in the room out of nowhere.

Zane yelled and lunged for him.

Drake grabbed Hope and clapped a hand on Paxton's arm. "Thanks for being here," he hissed.

Then they plummeted through time and space into absolute darkness.

* * * *

Paxton's head felt as if his skull had caved in and then blown out. Through the overwhelming pain, he tried to focus and force his eyelids open. There was only darkness and air and heat. Even so, he reached for Hope, knowing she was close. Just as he closed a hand around her biceps, a blinding light pierced his eyes, and he landed hard on icy packed dirt. Going on instinct, he yanked her against him, flattened her against his body and rolled, trying to protect her.

Then silence.

She was ripped away from him, and he growled, leaping to his feet. It took him a moment to focus. He was in the middle of what appeared to be some sort of camp, complete with wooden cabins and a large, handcrafted log lodge, covered with snow. Although dawn had arrived, there was still a bright spotlight shining down, illuminating the center of the camp. Forestland surrounded them, mountains rose high in the distance, and a river bubbled nearby. He smelled pine, dirt, and oil. They could be anywhere.

Kurjan soldiers surrounded them, all with weapons at the ready and trained on his body.

Drake held Hope, who was pale, her eyes blinking as she obviously tried to focus. The sight of her starting to fight the hands holding her nearly threw Paxton into a rage. He took a deep breath, centering himself so he could fight.

"Shoot him," Drake ordered.

Hope cried out in protest, and Paxton reacted on instinct, his fangs dropping low and fire blowing through his blood. Almost instantly, darts of all kinds struck him from head to toe, followed by lasers that turned into bullets with piercing agony. He flew back against a cage surrounded by iron bars. The pain was excruciating. Even so, he ducked his head and tried to get to Hope. She was the only thing that mattered in the entire universe.

"Lock him inside," Drake said with a casual flick of his wrist, looking around the area.

Hope fought him, kicking back and turning to punch him in the stomach. But she was no match for the Kurjan. He easily subdued her, grabbing both of her wrists and twisting her around to face Paxton while yanking her up against his body. Her head shot back in a spurt of temper, and she blinked, the corners of her eyes wrinkling in pain.

Drake didn't seem to notice she'd headbutted his chest.

At least five soldiers darted forward, and Paxton fought brutally, but whatever they'd shot into his bloodstream was rapidly taking effect. The darts were all over his body, and between punching and kicking, he tried to tear them out.

Somebody opened the cage door; it took four of them to shove him inside. The door clanked shut. He charged the bars, but they didn't move. They were solid iron. He wrapped his numb fingers around them. "Let her go," he hissed, uncaring that he was going to go down fast. He had to get Hope out of there.

The world swirled around him, and it took every ounce of stubborn will for him to keep his feet on the ground where they belonged. "Hope," he called. How could he get her free?

She pushed against Drake, but he held her fast. Shock covered her pale face, and tears filled her wide blue eyes. She looked around. "Where are we?"

"Far away from where you want to be," Drake admitted.

Paxton's fangs dropped and then retracted. "Wait, wait a minute. You can teleport?"

The Kurjan threw back his head and laughed. "Yes, quite the situation your Seven created when they violated the laws of physics. While they took the ability to teleport away from both demons and fairies, somehow the Kurjans gained the skill." He cocked his head to the side, holding a now subdued Hope to him. "You might want to get your rest, Paxton. I plan to kill you very slowly."

Paxton snarled and tried to call out to Hope, to give her something even if it was just a promise. But the darts and the bullets took effect, and he started to fall, the world disappearing for now.

Then there was just darkness.

Chapter Twenty-Seven

Hope felt as if the inside of her head was bleeding. She had never teleported before and had no idea if it was always that painful.

She struggled against Drake, trying to reach Paxton. He'd gone down onto the dirty snow-covered ground and appeared to be unconscious. Blood flowed from the many bullet wounds in his body, and there were several bright yellow-and-red-tipped darts still embedded in his skin. Panic made her voice hoarse. "What was in those darts?"

"Doesn't matter." Drake, still holding both her wrists in one hand, turned and started to drag her toward the main lodge. She fought him, but she was no match for his strength. At about six foot eight and three hundred pounds, he was solid muscle and unbeatable at the moment. She still couldn't regain her equilibrium after the teleportation.

They walked inside the building, and three women instantly got out of their way. They were dressed in long skirts and long-sleeved shirts, and while one seemed to be dusting and one vacuuming, they scurried to the side, their eyes downcast.

A chill swept through Hope. "Drake, what are you doing?" she snapped, trying to regain some of her strength.

He didn't answer, but instead, pulled her to the far end of a massive great room and up a set of stairs. She walked with him, trying to jerk her hands free. Finally, they reached a door that he opened and then not so gently nudged her inside a bedroom. In a word, it was opulent. There was a beautiful four-poster bed, a filigreed gold settee, a desk, and a vanity. It was like a starlet's bedroom from the 1950s.

She turned to face him and backed away on luxurious carpet that was the color of grayish blue clouds. "What are you doing?" she repeated, her voice trembling as she tried to find her childhood friend in his hard eyes. He shut the door and leaned against it, a solid block of male that she couldn't get through.

"It was a 'two birds, one stone' situation," he admitted. "You're here to become my queen, and Paxton is here to die. While I know he means a lot to you, the fact that he killed my father can't go unanswered. He will suffer, Hope, and I'm not going to lie to you about that."

"Apparently you've lied to me about everything else," she said.

"That's not true," he said. "Or if I did, it was to protect you or my nation. It's that simple." He glanced at his watch. "I do want peace, and that will come when all my enemies are dead. However, for you, I'm open to ruling the Realm if you can help make that happen."

She took a step back. "Ruling the Realm? You'd have to kill every Kayrs and Kyllwood alive today. All of my family."

"I know. I'm your family now. Get used to it." He glanced inside the spacious room. "Choose a dress from the many in the closet and then come downstairs. There will be soldiers outside waiting to escort you."

She shook her head, thrown off-balance. "So it was all a lie?"

He shrugged. "No. I would like to entertain a plan to kill Ulric. He doesn't know that, and I'd like to keep it that way. I strongly advise you not to mention it to him."

She jerked her head. "Ulric is here?"

"Yes. This is one of the satellite bases we work out of when we're seeking enhanced females."

Her jaw dropped. But she'd seen an actual crown in her dreamworld. She was somehow still meant to mate this monster? "You really are behind the kidnapping of enhanced females?"

"Yes." His eyes were a hard green with purple rims. "I'm not going to lie to you, as you're going to be my queen. You're going to have to accept the way things are here. Your life will be comfortable, luxurious, even. I'll give you everything you could ever want."

"Oh yeah? How about freedom for the enhanced females?" She scouted for a weapon in the pretty bedroom.

"Done," he said, smiling.

She narrowed her gaze. "What do you mean, done?"

He lifted up his hand. "I've always had every intention of freeing them, after a short period of time."

"What does that mean?"

"It doesn't really matter, and it doesn't concern you," he said. "Again, dress."

She looked down at her yoga pants and tank top. "I'm fine with what I'm wearing." Actually, she could use a sweater. "Do you have a coat or anything I could use?"

"The queen will wear a proper dress. Put one on, or I'll put one on you myself," he said. "Now is not the time for you to defy me, Hope. That can come later. For now, since we just declared war on the Realm by kidnapping you, we need to confirm you a queen as soon as possible."

"I say no," Hope said, putting her hands on her hips.

"That isn't an option."

Hurt wandered through her. "You're not who I thought you were."

His expression didn't change. "I've never hidden who I am or my destiny from you." His eyes swirled purple for a moment and then returned to the green color she knew. "My loyalty has always been to the Kurjan nation. Period."

She swallowed. That was true. Any higher attributes she'd given to him had come from her imagination…or her faith that destiny would be kind to them all. So it turned out that she would have to truly sacrifice herself. So be it. "Let Paxton go, and I'll mate you."

"You'll mate me regardless." Drake turned, opened the door, and shut it. She instantly ran for it and yanked the heavy wood open to find two Kurjan soldiers across the way. A quick glance down the hallway confirmed more sentries. They must have waited to take position until Drake had brought her to the room.

She was a trained fighter, but she wasn't that good, and she was still off. She slammed the door and quickly searched the room for anything that could be used as a weapon. There was nothing. Shoving away her headache for now, she stomped into the closet to find several gorgeous gowns with diamonds, rubies, and emeralds sewn onto them.

Lined up beneath the dresses were sparkly, delicate flats and heels, nothing that would make good fighting footwear. A dresser at the far end of the closet revealed piles and piles of lingerie, from sweet to sexy. There was absolutely nothing she could use for a weapon. In the attached bath, she again found feminine supplies, makeup, perfume, and lotions. No weapon.

A knock sounded on the door, and she hustled to the window to look out. She was on the second story, but she could make it out. However, her room faced that center courtyard, and she could see soldiers posted everywhere. Pax still wasn't moving in the cage, and her heart stuttered. Movement caught her eye to the left, and she leaned to see a Kurjan soldier stationed on the roof. The minute she stepped out there, he'd see her.

The knock came again, and then the door opened. Two women walked inside. One met her stare boldly, and the second looked down. Hope looked back at them. "Hello?"

"Hi," the bolder one said. "We're supposed to help you put on a dress."

Hope held up a hand to ward her off. "I don't need help putting on a dress."

The woman threw up her hands. "Good. Well, that's something."

Hope chuckled, even though she wanted to scream. "I'm Hope."

"Oh. I'm Lyrica," the woman said. She stood to about five six and was very curvy. Her dark hair was secured in an elaborate braid, and she had sparkling, light brown eyes. She glanced beyond Hope and gasped. "Oh, check out all the sparkles." She rushed into the closet. "These are gorgeous." She held up a pair of Manolo Blahniks, complete with sparkling square.

"I'd rather it was a weapon," Hope said slowly.

Lyrica looked toward her, her gaze hardening. "Yeah, me too. Can't really stab anybody with a Manolo, though."

"We might have to try," Hope said grimly. "Who are you?" she softly asked the other woman.

The woman shrugged.

Lyrica shook her head. "She's kind of traumatized after being kidnapped and finding out how evil our captors are. She got into an argument with one of the Cyst generals her first day here, and he beat her up pretty bad. Her name is Genevieve."

"Hi, Genevieve. I'm Hope. I'm going to help you get out of here."

Genevieve's head came up, and her eyes widened. They were a pretty bluish green, more blue than green. She had to be about nineteen, and her hands trembled when she clasped them together. "There's no way to get out of here. I've looked," she said softly.

"I'm looking too," Lyrica said. "I almost made it the other night, but those soldiers are everywhere, and they vary their patrols so there's no set pattern. I'm a mathematician. I study patterns." She looked again at all the sparkly dresses and shoes. "And shoes. I'm all about the shoes."

It was good to find allies so quickly. "When we get out of here, you can take those with you," Hope offered.

Lyrica snorted. "I don't care about them that much. I just want freedom." She had to be in her early thirties.

"Are you both enhanced females?" Hope could tell with Lyrica, but she wasn't entirely sure about Genevieve.

"Unfortunately," Lyrica said grimly.

Hope could understand the sentiment. "Yeah, you and me both." She doubted the three of them could take on the guards outside. She had a better chance escaping from Drake. How could he do this? What exactly was his grand plan? Her brain still felt sluggish from teleporting. "I have to ask you. Have you seen a couple of sisters from Paris? Natalie and Annette Toussaint?"

"Yep," Lyrica said. "They're here, and I've been learning French. It gets a little boring just cooking and cleaning. They're tough and will stand with us if we make an escape."

Relief filtered through Hope. Good. At least they were alive, and now she knew where they were located. "I'm glad they're okay."

"So you're going to be queen, huh?" Lyrica asked. "That kind of sucks."

Hope stared at the dresses. "I am not going to be forced into anything." Yet she might be forced to cooperate to save Paxton's life.

"You should at least put a dress on," Lyrica said, eyeing the fabrics.

"I don't think so," Hope retorted. "What are they doing with the enhanced females?"

Genevieve gave a small squeak and moved to the side, away from them both.

Lyrica rolled her eyes. "Stop being so scared. We will get out of here somehow." She softened her tone. "It'll be okay, I promise. For now—" She looked at Hope. "Drake said to tell you if you didn't put a dress on and come downstairs, he is going to cut off parts of Paxton's anatomy. He wasn't bluffing."

Hope shivered, shocked by the brutality of her old friend. She wanted to cling to the idea that he didn't mean this, and he wasn't really going to go forward with anything he'd threatened. But even inside her head, the words rang hollow. "Fine," she said. There was more material in the dresses than her yoga pants and tank top, so she actually didn't mind changing if she had to be seen by anybody. However, she wasn't sure she could fight as well in one of the heavy skirts. "Which one?" she asked.

Lyrica instantly reached for a blue one that had diamonds sewn along the V of the waist. "This one. It's the lightest material, and if you have to, you can tuck the bottom into this band around the waist to fight," she said.

"Excellent choice," Hope said, glad to have found an ally. The dress looked a lot like the one commonly seen on Cinderella. She quickly changed into it and had to suck in her breath so that Lyrica could secure the bodice. The woman had to put a foot against Hope's back and pull the strings in order to tighten and tie the corset.

"Man, these people are stuck in the last century," Lyrica sputtered.

"No kidding," Hope said, looking over her shoulder. She wasn't wearing shoes and needed to remedy that. Her heart hurt. Drake wasn't the person she'd thought, and she felt stupid. He'd been good at manipulating her; she'd wanted peace so badly. "Let's pick out the most pointed ones we can find just in case I need to kick somebody in the eye." There wasn't a lot to choose from, and in the end, she went with the Manolo Blahniks.

Genevieve still cowered by the bed. "They like us to wear our hair braided and away from our faces."

"Good to know," Hope said. She flipped her head over and ruffled her hair, making the strands even bigger and fuller. And then she tossed it back, letting her waves fall around her shoulders and down the dress. "I'll go like this."

Lyrica cracked a smile and smacked her on the arm. "Good on you. Now, let's go tell that asshole you don't want to be his queen."

Chapter Twenty-Eight

Paxton came to with his brain feeling as if missiles were exploding in his head. He stilled, knowing instantly he was in danger but unable to remember how or why. He forced his eyelids open and saw the top of a cage. Memories came rushing back. In one smooth motion, he rolled onto his feet and then staggered.

The outside cage had bars on all four sides, and the top was tall enough he could barely touch it on his tiptoes. People scurried around him. There were soldiers patrolling, and every once in a while a female or two would walk by with food or laundry. Their heads remained down, their movements fast.

Most ignored him, although occasionally a soldier would stare, trying to intimidate him. He barely kept from rolling his eyes. He tore all of the darts out of his body and focused on pushing the other bullets out. He was definitely weakened, and something was happening to his muscles. Whatever had been in those darts was the same drug already destroying his system, so now it was just going to happen quicker.

He had to get Hope out of there and to safety before he died. He didn't know how a drug could kill him, but everything inside him told him the crap chugging through his veins was deadly.

Drake strode out of the main headquarters. He was tall and broad in that Kurjan black uniform with all the silver medals on his chest. His gaze scanned the area, and then he clomped down the stairs and walked across the packed snow to reach Paxton. "You're up sooner than I would've expected." He held a well-worn leather-bound book in his hands.

Paxton squared his stance. "Where's Hope?"

"She's inside, preparing to become the queen of the Kurjan nation," Drake drawled. "It's going to happen, so you might as well stop clenching your fists. You're going to need all your energy." His lips ticked up.

Paxton looked up at the sun, which had started to shine.

Drake followed his gaze. "We're getting better," he said, pride and anticipation in his tone. "We can stay in the sun for about four hours now. Our scientists are close to making it permanent. How are you feeling with that sun, Paxton?"

Actually, he wasn't much liking it. The heat touching his finger around the bars felt like a burn. "What was in that drug?"

"Doesn't matter."

"Hope really believed you wanted peace." There were times Pax had hoped for that outcome as well, but he'd never trusted Drake.

"I will have peace once the Realm falls." Drake clasped his hands behind his back.

Paxton stared evenly at him. "Should've paid attention to Tacitus. 'They make a desert and call it peace,'" he quoted.

Drake smiled. "I quote myself, hybrid."

A truck roared to a stop near the other vehicles to the north, and two soldiers jumped out, hurrying toward Drake. Paxton straightened.

Vero was the first to reach them. "What have you done?" the young soldier hissed, throwing up his arms and looking from Paxton to the lodge. "We just got word that you kidnapped Hope Kayrs-Kyllwood."

"You can't kidnap your own mate," Drake said, looking at Vero and dismissing the other very quiet soldier.

Paxton gave a short nod to that silent male, glad to see Hunter Kayrs still alive and in place. He was the king's kid, who'd been undercover with the Kurjan nation for far too long. He'd even undergone surgery to make him look more like a Kurjan. Power emanated from him, and it was shocking that Drake couldn't feel it. He and Vero both stood to about six foot six, which was short for Kurjans, but they were wide and incredibly fast. Pax would need help getting to Hope and helping her to safety.

Hunter shook his head. "You just declared war, Drake."

Drake turned on him. "Harold, you shouldn't even be here. You should be, I don't know, gathering roots and berries with the women. I've seen you fight."

Actually, Drake hadn't really seen Hunter fight. He obviously didn't *see* Hunter.

Paxton started to formulate a plan.

Hunter flicked his gaze at him and then back. "This is crazy."

Vero nodded vigorously. "I agree. If Hope is meant to be your mate, she will be, Drake. You didn't have to kidnap her."

"There is no doubt my father allowed you too much time with the females. You're soft, Vero. I should've kept Karma away from you." Drake's lip curled.

Vero's chin lowered. "Karma was a kind female, and she taught me a lot. Especially that kindness and love don't make you weak." He glanced at Paxton. "Then she was taken by Benjamin Reese, a member of the Seven. He had better not be hurting her." Fire glowed in his odd blue eyes.

"He's not," Paxton said. "They're mated and are about to have another kid. She's happy and in love...and very safe."

Vero's expression didn't change. "Good. For now, we need to figure out what to do with the Realm princess."

"Hope will be my mate—she doesn't have a choice about that," Drake said slowly. "You two get back to your duties."

"No," Vero said, setting his stance.

Hunter stepped up to his side.

Paxton stiffened. He didn't want to see either one of them get hurt

"Where is the woman?" Hunter asked.

"It's none of your business," Drake said. "You'll see her when she's my queen."

Hunter looked toward the lodge and back at Vero. "We can' let him force a female to be his queen."

"Oh, she'll make the choice," Drake said, looking directly a Paxton. "I promise."

"Why is that?" Paxton asked, his blood feeling as if biting ant were crawling through his veins.

Drake looked down at the white leather-bound book. "Because of this. Even now I can't believe they pulled it off."

"Pulled what off?" Vero asked.

For an answer, Drake handed them the book. "You might a well read it. The journal belonged to your father."

Vero jerked. "My father kept a diary? I can barely remembe him. He died when I was a toddler."

Paxton thought through what he knew of the young soldie Vero's father, Talt, had been killed, leaving behind his two brothers Dayne and Terre. Dayne had been the leader of the Kurjans, and Drake was his son. Terre had been a brutal soldier who'd died while back. Terre had been the one to take in Vero, the poor sap Drake and Vero, thus, were cousins.

Vero started reading the pages.

Drake rolled his eyes, grabbed the bound book, and opened i to a page near the back. "Start here. We don't have all day."

Vero started reading. He stiffened and his eyes widened. Hi jaw dropped, and he flipped over another page, then another. He slowly looked up at Paxton.

"What?" Paxton asked. "What did...?" Dread slithered dow his spine. He opened his mouth, but he couldn't speak.

Growling, Hunter yanked the book away and read it quickly. "Holy fuck," he muttered, scanning another page. "Seriously?" He looked toward Drake, then Paxton, then Vero. "How is this even possible?"

Paxton remained silent, searching again for a glimpse of Hope in any of the upstairs windows of the main lodge.

Drake chuckled, and the sound was grating. "Apparently the Kurjans have been conducting experiments for much longer than anybody realized."

"Meaning what?" Paxton asked softly, returning his attention to the bastard who'd kidnapped him.

"Meaning you're not a vampire-demon hybrid, Paxton Phoenix," Drake said.

Pax remained silent, knowing Drake would continue. In the quiet, Drake looked at Hunter and cocked his head. His gaze became speculative. "Drake? You going to sleep there?" Paxton drawled, yanking his attention back where it should be.

Drake slowly turned to appraise him, near glee in his bizarre eyes. "You are a Kurjan-demon hybrid. You and Vero shared a father. Talt was a real bastard who liked to kill people slowly, and I have no doubt you're just as twisted." Drake threw back his head and laughed. "Welcome home, cousin. It is fitting you shall die amongst your own people."

* * * *

Just as Lyrica finished speaking, the door opened. All three women took a step back.

General Ulric stepped inside, more imposing and terrifying in real life than Hope had feared. She'd met him in his horrific prison world during a dream, but now that he was free, it appeared he'd rebuilt his health.

He stood to about six nine and was four hundred pounds o solid, raw muscle. His face was so pale he looked like a ghost and one long line of white hair bisected his too-pale scalp and was braided down his back. He wore the battle gear of the Cyst and the Kurjans: black combat pants, a black vest with a multitude of medallions on his left breast, and black boots that had to be size twenty-four.

"Get out," he ordered.

Lyrica and Genevieve scrambled to edge around him and flee Hope couldn't blame them.

She felt ridiculous in the fairy-tale gown, but even so, she pu her shoulders back and her chin high. "It's been a while, Ulric." She was shocked that her voice didn't tremble.

"I remember," he said. "It was kind of you to visit me in my prison world."

"Eh." She lifted a shoulder. "I didn't have anything going on that day."

His gaze raked her body. "Do you know where my Intended is right now?"

"Nope. She's mated. It's too late for you to find her."

He leaned closer, staring at her. It was an intimidating look "My Destiny. I can't wait to have her back in my hands."

Dessie was currently mated to Garrett Kayrs, which mean there was no way she'd end up anywhere near Ulric again.

"You keep telling yourself that, buddy." Hope tilted her head "You know, I do wonder though. Since she's an immortal mate who will live forever, does that mean you won't get anothe Intended?" To her knowledge, there could only be one Intended living at any given time.

"I've found my one. I shall retake Destiny as soon as I finish our current campaign."

"What is that campaign?"

He looked her over from head to toe. "You appear mighty breakable to me, Lock."

A frisson of fear crept down her spine, but she didn't let him see it. "I imagine most females look breakable to you." It was good that he underestimated her. She didn't know how, but if the chance came to kill him, she would take it.

"Tell me about the final ritual. Do you know how to kill me?" He drawled the words as if playing with her, but an intense curiosity swirled in his creepy purplish red eyes.

"Yes," she lied. "We're ready. In fact, I'm not even needed."

His smile showed razor-sharp yellowed fangs. "That's what I thought."

It was odd they were in the same space while she was wide awake. In the dreamworld, there had been a haze between the two of them. With no haze, she could feel the evil emanating from his pores. Centuries ago, the only way to contain him was to mess with the laws of physics and create a prison world. Now they had the Keys, Lock, and the Keeper of the Circle. "You must be terrified that the Realm has the ingredients to destroy you."

"Yet you're here," he said. "I don't feel terrified. Rituals always work in my favor."

"You know, I'm fine with dying if it means you go with me," she admitted.

"I'm not going anywhere," he said. "But I will tell you a little secret. I do plan on performing the ritual again, for all of my Cyst soldiers. They need to be invincible as well."

Her stomach lurched. "You're going to kill hundreds of enhanced females?" It had taken the blood of a hundred women to make Ulric's body impenetrable. "You can't."

"I shall. Just for a chosen few." His smile revealed sharp fangs.

"Why tell me your plan?" It didn't make sense.

His chuckle poured evil around the room. "I want you to dream about it. When it happens, and it will, I'll let you have a front-row seat."

She needed to throw up. "You're evil."

He shrugged. "Now, if you'll excuse me." He grinned at his own joke, because he obviously didn't care if she excused him or not. "There are two more enhanced females we just found in a nice little tavern outside of Anchorage, Alaska. You may meet them when I bring them here."

"There is no need to perform that ritual again, and you know it. After spending centuries in a hell world, didn't you do any introspection? It's not too late for you to do the right thing. Save your soul." She threw up her hands, noting how the long sleeves bounced and flounced and sparkled.

His gaze caught on the sparkles and then traveled to her breasts. "My soul will live forever back on this world. You're such a pretty pet. I wonder what it would take for Drake to let me spend time with you before he mates you. You're not safe right now."

It was true. She wasn't safe until she mated somebody, and then anybody who touched her would get a horrible rash. She met his gaze directly. "You're not my type. Way too old."

"That is permissible. I could live with the age gap," he said.

Her knees trembled, but the stupid skirt hid the weakness.

"For now, your king awaits." Ulric stepped to the side. "You should hasten to obey his orders. He may appear patient, but you've only witnessed that side of him. I look forward to your meeting his true countenance. You may then come crawling to me for solace."

Chapter Twenty-Nine

The guards escorted Hope across the main living area to a heavy, shielded door on the far side of the fireplace. They knocked before opening it and then gestured her inside. She followed their directions and stopped at the sight of Drake sitting on a heavy leather sofa across from two matching chairs. The room was a large office complete with a conference table and several monitors on the wall.

An unmanned computer area formed an L-shaped desk in the far corner. "Come in," he said, gesturing toward one of the chairs. His gaze swept her. "You look beautiful."

"I feel like I'm dressed up for a Halloween party," she said, holding the skirt so she could walk across the floor without tripping on the voluminous folds.

He poured two cups of tea, his gaze heated. "If you were, you would be dressed up as a queen." Next to his cup sat a glass full of what looked like Scotch.

"I'm not a tea drinker." She sat gracefully in the seat and stared at him before leaning forward and snagging the glass. The liquid heated her stomach, and she'd bet it was Glenlivet from a good year. "Not bad." She placed the heavy crystal down.

His eyes warmed, and he sat back, smiling. "We need to speak before making our announcement tomorrow at dawn."

"Speak?" she repeated, her spine straightening. There had to be a weapon in this room somewhere, although she wasn't quite sure what she would do with it. "What would you like to talk about, Drake?" Sarcasm loaded her words.

"I can tell you're upset."

"No shit," she snapped.

His nostrils flared. "There's no reason to swear. Queens don't swear."

"How do you know? Have you known any queens?" She gestured around the room, her attention focused on the large monitors in the corner. "What are those yellow dots?"

"They're enhanced females," he said, his gaze remaining on her. "We have systems all over the world, and now we're using satellite technology to identify them by energy signatures."

So he admitted to tracking them. "We've done the same by hacking into the sensors you placed in various cities," she admitted. "We know about the satellites too. What we don't know is why." She focused on those greenish purple eyes she'd known since childhood. If he wanted to kill Ulric, then he didn't want the females so Ulric could allow his soldiers to partake in the devastating ritual. "Why are you kidnapping enhanced females?"

Drake waved a hand in the air. "It's irrelevant. It doesn't have anything to do with you, so you don't need to worry about it."

"You know, as a condescending dick, you're doing a great job." The skirt was hampering her movements. If she needed to kick, it was going to be difficult.

"I hardly think name-calling is necessary," he said. "If you're trying to get me to lose my temper, I don't have one."

Everybody had a temper. "I thought you and I were going to work together."

"We are," he said. "Between the two of us, we will broker peace, after we kill Ulric."

She couldn't tell if he was lying or not. "So you really do want him dead?"

"Yes. He's undermining my authority, and his appetites are uncontrollable. He harms women. He harms everyone, actually, and I don't like it. In addition, he wants to duplicate that ritual he performed long ago, and I can't let that many enhanced females die."

For the first time, a kernel of hope unfurled within her. "You don't want to hurt people?"

"No. We need them for mates." Drake appeared long and lethal on the leather sofa. "I really do want peace. Once the Realm is destroyed, I'll have it."

Her throat hurt from trying not to scream at him. "Then what are you doing kidnapping enhanced females, if you're not helping Ulric?"

"It's none of your business," he said slowly, enunciating each word. "I understand things are different in the Realm, but in my nation, everybody has a place. Our society is very organized."

One of her eyebrows rose on its own, and she realized her head still hurt from teleporting. "What exactly is my place, as you see it?"

"As queen, you can have anything and do anything you want."

"What if I want to help enhanced females escape?"

He looked away and then back. "That is not going to happen. You can beat your head against the wall as much as you want, but they're here as long as they're useful, and then I set them free."

"What does that mean?" she asked, the skin prickling along her nape.

"None of your business," he repeated.

Was he just bringing the women here to see if the soldiers wanted them and letting them go if they didn't? It didn't make sense to her. "What about Ulric's grand plan to kill all enhanced females?"

"That was never his plan," Drake said, gesturing to her tea. "Drink. I promise you, so long as there isn't an accident during the acquisition phase, none of these females get harmed."

Her head jerked up. "The acquisition phase? Is that what you're calling kidnapping? Nice." She'd heard of euphemisms before, but that was a new one to her. No way was she drinking that tea.

"Thank you," he drawled. "I do my best."

She looked at him, trying to find the boy he'd once been. "I thought we were friends."

"We were." He shrugged. "I still consider you a friend. I think you'll make a fine queen, as I said."

"You know I'm human, right?" The words escaped her before she could stop them.

He studied her for several long moments. "I don't understand."

"Neither do I," she admitted, looking away. Several books were carelessly piled on the bookshelf. One with black scales was tipped to the side. Her heart beat faster, and she hid her excitement. "However, as you know, all immortal beings take on the characteristics of one species only, regardless of their lineage. Apparently, I've taken on the aspect of being human. I probably could die, Drake."

It was impressive that he sat there with his eyes barely moving. Chaotic thoughts were no doubt skittering through his brain, but he revealed nothing. As a fully grown male, his face had sharpened with age. His skin was pale, and long lashes surrounded those odd green eyes. He was conventionally handsome in a sharply defined way, and yet she could still glimpse the boy he'd been.

He leaned forward. "Well then, you won't be human after we mate. Perhaps your dormant genes will awaken, and you'll be more powerful than you hoped."

As an idea, it wasn't a bad one. "I think you could have just asked me to mate you," she said. "You didn't have to kidnap me." To think she'd been prepared to do just that, but now he'd shown his true colors. He was cold and unfeeling, and he'd kill anybody to get what he wanted. Even her.

"No, I didn't need to kidnap you. But it was the most expedient method, and I wanted Paxton Phoenix here. When you agreed to meet in the dreamworld, I knew that the two of you would be in the same place in the real world, and I took a chance that you'd be in your bedroom in Realm territory."

The more information she could get from him, the stronger she'd be. "How long have you known you could teleport?"

"About ten years," he admitted, and he'd kept that secret the entire time. What else had he kept from her? "Isn't it ironic that the Seven created this situation for us?"

She ran through the events of the last couple of decades. What else had Drake lied about? "Do you remember when my uncles were taken by the Kurjans?" Sam, Logan, and Garrett had all been kidnapped at one point and tortured mercilessly before they'd escaped. "You told me at the time that you had no idea they'd been taken. Was that the truth?"

"No," Drake said. "I knew where they were, and I knew who was torturing them. My father was one of the people questioning them."

"So you lied to me," she said.

"Only because I had to. You don't understand the way war works."

"Nobody understands the way war works." She threw her hands up. "The whole point of our connection was we wouldn't be at war, that we would trust each other and be honest."

For years, Paxton had been warning her that Drake was lying and that he wasn't the person she wanted him to be, the person she needed him to be. "I don't know what my path is," she muttered. "I do know that we're supposed to find peace together."

Drake reclaimed his glass and swallowed the rest of the Scotch. "I do know your path. You're going to be my queen."

"What if I don't want to be queen?" She stood, ready to fight.

His gaze was cold. Frozen. "Irrelevant. I would prefer to have your acquiescence, but I don't need it."

"Are you truly so unfeeling?"

He sighed as if annoyed she didn't understand him. "This is who I am. My path has always been clear. I knew I would lead the

Kurjan nation, and I knew I would take down the Realm, from within if necessary."

"Lying to me through the years, even when we were kids, was an acceptable way for you to do that." It was strange, but his betrayal hurt. She had thought they were friends. He had known they were enemies.

"Sit down," he ordered.

She sat, trying to find some sort of way to get through to him. "I won't be forced into a mating."

If anything, he looked bored. "You'll be forced in any direction I want you to go. It is completely up to you what kind of life you have with my people. You can be queen and have all the freedom, riches, friends you want, or you can be queen and be kept in nice little gilded cage. It is up to you, but you will give me sons."

Her mouth went dry. There was nothing soft or relenting about him. Worse yet, there didn't seem to be any emotion. He'd never shown a lot as they'd been growing up, but she had figured that was just since he was out of his element in the dreamworld. She now realized he'd been far nicer there.

The door opened, and Vero and Hunter, disguised as a Kurjan, strode into the room. "How could you not tell me?" Vero asked, his voice a low rumble of anger.

She turned to keep him fully in her sights. She'd only met him in dreamworlds, and he'd always seemed pretty mellow. He was anything but that right now.

"I didn't think you needed to know," Drake said.

Vero just stared at him, and for a moment, Hope thought he might take a shot at Drake. "Well, you're a fucking bastard."

She caught her breath. So much for those two being on the same page.

Drake glanced at Hunter.

Hope was very careful not to look at her cousin. She couldn't give him away, so she kept her focus on Vero. "What's going on?" she asked.

Rage mottled Vero's handsome face. "I have a brother."

"Not for long," Drake said. "As soon as we announce this mating, I'm going to spend a good few days with him. There isn't going to be anything left, I promise."

Hope looked at Drake and then Vero. "What do you mean you have a brother?"

It was Hunter who spoke. "Apparently Paxton's true father was a Kurjan named Talt. He was also Vero's father."

Hope's world spun away and came back. "Wait, what? Pax is a Kurjan?"

Chapter Thirty

Hope couldn't breathe as she looked at the males around her. "Pax is not a Kurjan." That was impossible; Drake was just messing with them all. "He can go in the sun. He doesn't look anything like a Kurjan."

Drake smiled, and the sight was not pleasant. "Apparently our scientists were hard at work pursuing more than one avenue with their research. Paxton's mother was taken during the last war. A few demonesses were experimented upon. It was a dangerous and new type of in vitro fertilization, because Talt had not yet mated Vero's mother. Most of the females died, but Paxton's mother lived."

"She must've been terrified," Hope whispered, horror filling her.

"Yes," Drake said. "But according to the journal, she was more frightened of the demon nation than of us. So when she discovered she was pregnant, she followed orders."

Hope sat back in her chair, feeling as if she might fall. "So how?" None of this made any sense.

Vero shook his head. "I can't believe it. I remember my father as being cruel, but I didn't think even he'd do something like this." He looked at Hope. "Apparently they genetically altered Paxton in the womb, so he would look mostly demon like his mother. They made the Kurjan genes dormant until..." He swallowed.

"He was hit by those darts?" Hope asked, her eyes widening. "Those were meant for Paxton, not for me." That's why the drug had disappeared from her system while it had seemed to take hold in Paxton's. It was all unbelievable. "What was Talt's grand plan?"

Drake shrugged. "From what I've read, the plan was for Paxton's mother to raise him in the demon nation, train and guide him, so we'd have somebody on the inside. It was brilliant, really. But then a few years in, apparently she changed her mind."

"Of course she changed her mind," Hope said. "She saw how people should live and how women should be treated. No doubt she knew instantly she didn't want her son growing up in your environment."

"That's what it looks like," Vero said, tapping the leather-bound book in his hand. "They ordered her death, and Paelotin followed through."

Hope's mind spun. "So Paelotin was working with the Kurjans from the beginning?"

"Yes. He was paid a fortune," Drake said.

"When did you find out?" Hunter asked Drake directly.

Drake looked at Vero and then glanced at Hope before turning to stare at Hunter. "I discovered Talt's journal about ten years ago."

Vero took a step back, his blue eyes widening and his shoulders squaring. "You discovered I had a brother a decade ago?"

"You don't have a brother," Drake returned quickly. "Paxton Phoenix is not your brother. Biologically, you may share a sperm donor, but considering he's going to be dead before next week, I wouldn't get too attached."

"I just saw him," Vero said. "I don't think he's going to survive the next couple of hours. You've shot him full of too many of those darts."

"That would be unfortunate," Drake said. "But it took that much of the drug to awaken the Kurjan genes. He needs to be half Kurjan before I kill him. I want to take him into the sun and

show him how much it hurts. He's always made fun of me for no
liking the sun—it's time for him to feel her bite."

Hope shook her head. "He never made fun of you, but he di
see the real you, and I didn't." She should have listened to Paxton
"So much for trying to find peace."

She looked at the other two warriors in the room. If ther
was ever a chance to cause a problem for Drake, this was i
"Vero, do you know what the Kurjans are doing with all th
enhanced females?"

Vero shifted his gaze to Drake before returning his focus t
Hope. "It's my understanding that they're just cataloging them.
He winced. "Kind of like wild animals. Like geese or moose."

Her jaw dropped. "You mean they're tagging the women t
keep track of them like scientists do for certain animal species?

"That's what I've been told," Vero said. "This is the first tim
I've actually been in this camp. It doesn't feel right, though." H
looked at his cousin.

"No, it certainly doesn't," Hunter said.

Drake's gaze wandered to his computer area and back. "Harolc
make yourself useful for once and escort the future queen to he
room. Vero, I need to speak with you. We have plans to make."

Hope's heart leaped. She tried to keep the outrage on her fac
as Hunter gestured her toward the door. "I'm not done with this.
she said, her head held high as she swept out of the room.

Hunter followed her and shut the door, his hand instantly o
her elbow. "Keep moving," he whispered.

She walked partially into the great room. Noting that the roor
was vacant, she turned and hugged her cousin. He'd grown an
filled out in the time they'd been separated.

He hugged her back, patting her shoulder. "Are yo
okay?" he asked.

"I am," she said. "How about you?"

"I'm fine."

It was time for Hunter to come home. "We have to save Paxton

Hunter's jaw visibly hardened. "This is a two-pronged mission. First I get you out, then I get Paxton."

"I am not leaving without him."

"You are," Hunter said, his fingers firm on her arm as he pulled her across the great room to the back, where a sliding glass door led to a massive snow-covered deck. A trail had been kicked through the snow on the other side of the deck toward a dark and foreboding forest.

Hope tried to pull away.

Hunter ignored her, staring outside. "I have transport waiting for you, but we're going to have to run."

She started to protest, but he cut her off.

"Trust me, I will get Paxton out of here. If you're both here, Drake will use you against each other. He'll hurt him to force your acquiescence. He'll hurt you to mess with Paxton. I have to take you out of play."

Hope took a big deep breath. "I just can't leave him, Hunter."

Her cousin's gaze softened. He didn't look right with the Kurjan features, and that surgery had to have been painful. "I know, I get it, but he's nowhere we can reach right now. He's in that cage in the middle of the courtyard, and we can't just walk out there. You need to trust me. I will get him free, and we will both meet you. Please."

Hope took a deep breath. She trusted her cousin almost as much as anybody in the world. He'd been undercover since he was sixteen within the Kurjan nation, and no doubt he had plans in place. "Can you trust Vero?"

Hunter winced. "I don't know. He's actually a good guy, but he has taken a vow to follow Drake. And he and Drake are blood like you and I are." He leaned in and kissed her cheek. "Come on, cuz. Let me get you out of here."

"All right." Hope had to go on trust. "But please tell me you'll get Paxton free."

"I promise. Follow me." Hunter opened the door, looked both ways, and pulled her out. He glanced at his watch. "The soldier are on a five-minute rotation today, so we have five minutes to get through the forest. It's going to be close. Are you any faster than you were before?"

"No."

"All right." He looked down at the dress. "We don't have time for you to change out of that thing, so you're just going to have to hold the skirt up and run. If it gets too close, I'm going to throw you over my shoulder. Okay? I want you prepared."

She hated that he might have to do that because she wasn't fast enough, but there was no other choice. "Understood."

Cold instantly slammed into her, and she ducked her head. There were so many layers to the bottom of the dress that her legs were warm, but the bodice was flimsy, leaving her skin exposed and chilled. "I'm okay, let's go," she said.

The shoes skidded on the ice, but she didn't complain. Instead, she ran as fast as she could behind Hunter. He had to slow down for her, but he dodged and wove through the trees as if he'd memorized the entire forest. He was impressive, and she would make sure to tell Uncle Dage that he should be very proud of his son.

They were in the middle of the dark forest when he paused, turning. "Are you doing okay?"

She panted, her breath filling the air. "Yes, I'm fine," she lied. "Are we close?"

"We're getting there," he said. "I know where most of the scout patrol, but every once in a while there's a random one. If I start to fight, you keep running. I have a car waiting for you."

"Okay," she said. "I'm ready."

Something cracked. "That's unfortunate," Drake said, coming around a corner up ahead. "I'm not ready to lose you quite yet, Hope."

Hunter jumped in front of her and set his stance. Soldiers dropped from the tops of the trees all around them, their guns out. Hunter tensed.

"No," Hope said, grabbing his arm. "There are at least twenty of them. You're good, but nobody's that good."

Hunter looked at Drake. "I couldn't let you force her to mate. As a Kurjan, I felt I was doing the right thing."

Drake laughed, his low voice roaring through the trees. "As a Kurjan? Give me a break. You're not a Kurjan."

Hunter blinked. "What do you mean?"

"I've known exactly who you are for at least this last year, Hunter." Drake smiled and addressed the nearest soldiers. "Take him, find another cage, and put him next to Paxton."

Hunter fought them, but he was outmatched. He did some serious damage to a couple of the soldiers, but there were just too many of them. Soon they had him trussed up, and they dragged him away.

The wind whistled, freezing Hope's skin, but she stood tall and faced the Kurjan. "If you knew he was Hunter, why did you let him live?"

Drake shrugged. "I didn't think it'd be this easy to get you here and thought there might be a trade necessary in the future." He grabbed her arm, digging his fingers in until she winced. "You need to understand this now, my queen. There is no escape for you, so you might as well stop fighting me."

Chapter Thirty-One

After a nail-biting afternoon during which Hope was locked in the opulent bedroom with nothing to do but pace back and forth trying to catch a glimpse of the now-missing Paxton and Hunter, soldiers escorted her back down to the same study, where a table had been set with white linen and crystal goblets. Drake poured two glasses of wine and gestured her to the other seat. "I thought I could show you how life might be with me," he said.

She looked at him. "You don't know me at all. I'm a strategist who likes to work. I'm happiest out in the field, Drake."

"That's unacceptable for a queen," he said. "Your other hobbies won't get in the way, I'm sure. Sit down."

She sat and once again eyed the bookshelf. There were several tomes she wanted to get her hands on—maybe there was something in one of them about killing not only Ulric but Drake. Maybe that was her destiny. "How familiar are you with these books?"

"Not very. Several of them were just dug up," he admitted. "Vero is usually the one poring over books. With Hunter."

Fresh concern welled up in her. "What have you done with him?"

"He's in a cage, much like Paxton. I don't want to start our life together on a contentious note, so I'm going to make you an offer." Drake nudged her glass toward her, and she picked it up.

A woman brought in two plates laden with steak and potatoes and placed them on the table. Without saying anything, she scurried away. Hope watched her go. "I don't like the way your females look around here. They appear terrified."

"Most of them have been recently kidnapped. I'll set them free soon," he muttered. "Human females scare easily. You know that." His gaze was appraising. "You, however, do not. I appreciate that in a mate."

"What's your offer?" She sipped the wine. It was rich and full-bodied, but the tannins hit her stomach and made her want to throw up.

He leaned back. "Here is the deal. I will let Hunter Kayrs go immediately, and I will let Paxton live after a week if he can survive that long. Take that as a mating gift to you. In addition, I will give you full access to our medical database and all of the kidnapped enhanced females. You may speak with them, you may advocate for them, and you may see what we're doing."

"If I refuse?" she asked.

"That would be unwise. Should you refuse, I will tear both Paxton and Hunter apart, inch by inch, in front of you," he said. "Then I will kill all of the enhanced females we have, and I will torture the ones we're about to claim. Finally, you will mate me." He shrugged. "So choose your path. You either come willingly or not, but one way, you will avoid monstrous pain for people you care about. Either way, you will end up in the same place."

She couldn't breathe. Her throat was closing, and the edges of her vision were narrowing. "Where are Paxton and Hunter right now?"

"I couldn't keep my men off them the whole time," Drake drawled. "I believe Ulric is having a chat with your cousin right now, and several of my men are interrogating Paxton. He's not holding up very well. I think the genetic manipulation may have weakened him more than the scientists thought it would. I will spare his life if you do as I ask, but I truly don't know what kind of life that will be."

She had to get out of there before she threw up. "I need to think about this," she said, her stomach aching. She stood, swiping a knife from the table into her sleeve with a sure hand. "I'm not hungry."

"All right, let me sweeten the pot," Drake said. "Not only will you be rescuing your friends and the enhanced women, but if you mate me, we will make peace with the Realm. There's no other avenue, so in effect, you'll be saving everybody. It's a small sacrifice to make, Hope, and I think you know that."

She had contemplated the sacrifice she'd probably need to make her entire life. When she had been younger, she'd believed that her path was meant to be with Drake, that maybe it wouldn't be a sacrifice, and somehow they'd fall madly in love as her parents had after meeting in the dreamworld. Now that she was here face-to-face with reality, she didn't know which avenue to follow. Any romanticization of the situation had long been blown away.

Her heart ached, and she needed Paxton. Right now. "So you're comfortable threatening or blackmailing me to be your mate," she said. "That's where you are in life."

"That's exactly where I am," he said, not rising to the bait. "If you want peace and safety for everybody you care about, it's a very simple decision. You may go now. Why don't you think upon it tonight? At dawn, you will speak into the cameras outside the lodge, telling my people and yours about your decision. I think we both know what it's going to be."

Giving him a look, she walked gracefully in her long skirt to the bookshelf. "Fine, but I'm going to read and let my subconscious work on the entire situation tonight." She tried to make her choice appear random as she grabbed several books, making sure to put the scaly black bound one in the center. She was sure it was the other half of the dragon book she'd read the other day.

"Very well. You may read all you want. Be ready at dawn, Hope, and don't disappoint me. There are a lot of people counting on you."

She strode to the door, her heart pounding, and made it nearly across the living area with her guards before Drake was suddenly there. "Wait a minute." He leaned over and studied the books, a small smile tilting his lips. "You impress me." He pulled the dragon skin–covered book as well as an ancient Greek book out of the pile and tossed them on a small table near the door. "Not those two." Grabbing her arm and digging in, he pulled her toward him, his expression hard. "Don't play games with me. Ever." He pushed her away.

Pain vibrated from the bruises he'd just left on her arm. She swallowed. "I don't know you at all."

His sneer distorted his handsome features. "You never did. But you will now, and only you can decide what kind of life you want with me." He turned, already dismissing her but addressing the guards. "Make sure she's locked in for the night."

* * * *

Hope had to get her hands on that book, but she also needed to save her friends. She had no doubt both Paxton and Hunter were being tortured that very minute, and there wasn't a thing she could do about it. More soldiers lined the roof outside, making it impossible to escape out the window. With the guards outside her door, she was truly secured for the night.

Lyrica appeared again to help her get out of the stupid dress. Together, they tried to find something for her to sleep in. "It's all pretty sexy," she said. "I don't see anything all that comfortable."

"There's got to be some sort of T-shirt." Hope pulled out the bottom drawer and rifled through it. It was full of silky camisoles with lace everywhere. "He's got a lace thing," she muttered. Finally giving up, she just pulled a pink-and-white silk sheath over her head. "Do you have any idea how I could get out of here?"

Lyrica threw up her hands. "If I knew, girl, I would've already gone that way. But we'll figure it out." She patted Hope's arm, forced cheerfulness in her voice.

"Sure, we will," Hope said. "Thank you for your help." She sucked in air. "What have they done to you so far?" She believed Drake's threat that he would kill all the captured females if she didn't obey him.

Lyrica looked at the door and then leaned in. "We have strict orders not to tell you, but fuck them. They've been injecting drug into us. Mostly in our arms, but sometimes in our heads. Do you know what it could be?"

Drugs? That was the last thing Hope would've expected. "Maybe." She thought through the facts but couldn't reach a solution. "The Kurjans experimented on females by injecting Ulric's blood into their brains and creating a sort of tumor. Then they hypnotized and trained them to kill. Are you being trained? Have you lost time?" It had all happened to Dessie, and then she'd tried to kill Garrett. But the doctors had taken the tumor from her head.

"No," Lyrica said, rubbing the top of her head. "Did they give me a freaking tumor?"

"I don't know," Hope admitted. "That doesn't make sense."

A guard opened the door. "Move."

"You bet." Lyrica took the dress with her as she went.

Hope chewed her lip and then pushed the nightstand in front of the door. It wouldn't stop anybody from entering, but at least she'd hear them come in.

Then she climbed into bed. She didn't know if this was going to work, but she had to reach Pax. She practiced several deep breathing exercises before finally dropping into sleep. She remained dreamless for a while and then forced herself to create a dreamworld, trying to build some sort of shield around it. Then she pulled Paxton in.

He landed on the snowy white sand and rolled over to sit up, his jaw fierce. "Are you all right?"

"I am." She rushed to him and fell to her knees, reaching for his face. "How badly are you hurt?"

He looked down at his arms. "I'm fine in the dreamworld." He shook sand off and noted the calm blue lake. Up above, the sky shone down, warming them both. "Are you okay?" He reached for her, his gaze intense, his body still healthy in the dreamworld.

"I'm fine," she said. "Drake told me they're torturing you right now."

Paxton's leg twitched. "Don't worry about me." His gaze flicked away and then back. "Did you hear that I'm half Kurjan?"

"Do you believe them?"

"Yes. I'm changing, and all for the bad. But none of that matters. We have to get you to safety. Is there any way we can reach the Realm from here?"

She had to save him somehow. "From the dreamworld? No. We're not really here, Pax," she said. "That's not how it works. We need a plan."

"Our plan is to get you to safety," Paxton said, his body jerking.

She clutched his arms. "What was that?"

"Nothing, don't worry about it."

Realization smacked her. "Oh my God. They're torturing you right this second, aren't they?"

He grinned, the look fierce. "They're trying to bring me back awake, but I like this unconscious state." His body jerked again. "Hope, no matter what you do, get free. I think Vero will help you. If he does, you have to go. Don't worry about me."

"I'm not going to leave you in Kurjan territory."

"Yes, you are." He grabbed her, kissed her hard, and then soft.

Conflicting emotions spun through her as she clung to him. "No, wait!"

He slowly disappeared from sight. They must have brought him back to consciousness. She pressed a fist against her mouth, trying not to cry. How in the world was she going to get him free?

She looked around the beautiful dreamworld she'd created and wished she could bring Paxton back in. Her gaze caught

on the green book lying open on a dark slate rock farthe
down the lakeshore.

That was it. She was done playing around with this thing. Sh
stood and stomped down the beach, willing it to stay in place
The book didn't move. A slight wind started to rustle the page.
Maybe she was supposed to be in Kurjan territory or in the sam
vicinity as both Paxton and Drake to reach it. She didn't know.

Her heart thundering, she sprinted the last several yards an
leaped across the sand to land on the book. The wind rushed ou
of her lungs, and the bound corners cut into her skin, but she hel
tight and yanked it off the rock, rolling several times on the beach

Sand coated her hair and her body, but she didn't care. Sh
sat up, holding tight, and then flattened the book on the sand. *
shut instantly. "Oh no you don't," she said, keeping her hand o
the leather-bound cover.

She flipped it open to see the face of a woman she didn
recognize. Words came into focus, darkening on the page, a l
of it in Old English. She read several pages about a woman wh
looked a lot like her, an ancestor of some sort. The urge to rea
the entire tome drove her, but she didn't have time right now
she wanted to save both Paxton and Hunter. Instead, she riffle
through the thick pages, heavy with ink and illustrations, an
then stopped cold at the sight of her parents as children. Jan
and Zane, their images perfectly captured by an artist's hand.

Unable to stop herself, she read about the first time they'd me
Lovingly tracing each line, she read about their romance, an
their difficulties, and their final triumph. Turning the page, sh
saw herself as a baby. Her heartbeat started to increase. Finall

The answers were coming.

She flipped the pages several times and found a full-pag
illustration of her in Kurjan territory, in that ridiculous gow
she'd worn last night. She might have looked like a queen, bu
she looked like a furious one.

She liked that.

Then she turned the page, and it was blank. She waited for the words to appear, for the page to darken.

Nothing happened.

Wait a minute. That didn't make sense. She flipped over several more pages and found them all blank. She carefully cracked open the book and patted it. "Come on, let's see what's there." Nothing. The wind picked up and rustled the pages back and forth.

She stubbornly flipped to the current page, right after the illustration of her in the dress. Nothing formed on the page. She pounded on the book. "Why won't you show me?" The words and illustrations, the directions she needed, didn't appear. Tears streamed down her face. She had believed. She had truly thought once she could read the book, she would know her path. Lifting her head, she screamed to the heavens. Then she went silent, her body aching.

A form wavered next to her. She gasped and fell to the side.

Paxton came into view on his knees, his eyes blinking. "I must be unconscious again," he murmured. "You're still here." His eyes widened. "You have the book."

She stared down at the useless book, her lips trembling. "It's blank, Pax. Everything after yesterday is just blank." She looked up, her entire body feeling stunned.

He nodded, his eyes gleaming more silver than blue in the dreamworld. Wisdom glowed in them, along with a fierce determination. "Of course it's blank, sweetheart. You make your own fate. She only records it."

Chapter Thirty-Two

Paxton sat back on the loose dirt in the underground cell, listening intently. He tried to send healing cells to his damaged organs, ignoring the open wounds across his body. It was odd that Ulric preferred a bullwhip to striking with his hands, but he certainly knew how to use it. "Hunter," Paxton called out. No answer.

Damn it, they still had him somewhere else, being tortured no doubt. Paxton couldn't see because his eyes were swollen shut, so he tried to spare some cells to get them to work again. His blood was flowing more freely, having finally accepted the additional drugs. It might be a good thing they'd shot him full of whatever it was that had jump-started his genetic alterations, because now that his body was accepting the change, he was getting stronger again.

Even so, he had taken damage to the heart during the last beating, and he had to fix that before anything else. Seeing Hope in the dreamworld had calmed him somewhat. For now, at least, she was safe.

Time crawled. His eyes healed within an hour, and he could open them even though he was still working on internal damage. His foot was twisted at an odd angle, so he tried to fix that bone as well. The healing cells were finally doing their job.

He couldn't believe he was part Kurjan. A lot of his childhood had been spent hating himself, and now he knew the reason why. Part of him was evil.

The drip, drip, drip of water in the background caught his attention, and he listened intently for any signs of Hunter. There was nothing. He didn't think they would kill the king's kid, but then again, he wasn't sure. It would be quite the statement to make.

He had to figure out a way out of this cell in order to find both Hunter and Hope—and somehow get them out of Kurjan territory. A door opened at the end of the tunnel, and heavy footsteps clomped downstairs. It wasn't Hunter. Even so, Pax forced himself to stand, putting most of his weight on his good foot.

Drake came into view through the iron bars. "Looks like the general took out his bullwhip," he said mildly.

"He does have a certain fondness for it," Pax said. "Where's Hope?"

"She's sleeping, probably."

Good. As long as she was sleeping away from this imbecile right now, she was safe. "What's your grand plan here?" he asked. "You know the last two times you've gone to war with the Realm... you've lost." The taste of blood kept filling his mouth.

"Yes, but this time I have an ace in the hole." Drake chuckled. "I do like that expression. I've been around a number of humans the last several years, and they have the sweetest little expressions, at least the females do."

"The ones you keep kidnapping?" Paxton asked. "Why don't you explain that one to me? We are cousins, after all." The thought made him want to puke up more blood.

Drake studied him, his metallic-green eyes sober. "It's odd. I was surprised, but I guess it makes sense. Our people turned to science long before the Realm did." He shoved his hands in his black cargo pants. "As for my temporarily collecting enhanced females, you're not going to live long enough to worry about it."

At least the soldier was finally laying it on the line. "You've been a liar all these years, and I've known it." Pax stepped closer to the bars. If he could just break one open, he could get to this asshole

Drake's expression twisted into a smirk. "Yes, it has been necessary. Hope's a sweet girl. She'll make a fine queen if she'll just accept her lot."

"She'll never be your queen."

"Then she dies," Drake said simply.

Pax wouldn't let that happen. He didn't know how, but there was no way he'd fail the woman he'd always love, in life and most probably in his imminent death. "She belongs to the Realm. You need to let her go."

"You believe she belongs to you?" Drake asked.

A rock-solid fist seemed to strike Paxton's gut. He didn't need anybody else to beat him up—he could do a fine job himself. "No Hope is way too good to be mated to a half Kurjan." He knew that fact to his soul, and part of him had always known she'd never be his. His role in life had been to protect her, and it would no doubt be the last thing he ever did. He would get her out of there. He would get her to safety, and then fate could take him. If his heart didn't heal, he didn't have a long time to live, anyway.

Drake laughed. "So you admit you're not good enough for her?"

"There's nobody good enough for her," Paxton drawled, his eye socket finally popping back into place. "But no, definitely anybody with Kurjan blood should be kept as far away from Hope Kayrs-Kyllwood as possible."

"At least we're partially on the same page." Drake looked at his watch. "I believe the general should be finished with Hunter within the hour. I'm sure he'll be back for you." He turned and walked away.

"Can't wait," Paxton muttered, going to work on his heart again. He had to repair the organ before the general drew out his knives once again. He worked in silence for about another hour hoping the general would hurry up and finish with Hunter so the kid could heal himself.

A door opened, and more heavy footsteps thumped down the stairs. He turned his head. To his surprise, Vero came into view.

Paxton didn't know the young warrior very well, but the blue eyes intrigued him. "Hello, brother," he drawled.

Vero snorted. "That was quite a surprise." His gaze sought Paxton, as if looking for something.

"I bet," Pax said. There was a kindness about the young Kurjan that he hadn't felt in many of the soldiers. He stepped toward the bars again. "I'm surprised your cousin didn't tell you the truth." It didn't make sense to him. Even though his family sucked, he'd seen how Hope's cousins treated each other, how brothers and sisters covered each other's backs. It was sad it wasn't the same in the Kurjan nation.

Vero shrugged. "It's who he is."

Paxton might never get this chance again. So he took it. "Apparently, we share a father. What was he like?" Curiosity took him. Even though his body was in so much pain, it was difficult to breathe.

"He was not a nice male," Vero said slowly. "In fact, he was a real jerk. He hit, he kicked, and it was almost a relief when he died." Vero's face lost all expression, making him appear even more dangerous. "Until I went to live with Uncle Terre, who was just as bad." He shook his head. "You know, the only father I've never seen hit his son was Dayne, Drake's father. He was proud of him and looked forward to Drake taking over the Kurjan nation someday."

"It's too bad Drake turned into such a jackass," Paxton replied.

Vero cleared his throat. "It's like that everywhere, correct?"

"No." Pax forced blood to his broken hand. "Even though my fake father liked to hit, the warriors in both the demon and vampire nations don't beat their children." He wiped at a wound on his elbow. "Neither do the shifters. You and I didn't have th best of examples."

Vero exhaled. "I would like to find a better way."

That was exactly what Pax had hoped to hear, but one thin; at a time. "You're a decent guy, Vero. I can feel it whether yo like it or not. Tell me you're not going to let Drake force Hope t mate him. You wouldn't let him rape her, would you?" He was a blunt as he could be, trying to make an impact. It was possible t force a mating bond, and the act would be brutal.

Vero stepped back. "No, I don't want to see Hope hurt, bu Drake is the leader of the Kurjan nation." His voice was low an hoarse with a thread of pain.

"He shouldn't be," Paxton said. "Anybody who thinks that a way to form an alliance or a family has no business leading You know that."

Vero studied him. "My entire life I wished for a brother. I trie to turn Drake into one, but his ambition and his alliance wit Ulric prohibited that."

"I wanted a brother too," Paxton admitted as his spleen finall mended itself. "I've seen some of the Realm kids with thei siblings. Not a lot of them have brothers or sisters because it's s hard for immortals to procreate. But the ones who do, it look like..." He trailed off.

"A safety net," Vero supplied. "Someone who alway has your back."

Pax had spent eons wanting that kind of support. He'd had taste of it working with Hope's team the other day. Being Kurja guaranteed he'd never work with them again. "Exactly. Hope an her cousins are like that as well," Paxton said. "I don't think I hav long to live, but I'm happy I have a brother, even for a short time He wished he had more time left to get to know Vero. He had younger brother. A surprising sense of responsibility and dut settled on his shoulders, but he cast it away, knowing it was to late. Still, maybe he could set Vero on the right path. "I'm going to save Hope, and you can help. Be the hero here, Vero. Let me out."

"I can't." Vero looked over his shoulder and down the tunnel. "Even if I wanted to, there are guards at every station. You wouldn't make it five feet, and then I'd end up in there."

It was a good point. Vero couldn't help Hope if he was imprisoned. "Then go free her. Get her to a vehicle and then step back." Pax's girl was a speed demon, and she knew how to drive. He just had to give her a chance.

"She's guarded as well," Vero murmured just as his watch dinged. He read the face and then concentrated once more on Pax. "I must go. If nothing else, I'm glad we found a chance to meet and speak with each other."

"We can do more than talk," Paxton said, squaring his shoulders. "We could fix all of this. We could create safety for everybody."

Vero's eyes glimmered and then went blank. "You don't know the Kurjan nation, my friend. Besides, do you really think Hope belongs with you?"

"No," Paxton said honestly. "It was a dream that kept me going for a long time, but now that I know the truth, hell no. She belongs with some strong warrior in the Realm, hopefully a purebred demon, not a mongrel hybrid like me." There was no doubt evil lived in his veins, so apparently Paelotin had been right. Who knew?

Vero looked down the hallway. "I need to go. I do want to check on Hope and make sure she's all right."

"You need to do more than that, brother," Paxton said quietly.

Chapter Thirty-Three

Hope walked down the stairs to Drake's study, her head held high, her heart beating too fast, and her dress way too heavy for her frame. Drake had sent it along with four women to help her get ready. It was an elaborate white ball gown strewn with too many diamonds to count. The skirt was floor length with a small train, the shape A-line, and the bodice corset style. It was perfect for a princess and disastrous for a woman ready to fight her way out of a Kurjan compound.

The guards left her at the door with a stern warning to wait for the king and a rough reminder that guards were everywhere.

She stood there for a moment and then saw the dragon-skin book still perched haphazardly on the table. Hurrying toward it, she snatched it up and looked around wildly. Her neckline was surprisingly revealing, with the bodice split down the middle, and her neck and shoulders were bare. Taking a deep breath, she yanked up the folds of her skirt and shoved the book up the back of one thigh, securing it in the side of her flimsy panties. When she let the material drop back down, the skirt was heavy enough to hold the tome to her thigh.

For now, anyway.

Drake entered the study in a perfectly pressed black uniform with his silver medals recently polished. His hair was brushed back from his face, and he stood tall and ready with an ornate wooden box in one hand. He'd be handsome if she didn't want to kill him.

He stopped cold. "You look beautiful."

"Thank you," she answered automatically, searching his face for any hint of the boy she'd once considered a friend. "You are really going through with this?"

"We both are." He strode toward her and flipped open the box to reveal a stunning sapphire-and-diamond tiara. "The stones match your eyes." Without asking, he slid it onto her head. "There you go. My queen."

She swallowed, ignoring the pain along her scalp. "I don't want to do this."

"I don't care." He exhaled, his gaze somber. "The nation and my leadership are all that matter. You need to learn that now." He glanced at his watch. "Once we step outside that door, I expect you to comport yourself as a queen, or there will be consequences."

"Meaning what?"

He straightened his already straight shirt, and when he spoke, his voice remained calm. "I really do want to find peace with your people. However, I'm prepared to finish this war as quickly as it began." He took her hand and led her across the room to the computer area, where he quickly brought up three screens. Her home in northern Idaho came into view.

"What is this?" she asked with a sinking feeling in her stomach.

"We've tapped into the satellites. We have missiles pointed at key targets, and I have a force amassed in the vicinity of northern Idaho. In addition, everybody here is prepared to go to war today," he said. "The Realm isn't expecting it."

She took a step back. He was right. The Realm was not expecting an attack. But they had defenses in place, good ones, so she took a deep breath.

His smile wasn't kind. "We know about the defense shield. The last time Paelotin was at Realm headquarters, we made good use of him."

She put a hand to her stomach. "He breached the defense shield?"

"He most certainly did. There are bombs all around the shield as well as inside the control unit, thanks to Paelotin. He turned out to be much handier than we thought. All I have to do is push a button and that defense goes down." He lifted a hand. "Oh, I don't doubt the Realm will fight and fight hard, but we'll have the element of surprise. And I promise you, I'll take out everybody you love."

She gagged, needing to throw up.

"Don't," he said sharply. "Don't even think about it. That dress cost me a fortune." He grabbed her hand and pulled her all the way back to the front door. "I hope you understand me."

"I understand you perfectly," she said, wishing she had a Kurjan blade. She'd take off his damn head right there. "My people are better fighters than you think."

"I've studied them my whole life," he said. "If you need more incentive, here it is. If you don't choose me in front of the cameras, then Paxton and Hunter will die in great pain." He sighed and looked down at her again. "Paxton is a mutt. A Kurjan-demon mutt with no real past and no future. He's a commoner. Too common. You can't want that life for yourself or your children. He's a nothing."

"That's not true," she said, heat boiling through her veins.

Drake let out a piercing whistle. "It is true, and you know it. Do you really think that the only female ever born with vampire blood in her, the heiress to both the Kayrs and the Kyllwood legacies, and the keeper of the dreamworlds is supposed to mate a common soldier?" He scoffed and grasped her arm. "Nobody in this world has ever chosen Paxton Phoenix. Not his birth father, not even his birth mother. Not my people or your people. Fate has decreed that you shall be a queen. Start acting like it."

The door slowly opened. "Why all the pomp and circumstance?" The heavy gown was weighing down her shoulders.

"A bit of pride, perhaps." Drake shrugged. "A long time ago, in one of your dreamworlds, I told Paxton Phoenix that one day you would choose me. I would like to see his face as you do so."

She tried to shake him off, but he tightened his hold, adding more bruises on her arm to the ones he'd left the night before as he pushed her outside. "You have got to be kidding me," she gasped.

"The Kurjans are entering a new phase of our history, and this is just the beginning." Drake smiled and strode out into the now-sunny day. The beams shone down on the snow, making each inch sparkle like the diamonds on Hope's dress. A red carpet led from the doorway to the center of the camp. Kurjan soldiers, all in their best uniforms, lined the way to the right, while Cyst soldiers, their white scalps shining in the sun, lined the left. The buildings were straight ahead.

There was no escape.

Several cameras, complete with camera operators, stood on the buildings, zeroed in on her. She wavered. "What in the world?" she whispered.

"New era for the Kurjans," Drake said. "We're getting married in front of the immortal world. The Realm will have no choice but to accept us."

"Why are you kidnapping enhanced females?" she asked suddenly, hoping to catch him off guard.

He smiled, his grip unrelenting. "Stay in your place, Queen." Then he strode down the stairs and along the red carpet, easily pushing her along.

"Where are the females?" She searched furtively around. There were no women anywhere in sight.

"They don't belong at state functions," he replied. "You'll meet some of the mates of my generals after we mate. We'll have a party—you'll like them."

This was surreal.

They reached the center of the courtyard and stopped. A door to one of the buildings opened, and soldiers shoved Hunter and Paxton out. Their clothing was ripped, and wounds covered their faces and bodies. A chunk of Hunter's jaw was missing, and Paxton's left arm hung at an impossible angle. Garrotes circled both their throats, and soldiers held them so tightly, the steel cut deep. Blood poured down their necks. Both males looked furious. Hope tried to move toward them, but Drake halted her with a hand on her arm.

Even across the distance, she could hear Paxton's low growl.

Vero stood next to Hunter, a Kurjan slicing blade in his hands. The blade, a new kind of knife, imbedded itself in flesh and then exploded, slicing in every direction. It was the perfect weapon with which to decapitate an immortal. No expression was visible on his face, but his eyes swirled a wild blue surrounded by a silver ring. For a second, she could see his likeness to Paxton.

"We would consider outlawing those knives in a treaty with the Realm," Drake said quietly.

Hope's gaze met Pax's. Fury and raw determination glowed in those silvery-blue depths.

General Ulric stepped forward, directly in front of two rows of Cyst soldiers. "The Cyst approve of this union, and I, as the leader of the Cyst, am present and willing to administer the vows. Our people are served well by King Drake, who will usher us all into a new and prosperous future."

Hope's legs trembled, but she kept her posture perfect and strong.

Across the distance, Paxton slowly lifted one hand, showing the mating mark. His was an intricate and deadly looking A surrounded by barbed lines. Beautiful and stunning but masculine, almost threatening.

Her bare back pounded, and the prophecy marks on both sides of her neck heated. She'd thought about his marking through the years, but she'd never imagined its rough beauty. Her entire body trembled

"I love you, Hope," he called, his voice hoarse and sure. "Always have and always will."

She opened her mouth, and Drake's fingers dug into her arm so hard a bone cracked. She winced, her breath catching. It was a struggle to remain on her feet. Dizziness pummeled her, and she gritted her teeth, trying to will healing cells to the fracture. Nothing happened except that the pain spread up to her shoulder.

Drake lifted his head and spoke directly into the cameras. "Thank you all for witnessing the birth of the new and stronger Kurjan nation." He looked down at Hope. "At my side is Hope Kayrs-Kyllwood, princess of the Realm. Today, she will agree to become the queen of the Kurjan nation and my mate." His voice rang out strong and sure. "But our people believe in females having a choice. So today, I ask you, Hope. What is your choice?"

Paxton reared forward, and the garrote pulled him back, shredding more of his skin. His eyes morphed to a bright emerald surrounded by a silvery blue rim.

She swallowed. The cameras wouldn't show Paxton or Hunter. The Realm wouldn't know they were even there.

Her entire life had come down to this moment...to this choice. There was only one right path. To save Paxton, to save Hunter, to save all of those enhanced females, there was only one choice.

As she faced Paxton, tears filled her eyes. Memories assailed her. The first time they'd met, when he'd taken a liking to her green dragon toy. The surprise on his face when her mother had given him a cookie. The moment he'd jumped in front of Paelotin to take a hit that could've killed her. The first time he'd kissed her. The last time he'd kissed her. The strength and protectiveness and wonder that was Paxton Phoenix. She'd loved him her entire life. Instead of searching for some great fate, she should've trusted her feelings. She should have told him. He deserved all of her, but the only thing she could do now was save his life.

In her heart, perhaps deeper into her very soul, there wa absolutely no choice for her. Some things transcended this world Even life...and even death.

Pax's nostrils flared. "Don't do this."

Nobody had ever chosen him. Those words echoed in her head digging deep. Hopefully he'd understand what she had to do.

She swallowed and lifted her head so the camera would have a better angle, but her gaze, that remained on Pax. "There is only one choice. For now and forever, regardless of the consequences I choose Paxton Phoenix."

Chapter Thirty-Four

There was dead silence in the compound for about three seconds, and then everybody moved at once. Drake grabbed Hope and shook her, yanking her toward him. Vero pivoted and sliced through the garrote around Pax's neck.

Paxton instantly turned and punched the two soldiers behind him, allowing Hunter enough room to turn and fight with his captor.

Soldiers rushed them from every direction.

Paxton knocked down the soldier he was fighting, grabbed the blade from Vero, and ran full bore for Hope. She struggled against Drake, reaching up to claw his face. He slapped her hard, and she fell back, the heavy train of the dress pulling her down onto the icy snow. Then he grabbed a knife and plunged down, slicing into her rib cage. She cried out as pain engulfed her.

The sound of thunder echoed as Paxton and Drake collided.

Hunter pulled Hope up, then whirled to fight off two Cyst, while Vero battled with two Kurjan soldiers. Hope stumbled away, searching desperately for a weapon, holding her bleeding rib cage with one hand. A Kurjan soldier reached for her, and she punched him in the eye rapidly with both hands, driving him back.

To her side, Paxton and Drake exchanged punches and kicks so quickly it was impossible to follow.

Drake lifted his arm, punched Pax with one hand, and then stabbed him in the stomach with the same blade he'd used on Hope. Blood sprayed across the snow.

Hope cried out, trying to get to them. How badly was Pax hurt?

In one smooth and impossibly fast motion, Paxton pivoted and shoved the Kurjan blade into Drake's neck. Drake's eyes widened and his hands scrambled to grab the handle, but it split in three directions with a clink of iron.

Everybody stilled.

Slowly, every eye focused on Drake. He frowned, blood burbled from his mouth, and then his head slowly fell from his body. It landed in the snow, blood pouring out to turn the crystals red. His body pitched forward, spraying red snow as it landed.

Hope rushed toward Paxton, who grabbed her and leaped across the field to smash into both Vero and Hunter.

Then they were falling.

Darkness pulled at her. Something evil shrieked and ripped at her arm. Heavy winds blew her hair in every direction. Pure darkness surrounded her, and she scrambled, trying to find Paxton. Then there was light, and they were falling even faster. He grabbed her and pulled her against him, and then they hit the earth with a solid thunk.

"Ugh," Hunter moaned loudly.

"What is happening?" Vero stumbled in the snow.

A roaring sound filled her ears, and Hope looked up to see barrels upon barrels of snow careening down.

"Avalanche!" Paxton yelled, wrapping himself around her and holding tight.

The snow hit them hard, throwing them through space, and they fell. He kept hold of her and bounced, rolling around wildly. Pain echoed through her body, but she clutched him tightly and held her breath. Finally, they reached the bottom of a mountain

Snow continued to pile up on them, and he kicked up, punching and kicking until finally there was silence. Her heart was beating so rapidly she could hear it.

Snow encased everything except her head. "Pax?"

"We're okay." He pulled her to stand and brushed yards of snow off her. It was nearly thigh deep, and she started to shiver. Her hair hung around her head, with the elaborate tiara lost somewhere in the snow.

"Hunter. Vero," Paxton called out, rubbing her arms, trying to instill some warmth.

"Here," Hunter said wearily, coming straight out of a snow berm.

Pax craned his neck, searching the area. "Vero," he called. "Vero?"

"Ugh. I think I'm dead," Vero said from behind a snow boulder. He pushed it out of the way, his hair covered with snow, bruises across his face. "Where did you land us?"

Paxton looked around. "I have no idea. It was the first time I teleported." His voice was demon low and hoarse.

"Why didn't you say something?" Vero said. "While I can't teleport yet, I could've at least helped you pick a direction."

"It was my first time," Paxton protested, brushing more snow off Hope's head. "I didn't even know if I could do it, considering I've been a Kurjan for less than a day. How bad is your side?"

She looked down to see the diamonds on her dress glittering with blood. "Not good."

His fangs dropped, and he bit into his wrist, holding it to her mouth. "Drink. Now."

She tried to protest because he needed his strength, but he grasped her head with his free hand and held her in place, not giving her a choice. When she started to drink, he looked around. "Does anybody have any idea where we are?"

His blood was like fine wine coursing through her veins, warming her. Filling her. Healing her. Finally, she pushed him away. "I'm good." She could feel her flesh stitching itself back together. Then she shivered and looked at the series of tall jagged peaks marching off to the horizon. They were in some sort of mountain range, but she didn't recognize it.

Blood slid from Hunter's left ear, matting his black hair. He studied Hope. "We need to get her somewhere warm. We're at too high an altitude for all of us right now."

"Agreed." Paxton rubbed at a bruise on his chin. "Vero? Are you absolutely sure you can't teleport?"

"Not yet," Vero said, his lip swollen. "Like the demons, not all Kurjans have the skill. You're young to have it."

Paxton pulled Hope to him and wrapped both arms around her. "You're shivering so hard, you'll hurt yourself. Take a deep breath."

Hope didn't know what to say. Her body was feeling better after taking his blood, which meant that his body would take longer to heal. "Did you know you could teleport?"

"No. But after talking to Drake, I thought there might be a chance." Paxton exhaled. "Let's see if I can do it again."

Nothing happened.

They all waited.

"I'm empty," Paxton said, looking around the now quiet wilderness. There were trees, snow, and more mountains extending in every direction. "Vero, you're lead. You need to create a trail. Then I'll trample the snow, while Hope and Hunter, you bring up the rear. Our goal is to keep Hope as warm as possible."

"I'm fine," she said, shivering so hard her bones ached.

"Right," Paxton said. "We need to find shelter, and fast. Move, Vero."

Vero looked at Paxton, his fangs sliding out.

Hope stilled. Were they going to fight?

Vero slashed into his wrist. "Here. We share blood, and you're injured. Need you at full strength."

Paxton studied him for a moment and then accepted, drinking his new brother's blood. "Thanks." He leaned back.

"Uh-huh." Vero looked around and then started down the mountain, scraping his feet, trying to widen a trail through the thick snow with his legs. Pax followed with Hope behind him, her hands tucked into what was left of his waistband. Both Pax and Hunter kept close to her, no doubt to provide body heat. They walked for at least two hours, and soon she couldn't feel her feet.

She stumbled on the long skirt and started to go down. Paxton turned and caught her, whipping her up, turning, and continuing.

"Put me down." She pressed against his bare and still-bloody chest.

"No." He trudged along, his body straight, wounded, and damaged. "I thought Hunter and I could keep you warm, but your feet must be frozen. Put your arms around my neck and take my warmth." His voice brooked no argument.

So she argued. "You need to preserve your strength, and this skirt weighs a ton. Put me down. I won't trip again." Despite her brave words, she snuggled into his heated chest and turned her cheek to his pec.

He sucked in air. "Your face is freezing. Just hold on."

"Pax—"

He looked down, still walking, his gaze intense. "Did you mean it?"

She gulped. "That I can walk?"

"That you choose me." His chin was up as if ready for a punch, but his eyes, well now. Those had gone demon hot.

"Yes." She forced herself to meet his gaze, and for some reason, it made her feel vulnerable. This was Paxton. Her Paxton. "I meant every word." She shrugged, and snow fell off her skirt. "I should've made the choice a million years ago, but I thought fate..."

He dropped a quick kiss to her nose. "Fucking freezing," he muttered, pressing her face against his chest. "We'll talk about it later, but it's done now. You're never taking that choice back."

She didn't want to take it back, although his tone hinted that the look of possession in his eyes was just the beginning. For now, she let his skin warm her face. Even bloody, bruised, and wounded, he smelled like her Paxton—worn leather and wild forest. She inhaled him, her shivers lessening just a little, but her feet feeling numb.

After a couple more hours, Vero pointed toward a clearing through the trees. "There's a river running along there, a wide one. There should be some cabins nearby. Maybe. It depends. have no clue where we are."

"Me either," Hunter grumbled from behind them.

They'd been silent, each concentrating on breathing and trying to stay warm. Black clouds swirled above them, hampering sight. The air was below freezing, and snow covered every visible tree and rock. Hope held tight to Paxton and could feel Hunter behind them. Vero was taking the brunt of the freezing wind; they probably needed to give him a break.

"I see something," he said suddenly. "There's a cabin near the river."

Pax stilled. "I'll check it out. You guys stay here." He placed her on her feet and waited until she'd regained her balance before kicking through the thick snow to the structure. Snow covered the dark, silent building. He kicked open the door and walked inside. Then he motioned for them. "We're clear."

Hunter took her arm and lifted her, nearly staggering. "This dress weighs a thousand pounds."

"You're telling me," she said, her teeth chattering.

He slogged through the snow, still bleeding from a wound in his head. They'd been working too hard to be able to truly heal themselves.

When they reached the cabin, Paxton drew her inside. "How bad are your injuries?"

"I'm all right. Your blood healed me." Now she needed him to heal himself. "How about you? Has the change to being Kurjan hurt you?"

"No. I'm stronger." He looked at the other two males. "I want you to hold on to me, Hope. I'm going to try to teleport again." The air popped around him, but they didn't move. "Damn it," he said. "It could have been a one-shot deal until I really learn how to do it. I don't know, but I'm not able to teleport now."

Hunter's face was grim, and he reached out to run a knuckle down Hope's cheekbone. "All right, cousin, I need you to dig deep. Pax is going to keep you safe, and you're going to be fine."

"I'm healed, Hunter." She looked at their temporary shelter. It appeared to be some sort of hunting lodge with several cots piled in a corner, plastic storage containers holding blankets, and open cupboards empty of food over a simple wood counter. There was no sink. A fireplace was already piled high with wood in the corner nearby. "I can keep going. We have to warn the Realm about Drake's plan. Even though he's dead, I can see Ulric and his soldiers still attacking."

Vero grimaced. "Drake has been holding Ulric back until he mated you, but now, the shackles are off. Ulric will regroup and attack at dark when the Kurjans are at full strength."

Panic flowed through Hope. She guessed it must be close to noon. They had to warn her family. "We have to go."

"You're staying here," Paxton said. "I'll go."

Hunter looked at Paxton. "You're still hurt, worse than I am, worse than Vero. You stay here, get warm, while we try to find safety. We're going to walk along the river until we find some sort of camp where we can call and warn the Realm. Then we'll find transport back home."

Paxton shook his head. "I'll go. You stay here with her."

"No," Vero said. "You still have broken bones and probably internal bleeding. I'm good, and Hunter is healing as we speak. If you regain the ability to teleport her out of here, do it. We'll find you." He shifted his feet. "You're both injured, and we might take days." His gaze flitted across Hope.

Indecision crossed Paxton's expression. It was sweet he wanted to take care of the younger warriors, yet he looked back at her, his gaze determined. "Okay. You two stick together and stay safe."

"We will," Hunter said.

Paxton reached out and tugged Vero in for a quick hug. "You're a good brother, Vero."

"I hope so. We just declared war," Vero said. "And neither or of us really has a place on either side." With that, he turned an shoved open the door. "But your job is protecting her."

Hope gulped. She'd chosen Paxton. Time wasn't on the side, they were at war, and she might be mortal. He'd want t mate...right now.

Hunter looked at Hope and then Paxton. "Stay alive. New! found Cousin Vero and I will be back." He winked, and with tha he followed the Kurjan soldier into the middle of nowhere.

Chapter Thirty-Five

Paxton had the fire crackling powerfully before he turned and unstacked the cots. He winced as his ankle popped back into place. He'd broken it twice over the last couple days, and then the avalanche had cracked it a third time. His healing cells were back to full force, though, and for that, he was grateful. Taking Vero's blood—his brother's blood—had definitely sped up the healing process. "Did you find blankets?" he asked, his senses tuned to the outside and any possible threats.

"Yes." Hope brought a stack of thick comforters from the nearest storage bin. "These look homemade, hand quilted." She frowned, looking fragile. "It's an odd thing to leave here."

He shrugged, his heart pounding. For her. "Let's get you out of that dress." It was wet and bloody, and she was shivering so hard, her lips were turning blue.

"Gladly." She turned around. "You have to untie this thing." The corset was intricate, and it was tied well, so in the end, he had to just rip the edges apart. When he released her, she sighed. "Oh, thank goodness. That was unbearable."

He finished tearing the delicate material open, and diamonds scattered across the cabin floor; they were probably worth a small fortune. The need he felt to protect her was overwhelming. She was everything. He couldn't believe that she'd chosen him. "Wha were you thinking?" he asked.

She turned, holding the material over her breasts with bot arms. "What do you mean?"

"You knew he was going to kill you if you chose me." Thoug he hadn't wanted her to sacrifice herself, he'd figured she'd say ye and then think of a way out. "I thought you'd acquiesce to gai yourself more time." He'd never forget, for as long as he lived, th second she'd chosen him. His blood heated until ancient drum echoed in his skull.

"I considered doing so," she said, her eyes soft, her gaze flickin away as pink filtered across her cheekbones. "But you remembe when we were little, and you told me once that you'd had a reall good day made up of a lot of perfect moments?"

He remembered exactly. He'd spent the entire day with he family, and her mother had fed him macaroni and cheese. An they'd baked cookies. Then he played his guitar while Hope ha played the piano. It wasn't her favorite thing to do, but she'd don it because it was what he'd wanted, and it had been one of th best days of his life. They'd been maybe eight or nine years ol "I remember," he said.

The firelight made her hair glow and her eyes glimmer lik sapphires, the real kind that were darker than those man-mad "I took that to heart. Life is full of moments. In that second whe I had to choose, when I had to say it out loud, there was onl one thing to say, and it was your name." She shrugged, lookin so beautiful his heart hurt. "I can't explain it, Paxton. Even if meant death, I chose you."

Nobody in his entire life had truly chosen him. She flayed hir right open. He should do the right thing and get her to safet away from him. His life had just imploded. As a half Kurjan, h wouldn't be trusted anywhere. Where would he even live?

But he couldn't let her go. She'd shown unbelievable courage i taking her stance, and he had to do the same, regardless of the futur

Hope Kayrs-Kyllwood was his future.

She kicked a foot against the sparkly dress. "Ice is forming on this thing."

"Turn around," he said gruffly. She did so, and he released the band around her waist. They had to get her out of the sopping wet dress so she could warm up. "You've been mine for about five hours, and I'm not taking very good care of you."

She stepped gracefully out and kicked the material, along with cute pink panties, to the side.

He tried to look above her shoulder, but her ass was perfect, curvy and full. His hands itched to touch. A scaly looking black book came unstuck from her thigh and fell to the floor with a loud thud. She reached for it and tossed it onto a spare cot. "It's the other half of the dragon-scale book."

He grinned, amusement taking him despite the danger facing them. The raw desire coursing through him wasn't going anywhere. Hundreds of years from now, even if he were half-dead, he'd still want her with the same intensity. "You hid half of an ancient book in your panties?"

She dropped the bodice and reached for a blanket to wrap around herself before turning to face him. "Yes. Drake didn't want me to have it, so I stole it." She met his gaze directly. "The book can wait. For now, I don't need the archaic 'mine' language." Her chin was up and her eyes a deep blue, while her wet auburn hair was beginning to curl around her bare shoulders. The woman looked like a sprite trying to be a warrior. A beautiful one.

"That's unfortunate." He cupped the side of her face and leaned in to kiss her before rubbing his thumb along her full bottom lip. She tasted like oranges and vanilla beans. It was a miracle. His miracle. He didn't deserve her, but he was keeping her. Forever. "You chose me. It's done." Then he took her mouth the way he wanted, full and deep, for the first time not holding anything back.

She moved into him with a soft sigh, her mouth so soft beneat
his. The woman had stolen his heart eons ago with a simple kiss
and it beat just for her. Hard and fast right now.

He slid his arm inside the blanket and flattened his palm acros
her entire lower back. Her skin was so soft it almost drove him to hi
knees. Pulling her even closer to his body, he bent her back, takin
and pouring as much of himself into her as he could. He caresse
her waist and didn't miss the little tremor that ran through her.

Her skin was so soft, he closed his eyes and just let himself fee
her for a brief moment. He'd always been gentle with her becaus
he knew the second she gave him the go-ahead, he would take fu
advantage. The decision had to have been hers, but she'd made i

Whether she understood that completely or not was
moot point now.

He deepened the kiss, flexing his fingers and showing a hir
of aggression. She gasped in need and pressed her body again:
him. Yeah. She was exactly perfect for him.

Blood roared in his ears, and then he calmed, needing her mor
than he would've ever imagined. He clasped one hand in her ha
and pulled her head back, his gaze on hers. Her eyes were so
and sleepy with desire. "Tell me you want this," he ordered. H
had to be sure.

She needed to be sure.

She blinked. Wariness filtered into her eyes, a soft hue c
vulnerability that was all Hope. "I do want this." Her voic
trembled. "Whatever happens next, it isn't going to be easy. Fc
either of us or our people."

"I've never wanted easy," he murmured. "I've only wanted you

Her eyes flared and softened. "Pax."

"I won't hurt you," he promised.

Amusement tilted her lips. "I think it will hurt a little bit." An
then she smiled—so damn sweet.

His heart rolled right over. So he gave her the absolute trutl
needing to know she understood him. He was no longer th

easygoing kid she'd known, and there was no way he could pretend to be anything other than who he'd become. "I cover and protect what's mine. You need to know that, Hope."

She steeled her shoulders in true Hope fashion and let the blanket fall to the floor. God, she was beautiful. From her little toes to the top of her head, he could spend an entire lifetime worshiping every inch. In fact, that sounded like a good plan. "I trust you, Pax."

The words hit him hard, and he took them in. He pressed his index finger against her clavicle and traced down between her breasts to her hip bone. She gasped as he did so, her pupils dilating. Her breasts were high and full, with pink nipples that he'd see in his dreams for the rest of his life. He couldn't help himself. He leaned down and tasted one. She ran her hands through his hair and tugged. He smiled, nipping at her. Her stomach sucked in, but she pushed into his mouth.

Yeah. She liked a little bite with her love. Good. So did he.

There had never been another female for him, and he had known it. He kissed her again. She was the one who reached for the shredded remains of his jeans and shoved them off him. He was hard, and he was ready, but he needed to be careful with her.

He spun her around and bit her shoulder. She laughed, and fire tore through him. He was aggressive and he was dominant, and he'd hidden those aspects from her all these years. But she knew him well enough to know that he'd never hurt her. Her ass was perfect, and he gave it a quick slap.

She jumped and turned around, pushing him in the chest, pink across her face. Her nipples were hard pebbles, and her thighs were damp. "Paxton."

Yeah, this could be fun too. He knew it. "You're so fucking perfect, Hope. You always have been," he rumbled, his body on fire. It was true. Even when she was being stubborn and hadn't seen that they were meant to be, she'd been his everything.

He'd loved her his entire life, and he'd been willing to sacrifice his very existence to save her. Still would—in a second. But he wanted to live to protect her. To love her and maybe see her swollen with their child, playing with their children. Forming a family.

There was no clear path for them to follow now, and he had no idea what their next step would be after he took care of the danger threatening her. But none of that mattered any longer.

She deserved a good life, a great life, and he'd find a way to give her happiness and peace. She'd bucked nations, fate, and maybe her own life to give herself to him, and worthy or not he was accepting her gift. He was going to take Hope and make her his forever.

He held up his hand, showing the mating mark that was burning a hole through his palm. "Before we get carried away, where exactly do you want to wear this?"

Chapter Thirty-Six

Hope faltered, so much need coursing through her she could barely stand. His mark darkened in front of her eyes, and for a moment she paused. This was for real and this was forever.

Then she looked up into his silvery-blue eyes and smiled, her heart stuttering. "Over my heart." Where he'd always lived, even when she'd pretended otherwise.

His eyes flared. Yeah, he liked that answer. He kissed her again, an edge to him she'd never tasted before. He was more aggressive than she had thought, but she liked it, or at least her body did. She was wet and ready for him, and she wanted to wear that marking more than anything in the world.

When she'd made her choice, she'd done so with her eyes and heart wide open. She could've gotten them both killed, and she'd known that at the time. But he was her choice in this lifetime and in any other, and that moment needed to be recorded for fate, and more importantly, for Paxton.

He kissed her again, one hand around her waist as he backed her onto a cot, laying her down. They were tall cots, but not very wide, not that they needed to be.

His body was heavy over hers, so much bigger and stronger than she'd ever be. Even if she gained full power, she'd never

match him in strength. Her body trembled. She moved agains
him, feeling him at her sex. He was huge and throbbing, and sh
felt a momentary panic.

"It's all right," he said, nibbling down her neck to sink hi
teeth into her shoulder. The sting flashed through her, landin;
between her legs, and she arched against him. He chuckled an
moved down to her breasts, taking time with each one until he
nipples felt like they were as needy as the rest of her aching body

"Paxton," she whimpered. "I think I'm ready." He had to d
something about this terrible ache inside her.

"I'm not." He nipped at each of her ribs and spent time on he
healed wound. "Are you all right?"

She moved against him, wanting all of him. Now. "I'm al
healed," she said, tunneling her fingers into his thick hair. "I'r
fine." Except she wasn't. She was about to disintegrate if he didn
make this horrible ache go away.

He enclosed her left hip bone and sank his teeth in, leaving hi
mark. It didn't hurt, but he made his point. "I love you, Hope. I'v
waited for you, for this, my entire life, and I won't be rushed."

Her heart swelled. Then his words caught her. "Wait a minute.

He lifted his head as if somebody had denied him a treat. "What?

She wanted him so badly it was difficult to think. "Matin
might make me stronger...or you weaker." She had to tell hir
the full truth. "I'm human. What if I make you human?" It wa
unthinkable. He was a strong warrior, much more powerful tha
even she had realized.

"Then I'll be human." He licked her rib cage. "It'll be the tw
of us, living a life together. It's all I've ever wanted. I don't car
if it's as demons, Kurjans, or humans. It's you and me, Hope."

Tears filled her eyes, and she nodded. There was no other pat
for either of them. He filled her, all of her, and she didn't want
any other way. She didn't know if soulmates existed, but he touche
something deep inside her. Maybe it was her soul.

She let him continue his wandering and then sucked in air as he settled himself between her legs and shoved them wider apart. His shoulders held her where he wanted her, and she'd never felt more vulnerable in her entire life. She slid her hands down his face, scratched her palms with his whiskers, and dug her fingers into his powerful shoulders.

His body was impossibly hard, like solid steel. Pax was a true warrior, and he was about to be hers.

He settled his mouth at her core and started to play, almost as if he was pleasing himself. His shoulders were unrelenting as they kept her thighs far apart. She liked the dominant side of him, but she'd never admit it. Although based on her body's responses, he probably already knew.

"God, you taste amazing," he murmured, sending vibrations up through her entire torso.

Need coiled high inside her, making the pressure unbearable. Her breasts ached as much as her core, but he wasn't in a hurry. If anything, he seemed to enjoy the little keening sounds she kept making. She'd never felt this alive. She knew for a fact that she'd never *been* this alive. How was it possible to feel such raw, pure pleasure? "Paxton," she cried.

"I've got you," he whispered. He used his fingers and his teeth and his lips and then his tongue, and all she could do was feel the different sensations quickly coming at her, driving her higher and higher until she was afraid she couldn't breathe. It was unbelievable.

Finally, something sharp crossed her clit, and she screamed, falling over the edge and fracturing into a million pieces. The orgasm tore through her, stealing her breath. When she whimpered, coming down, he kissed her clit.

"Oh, we're gonna do that again," he said.

She reached for him, feeling more vulnerable than ever. He held himself above her, caught sight of her eyes, and leaned down to kiss her gently.

"I've got you, Hope. I'll always have you."

A tear slid out of one of her eyes. The male was everything to her, and she trusted him. Completely. He licked the tear away and then kissed both of her eyelids. She widened her thighs and reached for his hip to run her hand around his butt. Even his butt was tight and firm and muscled. She smiled and leaned up to nip the skin between his neck and shoulder.

Pain flashed in her mouth, and she winced before touching her tongue to a sharpened canine. Holy crap, it was a fang. "I have fangs," she said. Finally.

His eyebrows rose, his cock pushing at her core. "You do. They're adorable."

She frowned. Even with her entire body on fire and needing him more than she would have thought possible, fangs were not adorable. "They're dangerous." She struck between his neck and shoulder, digging deep. Blood instantly bubbled into her mouth, and she sucked, knowing his taste already. He was spicy, and he was strong. He chuckled, but the sound was pained.

She retracted her fangs. "Did I hurt you?" she asked, quickly licking the wound closed.

"That's not what hurts." He dropped his forehead to hers. "I'm keeping that bite mark for the rest of my life. No healing cell will touch it."

Was it possible to feel this happy? She smiled.

"You can play more with those later," he said. Then he kissed her again, his body slowly penetrating her.

She returned his kiss, running her hands over his entire back. So much strength, so much power. She had seen both in him, but she hadn't felt him. Not like this. He pushed more, and she winced. He was so big. He kissed her again and then bit her ear. The pain slashed through her, and her body relaxed, more wetness spilling from her.

"You like that."

Apparently so. She widened her thighs even more. He reached the barrier inside her and paused. Then he kissed her and shoved deep inside her with one hard push.

Pain rippled through her, and she sucked in air. Heat flashed on her palm, adding more pain.

He paused, leaning down to capture the tears sliding from her eyes. She breathed out, slowly forcing her body to relax. As she did so, a low throbbing pulsed through her.

"There we go," he murmured. Grasping one hip, he gently pulled out and then thrust back in. Electricity arced inside her as if live wires had become tangled.

Her eyes widened. "Do it again."

"Gladly." He pulled out and pushed back in, his movements powerful and controlled.

Fire roared through her, and she lifted her knees, pressing against his hips. It was all the encouragement he needed. His grip tightened on her hip, and he started to move slowly and then quicker, faster, harder inside her.

She closed her eyes to feel the incredible fullness of Paxton. She marveled that she could even feel his heartbeat inside her. She tilted her hips, and more ecstasy flowed through her. He started to pound harder and faster, taking them both up. This was new for them both, but they moved together as if they'd done so for years. For centuries. For lifetimes.

She climbed, and pleasure detonated from where they met. She cried out his name, digging her nails into his skin. As the climax tore through her, stealing everything she'd ever be, she slapped her hand over his heart, searching for stability. Murmuring, she came down.

Her palm felt better.

Her eyes widened, and she looked at her palm to see the Kyllwood marking. Huh. "You just became a Kyllwood."

He looked down at his chest and laughed. "I wondered about that."

"So did I." Since she didn't have any other vampire attributes, or demon ones, either, she hadn't thought she'd get fangs or the mating mark. Satisfaction filled her at seeing it on his chest, right over his heart. She gulped as she realized he was still hard and pulsing inside her.

He kissed her, his tongue sliding inside her mouth as he began to move again. Slowly at first and then with increasing speed and power.

Pleasure pummeled her. He started pounding, one hand streaking up her torso to grasp her neck, holding her in place. His fang grazed her ear.

She gasped, climbing again fast and hard. He drove her up and then suddenly she was exploding again, undulating around him. His fangs pierced deep into her neck, and she cried out as the orgasm spiraled out of control edged with such intense pleasure there was a hint of pain. Delicious and decadent. Heat hinted above her breast, and then flash fire burned right through her. She gasped as the orgasm roared back in, continuing on and on until sparks flashed bright behind her eyes.

Finally, he shuddered with his own release, kissing and calming her until her body relaxed. Hope gasped, panting, trying to bring her heart rate down. He removed the brutally hot hand with his marking and then kissed her right where she burned, over her heart.

This was how it was always meant to be. She glanced down at the jagged and dangerous looking *P* over her heart. It was both deadly looking and beautiful. They'd given each other their hearts. Literally.

Gently, he kissed her, covered her, held her tight. She gulped, trying to focus. He licked along her jaw up to her ear, where he nipped her earlobe. "Mine, Hope. Forever," he whispered.

Chapter Thirty-Seven

Paxton lay on his back with Hope sprawled over him. The scent of orange spice and vanilla beans surrounded him. He'd never, in his entire life, felt this good. For years he'd wanted Hope. Her gift of herself was more than he'd ever deserved. However, he would never let her go now. There was barely room for the two of them on the narrow cot, but he didn't care. All hell was breaking loose in the world, and right now, all he felt was peace.

Finally.

He'd stoked the fire not long ago, so it crackled, spreading heat throughout the small structure. A quick glance at the splintered door showed light still coming under it, but the afternoon was half over. Night would arrive within a few hours, and the Kurjans would attack the Realm.

There was no doubt he needed to be there.

"I wish we could stay here forever," she mumbled, her mouth moving on his shoulder.

So did he. "We'd starve."

She moved her compact body against him and awakened his interest again. "Might be worth it."

"Definitely worth it." He kept his voice light. Even in this moment of bliss, he couldn't stop worrying about Hunter and

Vero. Had they found shelter? Had they found help? It frustrated him that he couldn't be there covering their backs. That he could only hope they were safe.

Vero hadn't expressed any emotion regarding Hunter's betrayal, but surely there had to be tension boiling up between them. Paxton had to believe that Vero was strong enough to deal with the situation at hand and face the personal crap later when there was time and space to do so. It was amazing how quickly he found himself caring about this newfound brother.

Hope stirred, her hand sliding across his chest. "I can't believe you killed Drake," she said softly, tracing a pattern across the mating mark covering his heart.

Paxton ran a hand down her thick hair and kept going, tracing the fine lines of her small body to cup her buttock. "I think Drake and I both knew it would always come down to that in the end," he admitted. "We just didn't know which way it would go." There had been no hesitation in his movements, even though he and Drake had known each other as children. When it came to Hope's safety, Paxton would never waver. That was absolute. Hopefully she understood, but even if not, he wouldn't be moved.

"The Kurjans never should have invented that knife," she said. "Any weapon that can decapitate an immortal so quickly should be outlawed."

Paxton couldn't argue with that sentiment, although he'd been happy he'd had the weapon at that moment. While he could live with killing the Kurjan leader, his Hope was a sweetheart with a kind soul. Even though she was a fighter, a warrior even, she'd had such dreams about fixing the world. "Drake didn't give us a choice. You know that, right?"

She nodded and her head bumped his chin. "I do know," she said. "He was going to kill you and Hunter, and at some point, me. I would've done it if I'd had my hand on the knife," she admitted quietly. "I'm not sure what that says about me. We've been friends since we were kids, and I still think I should have been able to find a way for us all to live peacefully together."

His heart turned over as it usually did when she showed her sweet side. He wouldn't allow her to blame herself for the outcome. "I wish we could have found peace as well, but that's not what Drake wanted. He didn't give either of us a choice."

She was silent for several long moments, no doubt thinking through his words. "Do you think there was ever a point, even for a moment, when he wanted to work with us? To make peace for everybody and not just his version, where he ruled the world?"

"No." Paxton had seen the truth in the Kurjan leader from the beginning. "Sorry."

She sighed. "Why do you think he captured those enhanced females and yet promised to let them go?"

"He was probably lying."

She shook her head and bumped his chin harder. "I don't think so. It felt like he was telling me the truth. The Kurjans are injecting something into the enhanced females. I don't know what. I don't know why. It's driving me a little crazy, and I'm worried about Lyrica and Genevieve, who are two enhanced females that were kind to me when Drake kidnapped me."

"We'll find them and free them," Pax promised. Having her naked body wrapped over him was killing him, but he'd already taken her three times, and she had to be sore. He forced himself to relax. He now had lifetimes to enjoy with her, and keeping her safe and comfortable and happy would always be his first priority. "We'll figure out the Kurjan plans. All of them. Vero didn't know, but at some point, we'll infiltrate their entire computer system and find out what the Kurjans are up to." He flexed his wrist, still feeling residual pain from yesterday's break. He sent healing cells to the fracture lines and to his fingers to repair the damage sustained during the torture Ulric had inflicted on him.

Hope kissed his chest, and he felt the small touch to his heart. Maybe deeper. "You're better? Your blood isn't sluggish any longer?" she asked.

"Yes. The Kurjans do seem to like their drugs lately." His blood was finally flowing freely as his body accepted the return to his actual genetic composition. He shifted uneasily. Even though he had evil Kurjan blood in his lineage, he wasn't letting her go. Maybe it was because of the evil. He didn't care. "Should we talk about the fact that I'm a Kurjan?" The idea made him want to hit something. Hard.

"Half Kurjan," she said. "Half demon. You're still Paxton. Does it matter to you?"

The sweet words eased something hard inside him, but he still thought about it for a moment. "Yeah, it matters to me." He needed to get his head on straight, and being honest with her was the first step. Hope had been a good sounding board ever since childhood. "I've hated the Kurjans my entire life, and to find out that I'm one of them—well, it pisses me off."

She chuckled, her breath warm against his skin. "What about discovering that you have a half-brother?"

He ran his hand farther down to her lower back and then settled on her sweet butt. "I like the idea that I have a brother," he admitted. "Vero seems like a good soldier, and he has a kindness in him I haven't seen in many of the Kurjans. I think taking his blood earlier helped me to heal faster, and it also completed the change in my blood. Plus, he helped us escape." Pax wished he could return the favor. Hopefully Vero was safe right now.

"Yeah, he did. His loyalty was to you and to Hunter, and maybe to me when it mattered," she said. "I think he's as lost as you are, Paxton. I think he needs a brother as much as you do."

Paxton kissed the top of her head. "Maybe, but I know he'll want to return to the Kurjan nation, and after betraying Drak, it won't be safe for him. There may be nowhere safe for him."

"We can give him a home in the Realm," she said. "Maybe he can help broker peace with the rest of the Kurjans."

It was a sweet thought, even if untenable. "Maybe," Paxton said. "I don't think Drake was alone in his determination to take down the Realm." There would be even more enemies coming for them now.

"Yes, but doesn't it come down to leadership?"

"Right now, with Drake dead, Ulric is their leader," Paxton returned. "He wants Destiny as his Intended, and he wants the other Keys butchered. We're at war. There's no question about that."

She made a small sound of distress. "I need to be home to direct my team when the Kurjans attack. I wish Vero and Hunter would hurry."

Paxton didn't much like the idea of her being in the middle of a battle, but he certainly wanted to be there. "We still have time." The Kurjans most likely wouldn't attack until dark. Even though it was December, the sun was bright over northern Idaho this week because of the frigid temperatures. "They won't attack while the sun is out, even though it doesn't harm them the way it used to."

She looked up, for a third time bumping his chin. Her eyes met his. "What about you? Does the sun weaken you?"

"I didn't feel great when I was in it yesterday," he admitted. "That's something we're going to have to watch. But perhaps since I lived most of my life in the sun, I will have some sort of defense."

She traced the ridges of his abs with one finger, shooting fire through him. His cock hardened instantly, which was his default setting if he was anywhere near her. "Most of the Kurjans can be in the sun for up to four hours these days, so if you have a few more hours' tolerance, you could be just fine. We'll just watch it." She kissed his chin.

"That sounds like a good plan." He couldn't believe that she was finally his. "Are you all right?" he asked softly. He'd awakened her two more times during the day, and he'd tried to be gentle, but that seemed not to be what either of them wanted.

"Yeah, I'm good," she said, her eyes a mellow blue "How about you?"

What a question. "I've never been this good," he admitted. H pulled her body up his and held the back of her head, kissing he unable to stop touching her.

A sound caught his attention, and he stiffened.

"What?" She looked toward the door.

He listened intently. "A helicopter, three clicks out."

She scrambled off him, naked, whisker burn reddening he entire body. "We don't have any clothes."

He stood and tossed her the blanket. "If they're allies, the brought clothing." Hopefully allies were coming and not the enemy He didn't even know where they were right now. There weren any weapons in the small shack, and there was nowhere for hir to hide her. He wrapped a hand-quilted blanket around his hip and strode toward the door. "Stay behind me, Hope."

Chapter Thirty-Eight

Hope shook out the stiffness in her muscles in case she needed to fight. The door was open, and she huddled closer to Paxton's broad back, seeking warmth. With him heating her front and the fire crackling behind her, she wasn't feeling the arctic chill, even though the sun was about to dip behind the mountain. "Can you see who it is?"

"Not yet," he said, his partially nude body tense and at the ready.

She gulped and tried to peer around him, but he was too big. Slowly, his muscles relaxed. "It's one of ours."

Relief filled her so completely her legs felt weak. Then she turned and snatched the black sparkly book off the cot.

He stepped to the side, and she ducked under his arm, clutching the book and blanket to her chest. A Realm copter blew snow in every direction, and clumps of the white powder fell off the surrounding trees. The vehicle was silver and gleamed in the waning sunlight. It dropped perfectly and then went silent. The door and the back hatch opened.

Both Vero and Hunter jumped out.

"Oh, good," Hope said. "They're okay." Her mind had been spinning, and she'd been trying not to worry.

"Excellent." Paxton ducked and lifted her in his arms, stridin
out, wearing only the quilt hanging loose on his hips.

"You don't have shoes," she protested. "At least let ther
bring you boots."

He ignored her. As he strode down the faint trail they'd created
the snow reached his thighs.

Libby poked her head out of the copter. She was dressed i
combat gear, and her thick auburn hair was in twin pigtails. Sh
smiled. "Thank God you two are all right."

Paxton reached the craft and settled Hope inside. She trippe
on the blanket, and Libby caught her, pulling her to the rear of th
craft. "Here, I brought you clothes." She handed over cargo pants,
black turtleneck, a bulletproof vest, combat boots, and some brigl
pink Ugg socks. "They're your favorite," she said. She hugge
Hope, holding her close. "I was so scared when you were taken.

"So was I," Hope said.

"Whoa." Libby yanked Hope forward and caught sight of he
chest. Her head whipped around to stare at Paxton and then back t
Hope. She grabbed her shoulders. "Oh my God, you guys mated

Heat blasted into Hope's face, the blush so hot it burne
her skin. "Yeah."

Libby hugged her tight. "Oh, congratulations. It's abou
freaking time."

Paxton settled into the craft. The other two jumped in, and the
shut the door. Hope looked around. Her entire team was ther
The twins were piloting the craft, while Derrick and Libby wer
in the back, leaving plenty of room for Hunter, Vero, Paxton, an
herself. Derrick tossed combat clothing toward Paxton.

"Is the Realm all right?" Hope asked, reaching for a shirt t
tug over her head. "Headquarters hasn't been attacked yet?"

"No, we got the warning from Hunter and Vero in plenty
time," Derrick said. "We're on the offensive. With Vero's hel
we traced the location of the camp where Ulric is. We're goir
to take them instead."

"We're going on the offense," Liam called out from the pilot seat.

"Hell yeah," Collin joined in.

Hope gulped. She hadn't intended on seeing battle so quickly after becoming mated, but it was her job. "All right, where are we right now?"

"Alaska," Hunter said. "So we're about two hours out from hitting the camp."

"An hour," Liam called back. "You wouldn't believe how fast this baby goes. Collin tweaked it last week. We should get there at the same time as the Seven."

Hope yanked the cargo pants beneath the blanket and pulled them up. It felt good to have clothes on, and even though the pink socks looked ridiculous, they were her favorite and they were warm. "The Seven are coming?"

"Yes," Libby said soberly. "They don't know the next time they'll have Ulric's location pinpointed, and this camp is not the main Kurjan headquarters, so half of their force is elsewhere. The compound is well armed from what we could tell by satellite, but we finally know where Ulric is based."

Hope settled into battle mode. "Did they bring the three Keys?"

"No," Derrick said. "They have the blood of the three Keys, combined with yours, which should be all that's needed. Their presence isn't required. They have the combined blood in bullets, they have it in bombs. They even have it in darts. If there's a way to get the concoction into Ulric, we're going to do it."

She reached for the black scaly book. "I don't think that's it." The book felt familiar in her hand.

"That's the other half of that book," Derrick said, reaching for it.

"Yeah," Hope said, pulling it back. He could read it after she did. "I think there's an answer in here somewhere." She hadn't had a chance to read it yet, and curiosity rode her hard. She only had an hour to figure this out. She flipped the book open to see an illustration of three keys. Her heart started to drum.

"What does it say?" Hunter asked.

She looked up. "I don't know yet. I'm still deciphering th
symbols." Then she narrowed her gaze on her cousin. He sporte
fresh cuts on his face and bruises on his jaw. She looked at Vere
who was similarly injured. "What happened to you two?"

Vero cut a look sideways at Hunter. "We found a cabin with
radio and were able to call the Realm, but they were two hour
out from reaching us with this amazing vehicle, and so..."

Hunter grinned. "We had some things to work out."

"Yeah, like the fact that you lied to me for five years," Ver
muttered. "I thought we were best friends."

"We are best friends," Hunter said logically. "We worke
together. We fought together. Crap, we nearly died together a coup
of times. We are best friends, but we just needed to work through
little anger before we reached that conclusion." He flashed a smi
at Hope, and a hint of Dage Kayrs showed in his face.

"I can't wait to see your real face again," she said.

Hunter snorted. "I know. It's hard to catch the ladies with this one

Vero punched him. "Shut up. Kurjans are better looking tha
demons or vampires. Everybody knows that."

Paxton snorted. "I would've disagreed last week. However, now..

The group chuckled. Libby winked at Paxton. "I can't believ
you're part Kurjan. That is so weird, but it is what it is. S
what happens now?"

Hope didn't miss the surprise that flashed quickly across Pax
face. Had he really thought his friends would reject him just becaus
he had Kurjan blood in him? He should have known better. "That
a good question. What does happen now?" she asked.

"Now we're at war," Paxton said grimly. He looked at the tean
"Hope, you have thirty minutes to read that book, and then w
need battle plans. I assume they're coming through your phone'

"Oh yeah." Derrick yanked the phone out of his back pock
and tossed it at Hope. Libby snatched it out of the air, her shift
reflexes making the movement too fast to see. "The Realm wan
you to coordinate with the other six squads they're sending i

There's a laptop in the bag to your right. The king wants you fully informed before we hit the ground."

Hope glanced into the bag. "Got it." That left her only twenty-five minutes with this book. The text wasn't in plain English but in symbols and archaic languages, but she knew them all. She painstakingly went through the text and once again found the lock in the shape of a heart. Her stomach started to drop as she finally deciphered the directions on how to take down Ulric. She sighed. That made sense.

"What is it?" Libby asked.

"I knew it would come down to a sacrifice," she murmured. "I just didn't realize how extreme." But she should have. Ulric was invincible, and there had to be balance in the universe. To be able to kill him, to be able to take him down, blood had to be shed.

"What does it say?" Paxton asked softly, a dangerous note in his voice.

She shivered because this Paxton she didn't know. This male was hard and unbendable. "It says that it takes the blood of the three Keys combined with the heart of the Lock."

There was dead silence in the helicopter for a moment.

"No!" Hunter burst out first.

"Not going to happen," Liam called from the driver's seat.

Even Collin, the more mellow of the twins, turned around, his gaze fierce. "We are not giving him your heart."

"I don't think we're supposed to give it to him." Bile rose from her stomach and she swallowed it ruthlessly down. "I think we're supposed to shove it down his throat." She wondered if it would still be beating, if there was something special about her heart that would keep it beating. Maybe it would blow up in his stomach. "Fate really is a bitch," she muttered. She couldn't help it. She lifted her gaze to meet Paxton's. He hadn't said a word.

His jaw was set hard, and his eyes had morphed to the green of a laser, piercing and sharp. "That isn't going to happen," he said, his determination all the more obvious in the quietness of hi hoarse voice. "Tell me you get me, Hope. Tell me that right now.

She opened her mouth, but nothing came out. Ulric was evi and he would do more harm in the world than she could explain. wasn't just the enhanced females, and it wasn't just his dedicatio to decimating the Realm. He was evil incarnate. He couldn't b allowed to walk the earth with everybody she loved.

She had known her life would require sacrifice, but she ha figured it would mean aligning herself with Drake, not actuall dying. Not really. She had finally found love, and she had finall dedicated herself to Paxton. She'd had three wonderful hours wit him, full of love and light, and a deeper understanding than mo: people would ever reach. It was probably more than most peopl ever found. She would have to take comfort in that.

"I don't have a choice," she said. "It's the only way to stop him

Paxton leaned his head back and crossed his arms. He didn turn his head. "Liam?"

"Yeah, Pax?" Liam asked, banking a hard left.

"When you set down, all of us are exiting except for Hope. want you to fly her at least five miles away from the battle zone

Hope jolted. "What? Wait a minute."

"No," Paxton said firmly. "You can direct your team from there His head remained back, but his gaze slashed to her, piercing an cold. "What exactly do you think happened earlier today?"

They'd mated. She'd move on from this world happy. Fulfille "Paxton," she started.

His chin rose, and the words stopped in her throat.

"What you seem to have forgotten is that your heart is n longer yours to sacrifice. Your heart is mine, Hope. Don't yc ever fucking forget it."

Chapter Thirty-Nine

Paxton finished tucking another knife into his boot. The Realm had copied the design of the Kurjan slicing blade, and he kept one in each boot. He didn't like using them, even against the enemy, because deploying such a deadly weapon seemed unfair. However, the Kurjans were all armed with the deadly blade, so he didn't have a choice.

He had guns strapped to his thighs and more knives secured in pockets throughout his cargo pants and his vest. "Where are we?" he asked.

Hope typed rapidly on her laptop. "Vampires are coming from the east, demons from the west, the Seven from the north, and we'll come in from the south. There are six teams, and we're coordinating from this position. We want to hit the ground at the same time."

"What's the go sign?" Paxton asked.

She kept her gaze on the computer screen. "There will be a missile strike from the Realm—the minute the missiles impact, we hit the ground using the explosions and the resulting confusion as cover."

Paxton nodded. "Who's on Ulric?"

"The Seven are on Ulric," Hope said, reading the screen. "We're to provide cover and engage and assist." She looked up at the team. "This is the best fighting force the Realm has ever seen. We're young, but we're strong and fast."

Pax eyed the soldiers. It was a good pep talk.

She continued. "The vampire teams are going to take on the Kurjan soldiers because there are more of them in this camp, while Zane's demon teams will take on the Cyst. Our team is to provide cover for the Seven as they get to Ulric. That means taking on both Cyst and Kurjan soldiers."

"Got it," Libby said, stretching one arm over her chest.

Hope extended her fingers, stretching them. "Once there's an opening and most of the enemy soldiers are taken care of, we need to find the enhanced females. The kidnapped women will be easy to corral, whereas females who have been mates of the Cyst for years, possibly centuries, may put up a fight. You have to expect to be attacked from every angle."

"We usually are," Derrick noted.

"Good point," Hope said.

Paxton sighed and looked at Vero. "You can sit this one out if you want." He felt an allegiance to this new brother of his, and he couldn't imagine the battle going on inside the young warrior.

Vero's eyes were a deeper blue than usual, fraught with intense raw emotion. "I've chosen my side," he said. "I chose you, Paxton, and I chose to avoid war. Now we're at war. I just want to end it. I've got your back."

The words slammed home inside Paxton. "All right. I have your back as well." He looked at the fighters in the small craft. "This is a team of partners. Liam and Collin, Libby and Derrick, and Vero and Hunter. You all have fought together before. You need to cover each other's backs. I'll take point."

Hope stopped typing and looked up. "Liam can't be with Collin if he's flying me five miles away."

"I'm aware of that," Paxton said easily. "Collin, stay with your brother—you'll both take Hope to safety." He wanted to leave guards on her, but Collin and Liam were needed in the battle.

There was no question about that. "It'll take you two about a minute to run five miles." The young hybrids were exceptionally fast, and he knew it. "Hope, the second they're gone, you lock this thing up, and if anybody comes at you, I expect you to shoot missiles and fly out of range." They all knew how to fly in case of emergency, and Hope was no exception.

Her jaw firmed.

"Done talking about it," he said, looking at Libby. "Libs? Are you ready?"

"Always," the shifter said. She nudged Derrick. "You ready?"

"I could spend a few minutes in battle," the witch said easily, forming a fireball in one hand. He was as well armed as the rest of them, except he would probably employ the plasma balls to start with. They could knock a full-grown shifter on his ass.

Paxton enjoyed being on Hope's team. It was where he'd wanted to be the last several years as he'd been training to kill. It felt right. Though everybody else had a partner, he considered Hope his, even though she would be behind a laptop typing furiously.

He liked that.

Although he needed to deal with her willingness to sacrifice her heart later. It wasn't going to be a lesson she enjoyed. If nothing else, she had to understand that she would not sacrifice her life. They'd only mated a few hours ago, and any immortal chromosomes that he could give her surely had not taken effect yet. At the moment, she was still vulnerable and still breakable. They had no idea how easily she could die, and he didn't want to find out. "Stay safe, Hope." He didn't like repeating himself.

She looked up. "You're not giving me a choice."

Good. Now she was understanding him. Drake had tried to kill her, and his generals had seen that action. Surely one of them would take it upon himself to fulfill Drake's dying wish. Pax wasn't going to let that happen.

"Our squad is in position," Liam said, looking over his shoulder and then back to the night sky. The craft hovered in the air. They all grew silent.

The only sound was the clacking of Hope's fingers over the keyboard. "We are Realm squad two for this mission," she said. "Squad one is in position." She typed more. "Squad two, ready."

They all waited. Pax's heart rate picked up, and he forced it to slow. He needed to be cold. It was the only way to fight, and he was good at it.

"Squad four in position," Hope said.

Several loud explosions rocked the world. The craft pitched and then settled.

"Go now, go," Hope urged, looking up from the computer.

Liam dropped the craft fast, and they hit hard. Paxton had the door open before the helicopter settled. He jumped out into air filled with debris. Fire burned all around, except for the area where the enhanced females were kept. Realm soldiers moved in while Cyst and Kurjan soldiers poured out everywhere, already firing guns and swinging knives.

He ducked his head and ran full bore into the battle.

* * * *

Hope could barely breathe. Smoke billowed into the helicopter as her team rushed out. Her heart was in her throat, and panic threatened to consume her. The idea of Paxton getting hurt froze her for the briefest of moments. She took a deep breath and started typing again.

Satellite images became blurry as the smoke rose in the air. She flipped on the cameras contained in her teams' vests to direct them in real time.

Collin jumped into the back of the craft and started to shut the door. "Go, go, go," he yelled at his brother. "We have to get out of here."

Something glinted, and Hope zeroed in on a Kurjan soldier positioned on top of one of the buildings, his over-shoulder rocket aimed at them. "Incoming," she yelled, ducking.

A missile instantly hit the back of the craft with a loud thunk and then exploded. Collin turned just in time and grabbed Hope, covering her with his body. Fire roared through the interior, and he bellowed, the sound filled with pain.

His brother was instantly there, grabbing them both and throwing them out of the helicopter onto the battlefield. Collin rolled several times, putting out the fire, and then stopped. "Hope, you okay?"

Her ears rang, and her body felt as if it had been through another avalanche. She'd felt a sharp pop in her leg. "I think so." Her knee was at an odd angle. "Except my leg's broken."

Yep. The pain came, fast and hard. She gasped for breath and then breathed out.

Colin rolled to the side, his entire back burned.

"Holy crap," Liam said. "Hold on." He slit his wrist with his fangs and held a hand to Hope. "Drink."

She drank several mouthfuls and then pushed him away. "Collin," she said.

Liam grabbed his brother and forced him to drink blood.

Collin drank and then pushed him away. "I've got it. I'm okay. I can heal myself."

"You're a fucking disaster," Liam said.

A Kurjan soldier came out of nowhere, and Liam turned, kicking and then slicing, punching hard and fast in a blur of motion. Hope gritted her teeth and tried to push herself up. The helicopter was smoking and burning behind them. As soon as that fire hit the fuel, the craft was going to blow.

"We have to move," she said, pain coursing through her entire body.

"Agreed." Collin forced himself to stand. Half of his hair wa burned away, revealing his scalp. Hope tried to help him, but h gestured her away. "I'm fine." He stood and staggered slightl before ducking a shoulder beneath hers. "You can't walk o that knee. Let me help you." The smell of burned flesh and hai clogged the air.

They looked wildly around for a safe refuge, but hand-to-han combat was going on all around them. A laser bullet zoome by them and hit the copter. Liam dispatched the Kurjan he wa fighting by slicing off the enemy's head and then kicking the bod out of the way.

His fangs dropped low. "Here. Over here." He put his shoulde under Hope's other arm, and the twins lifted her off the ground an started running with her between them. She tried to send healin cells to her broken knee and actually felt something happenin; Liam's blood was helping too. Slowly, her knee popped back int place. She shrieked at the pain and then calmed. Okay, that wa better. They reached some sort of toolshed, and Liam released h as Collin did the same. She stood on one foot.

"Get healed," Liam ordered his brother.

Collin shut his eyes and concentrated. The air popped all arour him as healing cells took effect.

Screams of outrage and pain filled the air as well as the sme of smoke and blood. The sound of steel on steel, metal on meta and fists hitting bodies reached a crescendo all around then Hope's gut hurt, and she wanted to throw up. Instead, she focuse on healing her knee. It took only a few minutes, but it seeme like an eternity.

Collin finally pushed away from the rough wooden shed. "I'; okay. Let's get in this thing."

Liam cut his gaze to Hope.

She shook her head. "Go. They need you." She no longer ha her laptop, but she had her ear communicator and her phone. Sl pulled it from her pocket. "I can see and direct all of you. Paxto

Vero, and Hunter need assistance. They're surrounded about two hundred yards to the north, over by the main lodge. You guys need to get there."

"We're not leaving you," Collin said, his hands clenched into fists.

There wasn't time to argue. She gingerly put weight on her now healed leg. "You don't have a choice. I can get inside where the enhanced females are."

"That's a good idea," Liam said. "All right, stay between us, and we'll take you there. If we're engaged and you need to run, do it."

"Affirmative," she said. The barracks where the enhanced females lived was less secure than some of the others. The Kurjans had relied on manpower to guard it, and right now they were all out fighting. She ducked her head and pulled a knife from the sheath inside her boot. "Let's go."

They were close to their destination. Even so, they had to engage several Kurjan soldiers on the way. The Cyst were busy fighting elsewhere, which was good. Collin killed two soldiers, Liam three, and Hope took down one on her own. She used the Kurjan fighting blade to her advantage and killed him. His blood sprayed across her face, burning her chin. She wiped at it frantically.

"Let's go," Liam yelled, his shoulder obviously broken.

They ran farther and finally reached the barracks. Three Realm soldiers were already guarding the facility.

"Good," Liam said, pushing her past the soldiers. "Is it clear in there?"

The first Realm soldier nodded. "Yes. No Kurjans or Cyst and no weapons. We made sure."

"Good. All right. Direct us," Liam said.

She read the face of her phone, her mind calculating distances and fighting forces. "Go assist Paxton," she ordered. "That way." She pointed past several clusters of combatants.

"On it," Collin said. He and his brother hurried into the fray.

Hope took a deep gulp just as she spotted Lyrica and Genevieve hurrying toward her.

Chapter Forty

Hope turned as two Kurjan soldiers barreled around the corner and tackled the Realm guards. A third followed up and grabbed her, lifting her off the ground.

"Oh, hell no," Lyrica yelled, running toward them and stabbing the Kurjan in the eye repeatedly. Genevieve followed and kicked him in the groin, ankle, and knees while shrieking the entire time.

He bellowed and backed away, swatting at the two females. Then a Realm soldier tackled him to the ground, and the other two took care of their attackers. Hope turned, ushering the women back into safety. Her breath panted. "Thanks for that."

"Sure." Lyrica's chest heaved, and she wiped blood off her cheekbone. "Snuck out and grabbed weapons for some of us. We're ready to fight." She winced. "Their blood burns."

"I know." Hope reached out and wiped off her friend's cheek.

Lyrica gulped. "We were just about to make a run for it. You want to come with us?"

Hope took out her phone to watch her team in action. "No, no. Don't go anywhere. It's not safe. There are more explosives, and the Kurjans will probably shoot you on sight. Your best bet is to stay here, and I'll let you know if we need to run in the case of breach." She looked around the main barracks area at the twenty or so enhanced females. "Are any of you mated to Kurjans?"

They all shook their heads.

"No," Lyrica said. "The mates are all at other barracks. To be honest, there aren't many here. I don't think the soldiers take them when they go to other camps."

That actually made sense. "Good. Excellent job procuring weapons."

"Thanks. It feels good to have a way to protect ourselves now. They've kept weapons away from us, obviously," Lyrica said. "Probably thought we'd stab them through the brain as if they had any." Today, the woman wore a light pink skirt with a V-neck top. She angrily unbraided her thick black hair. "I really want in that battle."

"Do you know how to fight?" Hope asked.

Lyrica set her stance. "Yeah, I know how to fight. I've been looking forward to this."

"I admire your dedication," Hope said. "But for now, how about we let everybody who has weapons and tactical gear fight the bad guys?"

"All right," Lyrica said, frowning. "But I'm telling you, if things look like they're going south for the good guys, I'm not waiting here."

Hope turned back to her phone. "Agreed."

Libby and Derrick were positioned with the far north fighting force, and Hope could see Realm soldiers around them. They were in good position.

She looked around for anything they could use to block the entrance to the barracks if necessary. The room only held cots and mirrors. It was kind of creepy. She didn't have enough weapons for all of the women. "Anybody against breaking some glass?"

"They're unbreakable," Lyrica sniffed. "I already tried. Thought I could use glass as a weapon. It's not even the real stuff."

"Figures." Hope looked back at her phone. Sounds of the battl were excruciating, and a couple of the women started to cry. "It' all right," Hope said, watching carefully. "We've outmanned then and we have better explosives. We took out their weapons depo as well as several of their missiles. They have a couple they ca still send. But we are deactivating them as we speak."

She could see what was happening in real time, but she wante to be out there. However, her skills were needed here, and thi was how she'd trained. She clicked her ear communicator. "Dage your force needs to move to the left. You guys are going righ and Talen's team doesn't need your help, whereas Garrett's doe: Maneuver toward the Seven, not the vampires."

"Copy that," the king said.

She could see on the map when they started to move. Goo "Does anybody have eyes on Ulric?" she asked.

"Negative," Paxton said, grunting.

A chorus of negatives came through the line.

"Keep looking," she muttered. "Where is he? We didn miss him, did we?"

The sounds of more fighting came over the line, an nobody answered.

"What's going on?" Lyrica asked, looking over her shoulde

"We're moving from the outside in," Hope said. "We're confinir those we can and killing any we can't."

Lyrica peered at the camera feed being transmitted from Liam vest. He was punching a Kurjan soldier rapidly in the moutl shattering teeth and then breaking bones. Finally, he knocked tl Kurjan down and punched him hard enough in the temple th. the soldier flopped down, out cold.

Lyrica gulped. "Are we sure we're the good guys here?"

"Today, we are," Hope said. She looked around the small grou "Can anybody besides Lyrica fight?"

Three other women raised their hands.

"Great. You all come to the front just in case. I don't see the fight coming this way, but if it does, we want to be ready." She looked at Lyrica and handed her a gun. "It's a laser scope. You shoot lasers that turn into metal as they hit immortal flesh. You know how to shoot?"

"Of course I know how to shoot," Lyrica said.

Hope turned back to the phone. "Collin, Liam, there are two Cyst soldiers coming up on your north. Be prepared. They're working in tandem, and they're moving fast."

"Copy that," Liam said.

"Got them," Collin said, turning on the screen.

She watched as the battle raged on. The smell of blood, coppery and sweet, filtered inside the barracks, and soon smoke began to accumulate inside. Two of the women started coughing. Hope looked over her shoulder. "Everybody sit down on the cots. The lower you are, the better the air. So far, the battle's not coming this way. If it does, I'll let you know. For now, preserve your strength and breathe."

They all followed her orders except for Lyrica, who remained at her side.

"Has anybody located Ulric?" Hope asked again.

"Negative," Talen said.

"Not yet," Dage said. Once more, everyone else replied in the negative.

Hope searched the camera feeds for a sighting of the Cyst leader. Where was he? Was it possible he'd left after Drake had died, expecting an attack? Hope chewed on her lip. She tapped the communicator. "Priority one is finding Ulric. Report in the second you identify his location," she ordered. If they could take off the head of the snake, perhaps they could end this thing.

Even as she had the thought, a trap door in the floor flipped open, and Ulric jumped out, grabbing her. "You wanted me, Lock?"

* * * *

Paxton sent healing cells to his pierced eardrum because h
needed to hear Hope's voice more than anything else. Her order
were quick and curt, but the woman definitely knew what she wa
doing. Even in the midst of battle, pride in her rippled through him
He didn't deserve her, but hopefully she'd never figure that out.

Because no way was he ever letting her go.

He turned and took another Kurjan soldier to the ground
knocking him out instead of decapitating him. After the firs
attack, all of the Realm soldiers were trying to incapacitate rathe
than kill. If they were ever going to have peace, they needed t
start now. Well, after they won this battle. Paxton kicked him
couple more times in the temple. He wanted to be kind, not stupic

A Cyst soldier came at him, and he stabbed the warrior in th
neck and punched him in the eye before beating on his skull unt
the monster went down. Pax took out half of the guy's throat bu
left the other half. The Cyst would live, but it would take him
while to heal. For now, he could swallow his own blood.

Paxton methodically went through enemy after enemy as Hunte
and Vero did the same at his side.

Vero covered his back nearly the entire time, fighting hard, h
face fierce and blood flowing down his arm. He'd been wounde
in the neck and hadn't healed it all the way.

"Heal that," Paxton ordered.

"Working on it," Vero replied, turning out and kicking a rushir
Cyst in the balls. He followed up with a series of punches th
sounded like a bat hitting a metal pole.

The trio moved steadily inward until they finally reached th
center of the camp. Pax spotted Dage and Zane—both king
panting, bleeding, but standing. It had always impressed him ho
the Realms' leaders were the first to fight, the first to bleed, ar
the first to die. He thought it was a good example that huma

should follow. The humans who sent soldiers to war remained safely at home. The system was messed up.

He paused as Realm soldiers lined up the wounded and defeated Kurjan and Cyst soldiers, positioning them on their knees near the main lodge. They'd spared a lot more than they had killed. He settled, his temper mellowing. It was a good thing they hadn't killed everybody.

Dage strode forward and tapped his ear. "Somebody give me a status."

Hope's voice did not come over the line.

Paxton tapped his ear communicator. "Hope, do you have the stats?"

Everybody had reported in to her during the battle, so she should have them. Silence. He shared a look with Zane. They both turned as one to race toward the barracks when Ulric emerged with Hope pinned in front of him, his knife at her throat.

Everything inside Paxton stopped, settled, and then boiled so hot he had no choice but to ice it all over.

Zane growled low next to him, the sight of his daughter in the hands of the enemy sending a shock wave from him throughout the camp. Several of the soldiers shifted their weight, all feeling the impact.

Ulric was at least a foot and a half taller than Hope, as well as about three hundred pounds of solid muscle heavier. He prodded her forward, one hand in her hair and the knife at her throat, until he reached the center of the clearing. "It looks like I have the Lock," he bellowed, his voice hoarse.

Paxton kept his eyes on the threat. That bastard would die today.

As one, the members of the Seven stepped forward in perfect formation to surround him. Sam Kyllwood, the brother of the demon king, stood next to Paxton. He began a low chant, one that sounded familiar but wasn't. Some of the smoke cleared from the air. A bright line of fire encircled the group outside of the Seven.

"What the fuck?" Zane muttered.

Sam shrugged. "The circle isn't located in one place. I create i when all the elements are here, and Zane, all the elements are here."

"Ulric has a knife to her throat," Paxton said, moving forward "That ends right now." He shoved past Garrett and Logan, th remaining members of the Seven, and into the circle. "Le her go," he said.

Ulric threw back his head and laughed. "That is not how this i going to happen. The problem is if I kill the Lock, another Loc will be instantly designated, and I'll never be free. So here is ou plan. King Kyllwood and King Kayrs, if you want the Lock t live, you'll kill every single member of the Seven right now. The I want my Intended brought to me."

Hope snorted. "That's never going to happen, you overgrown ape.

Ulric hissed and pressed the knife into her throat. Blood sli down over her delicate neck to her chest.

"Knock it off," Paxton ordered, not looking at her. She had t at least appear to cooperate until he could get her free.

"It's true," she said, goading Ulric. "You all know that we'r not going to sacrifice every member of the Seven or hand ove Dessie. Give me a break. We have always been traveling in th direction, Paxton." She gestured to her chest and then looked the members of the Seven. "One of you has to take my heart."

Dead silence met her statement. One of her uncles spoke firs "Absolutely not," Logan said.

"It's the only way," she said.

"I'm going to take your heart if you don't shut up," Ulric sai "I have made my demands. I know what this prophet means t you. I know what this female vampire demoness means to yo You will sacrifice anybody and anything for her."

Paxton needed an opening. There was no way Garrett woul sacrifice his mate, Ulric's Intended. If Paxton thought killing a of the Seven would save Hope, he'd consider it. But he probab wouldn't do it, because she'd never forgive him, and that was r way to live. His gaze caught on hers. "I love you."

Her eyes widened. "I love you too. This is a weird time to say it, though."

God, he loved her. Only she would give him a hard time about his chosen moment. Even though they were both probably about to die, he grinned.

"You're not listening to me," Ulric said, pressing the knife in deeper. "I will kill her."

As if on cue, every member of the Seven lifted a weapon. Paxton had no doubt each held the blood of the three Keys and Hope.

"Now," Benny yelled.

They all fired. Multiple bullets hit Ulric's face, striking eyes, nose, even in his mouth. More than one of the bullets made their way inside him. He jerked back.

Hope took full advantage, lifted her leg, grabbed a knife out of her boot and slammed it into his thigh. He jolted and lowered the knife just far enough from her neck that she could slide out of the way. Her blade bounced uselessly off his thigh because it was impenetrable, but the blow had still surprised him.

Pax instantly dodged forward and tackled the Cyst as Hope rolled out of the way. As one, the members of the Seven piled on. Ulric fought valiantly, and soon it became evident that the blood that had been shoved into him didn't do a damn thing.

They'd never be able to kill this beast.

Chapter Forty-One

Hope rolled to the side, her neck bleeding profusely. Eve[n] so, she came up on her knees and then her feet, running towar[d] Garrett. She grabbed him before he could jump into the figh[t.] "Uncle Garrett, I need the combined blood."

"What?" Blood poured from a wound in his temple, and h[e] was favoring one foot. He looked down, his eyes a deadly metall[ic] gray. "Hope, no."

"Yes, I need the blood." She searched his pockets for bullets [or] darts, careful not to touch him anywhere he seemed to be bleedin[g.] "Come on, you must have some liquid."

He yanked out a vial. "Here. Throw it at him if he gets close[r.]"

"Thank you." She took it as he jumped into the fray again.

Ulric tossed Logan across the clearing, causing him to sma[sh] into the front door of the main lodge, which shattered into thre[e] large pieces. He rolled and came up, running back into the battl[e,] leaving a trail of blood in his wake.

Hope flipped open the top of the vial and drank down th[e] contents. The mixed blood tasted sweet, like oranges and vanill[a.] Interesting. Then she waited, holding her breath for some sort [of] miracle to happen. She watched the fight, as did everyone else[.]

Ulric was more than holding his own. No matter what weapon the Seven soldiers used, his skin didn't bleed. It didn't bruise and it didn't crack. He grunted several times as if he felt pain, but they couldn't get to him. They couldn't really hurt him.

After a few minutes, she figured the blood had done whatever it was going to do. She reached for the remaining Kurjan blade in her boot and walked slowly toward the center of the circle. "Stop," she yelled, holding the blade to her heart above her breastbone, right where Paxton had marked her.

Startled, the entire group stopped fighting. Her uncles were bloodied and bruised, while Ulric was only panting heavily. It had been a difficult fight, but he definitely had the advantage.

"You can't kill him. You can't even hurt him," she said.

"What are you doing?" Uncle Logan snapped, moving toward her.

"Stop," she said pressing the knife in. If she put it directly above her heart, it would split in three and shatter her breastbone. "One of you is going to have to take my heart." They all looked at her, stunned anger in their gazes. "It's the only way," she said. "I can open myself, but you'll have to actually take the heart and shove it down his throat."

"Your heart is mine," Paxton growled, his voice carrying easily on the frigid air.

Adare and Ivar pivoted around Ulric and secured his arms, kicking him in the back of the knees and knocking him to the ground. He struggled, but they could hold him in place on his knees. They just couldn't hurt him.

Ivar shook his head. "That's not the solution. We're going to put everything we have down his throat. There's enough blood to commingle in there and do something."

"No," she said softly. "There isn't. I'm sorry. I've read the dragon-skin tome. I know what to do. My heart is the only thing that will work." She tried to avoid looking at Paxton, but finally she couldn't help it. Then she was sorry she did. His eyes had gone cold, flat, hard. They were silvery-blue metal, and they could freeze her in place.

"Don't," he said. One word fiercely spoken, his voice soft a always with that thread of danger.

She shivered. "Pax."

"Are you absolutely sure?" he asked.

She bit her lip until she tasted blood. "There is no question I read the ancient book, and I feel it in my soul. My heart is th sacrifice, Paxton. I already drank their blood. It's inside me. There no other way." She willed him to believe her and let her go.

"No." Blurring with speed, he was on her, moving faster than sh would've ever thought possible, grabbing the knife and throwin it across the field.

"Damn it, Pax," she snapped. "That was our only option."

"Wrong." He lifted her with one arm around her waist, tangle his other hand in her hair, and yanked her head back—not gentl not even close. His fangs sliced into her neck. She cried out as h drank, taking what he wanted.

Finally, he stopped, licked the wound clean. Then he kisse her in front of everybody. Her family, the soldiers, the enem He kissed her hard, making a claim that nobody could miss. Sh kissed him back, knowing he was everything she could ev want. He was hard and he was demanding, and yet he was sti Paxton. Still sweet. Maybe not at the moment, but she could tas it on his tongue.

Then he released her and placed her back on her feet. Sh staggered for a minute and then settled, her eyes wide, her min fuzzy. His nostrils flared, and crimson slid across his cheekbon for a moment. He swallowed and took several deep breaths, sti silent and predatory. "Who is your heart, Hope?"

She blinked. "What?"

"I told you, your heart belongs to me. Is that true?"

She couldn't see a way to answer that would get her out of doing what she needed to do. But then again, she could never lie to Paxton. "Yes, you have my heart."

"You are mine," he said. "And you know what? I think I'm yours."

He reached for a Kurjan blade from his boot and drew it out.

"No," she cried out. "No, that's not what I wanted."

"Too bad. This is how we're going to end this," he said.

He jammed the blade into his chest and hit the mechanism. It split into three, slicing open his breastbone above his heart, right where she'd marked him. "Jesus," he muttered.

Blood flowed, spraying in every direction.

"Holy fuck," Dage snarled.

"Vero." Paxton looked at his brother. "I need another knife."

Vero stepped up. "I'm not letting you do this."

"Only take half," Paxton said.

Vero's eyebrows rose. "It's an idea." He drew out a knife and yanked Paxton's chest toward him.

Paxton gasped and dropped to one knee. "Make it quick," he ordered.

"Stop," Hope said, grabbing Vero's left arm.

"No, he is right," Vero said. He shoved the knife into Pax's chest and sliced, bringing out a quarter of Paxton's heart. The entire area was deadly silent. He lifted it up.

Paxton groaned and clutched his hand to his breastbone, shoving it back in place. "Help me up."

Vero ducked his shoulder beneath Paxton's arm while Hunter ran forward and took the other one, both of them helping Paxton to his feet. Paxton was stark white, and blood still flowed from his chest.

"Here." Hunter sliced his wrist open and pressed it to Paxton's mouth.

Pax drank quickly, his gaze hard on Ulric, taking the piece from Vero.

Ulric watched the proceedings, his mouth slightly open as if he couldn't believe it.

Paxton pushed Hunter's wrist away. "I'm okay. Get me to him."

They strode across the battlefield to where Ulric struggled on his knees. "This isn't going to..." the Cyst leader started.

Paxton shoved his heart in Ulric's throat, his fist going all the way in.

Ulric bellowed and snapped his fangs into Paxton's arm.

Paxton growled and yet didn't move.

Ulric ground down as if he was going to bite through Paxton's entire arm, and then his terrifying red eyes opened wide, his jaw going slack.

Paxton pulled out his bloody and scraped arm before taking a step back. The members of the Seven did the same, everybody watching Ulric.

Hope caught her breath, holding it. This was insane. Everybody watched mutely. Ulric shoved himself to his feet and staggered then coughed several times. He held his stomach.

Thunder rolled in the distance, and lightning zapped across the mountains. A dark shadow crossed the sky and molested the sun, as if an eclipse had come out of nowhere.

Ulric lifted his head and bellowed. Sparks flashed through the air. Electricity arced, and the ground rumbled as an earthquake hit. Buildings began to topple.

The Seven moved as one up to the fiery ring of the circle. Benjamin, Adare, and Ivar put their heads back and yelled to the heavens, seeming to push some of the shadows away from the sun.

Brothers Quaid and Ronan lowered their chins and focused sending visible demon energy toward Ulric in the center of the circle. Logan and Garrett stood shoulder to shoulder, hands out seeming to harness the wind.

The fight was brutal. The wind keened, the earth cracked again and more darkness flooded the sky. The air was electric, and burned Hope's skin. She gasped. She couldn't think, she couldn't breathe. Her body trembled and her soul shook.

It wasn't enough. The Seven were destined to do this, but Ulric had more power than any of them had realized.

Ulric seemed to be harnessing the power of the universe. Had he gotten some sort of extra strength being in that prison world so far away?

The entire world started to shudder and struggle.

Hope cried out, running forward to grab Paxton's hand and drag him to the circle. Blood flowed down his chest, but he stood tall with Vero on his other side. Her team followed suit, flanking her, and then three of the most powerful immortals ever born, Dage, Talen, and Zane, ran up to finish closing the circle.

Together, they surrounded Ulric.

Hope's body trembled, and her lips shook. "Now," she yelled, flinging every ounce of psychic energy she could pull from the universe toward Ulric.

As one, everyone's heads lowered, and they focused on the undulating killer in the middle of the circle. All had demon blood in them, and they harnessed the power of a demon mind attack and laser-focused it on Ulric.

The pressure had to be unbearable.

The earth rumbled again. Lightning zagged down and struck the earth all around Ulric, throwing up ice and snow. The smell of ozone burned Hope's nostrils.

"That's enough! Everyone back but the Seven," Garrett yelled. "Trust me."

Pax lifted Hope, turned, and started to run from the circle.

She looked over his shoulder, holding him tight as the members of the Seven formed a tighter circle and moved even closer to Ulric. The energy between them was visible in sparks and zapping plasma until the air morphed from a gaseous state to a thickly violent liquid.

The Seven halted right around Ulric and propelled that glue-like liquid around him.

Then everything went silent. The sun remained darkened, bu the earth stopped trembling and the wind fell silent. It was th calm before the storm.

Then Garrett's head jerked up. "Run. Retreat now!" The Seve turned and started to run away from the circle, pausing a fe yards out to turn and watch.

Hope held her breath.

The atmosphere changed, grew heavy. The earth roared; the sk crackled. Ulric turned and looked at her, shock sizzling across h face. Then he exploded. As if he had eaten dynamite, his entir body splintered into pieces that flew in every direction.

Hope ducked as a femur careened by her head. Gasping, sh turned to look at where the Cyst leader had stood. The eart held a perfectly scorched outline of his feet and nothing els Everybody was silent.

Benjamin Reese, one of the Seven, appeared next to Hop "Well, that just happened," he mused.

Paxton looked around at the assembled group. "Did it work? He groaned, his hand to his chest as he placed her back on h feet. Her chest was covered in his blood, and she kept a hand o his arm to steady them both.

"Certainly looks like it," Dage drawled, his face slack. "I'v never seen anything like that. How's your heart?"

"Mending," Paxton said. "It'll be fine."

Hope looked at him, love all but consuming her. "You saved me

"Yeah, and we're going to have a discussion about you bein willing to cut out your own heart a little bit later, sweetheart," l said grimly, pulling her into his side.

Yeah, she was up for that.

Paxton looked at the group. "I would like to see peace betwee the Realm and the Kurjan nation. Are those cameras on?"

"Yes," Dage said. "We made sure they recorded the enti battle. We wanted the Kurjans to see that we didn't kill many their soldiers when we could have. We do want peace. It's time

Vero stood next to his brother and spoke in a clear and authoritative tone. "I agree. My name is Vero, son of Talt, cousin to Drake, who was the leader of the Kurjan nation until a few hours ago. As you know, the line of succession is clear." He gestured toward Pax. "This is Paxton Phoenix, my older brother, son of Talt, cousin of Drake. Let them stand." He pointed to the kneeling Cyst and Kurjan soldiers.

Dage nodded. The Realm warriors took a step back, and slowly, all of the injured but still living Cyst and Kurjan soldiers stood.

Vero stared at them, his gaze hard, his jaw set. "I align myself with my brother, Paxton. You have a choice, and you have free will. You accept him as your king, or you leave here and never look back. That goes for every Kurjan and Cyst soldier alive." He flicked his gaze to the camera.

Paxton jerked next to Hope. "What are you doing?" he snarled.

Vero looked at him, his gaze serious. "This is how it's done. The line of succession in the Kurjan nation is clear." He turned back to the soldiers. "Paxton Phoenix is now our king. Declare your allegiance or leave. You are free."

The assembled Kurjan soldiers looked at each other and then at Vero and then at Pax. One by one, they dropped to one knee and pounded a fist over their heart. Several of the Cyst soldiers did as well, but at least three turned and strode out of camp.

Hope gaped at Paxton, her eyes wide. Pax looked at the group. What in the hell had just happened?

Chapter Forty-Two

Christmas music played in the background as Paxton sat in the Realm conference room, negotiating peace with the Realm. He sat with Dage, who represented the Realm; Talen, who represented the vampire nation; Zane, who represented the demon nation; Brenna Dunne-Kayrs, who represented the witch nation, Jordan Pride, a shifter who represented all the shifter nations; Garrett Kayrs, who represented the Seven; and Hope, who was a strategic liaison between them all. Apparently, he now represented the Kurjan nation, which was a shock to his entire system.

"I don't want to be the king," he said. Both Dage and Zane threw back their heads and laughed as if he'd just told the world's greatest joke.

Dage sobered first. "Nobody wants to be king. I would give my position away in a heartbeat if I could. Sorry, kid. Welcome to the club."

"Yeah," Zane muttered. "Believe me, we all know that Garrett going to take over for Dage at some point, and then Hunter will probably give Garrett a break when he needs one. At some point Dage will most likely take over again. But we're talking hundreds of years from now. If I could find somebody who'd be willing to give me a break, it would be fantastic."

"Quit your whining," Talen said. "Both of you. You've got jobs to do."

Paxton wanted to smack all of them. "You all knew you were going to be king from birth. I didn't."

"Neither did I," Zane said. "I had to cut the head off my uncle to become king, and I still didn't want the job." His green eyes were appraising. "You're king. Step up."

Of course Paxton was going to step up. It's what he did. He didn't want to do so, however.

"What's the status right now?" Dage asked.

Paxton rolled his neck. His body had healed from the battle two hours ago, and yet here he was in Realm territory. He should be with his brother. "The soldiers who swore allegiance to me are being led by Vero and Hunter back to the main headquarters in Canada. I'm going to go there and submit to some coronation celebration before taking over."

Hope looked up. "Hunter is still a Kurjan in disguise?"

"Yes," Paxton said. "We decided he should remain so for the time being in order to help facilitate the takeover. Vero will need backup, and Hunter is an excellent warrior. I know you want him back home, King. I appreciate your letting me keep him for a while."

Raw emotion glinted in the king's eyes before a veil dropped down. "I do want him back home. As soon as things are stable, I expect you to send him."

"Not a problem. I understand," Paxton said. He still didn't want to be king. This turn of events was the craziest thing he'd ever experienced. "Maybe Vero will want to take over soon."

Both kings laughed again, as though he was purposely telling jokes.

He was not amused. "All right, let's get the treaty going," Paxton said, in no mood to deal with any levity. He had a nation to fix. He looked at Hope. "We're going to need to bring the Kurjans into the modern age, and it's not going to be easy. Are you on board?"

She looked up, her eyes gleaming. "Oh, I am so on board. I can't wait to liberate the Kurjan females. I'm sure it'll be difficult, but they deserve freedom." She glanced at her father and then back a Paxton. "Some of them may not want to remain mated, and we'l need to offer them the virus that negates the mating bond. Tha is going to cause all sorts of problems within the Kurjan ranks.'

"I'm aware," Paxton said. "But I agree. Everyone gets a choice and that's the first thing we're going to change when we get there The soldiers and the Cyst also get a choice. Every single one of then can leave without repercussion. Just like the soldiers earlier today.'

"They'll form a group, and they'll fight you," Zane said quietly

"I know," Paxton said. "But it's their right and their freedon to do so." He wasn't going to hold anybody captive.

"Agreed," Dage said, admiration in his eyes. "Plus, once w sign a treaty, you'll have the full force of the Realm behind you.

Paxton nodded. "I'll need it. Hope, will you negotiate with th Realm on behalf of the Kurjan nation?"

She hopped in her seat. "Absolutely."

"Hey," Zane said. "She's the best strategic mind we have."

"She's mine now," Paxton said.

Zane's eyes hardened. Yeah, they hadn't really talked abou that, now had they?

The door opened and Emma walked in. Everyone stiffened. Sh looked harried with her beautiful black hair wild around her hea and her blue eyes frazzled. She wore faded jeans, white tenni shoes, and a T-shirt with a very faded Big Bird on the front. He lab coat was askew. "Hi. Okay, so I conducted a myriad of tes on the captured females."

Paxton stiffened. "Are they okay?"

"Yes," she said, frowning. "However, I believe the compoun injected into them makes it impossible for them to be mated b anybody but a Kurjan. As far as I can tell. It's not like I've ha live tests done."

Paxton frowned. "Sounds like just the kind of sick thing Ulr would think of."

"But why?" Jordan asked.

"The legend said that Ulric wanted to kill all enhanced females in order to hurt the Realm," Pax mused. "This doesn't kill them but makes them only useful to the Kurjans." It was an evil and pretty brilliant plot, really. "The Realm needs enhanced females for mates. Sure, vampires and demons can mate with other immortals, but there aren't that many out there. If all enhanced females were off the table, theoretically most demons and vampires and even shifters would slowly die out. It's a long game, but Ulric believed he had all the time in the world."

Hope shook her head. "But how did he know it could be done? I mean, these legends go way back, and we're talking about current science."

"Yes," Emma said slowly. "But the injections are full of his blood. It has always come down to Ulric and his blood because it had properties found in no other being. The same technique they used to program Dessie and those other assassins to kill could be used to alter enhanced females on a genetic level."

"Can you reverse it?" Paxton asked quietly.

Emma rubbed a temple with her right palm. "I'm still learning about Ulric's blood. I don't know if I can reverse the damage or not. From what we can tell, there have been about one hundred fifty enhanced females affected by this."

"That's a lot," Dage muttered. "There aren't that many enhanced females out there."

"Right," Emma said. "If the ability to mate only with Kurjans is genetically transferred to offspring, there could be thousands of future enhanced females affected. I don't know enough about the Kurjan forces, Paxton, but their scientists, your scientists, enacted this program. Hopefully, they'll help reverse it."

He could guarantee they would, like it or not. "They will if they want to stay in the nation."

"Good." Emma smiled, patted his shoulder, and turned. "All right, back to the lab." She was gone as quickly as she had arrived.

"That's one question answered, at least," Dage said. "Are you ready for this, Paxton?"

"I don't know," he said honestly.

Dage and Zane laughed again.

He rolled his eyes and stood. "All right, it's well after midnight Let's meet again in the morning. Come on, Hope. You need sleep."

Zane tilted his head. "I'd like a word with you, Paxton."

Hope jerked and looked up at her father. "Hey, I—"

"Thanks, Hope. I'll see you later," her dad said.

Garrett slung an arm over her shoulders and all but dragged her from the room. "There's ice cream in the fridge. Let's go," he said. The rest of the group filed out, leaving Zane and Paxton

Paxton sighed. "Listen, I'm sure the last person in the world you wanted your daughter to mate was a Kurjan hybrid. But she's mine, Zane, and I'm not letting her go." He looked up and faced the king of the demon nation squarely.

Zane studied him for a minute and then slowly smiled. "Paxton I've always liked you. You know that. I've always seen a good future for you and Hope, and I'm glad you're finally together. You have my full support, and I know you'll keep my baby girl safe.

Paxton didn't react visibly, but something exploded deep within him. "I'll move this entire world to keep her safe."

"That's all I wanted. Welcome to the family, son." Zane stood

Surprising emotion welled up in Paxton, and damn if his eyes didn't sting. "Thanks."

Zane met him at the door and slung an arm over his shoulders "Come on, let's get to the ice cream before Garrett eats it all."

* * * *

Hope snuggled down in the warm bed next to Paxton, her body slightly sore from an energetic bout of naked Paxton. He was sexy in a way she had never dreamed, and he was all hers. "How'd it go with my dad?" she mumbled.

"Surprisingly well." He ran a hand from her neck to her breasts, as he seemed to like to do, tracing the lines of the mating marking. "He seems to have always thought we'd be together."

"I think most people did," she said. "I should have seen it earlier, but I was caught up in the prophecy, and fate, and that stupid green book."

His hand was warm and already arousing her. Again. "Well, my little prophet," he said, "I'm sure there's a lot more you have to do. I don't think you get to fulfill just one prophecy."

"I know," she said. "But for a while, we have a lot of work in front of us reforming the Kurjan nation." She couldn't wait. She was so excited to assist those women who needed it, and maybe some of the men too. Now she could actually help and see the fruits of that work. "You're going to make a good king, Paxton."

He snorted. "I don't know how to be a king."

"I think it's probably something you figure out as you go." Not that they had much choice. "I like that Hunter and Vero will be with us."

"You don't mind leaving Idaho?" he asked.

She nipped his jaw.

He pulled her head back and kissed her, his lips lazy and firm. Her mind fuzzed the way it always seemed to when she was near him. She cleared it when he released her.

"I don't mind. I'm excited about it. Where you go, I go," she murmured.

"I like that," he replied, kissing her again. "You know you've been my heart from the first day we met, right?"

She'd always known that, and she'd grown up with a warm sense of safety, thanks to that very fact. "I do. I think my heart was yours from that first second as well. Something in me recognized you." Something in her had known, deep down, that she belonged to him the same way he belonged to her. Always and forever. She hesitated for a moment.

"What?" he asked. "Tell me what's wrong, and I'll fix it."

She winced. "I was talking to my mom and Aunt Emma earlier today, and by the way, they're thrilled we mated. But..."

"But what?" He tugged on her ear.

"They want a wedding. A full-on, white-gown, huge-family celebration wedding."

He swallowed. He'd rather fight a cadre of angry wolves than wear a tux. But if it made Hope happy, he'd do it. "How about we plan a huge wedding in June? That was the month we first met, on the fourteenth, to be exact. I like the idea of getting married on that day."

"Paxton," she said, her entire heart warming. "That is the most romantic thing I've ever heard." She had no idea they'd met that day. She loved that he knew the exact date.

"Good. You became my destiny with one little smile that day, and even as young as we were, I knew my job in this life and any other was to protect you. At any cost." He kissed her nose. "Also, if we wait until June, hopefully we'll have the Kurjan nation in line and can invite new friends. It could be an introduction of the Kurjan nation to the Realm."

She rolled onto him and bit his neck, then leaned up to kiss him. "Now, that's strategically brilliant. I love you, Paxton Phoenix."

"I love you too. I always have," he said. "There were times in my life that were very dark, and there were times I couldn't see any good end for me, but I knew if I held tight and made sure you were safe, I would always find what I needed."

She stretched against him, surrounded by his heat. "What was that?"

His eyes blazed a familiar silvery blue. "My Hope."

DON'T MISS THE NEXT EXCITING ADVENTURE IN
REBECCA ZANETTI'S DEEP OPS SERIES!

FROSTBITTEN

"ZANETTI IS A MASTER OF ROMANTIC SUSPENSE."
–*Kirkus Reviews*

Enigmatic. With a wildly gifted mind, and an untamed head of hair to match, petite powerhouse Millicent Frost is brilliant when it comes to gadgets and electronics—less so with people. After an attempt to bust a bank scam goes awry, Millie is in hot water with Homeland Security and targeted by lethal enemies. In the midst of the trouble, she heads home to help out with the family hunting and fishing business. But when their rival competitor and Millie's ex is murdered, she's the number one suspect . . .

Irresistible. Former Marine turned lawyer Scott Terentson devotes himself to getting his clients out of tricky binds. A loner, the last thing he wants is to belong to any team, yet the Deep Ops group considers him one of their own—and he pays the price by getting shot at by their enemies. Now Millie is seeking his help—just as he's dealing with a brutal fail regarding a recent trial. Both are a headache, yet he's drawn to Millie in spite of himself. They're opposites, but maybe the old adage is true . . .

Electric. Working together, Millie and Scott soon have more on their hands than they bargained for as the danger escalates—along with the sizzling heat between them. And when a disappearance is thrown into the mix, all bets are off . . .

Praise for Driven

"Zanetti still makes time to dig into her characters' psyches in the midst of the action, adding nuance to the exciting plot."
—*Publishers Weekly*

"The story moves fast, and there's an unexpected twist or two, as well as a
scene-and-booze-stealing German Shepherd that provides a little levity to this dark and satisfying romantic thriller."
—*Bookpage*

Printed in the United States
by Baker & Taylor Publisher Services